Torrents of Blood

A light and gentle, gruesome period murder mystery

Anthony Drake

© Anthony Drake 2015

All rights reserved, including the right to reproduce this book, or portions thereof in any form. No part of this text may be reproduced, transmitted, downloaded, decompiled, reverse engineered, or stored, in any form or introduced into any information storage and retrieval system, in any form or by any means, whether electronic or mechanical without the express written permission of the author.

ISBN: tbc

PublishNation
www.publishnation.co.uk

In Memoriam

HULL GRAMMAR SCHOOL

1479 - 2005

Sources of the Quotations

Title Page: *Torrents of Blood* from Travels in France, 1789 by Arthur Young, p.199. Sub-Title Page, Part I: *Foul and Midnight Murther* from The Bard by Thomas Gray, Triad II, Strophe 3, line 88.

" *Therefore the winds...* from A Midsummer Night's Dream, II,i, 88-92

Page 38: *Grace was in all her steps....* from Paradise Lost, Book viii, pp.488-9.

Page 54: *Though the rain it raineth....* from King Lear, III, ii, 77.

Page 68: *We"ll have a posset....* from The Merry Wives of Windsor, IV, i, 7.

Page 93: *Awa', Whigs, awa'....* a poem by Robert Burns.

Page 110: *green eyed monster....* from Othello, III, iii, 170 -1.

whereby hangs a tale.... ditto III, i, 8+9.

Page 112: *this unwholesome humidity....* from The Merry Wives of Windsor, III, iii, 34.

Page 120: *first attack of Satan....* from Johnson's Dictionary under *Satan*.

Page 124: *If music be the food of love....* from Twelfth Night, I, i, 1.

Page 125: *thus spake the Fiend.....* from Paradise Lost, Book iv, 393-4.

Page 135: *Far from the madding crowd's....* from Elegy Written in a Country Churchyard by Thomas Gray, line 73.

Page 136: sub-title: *Bleeding Trophies* based on The Story of Civilisation: Rousseau and Revolution by Will and Ariel Durant, Book 4. page 963.

Page 136: *It will have blood....* from MacBeth, III, iv, 122.

Page 148: *that wicked imp....* from A Long Story by Thomas Gray, line 44.

" *Papers and books....* ditto line 66.

Page 221: *Hear how Timotheus....* from An Essay on Criticism by Alexander Pope, lines 374-377.

Page 236: *Life is a jest....* John Gay's epitaph on his tomb in Westminster Abbey.

Page 247: sub-title: *The Web is Wove* from The Bard by Thomas Gray, triad III, strophe 1, line 100.

" *Let the wicked fall....* Psalm 141, line 11.

Page 301: *Strange, that men from age to age....* from Caleb Williams by William Goodwin, Vol. 3, chap. 1.

Page 325: *But winter ling'ring....* from The Traveller by Oliver Goldsmith, line 172.

" *What is a Church....* from The Borough by George Crabbe, lines 11-12.

Page 326: *I am afeard....* from Henry IV, IV, I, 141.

Page 341: from Joe Miller's Jests written by Joseph Miller (1684 – 1738), an English actor, published just after his death.

NB The 17th Century Hull poet Andrew Marvell's surname is almost always mispronounced. So as you read please think *Andrew **MAR**vell,* p.82.

Part I

Foul and Midnight Murther

Therefore the winds, piping to us in vain,
As in revenge, have sucked up from the sea
Contagious fogs; which falling in the land,
Hath every petting river, made so proud,
That they have overborne their continents.

The Town and County of Kingston upon Hull, 1796
Monday 23rd November

A dismal, damp grey fog was crawling slowly over the shores of the North Sea and inland across Holder Ness, mixing with the miasmas exuding from the marshy land. The towns of Hull and Beverley and all the surrounding villages would soon disappear under this shroud that was creeping westwards. Only a few church spires and windmills would be tall enough to push their heads through and peer into the clear night sky. The only sounds that would be heard would be the muffled barking of the occasional dog, or a distant church bell sounding the hour.

By the early morning when the towns and villages were coming to life the fog was beginning to settle as though preparing to sleep, and by midday had become becalmed and quiescent.

It was market day in the town of Kingston upon Hull and, in spite of the fog, it was in the middle of its usual busyness. There was a tumult of people, as well as horses, dogs, barrows and carts, hackney-chairs, all coming and going hither and thither. The poor had been out the earliest scrabbling about amongst the hucksters and pedlars to catch the best bargains, but many of the wealthy from the outlying villages had foregone the journey because of the fog. From the odorous Fish Shambles at the south end up to the richer north end there were taverns, alehouses, coffee-houses and dramshops full of bustle and clamour.

A man swept down the High Street in great haste. He swerved into the Black Boy Tavern, his greasy black pigtail swinging out as he turned in and sped past the rabble in the bar. He was wearing white sailor's trousers and a blue coat over a yellow waistcoat. Half his right ear was missing above the gold earring that pierced it and his skin was like tanned leather. He ran up the stairs two at a time, his hand gripping his cutlass to hold it steady and he entered a room at the top of the stairs.

'Get up, Norski, get up. The horses are ready.'

The other man groaned then coughed violently as he rolled off the bed.

'You've been at the grog again, ain't yer? If you mess this up I'll rip your head off. Get ready, quick.'

He pulled the other man up on to his feet.

'Why was I lumbered with the likes of you? Yer goin' to 'ave more gold than you've ever seen and yer still dragging yer 'eels. Get that cutlass on.'

The Norwegian, although much bigger than the other, was submissive. His straw hair was short, without a pigtail, and his whole demeanour was neater and cleaner.

'Don't worry, Jack, I know exactly what I'm doing, *and* going to do.' He spoke good English but with a distinctive Scandinavian rhythm. He gathered up his cutlass and knife, took his purse off the table and put it in his pocket then donned his cloak. 'You can trust me.'

'Yeah, sure, as far as I can throw yer. And remember, you useless foreigner, no names when we leave this dump. Now let's be off. You carry that box.'

They left the room and went downstairs. By now half the men in the bar were drunk and the women were laughing and cackling like witches. The stench of stale ale and tobacco was oozing out into the street. Once outside the two men turned left and marched along the narrow street as fast as the crowds, the traffic and the fog would allow. Then past the Tudor splendour of the King's Head Inn, past countless other alehouses, shops and offices, past the house of William Wilberforce then down Salthouse Lane, eventually to emerge on the Dock Side.

'There, on the left.'

They entered the stables and ten minutes later were riding out towards Low Gate.

'Remember we've got a good two hours head-start. No hurrying! We should be there in three hours with time to spare. It'll be dark by then.'

They turned their horses down White Friar Gate and headed towards the Beverley Gate.

'It'll be over by 5 o'clock. Just be thinking about all that gold, Nordski, *keep* thinking about it and we'll be back in Hamburg in no time.'

The Norwegian knew that this talk was not for his benefit but for the Englishman himself. However, anyone looking at his face would see in it the darkness of fear and apprehension all rolled into one.

The street lights in the Market Place had been lit earlier than usual and little haloes of light had grown around the gently flickering flames, like some ghostly objects appearing out of the hidden sky above. The multi-paned windows of the smart new shops were casting networks of light onto the pavements.

Amongst the people who were out and about in spite of the fog was a gentleman, his gait erect, who was striding out through the turmoil and weaving his way along the Market Place towards North Church Side. There were so many people about that he couldn't swing his Malacca cane so he was holding it upright in front of him. He was tall and slender, and there was a sharpness about him - everything was sharp, his face, his nose, his eye movements, even his voice. He had blue-grey eyes that were penetrating. He was wearing a cocked hat above a black cloak that covered a green jacket and brown breeches. He bore hope and confidence like a sanguine rose in the lapel of his coat.

He had just passed the statue of *King Billy* when he turned his eyes to the right and saw through the fog the Royal Mail Coach parked outside the Cross Keys Hotel preparing for its 3 o'clock run to York. It was being loaded on the top with an assortment of trunks, boxes, bags and packages. The man continued on walking, passing by the Holy Trinity Church and then, turning left into North Church Side, he entered Tom's Coffee House.

The Mail Coach started to take on its passengers – an elderly gentleman bundled up to the hilt and carrying a stick got on first; he was followed by a young lady smartly dressed in fur. She was followed by another man, not so elderly, dressed in black; and finally a third man, taller than the others, with a stern visage and wearing a blue coat. The coach's headlamps were sending out beams of light into the fog ahead, lighting up the postillion who was waiting at the front ready to mount. The driver was giving the harnessing a final check. There appeared to be no outside passengers on today's journey. The guard in his distinctive uniform was already high up standing at the rear loading his two pistols and blunderbuss. A small group of boys and old men was gathered nearby watching, fascinated by this recent addition to the life of Hull's Market Place.

The coach left every day, as did many other coaches, but this one was special – quite a spectacle to see as it raced off fully laden in its fine black and red livery, the guard's horn blasting its warning notes to clear the way ahead as it sped along the streets. People would leave their homes and businesses just to watch it go by. Nothing stood in the way of the Royal Mail Coach – its journey timed to the minute was not to be hindered by man or beast. At Market Weighton they would change horses and driver in less than a minute. At 6 o'clock and it would be off again to arrive at the York Tavern at 9 o'clock, the horses bellowing steam out of their nostrils as they came to a halt.

The bells of the Trinity Church struck three, the guard's horn sounded and the coach moved off, gathering speed, mindless of the fog, and headed north. It turned into Silver Street and on down White Friar Gate, and then through the remains of the Beverley Gate and out of town.

By the time the coach was approaching Beverley forty minutes later the fog was thicker and wetter, and the full darkness of the night had descended. The beams of the headlamps could penetrate no more than a few yards and then only to reflect back the great wall of fog ahead. The horses and the driver knew every inch of the road but progress was slower than usual. The guard's horn was a continual ear-piercing blast as maximum speed was being made in the hope that no obstacle was lying in wait in the road.

The older lady sat with her eyes closed, the younger one was looking out through the window into the dimness, trying to avoid eye-contact with the man sitting opposite. The second man, deep in thought, was sitting with his head back, staring ahead. Lights became visible as they reached the centre of Beverley so they increased speed through the Saturday Market. The guard grabbed the mailbag from the waiting postmaster without stopping as they headed towards the North Bar.

Once they were through the narrow Bar it darkened again as they drove towards the village of Molescroft. The beams of the headlamps of another coach became visible as it came towards them from the opposite direction, but going much more slowly.

'Fog's thinner yonder,' yelled the driver as he passed by. Inside, the passengers were restless, sitting in silence, swaying this way and that unable to read, sleep or talk because of the sound of the horn and the rumble of the wheels. As the coach approached Bishop Burton it slowed down slightly as it came to the bends in the village where the fog was hanging thickly in the basin in which the houses nestled. The sound of ducks quacking on the pond could be heard but not seen. The lights of the inn on the right were faintly visible in the darkness.

The road started to rise steeply as it left the village and the fog began to get slightly thinner. There was still plenty of strength left in the six horses but the hill slowed them down. Nearing the top of the steepest part of the road they had slowed down almost to a standstill. Suddenly a voice boomed out of the fog.

'Guard, put your pistols and blunderbuss on the floor or you and the driver will be shot. There are four pistol barrels pointing at each of you.'

The coarse voice was coming from a barely visible muffled figure who had emerged from the roadside. He was holding two double-barrelled pistols and pointing them directly at the guard, a mere two yards from him. Another shadowy figure was covering the driver. The guard obeyed the man.

'This is a hanging offence and you...,'

'Quiet! Do not move an inch. Driver, put the brake on and get down from the coach.' The driver descended proclaiming, 'You *will* hang!'

'I said keep your mouths shut. Another word and they will have cause to hang us. Now, we want that man inside the coach. You in the blue coat, get out of the coach now. If you have a weapon throw it out. If you think you can use it, think again.'

The door on the left opened. There was a slight pause.

'Weapon!' yelled the footpad. The pistol landed on the ground, followed by the man in blue.

'Driver, mount. Guard do not move.'

The driver ascended and took the reins.

'Drive on, with haste,' yelled the footpad.

The coach moved on. It was all over in less than two minutes. The hill was less steep now and the horses and coach soon picked up speed and disappeared into the dank mist.

As the sounds of the departing coach faded away all became silent again, except for the crunching of horses' hooves, cart wheels and boots on the gravel as they made their way down a narrow lane to the south. The shadowy figures were moving on, the man in blue being pushed on ahead by the Norwegian.

Some minutes later they stopped.

The Norwegian whipped out a Spanish garrotte from his coat pocket and swiftly swung it around the victim's neck, tightening it until blood appeared. He kept on squeezing until the man stopped struggling and went limp.

'Very good, Nordski, now, put him face down,' said the other man as he grabbed the victim's right arm, 'then get that box ready.'

He twisted the man's arm so that it was facing away from him towards the hedge at the side of the lane. With his left hand he held the arm tightly while pulling his dagger out of its sheath. He then slashed it across the man's wrist. Blood spurted out as though a fountain had just been turned on, shooting through the hedge bottom onto the field at the other side.

After a few minutes the spurt subdued and eventually stopped.

'Now Nordski, it's your turn again.'

The Norwegian already had his sword out of its scabbard. He raised it with both hands high into the air and with one tremendous sweep sliced the head off. He wrapped it in tarpaulin, placed it in the box, double-wrapped it in more tarpaulin and bound it securely with twine. The other man rolled the rest of the body up to the hedge and covered it as best he could with debris of dead leaves, twigs and gravel.

They mounted the cart, then they too disappeared into the mist, disturbing its inertia as they moved through it.

Anyone standing nearby would have heard the crunch on the gravel slowly receding as the cart went down the lane towards Walling Fen and then faded into the distance.

The disturbed fog settled and everything returned to stillness and peace save for water droplets falling from the trees like tears in the darkness.

2

Two weeks later, Monday 7th December
A Company of Redcoats of the York and East Riding Regiment of Foot were on their way from York Castle to join the garrison at Hull.

At the same time a company of the 68th Durham Regiment had left Hull and were on their way to Scarborough Castle. Both journeys were long and strenuous one-day marches.

'Halt, men!'

Lieutenant Read, the Company leader, had stopped and turned to address his group.

'At ease! Five minutes to relieve yourselves or whatever. Just five minutes. Then another couple of hours and we'll be in Hull.'

The men removed their packs and put them down on the side of the road together with their muskets. Their shoulders relaxed into a slump. There were a few gasps of *phew* as they sat down. Some peed into the nearby field, some lit their pipes, and one man went off down a track for another kind of relief.

He'd gone several yards, started to unbuckle his coat and trousers when he spotted something in the dead vegetation further down at the side of the track. He walked towards it, holding up his trousers with both hands.

Then he yelled, "Lieutenant Read, sir, come here quick."

At that point he spewed up half of his day's rations as the Lieutenant approached.

'What on earth is it, Private?'

'Here, sir, quick!'

'Private Clifton, you haven't called me over just to nurse you for being sick have you?'

'No sir, look there.'

He pointed to a heap covered in debris.

The Lieutenant started to walk towards it while the Private started to clean himself up, looking the other way at the same time.

'Good God, what a mess! Go back to the road and get Sergeant Brown and Sergeant Judd to bring a tarpaulin from the cart, double quick!'

'Yes, sir,' and he half-ran trying to fasten up his trousers and coat as he went.

Some of the other men started to move towards the track.

'Get back to where you were, you men, stay there and don't move.'

The men turned back mumbling to each other.

The two sergeants arrived with the tarpaulin.

'There's a body here. It's in a helluva mess. Get it wrapped up and back to the cart. Tie the tarpaulin down and don't let the men see what's in it. Don't say a word to them about it. Is that clear?'

'Yes sir, absolutely clear.'

When they saw what they had to wrap up they both went white. They were hardened soldiers but neither of them had seen anything like it before.

The body was wrapped and carried to the cart, loaded and tied down securely on top of the other equipment. Another tarpaulin was used to cover the whole cart and tied down.

The Lieutenant wanted to get his men back on the march as quickly as possible and within a few minutes they were off, moving in unison, silent but for the clatter of their boots on the road. The Lieutenant knew that word about the body would get around among the men in no time. He couldn't stop that.

Night was beginning to fall as they passed through Bishop Burton and on towards Beverley.

3

The next day, Tuesday 8th December
Tom`s Coffee House was full with people and chatter. A man with the Malacca cane walked over to a table at the back of the room and sat down.

'Good morning, Robert.'

He was Nicholas Twygge. He earned a living as a bookseller and stationer. His home, workplace and shop were in a single building in the low end of the Market Place, by Myton Gate. He had a live-in widowed housekeeper, Mrs Hannah Field, and a live-in young assistant-cum-apprentice, Samuel Parker, who was also a surrogate son. Twygge himself was a widower with no children. His wife Elizabeth had died fifteen years earlier from puerperal fever and their child was still-born. He'd not remarried but devoted himself to his business, his friends and his interests which were wide-ranging. He used his books to fill his spare time which otherwise would have been devoted to the family he didn't have. Over the years he'd become thoroughly learned. People would come to him with their weird, their wonderful and their mundane queries. He knew everyone, rich and poor, within this tight and crowded town of Kingston upon Hull and he was liked by all.

'A very good morning to you, Nick.'

'I see you've beaten me to it. It's not always easy to abandon my customers in mid-flow. I do apologise for my tardiness.'

'Think nothing of it, Nick. Business first as well I know, especially murder. I hope I find you well.'

Twygge was suddenly taken aback but he said nothing.

Robert Wray was the owner of the Coach and Horses Inn on Myton Gate, and was also one of the constables serving the people of Hull. He was tall and thickset with fair hair and a somewhat rubicund complexion. He was about the same age as

Twygge and they had been friends for many years. He was avuncular and ursine and, unlike the 'sharp' Twygge, he was blunt, not blunt in his demeanour but blunt in his appearance – rounded features and ample body, rather like a teddy bear. There was nothing sharp about him at all. But he could be firm and authoritative when the need arose, particularly in his rôle as constable. They do say that opposites attract. Wray was not married and for a long time Twygge had put pressure on him to find a wife but he never did. He made it quite clear to Twygge that he had no time – running the Inn and his work as constable kept him too busy. Twygge eventually gave up and it was not mentioned again. Wray was now a confirmed bachelor.

'Very well indeed, Robert. How could it be otherwise on a splendid morning like this? I see you have cake on your plate. Would you recommend it?'

'Certainly, it's a slice of Mistress Usherwood's delicious nun's cake.'

'That's good enough for me. Then I shall order some for myself — 'nun' too soon as I'm ready for a hearty bite!'

'*Please*, if you don't mind, Mr Twygge, you're spoiling my enjoyment of this superb confection.'

'But, Mr Wray, the *nun*'s a pun, as well as a perfect rhyme, and as the verbal device of wit it was frequently exploited by the gargantuan figure of Mr Shakespeare himself. I feel entitled to use the same, to wit — the pun!'

'Ah, once again, Robert, you've out*wit*ted me.'

'Excellent, my friend, you're catching on admirably. Mistress Usherwood, your timing is perfect, you should enter that noble profession, the theatre.'

'Come now, Mr Twygge, how could I do that at my age? Anyway, the cavortings and carryings-on at that place on Finkle Street are a disgrace to the town.'

'You're quite right, Mistress, I'm afraid the place is sinking rapidly into an abyss of depravity. There was a time not very long ago that Mrs Siddons was captivating us with her magnificent performance as Lady Macbeth.'

Mistress Usherwood departed stut-stutting.

Twygge had been on tenterhooks waiting to ask Wray what he'd meant by 'murder….'.

'Robert, what's this about a murder?'

Mistress Usherwood suddenly appeared, a little belatedly, with the coffee and cake.

'I thank you, Mistress, your service as well as your excellent food is commendable, as is your beauty!'

She gave him a nudge on the shoulder.

'Ooo, Mr Twygge, you flirt with me. I know as well as you that I've been a bit tardy with your cake, so be careful — my husband will be after you with his blunderbuss.'

'Now, there's a new word – *flirt!* But I do not *flirt* as you say, I merely state a plain and obvious fact.'

She gave him another nudge and went off to another table. He took a bite of his cake.

'This is exquisite. I may even have another slice.'

Mistress Usherwood left the table.

'Now Robert, my Samuel told me that you have something important to talk about. Is it murder?'

Wray lowered his voice to a whisper.

'There's been a discovery of a body. Captain Sanderson of the Garrison has requested my assistance. The coroners wanted him to deal with it because his men found the body out of town, but he's too busy running the garrison because of the war. I'm asking for *your* help because I know you like a challenge. The coroners have agreed to this, particularly in view of the fact that we know the town and the people better than the military. However, the Captain will still be in overall charge — we must report to him from time to time or when necessary. He's expecting us at the Citadel later this morning.'

'Suddenly, the tenor of this meeting has turned *volte-face*, Robert. I've been blown a little off course. However, I *am* intrigued and delighted that you want me to work with you on this, but can we spare the time — we have businesses to run?'

Twygge was hesitating – he knew nothing about dealing with murders. He'd never even seen the body of a murder victim.

'I realise that but I think my staff will be able to take care of everything for a while now and then. As you know, as a constable I must be expected to be available when and as necessary.'

'True, and I'm certain my business will be safe in my absence. But from what you've said so far it does sound as though it might be somewhat too demanding of us.'

'We shall have to wait and see. We can't talk about it any more here, there are too many ears.'

He took out his pocket watch, looked at it and returned it from whence it came. He stopped whispering and resumed his usual hearty tones.

'We shall finish our coffee and make our way directly to the Citadel.'

'This is quite a mystery you've dragged me into. Indeed, Constable, if you're going to make a habit of this I shall have to abandon my shop and then declare bankruptcy.'

This touch of levity brought light relief to the moment.

'Don't forget, Nick, your assistance will be valued by many others of this town,' he lowered his voice once more, 'and probably elsewhere if we find the perpetrators of this gruesome murder.'

'*Gruesome* you say! Are you sure I'm your man? And how do you know if it was murder?'

'Not *if*, Robert, *when*! And you shall see for yourself why it was murder. Whatever evil has been committed we shall find the culprits, shall we not? Let us pay our bill.'

They paid and left the Coffee House.

'The Captain said he would meet us at the garrison officers' building where he has his own office, at 11:30. Being a military man he would expect us to be prompt, of course. He said there would be a sergeant waiting for us at the South Bastion to take us in.'

Wray continued to prepare Twygge for what was to come.

They'd reached the end of the Myton Gate when Twygge interrupted.

'I must call in to explain to Mrs Field that I shall be late for my dinner. Have you any idea how long the meeting will take?'

'Sorry, Nick, I don't. I could hazard perhaps an hour.'

They entered Twygge's premises.

Mrs Field was a very amenable and robust middle-aged woman, slightly ruddy of complexion and well-presented. She was a superb cook and didn't complain when he told her about missing his dinner. She was used to his erratic comings and goings.

'Well, My Twygge, what will you do? You must eat you know,' she chided.

'I shall be quite all right, Mrs Field, nobody ever starved by missing one meal. It will do me good. I have no wish to finish up like the Constable here, do I?'

This was said in the lightness of spirit that Wray had gotten used to over the years, in fact he felt rather glad - such remarks can only be said between the best of friends.

'My dear Mistress,' said Wray, 'if you cooked for me I'd be twice the size I am now, *and* I wouldn't care a jot.'

'Be off with you and see to your business, whatever it is. I'm too busy to stand here blethering,' she said good-naturedly and off she swept.

4

The same day, Monday 7th December
Wray and Twygge made their way south along the Butchery and down Queen Street.

They turned left and entered the South End where a ferry at the mouth of the River Hull would take them the short distance to the southwest corner of the Citadel. Twygge looked at his watch.

'See that queue! Do you think you can use your influence to get us to the front: this *is* serious business you said? It's not to my liking but needs must sometimes.'

'I think I can do that.'

He moved forward and raised his voice.

'Make way, make way for the Constable, urgent business, make way!'

People began to step aside and the two men got through in spite of some frosty mumblings and grumblings. When the ferry had discharged its human cargo Twygge and Wray boarded first.

'As quick as you can, ferryman, we have an important meeting with the Captain.'

'I can only do my best, sir. The tide's coming in, ships are coming and going non-stop, everybody's in a hurry – I can't perform miracles. If the Lord had meant us to go faster he would have given this boat wings. I'll take your fares if you please.'

They handed over their farthings. By this time the boat had reached the small pier on the eastern bank. They got off and walked to the gate a short distance away. Two guards were posted outside.

'A very good morning to you, gentlemen. We have an appointment to see the Captain.

I am Constable Wray and this is Mr Twygge.'

'Yes, sir, I know you Constable, and very pleased to meet *you*, Mr Twygge. Follow me please.'

They entered the garrison. It was bustling with activities — drilling, parading, and heavy artillery was being shifted from here to there, hordes of men were on the ramparts setting guns in position, pointing them to the west to cover the river and south to cover the estuary. Soldiers were going hither and thither everywhere.

After the French Republic had declared war on Britain and since a French privateer had been sighted off Holderness, that expansive, low-lying marshy peninsula between the North Sea and the River Humber, preparations for war had begun and daily vigilance was being maintained. The people of Hull had by now become inured to the idea of war and continued with their daily business with pragmatic resignation, gaining some degree of comfort knowing that the town was well protected by masonry as well as by soldiers, while at the same time they were vaguely aware of what a siege *could* mean if it ever happened — stories of the Civil War had been passed on down the generations.

The citadel had been built a hundred years previously after the lessons of the Civil War but then was neglected for many years. It was brought back to life in the 1740s as a result of threats from France over the Old Pretender and the Jacobites, threats which never materialised into a conflict. A decade or so later, there was yet another attempted invasion, in which the French were defeated. Then, of course, the American Revolution brought further attempted invasions from the Americans, *and* the French after England declared war against them for siding with the Americans. The exploits of John Paul Jones along the east coast of Yorkshire were still fresh in people's minds. Yet again, the French, as well as the Spanish, were defeated by the English throughout Europe and the West Indies.

The citadel was built mostly of local brick, with substantial blockhouses on the two western corners and massive curtain walls. Twygge guessed the sides of the triangle to be at least a third of a mile long. He was taking everything in with the eyes of a secret agent as the men walked through. He'd seen the outside of the citadel many times of course — it was a major feature, as were the town walls which stood at twice the height of a man. This was his first visit to the interior. Wray was already familiar with the garrison, having being several times on official business.

'It seems very busy today, Private,' observed the Constable, 'any news about an invasion?'

'Not to my knowledge, sir. Things have slowed down somewhat in recent weeks. Maybe there'll be no war after all.'

'I'd not be so sure, Private, we can never trust the French – history has taught us that. But you're too young to remember.'

'Yes, sir.'

'I notice by your speech, Private, that you're not from these parts,' said Twygge. 'May I hazard a guess that you were born and raised in Nottinghamshire?'

'I was, sir. If you don't mind my asking, sir, how did you know that?'

'Two ways, you speak with that distinctive Nottinghamshire accent, and you're wearing the trappings of the Nottinghamshire Regiment. Did you see, Constable?'

He looked at Wray with a wry smile and a twinkle in his eye — obviously pleased with himself.

'I did not, Mr Twygge, but then I don't have your genius – I'm just a plodder.'

'We're all plodders in our own ways Robert, we just don't all train our minds and senses the same way. *Your* skills are your own – ones that I don't have.'

The three men approached the officers' building and, led by the Private, they entered. They went down a corridor. The Private stopped at the door and knocked.

'Enter.'

The Captain's office was in the barracks just by the South wall which faces the Humber. The room they entered was not very spacious. The walls were panelled and the Captain was sitting at his desk beneath the window and facing the door. A cosy fire was blazing in the wall to the right of the Captain. Two empty chairs were in front of the desk. Sitting in a third chair to the left of the Captain was a man in civilian clothes. Captain Sanderson had the face of the basset hound but with hard eyes. One couldn't imagine his tail ever wagging. Although, Twygge thought, unearthing certain breeds of human foxes would no doubt give him great deal of satisfaction.

The atmosphere, in spite of the roaring fire, was hanging with a heavy gloom. The faces of the seated men bore a grimness that bespoke of the matter in hand.

'Good day, gentlemen. This, as I'm sure you will recognise, is Mr Melling. Mr Melling, this is Constable Wray.'

'And this is who, Mr Wray?'

'This, sir, is Mr Nicholas Twygge, a gentleman of Hull who has a superb mind, and, I can guarantee, will be of great assistance to us.'

'I don't want any old Tom, Dick or Harry meddling in this, Mr Wray. But I shall take your word for it and trust your judgement.'

The Captain's manner was brusque, with a touch of irony in that final phrase. Twygge, too tolerant to be affronted, recognised this type of military man who has no time for civilians.

'I'm very pleased to meet you, sir, *and* you, Mr Melling, whom I know by personal experience and reputation – the most able and learned surgeon the Town and County has ever had the privilege of owning, if I may use that word. As for having a 'superb mind', Captain, that is an absurd exaggeration perpetrated by the Constable for malicious ends and I shall sue for libel one day!'

The Captain scowled at Twygge. Ever alert to people's reactions, Twygge continued, 'I do apologise, gentlemen, the seriousness of this business does not allow for such frivolity.'

This is not a good beginning to our relationship, thought Twygge.

'It certainly does not, sir, as you shall see.'

Twygge lowered his head slightly in recognition of the reproof. He realised now that Captain Sanderson had taken an instant dislike to him.

'I want you to come with me toward the Main Gate shortly. No doubt the rumours have spread, as they do, with celerity, so you probably know what to expect.'

'I beg your pardon, Captain Sanderson, but I know nothing,' said Twygge, 'The Constable merely used the word 'gruesome' to describe what has happened.'

'Well, let's go now. Follow me to the Main Gate.'

The Captain took out a large key from his desk drawer and a lantern from a small table, and they left the building. The Main Gate was in the eastern wall of the citadel and the four men walked briskly towards it, skirting the barracks square. The day had started fine but heavy rain clouds were now rolling in from the west and the sun, now past its zenith, had darkened. Once inside the vaulted passage off to the side just inside the gate they turned left and came to a heavy, studded door with a small iron grille that had been covered from the inside.

'This is the prison vault, gentlemen.'

The Captain placed the key in the lock and turned it, the heavy door squeaked and creaked as he opened it. They entered.

The cell was cold, dark and dank, although the small amount of light coming in through the door was sufficient to light up the table in the centre over which was spread a rumpled canvas with something underneath. There was an unpleasant smell. The Captain lit a lamp that was fixed to the far wall, then he lit his own lantern and held it over the object on the table.

'We've kept the body as best we can with ice and the severe cold weather has delayed the decay somewhat. But, no doubt, as you can tell by the smell it won't keep much longer so this will have to be a thorough scrutiny. There will be no opportunity after today. The body will have to be buried. Constable would you help with this?'

They slowly removed the canvas, rolling it back from one end to the other. First the feet appeared, then legs, then the stomach – it was clear now that the body was naked, grey-coloured and male. A considerable part of the legs and arms appeared to have been eaten away. Finally the canvas exposed the chest and neck. As the cover dropped to the floor there was a gasp from two of the four men present - there was no head attached to the body. Had there been more light the sudden whitening of their faces would have shown the depth of their shock.

Wray turned his head away immediately and looked at the ground as his stomach began to turn. Twygge reacted by diverting his eyes to the other men in the room. He was concerned about the fate of the nun's cake he'd previously consumed.

'I'm sorry, gentlemen, for not giving you a prior warning. We don't want this to be broadcast abroad. You know the people of Hull and how easily they can be infected by rumour. Who knows what stories may be invented and begin a simmering which could eventually boil up into hysteria?'

The veiled threat was clear, *keep your mouths shut*! No one spoke.'

The Captain continued, 'Now I shall give you all the information I can. Mr Melling has already seen the body so he will enlighten you regarding anatomical and surgical matters. You recall that the Mail Coach was robbed at Bishop Burton two weeks ago? Not the robbery of the mail but of a man. They kidnapped a man, took him away and then robbed him. This hold-up was reported by the driver as soon as the coach reached Market Weighton. The description of the footpads was very vague because of the fog but one was believed to be local by the sound of his voice. All anyone could remember of the victim was that he didn't speak at all on the journey and that he was wearing a blue coat, was tall and he was carrying a pistol. We know this because he was forced to throw it down as he descended the coach. The man's headless body was found behind shrubbery on a lane running south west, just off the York Road a few hundred yards or so beyond Bishop Burton and brought here two days ago. There was a small company of soldiers of the York and East Riding Regiment on a march from their headquarters to this garrison. They stopped to rest in the lane by the main road. One of the men found the body when he was relieving himself. We think this body is that of the kidnapped man. He was wearing a blue coat,' he pointed to the dead man, 'and he's tall, well he would have been!'

Twygge was taken aback by the Captain's brief moment of what sounded like levity.

'Some time later the body of another man, with his head *in situ* I might add, was found several hundred yards down the same lane. He's believed to have been a foreigner by his appearance, his tall stature, his features and his very blonde hair. Because he also was murdered we assume he must have been an accomplice and of no further use.'

Twygge hesitated, but by now he'd regained some of his self-composure which was, in fact, slowly beginning to turn into curiosity.

The Captain continued.

'Mr Melling has examined the body and the only thing he can conclude is that he was beheaded by a very sharp object most likely a sword, a very high-quality sword at that judging by the cleanness of the cut. Mr Twygge would you care to examine the body?'

'Certainly, Captain. Was there any attempt to search the area the following day?'

'No investigation was made at the time. The coach got to York safely, albeit a little late and nothing was taken. There appeared to be little chance of finding the culprits.'

'I see,' continued Twygge. 'I presume the legs have been got at by foxes, birds and suchlike. Would that be correct, Mr Melling?'

'I believe so, yes. There are dog-like claw marks as you can see here,' he pointed them out on the thighs.

Twygge inspected the hands that were intact but there was a distinct cut across the inside of the wrist of the left arm.

'What do you make of this, Mr Melling?'

He pointed to the cut on the wrist.

'I would say that that was made with a sharp instrument, a sword or most likely a knife.'

Then he inspected the neck, or rather what was left of it.

'Could you tell us how old you think he might have been?'

'I would hazard somewhere between forty and fifty, give or take...'

'Thank you.' Twygge continued with his inspection. 'Obviously he was a man of class, his hands, nails and general condition indicate such. Do you agree?'

'We believe so,' replied the Captain, 'and his clothes appear to be of the very finest quality.'

'Are his clothes available for us to have a look at, Captain?'

'Yes, we have them in a trunk in my office.'

'Excellent. There is a surgical question I would like to ask you, Mr Melling.'

'What is that, Mr Twygge?'

Twygge bent over the body as his composure was now fully recovered.

'Take a look at this mark on the neck.'

He pointed to a faint thin line slightly darker than the surrounding skin, near to where the skin had been cut.

'Yes, I see it.'

'Captain, could the body be turned over please?'

'Yes, give me a hand please, gentlemen.'

The four of them managed to turn the body over onto its front. Twygge scrutinised the skin of the neck once more.

'I believe there are more traces of that dark line, do you see, here, Mr Melling?'

The doctor bent over to inspect the marks.

'Yes, yes I believe so,' he said hesitantly, 'I cannot give you an explanation, gentlemen. They don't appear to have any connection with the cutting of the neck by a sword.'

'Would you be able to deduce, Doctor, whether or not the man was dead when he was beheaded?'

'Well, Mr Twygge, the body has been too long in the open to know that, and I cannot conclude from the evidence now before me that that may be the case. But I cannot see that it would be likely anyway, what would be the point?'

'I shall have to think further on the matter.' Twygge paused for a moment. 'Captain, was the body washed or cleansed in anyway since it was discovered?'

'Not to my knowledge. I didn't think it necessary.'

'Is there anything, Doctor, of a specialist nature that you can tell us regarding the condition of the body? Anything about the internal organs and tissues of the neck, for example?'

'There is nothing out of the ordinary as far as I can see.'

Twygge was peering closely into the interior of the exposed neck. Wray turned his head away in disgust.

'Doctor, I find this very interesting. The organs and tissues are not what one imagines, if one *does* imagine such things. They're all quite neat and tidy, a little damaged perhaps but quite distinct. Fascinating!'

'Sir!' The Captain spoke, 'if you wish to take a lesson in anatomy would you please arrange it with Mr Melling in your own time? Are we finished here? Any more questions that are *relevant* to the circumstances? No? Then we shall return to my office. Take the cover, gentlemen.'

They replaced the canvas over the corpse. The Captain dowsed the lights, opened the door and they came out, he then locked the cell door behind them.

'Captain, there's one more....'

Twygge was abruptly interrupted.

'Mr Twygge, there's nothing more to be said. You have all the information there is.'

Back in his office, the Captain opened the trunk that was placed against the wall by the door.

'The dead man's clothes.' He proceeded to take the items out of the trunk one by one, placing them on the floor for want of space:

'First, the aforementioned blue coat... breeches... waistcoat... stockings... shirt... and so on. Make of them what you will.'

Constable Wray and Mr Twygge began to handle the items.

'There appears to be blood stains on the left cuff of the coat and shirt, clearly from the cut on the wrist. But only very small stains on the collar of the shirt and coat. Interesting!'

'Did the pockets contain anything?' asked Wray.

'Very little. A gold watch and a handkerchief.'

'No money?'

'No, nothing else.'

'He must have had money with him. So robbery was clearly part of the kidnapping. Did the victim not have luggage with him on his journey?'

'It appears not. Nobody saw him take any onto the coach, nor was there any when the coach arrived at York. Very strange indeed!'

'Do you have the watch here, Captain?' This was Twygge.

'Yes, it's safe here in my office.'

'Is there anything about the watch that may help us – engraving of any kind?'

'Other than it was Swiss-made and of very high quality, no. It seems to me, gentlemen, that the clothing offers us nothing in the way of clues that would help us solve this murder.'

'That may be true, Captain' retorted Twygge, 'but I have had some thoughts on the matter. May I possibly borrow them for a few days?'

'That's a very odd request,' said the Captain. 'Would you mind enlightening us?'

'Well, it might be possible to find out where the clothes were made before they were bought. There are many tailors and seamstresses, and countless premises in Hull where clothing and footwear are sold, not to mention all the drapers and mercers. I'm sure someone somewhere will be able to tell us something.'

'Very well, Mr Twygge, you may take them all but you must not let out what you think even if the most meaningless piece of detail concerning this affair is mentioned within earshot of anyone. Do you understand? And that applies to you all, gentlemen. Do I have your word?'

Collectively, 'You do!'

'If you bring a cart and a small trunk with a sound lock, Mr Twygge, as soon as possible you may take them. You must come in person with no one else, except perhaps the Constable here to assist you. I shall be here in my office until four o'clock this afternoon. Good day to you and thank you for your assistance in this business.'

The Captain walked over to the door and opened it. 'Is it not enough that we have to contend with the possibility of a French invasion without having to deal with civilian murders as well!'

'We shall do our very best, Captain,' promised Wray. 'You can leave everything to us. You may return to your official duties and if we learn anything of value we will inform you immediately.'

'Oh, one more question,' said Twygge, 'Were any of the three remaining passengers on the coach able to remember anything about the man?'

'I'm afraid not, they reached York and went their ways. But the guard, who reported it to the Post Office authorities in York, noticed that the man was wearing yellow breeches – quite conspicuous for Hull!'

'So that proves that the body is that of the same man who was abducted,' said Twygge.

'I would have thought that was glaringly obvious, regardless of the breeches, sir.'

'The law always requires positive proof...'

The Captain ignored that and interrupted Twygge before he'd finished.

'Part of the guard's job is to scrutinise the passengers as they get on the coach. Nothing more was done after that because the authorities were only concerned about the delay caused by the fog and the hold-up. It was also noted by the guard that both of the kidnappers were sporting double-barrelled revolving flintlock pistols – very expensive weapons, I might add, and unusual for regular footpads. Now, I know you have your own work to attend to, gentlemen, but if you can solve this as quickly as possible I will be in your debts. Good day to you. The Sergeant will see you to the gate. He is by the door downstairs.'

At that, the door closed and the three made their way out, Mr Melling going to the main gate to his waiting carriage that would take him to the turnpike road to Wyton, and Twygge and Wray returning towards the town.

Once across the river Twygge broke the silence.

'Robert, why rob a man, take his money but leave behind a very expensive gold watch? And why hack his head off and then murder his accomplice?'

'I have absolutely no idea, Nick.'

'Well, we shall have to find out then.'

5

The next day, Tuesday 8th December

Sam Parker was sitting at his desk facing the window of his room. A sprinkling of snow had fallen in the night and covered the garden down below the window from where he was writing. In his hand was a quill. Several books lay on the desk, two of them open. His room was in the building that was *Nicholas Twygge, Bookseller*. Nicholas was his guardian and his mentor. Sam was sturdy, fair, with pale grey eyes and a firm face, bright, conscientious and eager. His eagerness and enthusiasm he had got from Nicholas. He had caught it like some benign infection, absorbed it over the four years he'd been with him, and turned him from an ill-nourished, ill-educated and ill-treated child into an exemplary young man. He lost his father when he was a small boy and his mother was unable to manage and she turned to the bottle. He was rescued when, bedraggled and wet from the rain, he was found staring at the books in Twygge's window and was invited in. Sam's mother had not objected when offered a goodly weekly sum to keep him at the bookshop.

For four years Nicholas had nourished Sam's mind and body, taught him to read and write, instructed him in business matters and introduced him to the craft of bookmanship, sending him to learn binding at William Bell's, in the Market Place, once a week. Each morning he was to study in his room, a different subject each day, and in the afternoon he worked in the backroom repairing books or occasionally tending the shop. Sometimes he was out delivering customer's orders – Twygge thought that this was the best way for Sam to meet people and to learn how to conduct himself. All of this he did with the verve that he'd got from his master. Twygge could have sent him to the Grammar School hard by the Holy Trinity Church but he had had reservations about Mr Milner's ideas of how and what boys should learn. There was no doubt that Joseph Milner was very learned and an illustrious master, as well as a good benevolent man. But he was *The Methodist*, one of those who some people would refer to as the *Bible Moth*, or a member of the *Holy Club*, although Twygge himself would not condone the use of such derogatory epithets - he was a believer in the practical as well as the intellectual and both were equally important for a person to achieve a full life.

The day was Tuesday and Sam's topic of study was History. In front of him was a copy of Oliver Goldsmith's *The Roman History*. He was pondering over the language of the Romans: how did they manage to use such an arid and, what sounded to him, formal language in everyday life? In Hull he'd heard bits of every language imaginable in various parts of the town over the years - French, Dutch, Polish, German, even Chinese, and they all sounded so natural, flowing smoothly, if not swiftly at times, like the tides of the Humber. Even though he understood not a word he was fascinated by the sounds, and the fact that he didn't understand what was being said made it all the more fascinating. But Latin, he thought, flows clumsily like the shallow and stumbling waters over a rock-strewn stream. Sam's mind was *like* the waters of a mountain stream - never stopping, for ever travelling, running this way and that, seeking a way around from one hurdle to another.

He was brought abruptly back to consciousness by a gentle tap at his door.

'Come in.'

It was Mistress Field, 'Your dinner's ready, Master Sam.'

'Thank you, I shall be down directly. What culinary delights have you prepared for us today, Mistress Field, I'm extremely peckish?'

'You shall have to come and see for yourself, young Sam, and don't let it get cold.' and off she went.

Sam arose from his desk, closed his books, wiped his quill and left the room.

In the dining room was gathered his Master and a guest Sam barely recognised.

'Ah, Sam, I'd like you to meet Mr Townend. We've done a lot of business between us by means of the General Post Office but this is the first time that we've ever met face to face.'

'I'm pleased to meet you, sir.'

"Tis my pleasure and honour, Sam,' and they shook hands.

'Now, let's be seated. I can hear Mistress Field approaching.'

They took their places at table as the Mistress entered with a large dish.

'And what have we for dinner today, my dear?'

'Salmagundy, and it's with veal today - a treat for you.'

'Wonderful, Mistress, it couldn't be better on such a winter's day.' She placed the dish on the table and proceeded to serve.

'Mr Townend,' continued Twygge, 'is also a bookseller and has come all the way from York to deliver by his own hand some rare volumes for me, *and* to have a day away from business, I presume? This must be your first visit to Hull, is it not?'

'Indeed it is, and a fine town it appears to be.'

'A small glass of claret, Mr Townend?'

'Yes please. I'm here Partly business with you Mr Twygge, but I came also to visit another gentleman of business, Mr Levi, the jeweller of Blanket Row. I haven't seen him in York for a year or so.'

'Will you be staying with him?'

'I have been invited to do so, yes. Do you know him?'

'Not personally, but he *is* famous for the quality of his work, *and* for his sartorial, er, shall we say, extravagance. He courted and married a Miss Brown of Wrawby, just over the water I believe. It was much talked about at the time. Just a few years ago if I remember correctly. This is a superb salmagundy, the veal melts in one's mouth. Mistress Field never disappoints. I think I shall marry her one day!'

Mr Townend and Sam seemed lost for words.

'Have I surprised you, gentlemen?' Twygge laughed. 'I mean it, although I fear now that I've said it I've committed myself, have I not?'

'Well,' said Mr Townend slowly, 'I *am* surprised, but on reflection I think it is a very good idea - a man needs a good wife!'

'I absolutely agree. And I think I've now fully recovered from the loss of my dear Elizabeth. I have a good, nay indeed, an excellent housekeeper and cook in Widow Field so what could be better than to have her as a wife as well? But hush, I don't wish her to overhear such talk. I shall wait until I am quite ready and prepared to make the proposal when the time is ripe. How *is* business, Isaac?'

'Not so good, I'm afraid, Nicholas. We have a surfeit of booksellers in York and the competition can be rather fierce.'

'It's getting that way here. We have at least half a dozen of them and some of those have to supplement their incomes with other things. There's even one, a Mr Foster, who does carving and gilding, and others like us have to sell stationery and do a bit of book surgery, or sell patent medicines. And that, Isaac, is within a population of twenty thousand people, a quarter of whom cannot read or write. Why many of those who can read don't is something we don't know, but it must be most of them.'

The conversation continued in the usual lively and diverse fashion until the meal was over.

'Now to work,' said Twygge. 'Sam, I have a delivery for you this afternoon to Mr Benjamin Sachs of Dagger Lane. Two books he ordered several months ago arrived yesterday from London. They've taken all this time to get here. They had to come from Berlin, so please apologise to the gentleman for me. There will be an invoice with them but tell him that he may pay me at his leisure. I have an important meeting later this afternoon.'

'I don't think I know his house. How can I find it?'

'Next door but one to the Chapel. There is a sign outside. Mr Crosswell has the books prepared for you downstairs.'

'I shall be off straight away then. It's been a pleasure meeting you again, Mr Townend. I do hope we shall meet again soon.'

'I hope so too, Sam. Good day to you.'

Sam rose from his chair, made a small bow, 'Good day, sirs,' and left the room.

'I shall have to be on my way, Nicholas, I need to be at Mr Levi's by two o'clock. I don't wish to hurry but we have had rather a long but yet delightful dinner. You have a very bright and amiable young man there. How he's come along over the years!'

'I have indeed. He is a credit to me. His diligence in his studies, *and* his work, are exemplary. I am a very fortunate man, Isaac.'

'Oh, by the way, Nicholas, I heard about that incident in Bishop Burton a couple of weeks ago. What was that all about, do you know?'

'Yes, Isaac, a little. How did you find out about it?'

Twygge could detect a slight frown on Townend's brow. He hesitated before he answered.

'There was a very small item in the *York Courant* about it at the time but there were not many details.'

There was a brief pause. Twygge could sense that there was something bothering Townend.

'Well, actually I believe I'm involved in it, Nicholas, but I can't tell you – it may cost me my life.'

For once Twygge was lost for words.

'How on earth can that be, Isaac? Surely you must be imagining it.'

'I don't think so. I've been threatened. But please, Nicholas, don't ask me. I came here really to find out what happened but I don't wish to involve you.'

'Well, actually I *am* involved in it. I've been asked by a Constable to help him investigate, under the supervision of the Captain of the garrison.'

'Is there anything you can tell me about it, Nicholas?'

'Nothing at all, only what's been in the Press.'

'I'm flabbergasted. Are you serious?'

'Never more serious, Isaac. But you really should tell me how you're involved – it may help us.'

'It's impossible, Nicholas. I'd be putting great danger on you and your constable as well as me. I just cannot.'

Twygge could see that Townend was deeply disturbed so he decided not to pursue the matter further.

'I do hope something can be done. Every day in York I feel afraid that something dreadful is going to happen to me. But now that I know that a serious investigation has been started I might feel a little safer. But thank you for the delicious dinner. I'm sorry we didn't have much of a chat with you, Sam, but maybe on another, more happy, occasion? I'm certain you're in very good hands with Mr Twygge. I must be going now to meet Mr Levi.'

'I'm sorry that things have turned out this way, Isaac. I'll go and get your coat.

Twygge went out and returned with Townend's coat and his own. They left the room.

Hannah Field came in and cleared the table.

Sam collected the two books for Mr Sachs from Mr Crosswell. They were two large tomes tied carefully with cord. He noticed when he looked at the spines the titles were in a form of alphabet he didn't recognise. Several customers were browsing along the shelves.

Sam turned to Mr Crosswell, 'I shall be back soon to help you, it appears to be rather busier than usual today.'

'I suspect I shall need you, Sam, it's almost as busy as a market day.'

'Short days, long nights - people need to be occupied of an evening. I shouldn't be more than half an hour.'

He left the shop and turned left into Myton Gate. He passed the gunsmith's and turned into Finkle Street with its notorious Theatre Royal, crossed the road towards the Coach and Horses Inn, continuing until he reached Dagger Lane, once the street of the knife-makers. He turned right and within a couple of minutes reached the premises of Benjamin Sachs. The building was not new like several in this area of the town but it was smart and the sign, *Silversmith*, outside was fresh and colourful.

He knocked on the door. He waited for a few moments but there was no answer.

He tried again a little more loudly. Soon he heard a bolt being drawn and the door opened.

'Good afternoon, I…' but he was interrupted.

'I'm sorry, sir, to keep you waiting but we always wait for a second knock before opening the door.'

The girl spoke with an accent but her English was good.

'Why should that be, Miss?'

'We often get mischievous children knocking on the door and running away, you see. A second knock means it must be real and not those naughty boys and girls. Come in. You want to buy?'

Sam only heard the first part of her reply, he was transfixed. In the doorway stood the most beautiful young lady he'd ever seen. She was dressed all in black, raven-haired, with soft gentle eyes as dark and luminous as jewels of obsidian.

'I beg your pardon, Miss…', he fumbled, 'my name is Samuel Parker. I have two books here for Mr Sachs from Mr Twygge of the bookshop.'

From inside the house came a man's voice, 'Ver is dot, Rokhele?'

'A mensh, foter. Er hat gebrocht tsvai bicher fun her Twygge.'

'Kumen,' returned the voice from within.

Rokhele showed Sam in and he followed her down a corridor and into a large room. Sam recognised the Israelite immediately, though not personally. It was the clothes he was wearing that bespoke his race. He'd seen others of his race occasionally in the town but there never were very many of them so he hadn't had any opportunities to make their acquaintance. Sam was now in the house of Hebrews. So, he thought, their books are in their language, but yet they speak German – interesting!

The man arose from the bench where he'd been sitting. He was wearing a flowered, lengthy loose waistcoat and a colourful tasselled cap, black breeches, and he sported a full long grey beard.

'Good afternoon, young sir, I have not seen you before. Mr Twygge bring the books.' His accent was very strong, much more so than Rokhlele's.

'He's very busy, sir, he has an important meeting to attend. I'm Samuel Parker his assistant.'

'Pleased to meet with you, Mr Samuel. Mr Twygge is a busy man.'

Sam handed the books over to Mr Sachs who took them and handled them very carefully. He stroked them, and his eyes lit up.

'Send Mr Twygge my thank you for these beautiful books. I miss him today, we have good talking when he come to my house. Thank you.'

'You have some beautiful things here, Mr Sachs. Do you make them yourself?'

'Yes, I make.'

'Why are they all inside out of sight?'

'They're here for every man to see. They knock on the door to see. I make to special order. I very busy, there are much people with lots money to buy silver.'

'I'm very glad for you, Mr Sachs, and it's been a great pleasure to meet you and a privilege to see your beautiful work. I hope I can deliver to you again.' And see his beautiful daughter again, he was thinking!

'Shalom. Peace be with you, sir.'

Rokhele led Sam out of the room, down the corridor to the front door and opened it.

'Good day, Miss. It was a pleasure meeting you.' He held out his hand but she didn't take it.

'Good day, sir.' She closed the door.

He hesitated for a moment then set off back down Dagger Lane with a noticeable spring in his step and a smile in his eyes. He hadn't realised that he'd forgotten to give Mr Sachs the invoice for the books.

He recalled some lines of Milton that had lodged themselves in his mind after he'd been reading them aloud to Nicholas on a previous cold winter evening:

Grace was in all her steps, Heaven in her eye,
In every gesture dignity and love.

6

The next day, Wednesday 9th December
Robert Wray's office was on the first floor at the back of the Coach and Horses Inn on Myton Gate. The building was old but in good shape and still bore the features of the best of the 17th century's architecture and fittings. It was one of Hull's main coaching houses.

It was a cold and dull day and the Constable was sitting by the fire with a glass in his hand when there was a knock on the door.

'Enter.'

Nicholas Twygge walked in.

'Ah, good morning, Nick, do come in and take a pew. I know you like a fine glass of hot negus especially on a morning like this. Please help yourself and sit down here.' Wray pointed to a chair opposite him by the fire.

'A very pleasant alternative to our usual coffee, Robert, thank you. We have a lot to do this morning so this splendid nectar will be the crack of the whip that we need. Your good health, Robert.' He raised his glass and drank, letting the liquid linger on his tongue awhile before he let it flow down, warming his throat gently as it descended.

'Excellent Robert - perfect! Now to business. I've made a list of everything we know about the man in blue.'

'I've done the same but no doubt yours will be the longer.' said Wray.

'Why should it, Robert?'

'You're much more thorough in these matters of the mind, and don't deny it. I'm practical, I *do* things, you know that.'

'It matters nought - let's begin. Here's what we have.' Twygge proceeded to read aloud from his notes. 'The man was beheaded with a very sharp implement, probably a sword, although inexplicable lines have been seen around his neck. There was a cut on his left wrist. He was of a good build and height. He was not a common artisan judging by his hands. Nothing else about his body was remarkable. His clothes were of the finest fabrics. They bore no signs of where they were manufactured. There was a gold watch of Swiss origin, coat buttons with the initials **MS**, and a handkerchief embroidered with **VG**. Why he should be bearing items of clothing with two separate sets of initials is also a bafflement. Perhaps the handkerchief was a gift, a memento from a lady friend. That, on the face of it, doesn't amount to much. Can you add anything?'

'No, my list is about the same as yours. However, I did find it strange though that the blue coat the man was wearing was of a rather cheap quality. Now why would that be when all the other garments were of a very high quality? That will require some serious thought. Also, I did think that the man's skin, in spite of the damage and discoloration, appeared to be darker than the average Englishman's. What do you think?'

'Well, Robert, I missed that one. You may be right, but it may be the consequence of decomposition – or, the lack of daylight in that cell. We can't be certain. But even if it was naturally darker, we have so many people nowadays from other lands that he may well have been a visiting foreigner or even a resident. As for the blue coat I've no ideas. But we shall keep all this in mind. Anything else?'

'No, that's all we have. I really don't see how we can get any further. Shall we be wasting our time?'

'I'm not sure, Robert. Let me add a few of my thoughts. First, I intend, with help of course, to take the clothes that the man was wearing around the drapers and gentlemen's outfitters in the town to try to determine the origin of the cut and fabric. It might help. It should tell us whether he could be a resident or a visitor.'

'Unless,' interrupted Wray, 'he was a visitor who bought his clothes in this country.'

'Of course, Robert, you're right. I find three other things curious: firstly, why two different sets of initials - the handkerchief's and on the buttons? Secondly, we need to check the gunsmith's concerning those double-barrelled pistols the abductors were carrying.'

'I can do that Nick. There are only two of them and I know them quite well.'

'Excellent!'

'Now the third thing are those marks on the neck. I believe he was strangled before he was beheaded.'

'But why on earth kill a man and then chop his head off?'

'That was the puzzle. I shall have to confirm my theory with a visit to a surgeon before I can pursue it further.'

'But don't forget, Nick, the head wasn't found. Perhaps it was buried, in which case it's not likely to be found.'

'Well, by whatever means the head was disposed of, it's missing, *at the moment*. Who knows, it may turn up? The only thing I can think of is that the head was cut off to prevent identification. The most puzzling question is why kill the man, behead him and then rob him? He must have been carrying money, especially if he was a foreigner who lately arrived in Hull. All this tells me that the motive was a complex one. It seems to me that the reason behind this murder is going to be difficult, if not impossible, to discover from what we know so far.'

There was a pause, a few moments of silence. Both men supped from their glasses.

'A man's character, his identity, almost his whole being, is held in his face, Robert. Even his hair's a part of what and who he is - without hair he's lost a large part of his personal identity, he becomes almost anonymous.'

'Without the head, I believe we'll be hunting in the dark, Nick. But don't lose *your* head about it!'

'Robert!!! Now we've got his clothes we can ask questions around the town to see if anyone's noticed him. There's a lot more we can do further.'

'You're quite right. I can always depend on you to keep my wheels out of the ruts.'

'One thing I was wondering, where did he stay in the town, or did he get off a ferry or a ship on the same day that he got onto the coach?'

'Of course! If he had stayed in the town we can enquire at the hotels. I think the Cross Keys Inn would be the best bet first. And that's given me another idea - John Pybus at the Mail Coach Office, he would have sold a ticket to the victim. He may remember him. We'll put him first on the list.'

'Yes, unless someone else bought the ticket in his stead.'

'If that's the case, Nick, we shall move on to the hotel, a mere two or three minutes walk away from Silver Street - two birds with one stone in a short time.'

'Oui. D'une pierre faire deux coups!'

' I beg your pardon?'

'Nothing, just words that came into my head. No more shilly-shallying, lead on!'

'Would it not save considerable time if we separated? I can see Mr Pybus and you can go to the Cross Keys.'

'It would certainly save time, Robert, but I'm of the mind that two brains are always better than one when there's a problem to solve.'

'Mmm... yes, I see your point'.

The two men entered the Mail Coach Office.

'Good morning, Mr Pybus. You know Constable Wray. We're here on behalf of Captain Sanderson, enquiring into the Mail Coach hold-up.'

'Good morning to you, gentlemen. The Captain has already been here. He came yesterday and said you may be coming to see me. But, as I told the Captain, I don't remember anyone buying a ticket who resembled the man in the Captain's description. It's two weeks ago, and many people have passed through here since then. I'm sorry, sirs.'

'How unfortunate. However, if you do think of anything or if anyone else talks to you please inform the Constable, if you would be so kind.'

'I certainly shall, gentlemen. I told the Captain likewise.'

'Good day to you, Mr Pybus, and thank you,' said Wray.

'Good day to you, sirs.' The two left the office.

'Not a good start, Robert. First enquiry - a total failure! Never mind, let us not be discouraged. I have an idea while we're here. Why do we not just cross Low Gate and call in to see your brother in Bishop Lane before we go to the Cross Keys? I know he was not part of our quest but he might just find us a clue.'

'We can but give it a try, Nick, although being a very busy man he may not be in his office.'

'I said, *let us not be discouraged*. He may be in so let's trot in that direction. You know, I'm getting a great thrill out of this. It's the challenge and the pursuit. Don't you feel the thrill, Robert?'

'Well, a little maybe, but it's really more of a necessary chore for me. I sometimes wish the Captain hadn't asked me to take over. Although, I must admit, having you to help me does lighten the burden considerably.'

'Splendid!'

They fought their way through the people and traffic across Low Gate and turned into Bishop Lane, past a shoemaker's, a pawnbroker's, a brandy merchant's, a doctor's surgery, and a wharfinger, before reaching the office of the Postmaster, John

Wray, also agent for the Royal Exchange Fire and Life Office, London. An assistant showed them into his office.

'Good morning, brother, I hope we find you well?'

'Good morning, Robert, this is a surprise. We see so little of each other these days. I'm very well thank you.'

John was older than his brother, of smaller build and had a much more serious disposition. He bore his two heavy responsibilities with a quiet zeal and a dutiful and diligent application.

'I believe you know Mr Twygge. A good customer of yours I suspect?'

'He is indeed. Good morning to you, sir. And what brings you both here?'

'Good morning, Mr Wray. Captain Sanderson of the garrison has requested Robert's assistance in trying to discover what happened regarding the Mail Coach incident at Bishop Burton and Robert asked me to help in the matter, which I readily agreed to do.'

'Well, gentlemen, I must admit to being very pleased to hear that something *is* being done. That business has cast a dark cloud over me, Mr Twygge. I do feel some degree of responsibility for the actions of the employees of the Post Office. The guard has taken the blame, of course, and in the circumstances he's been treated quite leniently by the authorities. But their interest was minimal however. Because there was no robbery and only a marginal delay, the Post Office were not overly concerned. Finding the perpetrators would ease the discomfort of the burgesses of Hull considerably though. So how can I help?'

'We shall do our damnedest towards that end, Mr Wray, but we wondered whether you might be able to offer any information, no matter how trivial, that might help. For instance, who took that day's mail to the coach? That person may remember the passengers. We do know that the man abducted was tall and was wearing a blue coat of high-quality.'

'The mail was collected by Mr Pybus' assistant. Have you been to the office to enquire?'

'We have but nobody can remember anything. It's not surprising considering how busy everyone is.'

'Yes, we can understand that - celerity is the word in Mail and Post Office business, is it not?'

'Most definitely. It is the basic principle of the whole operation and it is vital, albeit fraught with dangers that excessive haste inevitably carries with it. I'm sorry indeed but I cannot help you.'

'There is one other idea that I've had. Would it not be of value if Mail Coach tickets were issued with the travellers' names on them? In this instance it would have been of immense value to us.'

'Well, that is a new idea, Mr Twygge, but I'm not sure whether the Post Office would think so. I tell you what, Mr Twygge, I shall write a letter to the General Post Office in London explaining our predicament. Although abduction of passengers must be quite a rare event the idea might be useful in other circumstances. Yes, a very good idea.'

His eyes told of the mild excitement he felt as a result of Twygge's suggestion – this could impress his masters!

'Well, now please excuse me, business calls as ever. There is some post due from out of town shortly. I wish you success in your searches and please keep me informed.'

'We shall, Mr Wray, and thank you for offering your time.'

'Yes, thank you for your help, brother, and we appreciate your concern. The Cross Keys is our next destination. We bid you good day and I'm sure that between us we will sort this mess out.'

'I do hope so, Robert.'

Twygge opened the door, allowed Robert to leave first then

closed it. They turned left retracing their steps back to Low Gate and thence to the Market Place.

At the Cross Keys there was the usual hustle and bustle of people coming and going. The dining room was filling up rapidly.

'I think we should first consider having some dinner here, Robert, it's approaching that time of day and the place is getting full. And my stomach is sending me little reminders.'

'Yes, we could. But I can offer you a very nice *ordinary* at my place and it would cost us nothing.'

'That's very generous of you. I shall accept the offer.'

They left the hotel and crossed the Market Place past the towering and magnificent gilded statue of King William III on horseback, looking northwards as though he'd just arrived into the town and was riding forth to save it from the threat of the Jacobites. It had been standing there nigh on sixty years. Known locally as *King Billy* it had been there in both rain and shine, forever glistening, never tarnishing, as a constant reminder of what might have been... although not *everyone* at that time was pleased with it's presence!

After their lunch Wray and Twygge returned to the Cross Keys and were questioning the man behind the reception desk when they were interrupted by a young lad.

'Excuse me, sirs, but I heard you talking about the day of the murder and I...'

'Don't interrupt!' said the man, 'What on earth do you know about it? This is private and you have no business listening in or interrupting. Back to your work!'

'But, sir, I think this is important.'

'Back to your business before I...'

'Please,' interrupted Twygge, 'let him speak. If you know something young man, however small, it could help us.'

'Well, if you say so, sir.'

'What have you to say, boy?' boomed the receptionist.

'Well, sir, I was here in the lobby that day and I saw the man in the blue coat...'

'How do you know it was a blue coat he was wearing?' interrupted Twygge quickly. He thought the lad may have heard things from the local gossipmongers, but not actually seeing it for himself.

'He looked a bit different, I mean, he was tall, sir, he looked... I'm... I don't know but he just seemed different. Then I saw these two rough-looking blokes watching him for a long time and then they left.'

'This *is* interesting! How do you know it was him that had anything to do with our being here? What else do you know?' enquired Wray.

'Everybody knows, sir, since yesterday.'

'How much do you know?'

'Well, sir, this dead man without a head was found at Bishop Burton and he was wearing a blue coat, that's what's going round.'

Twygge was right about the gossip. 'Why do you think it was him that had anything to do with our being here? '

'Well, it's Constable Wray, sir, everyone knows him and he was seen with another gentlemen going into the garrison. They said they'd been to see the Captain. I just thought...'

'Gracious me,' interrupted Twygge, 'I'm quite amazed. This lad is very bright indeed, gentlemen. How old are you?'

'Fifteen, sir.'

An undernourished fifteen, thought Twygge, 'What's your name?'

'He's Joseph Heron,' said the man behind the counter.

'I'm sure he's capable of answering for himself,' said Twygge, 'Where do you live, Joseph?'

'Behind the Friary ruins, sir, at the bottom of Grimsby Lane.'

'Very good young Joseph, I do believe we might call on your assistance in the near future. One more question, tell us about the two men you mentioned.'

'It's like this, sir, they just stared at him all the time he was paying his bill.'

'Did they speak?'

'No sir.'

'Describe their appearance.'

'They looked like sailors, sir. One of them I think was foreign. He was very tall and had yellow hair, and his clothes were different.'

'What made you think that?'

'I don't know, sir, you know, people look different somehow, you just know, sir.'

'Very good Joseph you've been extremely helpful, more than you realise. Back to your work now.'

'Yes, sir, thank you, sir,' and off he went.

'That lad is quite a character. He has a natural instinct for careful observation. Given the opportunities he could do well for himself. We could use him again, Robert..'

'Yes, he's a very bright lad. Now we seem to have learned *something*, but what next?'

He addressed the receptionist, 'Thank you for your co-operation and good day to you.'

'Good day, gentlemen.'

They both left the hotel.

'On thing bothers me, Robert. That lad just now said he thought one of the two men was foreign. The Captain told us that the people in the coach at Bishop Burton thought they were local.'

'Those two men the lad saw were not the murderers then? '

'We shall have to keep open minds. *Looking foreign* is a rather vague description, but we cannot eliminate them as suspects so soon. Anyway, the next thing, Robert, is to see what we can learn from the dead man's garb.'

'And how shall we do that?'

'I intend, with the help of Sam to visit drapers and clothiers and see what, if anything, they can tell us.'

'And when shall we do that?'

'The sooner the better. I think we should start this today, if that's not overdoing it? Have you some spare time, Robert?'

'Could we start tomorrow? I have one or two other duties to perform.'

'I quite understand, Robert. You have a demanding business, not to mention your duties as Constable. Look, I shall divide the work between Sam and myself. It won't do any harm if he misses a morning's study for once. He's been extremely diligent over the years. I'm sure we can cover the ground between us.'

'If you're certain Nick. I hesitate to put all this part of the job onto your shoulders, considering I dragged you into it in the first place.'

'Think nothing of it Robert. You get off. Shall we meet as usual tomorrow?'

'Would the afternoon suit you? That would give me more time.'

'Of course it would, it would also be better for Sam and me. Shall we say four o'clock?'

'Four o'clock it is, and thank you again for helping me out.'

'My pleasure as you know, dear friend. Tomorrow then?'

'Tomorrow.'

They parted. Twygge went to his house to collect some clothing and to instruct Sam in his new-found occupation as a criminal investigator.

Immediately after lunch on that same day, Sam Parker went back to Mr Sachs' house to deliver the invoice he'd forgotten to leave the previous day. He knocked on the door, waited a minute then knocked again. He heard footsteps approaching and the unbolting of the door. His heart was beating at a higher rate than normal. The door opened.

'Ah, Mr Parker, good day.' Sam was unprepared. This was apparent by his silence and blank look.

After a pause, 'Can I help you?' It was Mr Sachs himself.

'I, er, forgot to leave the invoice yesterday, Mr Sachs, here it is. Mr Twygge said you can pay it at your convenience.'

'Thank you, sir, I will pay now.' He went indoors and returned with some money. There was no sign of Rokhele. He dare not ask, it would be unthinkable.

'Thirty five shillings,' he counted it out. 'There, and thank Mr Twygge very much. I will again order books from him. Good day.' He closed the door. Sam's heart sank. He had so many questions to ask Rokhele. He turned back down Dagger Lane, walked to the end, hesitated, and returned along the opposite side of the road to the other end of the Lane. Then he walked back again slowly. He did this twice in the hope that Rokhele would leave the house. She didn't. He returned home and bore the heavy burden of disappointment on him for the rest of the day.

When he got home he found Twygge waiting for him.

'Sam, I was surprised to find you not here just now.'

'Sorry, I forgot to tell you that I had forgotten to give Mr Sachs the invoice for the books yesterday. I only remembered this morning, and you were out so I decided to go back to his house with it straight away after dinner. I left the money in your office.'

'I said he didn't need to pay immediately.'

'I told him that but he insisted.'

'Yes I can see that, he's that kind of man. Well, let's put that behind us. I have another job for you. Come to my office.'

Twygge led the way through the door. Sam followed and the entered Twygge's office-cum-study. Twygge opened the small trunk containing the dead man's clothes.

'Now, I can't go into any details at all Sam, but I would like you to take this pair of boots. I know it seems a very strange request to make of you but I would like you to put them in a bag and take them to as many of the boot and shoemakers and dealers in the town as you can find. I need to know where they might have been made. As I said, it is an odd request but it is important and urgent, but do please try to avoid a discussions concerning anything else except their manufacture.'

'I quite understand, sir. I shall do exactly as you say.'

'Good lad. Now it's getting a bit late in the afternoon so see if you can fit in an hour's worth now and if you have no luck you can continue in the morning. Start on the Market Place, up one side and down the other. I'll see what I can do with some of these other clothes.'

'Yes, sir, but what about my morning studies, it's Thursday tomorrow, geography, my favourite?'

'It won't do you any harm to miss it for once. You've been extremely conscientious in your studies, Sam, and you know how pleased we are with you. You wouldn't really mind missing one morning would you?'

'No, sir. I shall put these in a bag from the shop and be on my way.'

'Thank you, Sam. Oh, by the way, if you don't find anything today and if you find something in the morning would you come along with it to Mr Wray's office at the Coach and Horses tomorrow morning at 11 o'clock?'

'Yes, sir.' Sam swept out of the room.

His earlier disappointment appeared to have diminished somewhat, but only temporarily. Out on the street he turned his head and looked down Myton Gate, his thoughts on Dagger Lane!

7

The next day, Thursday 10th December
Having had no success the previous day Sam and Twygge were continuing their separate rounds the following morning. It was raining so Twygge was pleased when he found the next tailor's shop.

'I am quite certain they were of French make, Mr Twygge.'
'Could you say why?'

Nicolas Twygge was in the backroom of the premises of David Hutchinson, high-class tailor of Low Gate. He had been doing the rounds of all the tailors and drapers with the coat, waistcoat, and breeches of the dead man. He'd started up High Street, turned along Chapel Lane, and was now working his way down Low Gate. One or two people had thought the clothes might have been foreign. That was all the information he'd been able to glean so far.

'Well, as you can see, they are much too ostentatious for English tastes. The cut of the coat front and tails for example, and the *revers* of both are far too exaggerated. *And* the quality of the wool is inferior. They could, of course, have belonged to one of those London dandies who might have fitted themselves out in Paris or perhaps had them made at home.'

'I see, Mr Hutchinson, very interesting.'

'Another thing, Mr Twygge – what's this stain around the collar?'

'I'm afraid I can't say.'

'Can't say or won't say,' thought the tailor.

'Could these clothes be very old?'

'Certainly not, the fabric of these is quite fresh. I would say they are not much above a year old.'

'What about the quality?'

'Some of the finest, except for the coat. A waistcoat of

exquisite silk. And another thing, by the way, silk has also gone out of fashion here.'

'Really? I don't notice these things, Mr Hutchinson.'

'Perhaps you should,' he thought, glancing at Twygge's attire.

'You haven't mentioned the breeches?'

'Ah, yes, well, I'm not sure about those. The buckskin is quite common but, I would say that yellow is somewhat unusual these days.'

'You've been a great help to me, Mr Hutchinson, I thank you very much indeed.'

'May I venture to enquire as to why you want to know all this, Mr Twygge?'

'As much as I would love to return your kindness with an explanation in answer to your question, I'm afraid I'm not permitted. One day it may be possible but at the present I would prefer it if you didn't mention my visit to anyone. I apologise for my having to be so secretive but it's in the hands of powers beyond my control. When I am allowed to talk about it I promise, Mr Hutchinson, that you will be one of the first to know. Although I suspect that you will read it first in the newspapers. May I thank you for such valuable information? It's been of the utmost importance, as you may one day find out. Good day, sir.'

Twygge turned towards the door.

'Good day, Mr Twygge. I shall be thinking about this mystery for the rest of the day.'

He continued on his mission and walked down Low Gate. Whilst he was at the bottom end of the town Twygge decided to walk to Dock Street and call in to see the surgeon Bacchus Huntington. He was sure the surgeon would be able to explain certain matters of blood circulation: *as per 'Exercitatio Anatomica de Motu Cordis et Sanguinus in Animalius'* (Frankfurt, 1625) by William Harvey, a rare volume that had once passed through

Twygge's hands.

After the visit and satisfied that he'd discovered all he needed to know from Mr Huntington Twygge returned up Low Gate and went straight on into the Market Place towards the Trinity Church. As it was only a few minutes after half past ten he decided it was too early to meet Robert Wray so he would spend some time in the reading room of the Coach and Horses. The room was quiet, there was only one other person.

'Good morning. Miserable rain we have today.'

'It's that time of year... *Though the rain it raineth every day......*'

'I see you are a scholar, sir. Are you staying at the inn?'

'No, sir. I am a bookseller. My shop is at the top end of Myton Gate not far from here.'

'Of course, I was even in there this morning. You must be Mr Twygge?'

'I am indeed, sir. Nicholas Twygge at your service. I don't believe we've met. And by your voice I don't believe you are from the north of England?'

'True. I'm from London. But I'm staying in York at the moment. James Harris,' he offered his hand, 'I'm in Hull on business.'

'I'm pleased to meet you, Mr Harris. May I enquire as to what business?'

'I'm employed by the Post Office but I cannot speak about my business here, Mr Twygge, I've been instructed not to. I apologise for that.'

'Not at all Mr Harris, I quite understand. I'm in a similar sort of situation myself. I've come here to see what's in the newspapers. It concerns a brutal murder that was committed in these parts recently. Do you mind if I have a brief look? I have an appointment with the landlord, Mr Wray, at eleven o'clock concerning some news that may be in print today.'

'Certainly Mr Twygge, but I have the very thing here that

you're looking for.' He handed over a copy of the *Hull Packet*. It was open at page 2.

'Really Mr Harris? How fortunate for me, you've saved me some time.' Twygge started to read, 'Mmm... oh dear...tut-tut...'

He begins to quote from the newspaper.

'...gruesome, bloody and sordid execution and decapitation of an innocent traveller has caused some serious concern to everyone in Hull and its environs.....people are afraid to come out of their houses at night and even in the daytime. They go about their business suspicious of every stranger they see. The authorities are doing nothing...'

Harris interrupts him.

'Quite, Mr Twygge, an abominable exaggeration, hyperbole at its worst. Is this the business you are here to see Mr Wray about?'

'It is, sir, and such a coincidence that an employee of the Post Office should be reading this as I walked in.'

'Not a coincidence that *I* am here but a coincidence that *you* are on the very same business. But it is a happy coincidence for me. I arrived early this morning on the Mail Coach from York. I've been sent to investigate thoroughly what happened at Bishop Burton that day. I have no contacts other than Captain Sanderson who's agreed to see me at two o'clock this afternoon. How are you involved, Mr Twygge, and why also Mr Wray?'

'It's a long story which I have no time to recount.' He took out his pocket-watch. 'It's approaching eleven o'clock. But you must come along with me to meet Mr Wray. You obviously don't know it but he's a Constable who's been commissioned together with myself by the Captain to do what you've been employed to do. The three of us being here together is an unlikely event that would normally only be found in the pages of a Gothic novel, would it not?'

'Indeed, sir, as would the manner of the murder itself. Shall we go?'

'Follow me Mr Harris.'

They left the reading room, mounted the stairs and Twygge knocked on the door of Wray's office.

'Come in.'

The two men entered. The Constable looked surprised.

'Robert, there has been a most remarkable coincidence in your reading room. I went in to see whether the report of the murder had been printed and in the room was sitting this gentlemen reading the very same piece of news. Let me introduce him, this is Mr James Harris employed by the Post office to investigate the Bishop Burton murder, would you believe? Mr Harris, this is Robert Wray a member of the Town of Hull Constabulary.'

Wray's expression was one of astonishment.

'I'm extremely, nay, unbelievably fortunate and very pleased to meet you Constable. When I arrived here nigh on five hours ago I knew know one, now suddenly, well, here we are!'

Wray, having recovered his composure asked the two men to sit down by him at his desk.

'Please take some tea.'

'Thank you,' said Harris, 'this is a luxury.' Smiling, he added, 'Smuggled?'

'Who knows these days, Mr Harris, but it is from a reputable dealer.'

Wray served the tea. He continued, 'So, a slight change of plan I think, Nick. We should explain to Mr Harris everything we know and our ideas on the matter concerned.'

'Yes,' said Twygge, 'but I forgot to mention that Mr Harris has made an appointment to see the Captain at two o'clock this afternoon. So your suggestion, Robert, is the best way to occupy our time. Do you think the Captain would object if we two went along with Mr Harris later? Otherwise we shall be four parties floundering around in dark waters without each other's help.'

'Let me say, Nick, that it's nonsensical for you *not* to go, and go you shall, and the Captain can take it or leave it.'

'Well said, Robert!'

'Well, I've been getting annoyed with his pomposity. Do you realise I've been called to see him twice recently and he's berated me for not having any news to give him? What does the man expect - an instant solution?'

'Don't take it personally, Robert. He has a difficult job. He is what he is, we can't change that.'

'He just...well...I don't know!'

'May I enquire, Mr Harris, why is the Post Office interested in this affair? I understood that no mail was stolen and the delay to the coach was minimal. It appears to be mainly a local matter.'

'That's a very good point, Mr Twygge. Perhaps we should wait until I've seen Captain Sanderson. That way we can all have the information together at one time and place.'

'Now, Mr Harris, are you *prepared* to face the demon figure of Captain Sanderson?'

'In my work I'm sure I've met worse, Mr Twygge. But please, gentlemen, call me James. I take it we are now a team? By the way, how is it that you two are involved in this business?'

The Constable explained the situation to Mr Harris after which there followed a lengthy account of the events of the past weeks. After an hour and a half James Harris knew as much about the murder as Twygge and Wray.

In the meantime Samuel Parker decided to begin his mission around the town with the pair of the murdered man's boots contained in a box. He turned left into Myton Gate. It wasn't a random choice, it wasn't instinctive, it was more of a yearn.

He scanned both sides of Myton Gate as he went along. He marched down and back along Vicar Lane, Finkle Street, Sewer Lane and Fish Street... there were no such businesses. He decided there was no point in going beyond Dagger Lane as it was so near to the town wall so he turned right into it, down one side and back the other. There were no footwear shops, *nor any sign of Rokhele*! He then realised that there was no point in going back down Myton Gate where he'd already been, so he went back up Dagger Lane intending to continue his search down Postern Gate. Now, he was totally unaware that on Postern Gate practically facing Dagger Lane was a synagogue when he saw it and then he realised the significance of the building: *Sachs* equals *Hebrews*, *Hebrews* equals *Jews*, *Jews* equals *synagogue*!

The people and their building had never featured much in his life, if at all. But now all of a sudden it took on a meaning that for him was perhaps even bigger then he realised at the time. He stopped to inspect the building. The door was closed, it was quiet and there appeared to be no activity of any kind. After a while he turned and continued up Postern Gate, feeling disappointed yet once more.

Eventually having covered several streets he came to Low Gate. There he found the shop of Thomas Allan, Boot and Shoemaker. He went in.

'Good morning young man. What can I do for you?'

'Good morning, sir. Are you Mr Allen by any chance?'

'No, sir, merely his assistant. Can I help you?'

'I'm here on behalf of Mr Twygge, the bookseller of Myton Gate.'

'Oh yes, I know of Mr Twygge, he has a reputation you know.'

'Yes, I work for him.'

'So, what would you like to see?'

'Nothing, sir. I've been asked to enquire about these boots.' He proceeded to take them out of the box. 'I've been along many streets but this is the first boot-maker I've come across.' He placed the boots on the counter.

'What about them? Do they need mending?'

'Oh no, they're in very good condition. Mr Twygge wants me to ask you if you can tell me where they might have been made.'

The assistant picked up a boot, inspected it inside and out and looked up at Sam.

'Well, I can't really say where they were made, there are no labels or markings as far as I can see.'

'Oh well.' There was a slight pause. 'Do you think Mr Allan might know?'

The assistant appeared to be somewhat put out.

'Now then young man, I've been in this business over twenty five years. I know all there is to know about boots.'

Sam reddens. A customer enters the shop.

'I do apologise, sir. I didn't intend to cause offence. Mr Twygge said it's very serious and I must endeavour as best I can to discover *anything* concerning the origin of the boots. I believe that sometimes two minds are better than one when there is a problem to solve.'

'That may be so but Mr Allan is not here today so there can be nothing more to be said. I must see to the gentleman customer. Good day.'

'I'm sorry, sir, and I *am* indeed very grateful to your time. Good day.'

Sam left the shop and continued down Low Gate. He saw between the bustling traffic another boot and shoe shop on the opposite side of the street. He crossed the road when he could and found himself facing the business of Robert Gould, Boots and Shoemaker. This one was impressive. There were two large window displays of dozens of pairs of all types of footwear. Sam entered the shop, the bell tinkled. There were several customers, all ladies, some of them trying on shoes. Sam felt uncomfortable and out of place.

After a while a lady assistant came over to him.

'Good morning. May I help you, sir?'

Sam had learned a lesson from his experience with the assistant in the previous shop.

'Good morning, Miss. Would it be possible to see Mr Gould please? I'm on an errand for Mr Twygge the bookseller. My name is Samuel Parker.'

'Oh yes, Mr Twygge. Well Master Parker, I shall go and see if he's available.' She disappeared into the back of the shop and emerged two minutes later.

'Mr Gould will see you. Please follow me.' She led him into a large office. Sitting behind a desk was a large red-faced, smiling gentlemen with a quill in his hand.

'Good morning Mr Parker, what can I do for you?'

'Good morning sir.'

Sam became a little more confident in the face of the amenable and jolly-looking Mr Gould.

'I've been requested by my master, Mr Twygge, to ask you whether you can tell me the possible origin of this pair of boots I have in this box.'

'What a peculiar request, Mr Parker! Could you enlighten me?'

Sam became hesitant. 'I don't wish to offend you, sir, but Mr Twygge specifically said that this was an urgent and serious matter and I was not to mention why he needs to know about the boots. In fact, he didn't need to tell me that because I don't know myself anyway, sir.'

'I see. So this is a mystery for all of us then, Sam?'

'Yes, sir.'

'Well then, take out the boots and let me have a look.'

Mr Gould arose from his desk and came around to the front. Sam handed him the boots.

'Mmm......*very* good quality. Not very worn. Very long turned-over tops. They do appear to me to be vaguely familiar. Let me have a look in the catalogues.'

He went over to a Cabinet of books and pamphlets and ruffled through several of them before picking one out from a pile. He flicked through the pages.

'Yes indeed, here we are. It's a new style, they call it *Directoire* but what that means I don't know. Have a look at this. Do you think your boots are similar to these?'

Sam felt flattered that he'd been invited to express an opinion.

'I think they are, sir. Yes, quite similar. But isn't this in French?'

'Very well observed, Master Parker, it is indeed. I get all the catalogues you know. You never know what the ladies and gentlemen will be wanting next of the latest fashions. But between you and me, I don't really care for this modern stuff. But business is business is it not, Sam?'

Sam felt flattered even more to be confided in on such matters.

'It is, sir, and Mr Twygge would entirely agree with you.'

'Very good. Now, Sam, I have to continue my work. Will Mr Twygge inform me of the outcome now that I've answered his question?'

'I'm sure he will, sir, when he is able.'

'I shall look forward to that moment. It's been very pleasant meeting you and pass on my kind regards to Mr Twygge for me.'

'I shall, sir, and thank you very much indeed. Mr Twygge will be exceedingly pleased that you have been able to assist him in this matter. And it's been a great pleasure meeting you, Mr Gould. Good day to you, sir.'

'Good day to you, Sam.'

Sam left the shop with a lighter mind. So much lighter that he felt that he must, yet once more, return by way of Dagger Lane!

As Sam turned left out of Postern Gate he saw her. A figure in black walking away down the lane towards Myton Gate. A tingle ran down his spine. He started to run.

'Rokhele!' He called, but she hadn't heard. He ran faster and called again, 'Rokhele!'

She stopped and turned. By this time Sam had caught up with her.

'Oh, Mr...er...?'

'Samuel Parker, Miss, do you remember me?'

'Yes, you brought some books for my father.'

'I did. May I walk with you?'

'Yes, I'm going to buy some vegetables.'

'May I ask you some questions? I'd like to know more about you and your family. I may be bringing more books again you see.'

'Well, what do you want to know?'

'Lots of things. Where your family is from for example.'

'I'm puzzled as to why you want to know these things.'

'I'm very interested. I know nothing of the Hebrews of Hull. I'd like to learn about your religion, your country. That sort of thing.'

'Well, my father came from, er, Preussen. I, er, don't know if that's also the word in English.'

'Preussen... let me think... geography is my best subject. It sounds as though it might be German. Does your father speak German? It sounds like a place I've seen on a map that we call Prussia.'

'Prussia, yes, I *have* heard it called that.'

'It's east of Germany on the coast of the Baltic Sea. See, I know my geography!'

'I'm sorry but I don't know geography.'

'I'll teach you one day if you will let me.'

'I don't think my father would allow that. By the way, my father does speak German but he doesn't use it very often.'

'But I heard him, at your house, when you opened the door. You spoke it yourself.'

Rokhele made a small laugh which made Sam's spine tingle again. She is relaxed, he thought, she doesn't mind me talking to her!

'It wasn't German,' she said, smiling at his ignorance, 'it was Yiddish. We speak Yiddish all the time. Except to Gentiles.'

'Gentiles? I've heard of Gentiles, they are in the Bible. What are Gentiles doing in this country?'

'You are one!' She said still smiling, 'Everybody who's not a Jew is a Gentile.'

'Are we really? But that Yiddish sounded like German to me.'

'I can understand how it would, some words do sound similar. But if you heard more of it you could tell the difference easily.'

'Can I ask you about your name, Rokhele?'

'Yes, it's from the Bible. In English it is Rachel. My father told me it means a lady sheep.'

'Rachel... a beautiful name. You don't look sheepish to me. I presume Rokhele is Yiddish then? May I call you Rachel?'

'You may.'

Sam was so light of heart he didn't notice that they'd walked right past his house and into the Market Place. He was the most joyful young man in the whole of the town of Hull, and probably the whole of England, if not the world!

8

The same day, Thursday 10th December

'Sit down. gentlemen. I didn't expect to see you today, Mr Wray, nor you Mr Twygge.' The Captain cast a frowned glance towards Twygge as he spoke, 'But in view of the developments, well…!"

The office of the Captain was now cramped with four people, and rather noisy from the activities going on outside.

The Captain continued, 'Now, I must have a clear account of what you all know. I would like to know exactly what you and Mr Twygge have discovered since Monday. I have already spoken to you but would you please repeat it for the benefit of Mr Harris?'

'How about it Mr Wray?'

'It seems that the clothes of the deceased were of French origin, Captain. Mr Twygge discovered this with the assistance of the high-class tailor, Mr David Hutchinson of Low Gate. The boots the deceased was wearing were also identified as manufactured in France, confirmed, apparently, by entries in a footwear catalogue by Mr Robert Gould also of Low Gate. It was also confirmed that the clothes and boots were of the finest quality, and were no more than about a year old, except for the blue coat which was manufactured from low-quality wool.'

'Yes, I believe I noticed that the first time I saw them,' said the Captain.

Twygge cringed, *'Did you really?'* he thought.

'Anything else Mr Twygge?'

'Yes, I enquired of Mr Levi, a jeweller, where he had his clothes made. The reason I did this is because Mr Levi is noted for his lively wardrobe. He told me he has had some of them made in Paris when he's there on business. So that points to the most likely source of the victim's apparel I also visited George

Wallis and Richard Bottomley, the only two gunsmiths in the town and both of them know a little about the weapons the footpads used. But those double-barreled pistols are not found in these parts nor do they deal in them.'

'Well, that doesn't appear to me to amount to much, does it?'

At this point Mr Harris interceded, 'Oh, I believe it does, Captain. You see, it's happened before, quite recently in fact.'

'Really!' The Captain was genuinely surprised. 'Do tell us, Mr Harris.'

'A headless body, a man's, was found at the Legal Quays in the Pool of London. His body was discovered in an ale barrel. You see, gentlemen, the Post Office *must* be informed of even the most insignificant event that interferes with the delivery of the mail. The London Office was informed by the York Office as soon as the Bishop Burton incident had occurred. But because a man was abducted I was sent to York to investigate. We don't want the people who travel on our coaches to feel under any threat of danger. They want to be able to travel safely and most of the time they do. I heard a rumour in York about a headless man being found so I had to investigate that also. Hence, gentlemen, my presence here.'

'But Mr Harris, did the London murder involve a Mail Coach?' enquired Twygge.

'Actually it didn't, Mr Twygge, but everyone knows of it. Whilst I was in York I heard the rumour of another beheading so I had to come to Hull. I was told by the York Office that the Captain here was in charge of the matter.'

'I sec,' said Twygge, 'it all makes sense now. Well, not the actual murders of course, but your being here.'

'Gentlemen,' jumped in the Captain quickly, 'what do we do next?'

'Does anyone believe these two murders are connected in any way, or is it a coincidence?'

'The only connection, Mr Harris, is the beheading and I certainly wouldn't commit myself to an opinion on that alone,' said Twygge. 'We need more evidence and how we find that could well be in the hands of Mr Harris.' He glanced at Harris.

'How may I do that, Mr Twygge?'

'Do you think that you could find out more about the man from the Pool of London? What he was wearing, what was on his person - money, possessions, that sort of thing?'

'Well, I suppose I could. The details may have been in the newspapers, I don't recall. I could write to my superiors at the Post Office. It would take several days and it would have to be sent to you, Captain, as I must leave Hull by tomorrow's Mail Coach.'

'Is this all really worthwhile? Personally, I'm of the opinion that in both cases it was a simple robbery – gangs moving from port to port watching out for rich foreign gentlemen to rob as they enter the country and beheaded to prevent tracing who the people were. Nothing to do with coaches or Frenchman particularly, just easy prey. Can we not now just close the matter?'

'That may be, Captain,' said Wray, 'but the Justices would have to decide.'

'Well, I shall discuss it with them, gentlemen. So if there's nothing else I have much to do regarding other matters.'

The Captain moved towards the door. 'I thank you all for your efforts. Your assistance has released me to deal with more important military affairs. Mr Wray, you in particular have sacrificed much of your valuable time, I'm extremely grateful, sir.'

'It's been, well, hardly a pleasure, but an *interesting* duty, and without Mr Twygge's assistance I fear I would have not achieved much at all.'

'Well, I hope that's the end of it now.'

He opened the door.

'Good day, gentlemen.'

Saying their good days they left and returned to the town. On the way there the Constable pointed out a rather obvious fact.

'The Captain's heart is not in this investigation. Do you not think we should leave it at that?'

'I think not Robert, although it's not up to me. You know, I believe I know the reason why the Captain is so brusque and miserable whenever he sees us.'

'Why is that?'

'I think he wishes he were doing what he *should* be doing – fighting in a war with France. He is a soldier. Here he's just an administrator, unless there is an attack on the Citadel of course, which seems unlikely at the moment. It hasn't happened in the years since the war started and no French ships have managed to get into the Humber. I have a feeling that there is a lot more to this business than meets the eye. In the Captain's office just now I was reminded of a report in the *Hull Packet*, oh, about two or three years ago. It concerned a certain Marquis de la Sierre. Apparently he was a refugee from the French Revolution. He'd arrived in Hull. If I remember correctly, he'd arrived from the Baltic port of St Petersburg and then travelled on. Where he went I know not.'

'I can't imagine how that could be relevant Nick,' said Wray.

'Let me suggest, gentlemen, if you have the time, that we repair to my office for some afternoon refreshment and have a further talk. What do you say, Mr Harris?'

'Well, I can, certainly Nicholas. I have no further business and I shall be returning to York tomorrow.'

'Robert?'

'I could. I kept the afternoon free to be at the Captain's office but the meeting was so brief I have time left.'

'Excellent!'

Twygge's office was full of books and stacks of papers. The room was light and airy, the walls were a pale blue, the shade of Mr Wedgwood's Jasper. It was a tidy room, Nicholas Twygge was a tidy man, and he carried around with him a head full of tidiness, but he was not fastidious.

'So how do we proceed or are we just going to talk about theories?'

'Theories it has to be, Robert. Without theories we cannot penetrate the unknown, gentlemen. We have theories, we try them out, and if they don't work we come up with another one. That's how understanding of the world progresses, is it not?'

At this point Mrs Field knocked and entered with a laden tray.

'Here we are, sirs, a nice hot posset and some pound cake to warm you up on a cold and wet winter afternoon.'

'*We'll have a posset at the latter end of a sea-coal fire!*'

'I beg your pardon?

'Just a few words of Mr Shakespeare's, Mistress Quickly. Oh, I'm sorry...Mistress Field. You know, my dear Hannah, you are a treasure. I shall have to have you as my wife.'

There was a stunned silence from the two men, and a gasp from Mrs Field as she reddened.

Twygge was quite clearly embarrassed. 'I do apologise Hannah, indeed I am deeply sorry, I forgot myself. Do forgive me, please!'

Mrs Field turned abruptly and swept out of the room.

'Well, I *have* put my foot in it! It's my weakness. I get carried away in my head and lose control of my mouth. But I'm not being frivolous, gentlemen, I do intend to ask Mrs Field for her hand in marriage. I've been thinking about it for some considerable time.'

They take up their posset and plates of cake and sit down.

'Well, well, well, Nick, I'd never have guessed. I thought you'd become settled into your widowhood.'

'Not so Robert, I have really found it very difficult.'

'I have had the opposite impression. You always seemed happy and contented as you were.'

'One can hide things, Robert, keep them bottles up, but I always say to myself 'get on with life', but it never quite goes away, that feeling of 'aloneness'. I don't mean loneliness, I always have good company around me, at home and elsewhere. No, it's that 'twoness' that one has with a wife that I miss. Do you understand? A twoness that really makes you both become a fused *one*, almost like Siamese twins. Is this comprehensible or a lot of fiddle-faddle?'

'I don't quite know, Nick.'

'Never mind. I apologise for being so personal but I felt my indiscretion needed an explanation. We shall sup our posset and eat our cake, then talk about the French. What about this revolution? It's certainly on many people's tongues these days. We had ours a century and a half ago. There was a lot of destruction and death, but, I believe that there was something good came out of it.. So I suppose the time had come for the French to have their turn at a revolution. So why *are* the French revolting? Is it that they live entirely on cloves of garlic and the odours...'

Harris's distinctly audible cough brought Twygge to a halt.

'I'm sorry, James, that was not called for. It was a pun, not meant to be taken seriously. Robert is used to my little bursts of levity, but this one was out of order, an abuse of our brief acquaintanceship. Dear, dear, I seem to spend half my life apologising, don't I? How people put up with me I'll never know. But it's a habit of mine. One can have deep feelings and strong opinions about certain things in life that if they are taken to extremes of sanctimonious solemnity as though sacred then we are in fear of losing our perspectives. Now, we were saying...?'

Harris responds, 'What is the French Revolution about?

Does it lead us to an explanation as to why two, or maybe more that we don't know about, apparently high-class French gentlemen, *if* that is what they were, we have no definitive proof of that, are beheaded and robbed in this country?'

'If you recall,' said Twygge, 'I raised the matter of the French Marquis who had passed through Hull as a refugee from the Revolution? Can one think of a possible connection between the two different events? Robert?'

'Nothing in particular occurs to me, Nick. What about you, James?'

'On the face of it they appear to be two totally separate events. But I'm willing to consider any possible theories if either of you gentlemen can produce one.'

'Let's have a look at the Revolution itself and what it has brought about in recent years.' Twygge leaned forward slightly. 'At its simplest the French Revolution is similar to our English Civil War: they were both started as a result of tyranny. In France it was the tyranny of Louis XVI and the aristocracy, in England it was the tyranny of Charles I, *and* both monarchs were executed for it.'

'Yes, Nicholas,' agreed Harris, 'but isn't that all they have in common? Wasn't the tyranny of Charles I religious, and the French one political? Two quite really different causes.'

'I thought,' said Wray, 'that Charles prevented the Parliament from doing its job. He even shut it down I believe. Isn't that political?'

'Quite correct, Robert. Have some more posset, gentlemen.' He topped up their goblets and continued. 'We are in danger of a common failure in discussions of this nature: oversimplification. We are trying to reduce all the events down to simple digestible portions.'

'And I am the most guilty when I reduced the arguments down to a matter of religion or politics,' added Harris, 'when they were clearly both closely involved in both revolutions.

Maybe I'm not equipped with sufficient information to formulate an argument.'

'None of us probably is, James, but discussing what we do know may give us a hint of a possible explanation for the two violent and gruesome murders.'

'That is possible, Nick, but are you not tending to convince yourself that there is a connection when all along there may not be?'

'I agree with you, Robert, but I have an instinctive feeling. I know it's not logical, therefore quite void as an argument but it is there fermenting in my mind and with more discussion, and information, it may become a logical theory. That is my hope. Another piece of cake, Robert? I see you haven't touched yours yet, James. Is it not to your taste?'

'It is indeed, I've been too busy thinking, trying to compete with your arguments. My knowledge of these matters is rather limited.' He takes up his pound cake.

'One of the things that I think makes the French Revolution different from the English is the behaviour of the aristocracy and the wealthy landowners,' continued Twygge.

'In what way, Robert?'

'Well, the French Revolutionaries blamed the aristocracy as well as the King for their troubles, and they are executing both, as well as political prisoners. In the English Civil War the aristocracy was divided by religion and politics, but they were not a target for mass slaughter. It was Charles alone really who was the tyrant because of his belief in the Divine Right of Kings, that was his downfall. The French aristocracy go in fear of their lives now.'

'Let me quote the Comte de Mirabeau, you've heard of him?'

Almost in unison, 'Well, yes...'

Twygge arose from his chair and went over to his desk and picked up a notebook.

'Mirabeau virtually started the French Revolution single-handed. Let me read something he wrote: 'Take care; do not disdain this people which produces everything; this people, which, to be formidable need only be immobile'. You see, gentlemen, the people were starving. The greed of the landowners had put up the price of corn when the crops were poor. The people were desperate.'

'It has happened in Hull,' added Wray, 'Corn prices rise so that people can't afford flour. Fortunately, of course, the desperately poor can be taken care of by the Corporation of the Poor. But I can see it happening again.'

'Yes, Robert, but hungry people will riot, remember the past year. We have to be diligent and not let people starve.'

'You should join Mr Fox and the Whigs in Parliament, Nicholas,' added Harris.

'I lack the necessary wealth, James, and, besides, I detect in politics a side of it that turns men into players of games for the sake of money and power. Although I believe Mr Wilberforce to be an exception. I doubt if his campaign to abolish the slave-trade will ever succeed. There are too many people who have financial interests in the trafficking of human souls.'

There was a pause.

'I apologise, sirs, I'm turning this debate into a lecture, if not a sermon!'

'Not at all, Nicholas, but this Comte de Mirabeau, *he's* a member of the aristocracy in France, and yet you say he started the Revolution.'

'Not *is*, James, *was*, he died two years or so ago. But yes, there's the irony. However, I think that saying he started the Revolution is too simplistic. I realise I said he 'virtually' started it, but he was more of a trigger to set off something that was going to happen eventually anyway.'

'Well, Nicholas, you are very convincing. I shall have to submit to your superior arguments,' said Harris, 'I'm out of my depth. I do think, though, that the Revolution in France appears to be much more vicious than ours was, and mob rule has occurred in many places. In this country it was a *war*, fought between armies, rather than a revolution. Tens of thousands of people have been guillotined in France.'

'Are you sure it was as simple as that?' Wray added. 'There was a lot of wanton destruction of property and suchlike in our Civil War.'

'True, Robert, but not the wanton destruction of *people*. It was soldiers killing soldiers was it not?'

'Would you care to smoke a pipe with us, James?'

'No, Nicholas, my physician forbade me. I've had a serious infection of the chest.'

'Oh, I am sorry to hear that. Shall we refrain?'

'No, no, gentlemen, I can enjoy a little of yours second-hand, can I'm not?'

'Are you sure, James?' asked Wray.

'Yes, of course.'

Pipes were duly lit. The room began to fill with that thuriferous heady aroma enjoyed by many since the days of Walter Raleigh.

'Back to your last point, Nick, concerning wanton harm to ordinary people. Weren't the sieges of Hull and Scarborough intended to harm innocent populations?'

'Yes, but had these sieges ever resulted in any deaths due to diseases or starvation?'

'Only because they didn't last long enough.'

'Gentlemen,' interrupted Harris, 'are you not doing what Nicholas said we shouldn't do in this discussion – losing sight of the main points? These minor details would not lead us towards a possible explanation to account for the beheading of two men.'

'No, they won't, James,' agreed Twygge, 'This is what happens ever so readily in such debates. *Mea culpa*, I'm breaking my own rules! Thank you for bringing us back down to earth, James. Nevertheless, we do need to know much more of what's been happening, and why, so we can stop it here in Hull. I wish we had time to continue but duty calls, for all of us, I believe.'

'Yes, indeed. I must prepare myself for the return to York.'

'Well, James, it's been a pleasure to have your company, brief though it has been. You won't forget to write to me when you discover more about the man from the Pool of London?'

'I shall not, Nicholas, even if it requires me to pursue it in my own time.'

The three men rose from their seats. Twygge let them out into the corridor where their coats were hanging. After donning them they made their way downstairs.

'If ever you are in Hull again, James, you must not fail to call on me.'

'I shall, Nicholas, you have my word. And if ever you're in London you will find me at the General Post Office in St Martin's-le-Grand. You will be most welcome.'

'You never know, James, one day I just might appear.'

James Harris left the building and then turned down Myton gate. Twygge and Wray remained in the doorway.

'You know, Robert, I wish I had invited young Sam to our discussion today. I think he's old enough now, and he would learn a lot from us. It will add some real life to his education instead of pouring over books *all* the time.'

'I wouldn't object, Nick, he's sensible, bright and pleasant. Who knows, he may be able to teach us a thing or two?'

Twygge laughed, 'I believe he just might.'

They went indoors and returned to Twygge's office.

9

Six weeks later, Saturday 16th January

'Now Sam, this repair needs a lot of work doing on it. Both covers are separated from the spine. You need to remove the cover completely off the spine as well.'

'Is it not possible, sir, to cover the whole book with some new leather, then add new endpapers?'

'No, no, that would be a crude repair, and weak. You see, Sam, a book is a valuable item, it's more than just paper, cord and leather. It must be highly respected, you must love it, repair it soundly as a surgeon would repair a damaged person – make it strong again.'

'I see, yes, of course. I must try to make it as perfect as it was.'

'Exactly, Sam, 'make it perfect again', I couldn't have put it better myself. I shall adopt that phrase for my business cards. Yes, that's it: 'If you need a book repairing we shall make it as perfect as it was!' How does that sound?'

'It sounds as though it would be very expensive.'

'Ha! You think it would frighten customers away? A good argument *but*, anybody who has a valuable book and values it enough to have it repaired will surely be wanting the job done well, Sam, and be willing to pay what it costs.'

'Yes I see that. I'm not yet familiar enough with people, sir, as you are.'

'I'm not sure if I really am, but one day you will know them better than you do now. You're a fast learner and the more you get out and about the sooner you will learn.'

It was the morning of a January Saturday, just after the height of winter and the shortest day. Twygge had proposed to Hannah Field on Christmas Day. She had accepted but no further plans had been made. The season was passing without any frosts, mostly just chilling fog and cold rain, with occasional appearances of the sun to remind everyone that it was still there. In recent days there had been strong winds and rain which lashed people's faces. Twygge and Wray had got no further with their murder enquiries over the past few weeks. They had met a blankness as thick and high as the town wall. They and Captain Sanderson were beginning to feel the matter slowly fading from their minds. They were fully busy now with their regular routines.

'You must very carefully remove the stitching using a very sharp knife, but first remove the leather from the spine. Begin with the bands, those are the cords that are sewn into the spine and then...'

Sam interrupted, 'Those must be the spinal cords then, sir?'

Twygge guffawed, 'Sam, you're a gem! But a word of warning – there's nothing like a good pun but many people don't understand, others just don't like them, they think they are trivial. So pick your person with care and only use them on people you know very well and who will understand.'

'Yes, sir, I'll remember.'

'Good, now let me finish. Removing the cords and stitching will take a long time so when you've done it come down to the shop so we can proceed to the next step. Oh, by the way, do take particular care to keep all the page sections in the correct order, otherwise it'll be a devil of a task putting them back together again.'

'I understand, sir. Thank you. Mr Bell has taught me well but this is my first repair. I haven't taken a book to pieces before.'

'Of course, Sam. Now, you can begin to repair this valuable tome and I shall repair downstairs to the shop.'

'You shall repair *what* in the shop, sir?'

'It was a pun, Sam.'

Twygge walked out of the room leaving Sam with a big smile

on his face.

Twygge and Wray were having their usual eleven o'clock coffee and cake at Tom`s Coffee House.

'Mr Wilberforce is a blessing on this town, Robert, he has put us on the map, made us known – this port at the end of a road which stops here and goes to nowhere. Hull now has something to be proud of.'

'And yet, Nick, he has upset many people.'

'Yes, but as I've said before, only those who have financial interests in making money from tearing human beings brutally away from their homes and families and turning them into slaves. Do they have a moral right to do that?'

'But are they not primitive peoples? Do they really think and feel as we do?'

'Who knows that they don't? Isn't it better to assume that they *do* rather than not, given our ignorance of them?' Twygge took a bite of his butter cake then a sip of his coffee, 'I'd rather give them the benefit of the doubt than risk being condemned to Hell for being inhuman.'

'It is very difficult, Nick. If we abolish the slave-trade we face financial ruin and the Empire will collapse. Which will hurt the most people?'

'That's a good point, Robert, but nobody would suffer or die as the slaves do. Only a small number of very wealthy men would become a little less wealthy, that is all is it not?'

'I don't know, Nick,' said Wray resignedly, 'it's too much for me. I shall let God decide.'

'I think God is on the side of Mr Wilberforce, but we shall see. You know, Robert, we in Hull don't see or know what actually happens in this slave-trade business. We never see slaves or slave ships. I believe Hull is the only port of any importance where slave-ships have never passed through.'

'Could that be because of Mr Wilberforce, or is there another reason?'

At this point a man in a soldier's uniform approached their table.

'Sergeant, I remember you,' said Twygge, 'good day to you.'

'Good day, gentlemen, I have an urgent message for Mr Wray from the Captain.' The Sergeant appeared pale and exhausted. 'Yesterday afternoon the Captain sent me to Barton by private boat. He'd received an urgent message from the Chief Constable there to go and see him as soon as possible. This morning he sent me back to Barton to get you rooms at the Waterside Inn and now I've come with this.' The Sergeant handed a sealed letter to Wray.

'There's no wonder you look ill, Sergeant - seasickness?'

'Almost but not quite, unless he sends me over the water *again*!'

'And I thought my dealings with the Captain were coming to an end.'

'It appears not, Mr Wray. Does the Captain require a reply, Sergeant?' asked Twygge.

'He didn't say so, sir. I shall have to leave you now, gentlemen. Good day.' The Sergeant turned and marched out of the building.

'That lad has been bounced around like a cork on a rough sea, Nick. Four crossings in this weather!'

Wray broke the seal, opened the letter and read it. Twygge watched him carefully and saw his visage darken and a frown appearing.

'Oh dear, Sam, our cosy little tête-à-tête is over. I think you may be permitted to read this.' He handed the letter over to Twygge. Shortly a frown appeared on *his* face.

'Ah, well, well! Robert, what do you think?'

'We shall have to do as he says.'

'Yes, Robert. Are you able to be away that long? You have more responsibilities than I.'

'By good fortune I have reliable people working for me, as you know. I couldn't do the work of the Constable without being able to depend on others to keep the Inn running smoothly.'

'And I can say the same, Robert. So, the Captain needs us both. It must be something to do with the murders, do you not think?'

'There can be no other reason as far as I can see, Nick. Having the Chief Constable of Barton to meet us tells me that something serious is amiss.'

'Well, and I was beginning to believe that we'd seen the last of it.'

'So was I, Robert, in fact it had almost gone completely out of my mind. Although I do now feel a sudden surge of interest and, can I say it, a little welling of elation? The challenge returns! Although I am not happy if another person has lost their life, that would be callous.'

'Sometimes, nay often, there are times when I can't quite make you out, Nick. We have many common interests and you provide me with a friendship which I value and which offers me respite frequently from the burdens of my work. But you're forever-enquiring mind overpowers me. Forgive me for sounding a little harsh.'

'Not at all, not at all, Robert. If there is one human being on this earth who doesn't understand me and becomes exasperated by the way I speak and behave it is me myself. I think you may know that. As I've said before, sometimes I can't stop it, it races along with such momentum, if I may use one of Mr Newton's new words, that it's barely stoppable.'

'I know not what momentum is but I can guess. Forgive me for talking in this way. *You* feel some excitement at the possibility that this is another murder whereas I feel a little put out. But it is my duty so we had better begin now and prepare ourselves for what is required of us. The Captain said the ferry and the rooms have been booked so all we need to do now is pack some items for overnight. The ferry sails at half past one so we shall meet at the pier at a quarter past one.'

'I thought the ferry left on the hour.'

'There must be a west wind, Nick, have you forgotten?'

'Of course, how foolish of me. I haven't used the ferry for a considerable time.'

'We haven't time now to call Mistress Usherwood so we shall leave the money on the table.'

They leave the coffee house and together stride up the Market Place towards their abodes.

10

The same day, Saturday 16th January
There was a brisk west-south-westerly blowing by the afternoon and the Humber was choppy. As the route to Barton was in a south westerly direction the ferry crossing was going to be slow and lively. For the previous two days the ferry was unable to run because the wind and rain had been too violent but today it had abated sufficiently for the ferry to sail.

'We're in for a rough journey, Nick, are you up to it?'

Wray could detect the slightest hint of hesitation in Twygge's reply - he was putting on a brave exterior.

'It does look a bit daunting I must say, but I think I shall enjoy it. It will be bracing so we shall brace ourselves, eh Robert? We mustn't contemplate the fate of Andrew Marvell *père*, must we?' It was a father of the Hull poet, also called Andrew, who had drowned in 1640 when the ferry boat making this very same crossing was lost in violent weather. The fate of Mr Marvell's father was being re-enacted in Twygge's imagination, which was vivid enough at the best of times.

The ferry boat tacked its way across the river, heavily laden and pitching and rolling without respite and making very slow progress. The spindrift was blowing viciously, forcing all the passengers to face towards the northeast, appearing, for all intents and purposes, like a church congregation at prayer.

By the time the boat reached the Haven at Barton it was almost dark. The passengers were considerably subdued. Only seasoned travellers and crew remained composed, even Wray was showing evidence of discomposure.

'I'm relieved that's over,' he said as they made their way off the boat and along the pier towards the Waterside Inn. A Mail Coach was standing outside the Inn.

'Is this another murder?' thought Wray.

The passengers were dispersing amongst a large crowd gathered outside the Inn. A large men approached Twygge and Wray. He offered his hand to Wray, a large hand. The man was a hulk and even taller than Wray. In his uniform he was quite an awesome figure.

'How do you do, Mr Wray? I see you've had a rough journey. I was watching the ferry boat bobbing its way in just now.'

'Good day, Chief Constable. Indeed we have. May I introduce Mr Twygge? Mr Twygge this is the Chief Constable of Barton and the villages around, Mr Thomas Stamp.'

'I'm very pleased to meet you, sir.' He felt the fingers of his right hand crunch in the grip of the Chief Constable's.

'I hear you've been seconded as a constable, Mr Twygge.'

'Hardly, sir, it is not an occupation that I'm suited for,' he said, rubbing his hand, 'You constables have to deal with people and incidents that I never could. You are all to be greatly admired and appreciated for what you do. I am merely a solver of puzzles and I've been helping the Captain and Mr Wray here to try to make sense of certain unusual events.'

'Thank you your generous compliment, Mr Twygge, then let us go inside and have some refreshments, and I shall explain why you've been asked to come here.'

The Waterside Inn was the fullest it had been for some weeks. Two days without the ferry had seen a backlog of people and belongings inside and outside the inn. The noise was more subdued than usual and the people were weary with waiting. Some were standing, some sitting and some lying down where there was a space. Some travellers had managed to find cheap accommodation in the properties lining Waterside Road that led into the town of Barton itself. Twygge and Wray were received and took their bags to their rooms. Not all the waiting passengers had the money to stay the extra nights at the Inn hence the two or three vacancies which were available for the two men. Chief Constable Stamp had offered his own home if it had become necessary. The Inn itself was very large. There were so many carts and coaches which used the Inn daily that stabling for dozens of horses was provided. Extensions had been built on over the decades so the site was almost a village in itself. Because the Inn was so full it was decided between them to have their supper and meet together in one of the rooms. They registered their presence at the front desk and went up to their rooms. After depositing their belongings they gathered in Wray's room.

'Now, Chief Constable, please explain to us why we're here. We have our suspicions but, of course, we may well be completely wrong.'

'If a Constable has suspicions, Mr Wray, he is usually right,' observed Stamp.

Twygge was sitting on the bed, he made a barely noticeable frown. *'Really,'* he thought, *'then why am I here?'* He was less affronted than annoyed that people can be so sure of themselves.

'In that case, Chief Constable, please tell us about the gruesome murder that has been committed hereabouts,' ventured Twygge, praying that he was right.

'Oh, so you have heard of it? I was hoping that we could keep it quiet.'

'Not at all, sir, we had our suspicions and we assumed. No such news has crossed the river as far as I know.'

Mr Stamp was clearly unaware of the contradiction he had elicited. Twygge knew that he and Wray must proceed with caution with Stamp with regards to detail and conclusions - a small town and country Constable!

'I think we are about ready to begin, sir,' said Wray.

There was a knock on the door.

'Come in.'

A maid opened the door, picked up a tray from a table in

the corridor and brought it in.

'Your supper, gentlemen.'

She placed the tray on the table by the window.

'Thank you, Miss.'

She arranged the plates and food, went back into the corridor to bring in another chair and then left.

'Very efficient that young lady,' said Wray. 'I find that usually girls are much better than boys at hotel work.'

They sat around the table and began their meal – cold venison pie and tea caudle with some saffron cake to finish.

'After that rough sailing across the Humber, gentlemen, I am very grateful the Inn hasn't been parsimonious with the servings,' said Twygge, 'and the caudle is nicely warming, is it not?'

'This Inn is almost at the end of a very long journey for many travellers, often very important people,' added the Chief Constable, 'It has to be welcoming and accommodating. It was not long ago that we had your famous member of the Parliament, Mr Wilberforce, here. I was required to be on hand. But now to business gentlemen, it is getting rather late in the day.'

'Certainly,' said Wray, 'we are ready. Please begin.'

'Yesterday morning, early, just as day was beginning to break, the manager of the brick and tile works just to the east of here across the haven, was making his usual inspection of the premises. His is one of the sites in the Brick Closes owned by Mr Grayburn. He said he noticed that some of the tiles had been disturbed – they are usually kept in neat and orderly stacks in the yard, he said. Some tiles from one of the stacks had been piled onto the ground in a jumble. He said he then intended to seek out a yard-worker to put it right when he noticed something on the ground by the heap of tiles. It was small and shining slightly in the dawn light, just enough to catch his eye. He moved two or three tiles and then he saw it – a hand with a ring on it.' He paused.

'What did he do next, sir?' enquired Wray.

'He said he thought of shouting for help to move the tiles, but he had second thoughts.'

'So what did he do?' asked Twygge.

'I'm coming to that, Mr Twygge. Instead, he thought to himself it may be better for everybody if he sent for me first, so he did, without telling the worker that he sent what the reason was. Then he returned to the tiles to guard it in case anyone should approach.'

'Why was he out so early, Chief Constable?' enquired Twygge.

'He prefers to make his daily rounds of inspection at the start of the day so there is time to put things right if necessary. Mr Alcock runs a tight works, gentlemen, Mr Grayburn the owner expects it. Barton is only second to Hull as the largest supplier of bricks and tiles in the region so it depends on speed and efficiency. There is so much new building going on these days since the Enclosures, not to mention all the rebuilding – people of fashion need to be seen to be modern, even if they are not wealthy enough to have a new house built they have their old houses re-fronted in the modern style. I have been to your fine town of Hull and seen all the splendid new streets for myself.'

'Yes, indeed, Chief Constable,' agreed Wray. 'I imagine there must be a house a day going up on the other side of the New Dock.'

Twygge was remaining silent, he didn't wish to be led away from the account of yesterday's events. He was anxious to know the details of the body, if it were a body and not just a hand or an arm.

'Anyway, we are not progressing very far with the matter in hand. What happened next?' continued Wray.

'Well,' said Stamp, 'I arrived and Mr Alcock and I began to remove all the tiles, replacing them neatly back on the stack. It was clear before long that a human body was underneath.'

'*It could hardly be any other than human with a hand with the ring on it,*' thought Twygge.

'As we removed more tiles we could see plainly that it was a man by his clothes. Then we saw something that shocked Mr Alcock so much that he staggered back and fell against the stack of tiles. By good fortune he was not injured. The body of the man who'd been buried under the tiles had no head.' The Chief Constable paused, whether for effect or to take a breath was not clear.

'So,' said Twygge, 'would you please tell us about the dead man's appearance, Chief Constable?'

'Yes, Mr Twygge, I could, but you can see for yourself tomorrow morning. I must return to Barton now. I've arranged with Mr Alcock for the four of us to visit the scene at nine o'clock in the morning – any earlier and it wouldn't be light enough.'

'But what about protecting the body, particularly from prying eyes? Somebody must be aware of these mysterious comings and goings, of you in particular. They must know you by sight.'

'Quite correct, Mr Wray. I have had the body securely covered with tarpaulin provided by Mr Alcock and one of my assistants has been standing guard and another will be on duty through the night. Neither of them, I might add, has been told what is underneath the tarpaulin and they've been instructed not to move it or lift it, under severe penalties if they do. Nor must anyone be allowed to approach them. Does that satisfy you, Mr Wray?'

'Yes, indeed, Chief Constable.'

'I shall be on my way now and I shall be here with a cart at half past eight tomorrow morning to take you to the body.'

The Chief Constable arose from his chair and went towards the door. 'Good night, gentlemen. I shall be looking forward to your conclusions after you've inspected the body.'

'Good night, sir. We shall do whatever we can.'

The Chief Constable left the room.

'Well, what do you make of him, Robert?'

'Oh, I think he's good at his job. Obviously a countryman, but I can't imagine he has to deal with anything as serious as this very often around these parts.'

'This sounds *very* serious to me, Nick.'

'Of course. I've never been called over to Lincolnshire before, although I did meet the Chief Constable once before in Hull at the office of John Clarkson our own Chief.'

'Policing Hull must be a very different affair from the backwaters of north Lincolnshire.'

'I'm sure it is. You must be tired, Nick, you've had a long and wearisome day. I shall leave you to your bed.'

'Indeed I am weary, Robert. At what time shall we breakfast?'

'I think half past seven would be early enough. That will give us a clear hour before Mr Stamp appears.'

'Half past seven it is. A good night to you, Robert. Until the morrow.' Twygge opened the door for the Constable.

'Good night, Nick.'

He disappeared down the corridor.

11

The same day, Saturday 16th January
Sam Parker had been in the workshop all of Saturday morning. He had found that taking a book completely apart was more difficult than he thought. He was still in the middle of cutting the thread and separating the folded sections of pages. But, of course, taking things apart is much quicker then putting them back together, albeit less creative. So, Sam realised he was going to be working on this task for several more Saturday mornings. He was not disheartened at the thought, however, because he had enough diligence to appreciate the skills it required and he could imagine the finished product as something to be proud of, *and*, he would make sure that it would be!

Mrs Field came into the workshop.

'Your dinner is ready, Sam. But I must tell you, Mr Twygge is having to go to Barton by this afternoon's ferry and won't be back until tomorrow. He didn't tell me why, but he's already had his dinner and wishes you to work in the shop with Mr Crosswell afterwards. He also said that he won't be able to accompany us to church tomorrow so we should go without him.'

'Thank you, Mrs Field, I shall be with you shortly.'

She left the workshop.

Sam tidied his bench, returning the tools to their proper places and left the room. He was dining alone with Mrs Field today.

'Now, young Sam,' she said as they were digging into their fish pie, 'I've noticed and so has Mr Twygge that since Christmas you seem to have become quieter than usual. I'm not saying you normally talk too much but I'm saying you talk less than you did. Am I right?'

'Delicious pie, Mrs Field. Is it flounder?'

'It is flounder. But you see my point – you don't usually ignore people's questions? There must be something wrong. We women, Sam, notice things that most men usually don't. We can see into people better and I know something's changed in you.'

'Forgive me, Mrs Field,' he said, clearly feeling the guilt of trying to avoid the question, 'but there *is* something that's been on my mind for several weeks. It's very difficult for me to explain.'

'Please try, Sam, it'll make you feel better. There's nothing worse than bottling up inside something that causes worry. We'd like to see you back to being your old self again.'

'If I tell you you'll laugh, I know, and that would upset me more.'

'Now, Sam, how on earth do you know that I will laugh? If something is upsetting you I'm not such an uncaring person as to make fun of you. You should know that.'

'I do, Mrs Field, but... but, it's very personal. I just can't seem to bring myself to talk about it. It's almost as though it's locked inside me and refuses to let me release it. I feel such a fool.'

'Let me have a guess, Sam, and do *please* trust me. I want to help you, make you feel better. You *will* feel better, I promise you, if you let it out. Some things can fester inside you like a boil and once pricked the pain will go and you'll feel relieved.'

'Well...' Sam was hesitant.

'Is it about a young lady?' she said gently.

Sam was taken aback. It was an arrow shot without warning and hitting the very centre of the target in a split second. 'She must know,' he thought.

'Now, just finish your pie and we can talk about it.'

Sam continued eating but with less heartiness than when he started.

'I don't know what Mr Twygge is up to today, gadding about with Constable Wray. Sometimes they are a mystery to me, Sam.' She was obviously trying to make Sam more at ease, to put him in a relaxed state of mind so he would be more willing to open his heart to her.

'Yes, I envy him Mrs Field but I'm sure he'll tell us all about it when he can. Anyway, you're going to marry Mr Twygge, should you be marrying a man you don't understand?'

'All men are a mystery to me, Sam, and no doubt women are a mystery to men but it doesn't stop them being married and being happy together.'

'You're very wise, Mrs Field. I wish *I* had your wisdom.'

'You will one day, Sam, it comes with age and experience. Now I'll take your plate and go and fetch the quince and apricot pudding I've made for us, then we can talk.'

She arose from the table, placed the plates on the tray and went into the kitchen, returning a minute later with a steaming pudding, a jug of cream and a pot of tea. She sat down and served the dessert.

'Delicious, Mrs Field, absolutely delicious.'

'Thank you, Sam.'

Soon the dessert had been consumed and tea poured.

'Tell me about the young lady, Sam. Is she pretty?'

She was trying as carefully as she could to break down the barrier within him.

'She is, Mrs Field, very beautiful.'

'Have I seen her?'

'I doubt it. You may have passed her on the street but then you wouldn't know who she was would you?'

'Has she ever been into the shop?'

'I've never seen her here, no.'

'Then how did you meet her?'

'Well, it was several weeks ago, before Christmas it was. I took some books for delivery to a house in Dagger Lane...'

It was obvious to Mrs Field that Sam was beginning to relax a little. She could hear him gradually opening up his heart and could see the relief in his eyes. He told her the whole story of meeting Rachel Sachs and her father and he was even telling her about his occasional wanderings around the streets in the hope of seeing her again, which, apart from the one time in December, he never did.

Mrs Field knew of Mr Sachs who had visited Mr Twygge on several occasions. She didn't have the heart to tell Sam about the Israelites, it would only drive him back into his sad and brooding state.

12

The next day, Sunday 17th January
The following morning the wind had dropped and a clear sky offered a splendid view across the river which was now much calmer. Twygge and Wray, having rooms at the front of the Waterside Inn, could see the sun beginning to rise and send its beams along the estuary of the Humber, giving a silvery shimmering sheen to the surface as the tide moved slowly westwards.

They breakfasted on eggs and meats with rolls and plenty of coffee. The inn was still full, despite the ferry returning to Hull yesterday evening loaded to the gunnels.

'Have you heard, Nick, that delays have been deliberately done to delay the ferry on its way to Barton?'

'Why should someone want to do that?'

'It brings extra custom for this Inn. If the ferry arrived at Barton after the London coach had left, those passengers would have to stay at the Inn and take a coach the following day.'

'How underhanded. Have the guilty people been found?'

'Afraid not, Nick, there's always some feasible excuse given by the ferry crew. Nothing can be proved but I bet you ten golden guineas that money changes hands.'

'That's got me wondering, Robert. Do you think we were delayed in this way yesterday? It did take a considerable time to make the crossing.'

'I doubt it. You see how full the Inn has been since the ferry was cancelled? The Inn would have nothing to gain.'

'Yes, of course. Who is the owner?'

'You know, Nick I couldn't tell you. It could possibly be Mr Uppleby, he owns a large amount of land and property in these parts. But who can tell who owns what these days? We don't notice it much in Hull but these country areas have suffered from having to hand over the common land to the rich.'

'You're beginning to sound like a Whig, Robert. I have a book on my shelves by a Scotsman. It's poetry. I don't think it'll sell, the poems are in Scots and can be difficult to read. But if not I'll keep it for myself. There is a verse in it that caught my attention,

> *Our sad decay in Church and State*
> *Surpasses my descriving;*
> *The Whigs came o'er us for a curse,*
> *And we hae done wi' thriving.'*

'You and your books, Nick, I don't know! Well anyway, there are certain things that are not just, Nick, and this Enclosure business is one of them.'

'Yes, but isn't much of this land needed to produce more food? The population is growing and needs feeding. The poor cannot afford to start up farms and the like, and we do need more of them. Look what the corn shortages came to – rioting in the streets?'

'Now *you're* sounding like a Tory, Nick.'

'No, just being practical and logical, Robert. Anyway, this is a raw subject and no doubt will be vigorously debated for years to come. I think it's time we met the Chief Constable. If I believe it is what I think it is I hope you can keep your breakfast down.'

The two men got up, gathered their belongings and nodded in acknowledgement to the gentleman at the front desk as they left the Inn. There was considerable activity at the wharfs along the Haven. The chimneys of the brickworks opposite were churning out plumes of smoke and a multitude of carts of all sizes were coming and going from the new Humberside Dock. The old Coward Dock was closed because of the Enclosures and now stood empty of ships and men, abandoned to face the destruction that would be meted out to it, slowly year by year, decade by decade, by the powerful river.

Twygge and Wray could see the Chief Constable approaching in his dog-cart.

'Good morning, gentlemen, this is a fine change in the weather is it not?'

'Good morning to you, Chief Constable, you're very punctual.'

'I do my best, Mr Wray. Would you gentlemen care to mount and we can be off? I think my Assistant will be ready to be relieved after being out all night.'

Twygge and Wray climbed onto the cart and stowed their belongings.

'We have to go the long way round but it'll only take a short time. I've arranged for the body to be taken away and buried later so you'd better make the most of it while you can.'

The cart went south down Waterside Road past some busy wharfs and past the Sloop Inn on the right.

'This is a new road it seems to me, Mr Stamp,' said Twygge.

'Yes it is. When other tracks and lanes were shut down by the Enclosures this had to be the new way into the town.. But as you can see, it's a good road with plenty of room for the Mail Coach to get through without delay.'

At the end of Waterside Road the cart turned left down Butt Lane. Here the Lane was not so good and the cart bumped along another 300 yards, with many other carts and barrows going back and forth. They turned left again into the entrance to Grayburn's land leading to the brick and tile works.

'Not far now, gentleman.'

The cart turned into a track leading to some drying sheds with acres of tiles stacked at the sides of the track.

'These are the common pantiles. There is a great demand for them at the moment as you can see by this maze of stacks.'

The Chief Constable slowed the cart down. 'We shall have to stop here. The Constable is over there. He's seen us.'

They dismounted and walked down one of the many aisles between the stacks, heading towards the Constable.

'Good morning, sir.'

'Good morning Constable, how as the night?'

'Quiet, sir. I had a pair of nosy young lads earlier but I soon saw them off.'

'So the tarpaulin's not been disturbed then?'

'Not at all sir.'

'Very good. Now, I've brought two gentlemen from Hull to have a look at what's under here. This is Constable Wray and this is Mr Twygge. I'm sure you're ready to be off. So go and get some breakfast and have a sleep.'

'Yes, sir, thank you.' The Constable picked up his bag and walked towards the track where the cart stood, then turned left towards Butts Road.

'When exactly will they be collecting the body?'

'I had asked them to be here at half past ten. That should give you plenty of time, Constable.'

'I believe so, yes. Shall we begin?'

'I brought two lanterns,' he reached into the front of the cart, 'here.'

'Do you mind if I take notes, Mr Stamp? I can't trust my memory.'

'Not at all, Mr Twygge, if it will help.'

The Chief Constable lit the two lanterns, handed one to Wray, and moved towards the heap on the ground. He removed the tarpaulin slowly and carefully. Twygge and Wray moved towards it. Both men had seen the very same thing before and as the body came into sight they were still shocked by it. Then Twygge made a short involuntary cough and fumbled in his coat pockets for his notebook and pencil.

'Well,' said Wray, 'it's amazing! Exactly like the other one.'

'I half expected it, Robert, but yet it still shook me up.'

'Me too, Nick. Shall we get a closer look?'

The two men crouched on either side of the body, Twygge with his pencil at the ready.

'The same blue coat. Body decapitated. Not much blood around the ground where the head would have been. Just a little blood around the coat and shirt collars. But look, a large pool of blood on the ground by his right arm.' Twygge inspected the wrist and found a deep two inch cut on the inner side.

'Exactly the same,' said Wray.

'Exactly! Now the neck.'

Twygge bent down closer.

'You know, gentlemen, this could be the very same body brought to Hull from Bishop Burton – a case of *déjà vu*, Robert?'

'It is quite puzzling, Nick.'

'Certainly it is. It hardly needs saying, gentlemen, but there is something very peculiar going on here – a mystery of mysteries. You see, Mr Stamp, this body looks more or less the same as the one found near Beverley, even down to the coat. What does one make of that?'

No response was elicited. It was clearly a rhetorically question.

'Have you looked in his pockets?' enquired Wray.

'No,' said the Chief Constable, 'we haven't touched a thing.'

'May we do so?'

'Please do.'

Wray began searching in the coat pockets and brought out a handkerchief. In one of the waistcoat pockets he found a watch. Wray handed both items to the Chief Constable. Nothing was found in the pockets of the breeches, nor any money.

'Don't forget the coat buttons, Robert.'

'Quite, yes, here. There you are, look, the initials MS, precisely the same as on the buttons from the first body, I believe. What do you make of that?'

'I couldn't say. Are they all there?' Wray checked them all.

'No, one is missing.'

'And the handkerchief, Mr Stamp, does it bear any markings?'

'Er, yes, in one corner there are some initials... CM.'

Twygge was scribbling hastily in his notebook.

'May we take the handkerchief and one of the coat buttons with us, Mr Stamp, they could be of great value in our investigations?'

'If you wish, Mr Twygge.' He proceeded to take out a knife and cut one off, and hand it over together with the handkerchief to Constable Wray.

'And the watch?' asked the Chief Constable.

'I don't think so, do you Robert? There's nothing personal about it is there?' The Chief Constable opened it up.

'In fact there is. See here, gentlemen.'

There was an inscription in French, including the initials CM. Twygge copied the inscription into his notebook.

'I believe,' said Twygge, 'that someone has made a mistake by leaving this watch behind. It confirms my suspicions. Excellent!'

'What shall I do with it, gentlemen?'

'Do you think we should take it, Nick?'

'It's not necessary, Robert. I have the inscription so you may dispose of it as you think fit, Mr Stamp.'

'Well, gentlemen, if you've finished then we'll just wait a few minutes for them to take the body away then we'll get you back to the inn.'

'No need, Mr Stamp. It's such a fine day I think we could walk back. The ferry won't be leaving until much later. What do you think, Robert?'

'I don't mind the walking but I'd rather take a private boat back across the river and get back as soon as possible, if you don't mind?'

'Not at all.'

The Chief Constable was replacing the tarpaulin over the body.

'Please yourselves, gentlemen. By the time the waggon arrives you may have reached the wharf anyway, and be back in Hull in time for dinner. This west-south-westerly will take you across in no time.'

'Well, Chief Constable, I hope we haven't wasted a lot of your time.'

'Not in the least, Constable, and I hope it's been of value. This is quite a mystery for us to solve, but I shall begin some enquiries locally and if any information is forthcoming I shall make sure you hear of it.'

'Thank you,' said Twygge, 'we shall ask a few questions ourselves on the way back.'

'Do so but, please, don't reveal too many details, Mr Twygge. No one knows what's under this tarpaulin save us three and Mr Alcock. And I'd hate the news to get out and cause ructions in the town. There'll already be rumours going around.'

'We shall be the paragons of discretion, Mr Stamp.'

'Of course,' said Wray, 'we've been doing our own investigations already in Hull and elsewhere, as you are aware, Sir.'

'In that case, gentlemen, may I wish you a good day and a safe journey back.'

'Good day to you too, Chief Constable.'

They turned and walked back the way they'd come.

'Nicholas, I do think you were a bit out of order with the Chief Constable today.'

'Why is that, Robert?' Twygge was somewhat surprised. It was a rare event for Wray to be critical with his friend.

'Well, yesterday you addressed him as *Chief Constable* and *sir*, as one should. But today it was *Mr Stamp* all the time. Why the change?'

'Do you think he was affronted? I saw no signs of him objecting at all.'

'That's not the point, is it? It's protocol or etiquette, or whatever you call it. It's good manners, and respectful.'

'Yes, but only within reason, Robert. Yesterday I got fed up with saying *Chief Constable* all the time. It's a mouthful, it's clumsy, it's repetitive, it's... it's, er, unpoetic, it doesn't trip off the tongue easily.'

'Quite. Well, in my position, Nick, it is expected, and I think he would expect it of everyone.'

'I think you're exaggerating, Robert. This is only Barton-on-Humber, not the City of London Constabulary. And as for respect, I believe that that is earned. It doesn't come automatically.'

'What on earth do you mean?'

'I can respect a man for what he is, not who he is. I allow a certain *general* degree of respect for all people before I get to know them, after that they either earn more or lose some according to how they behave. I don't respect someone just because they have a title.'

'But surely, *Chief Constable* is a word enough to show respect, Nick?'

'No, Robert, you've not understood my point, *chief* and *constable* are just words, how can one respect words?'

'I just don't understand the difference. Anyway, I think we should agree to differ on that. Let's leave it there.'

'I think we should, Robert. We'll deal with the business in hand.'

They continued their way, turning right into Waterside Road and then stopped to make enquiries at the Sloop Inn and imbibe a little refreshment.

After leaving the Inn they began questioning the men at work at the wharfs along the Haven, then finished up at the Waterside Inn. They drank coffee and ate some cake before finding a boat that would take them back across the river to Hull.

13

The next day, Monday 18th January
At nine o'clock on Monday morning Nicholas Twygge opened his shop. It was going to be a quiet day for business, Mondays always were. At fifteen minutes past nine Henry Crosswell arrived to assist him. Twygge would probably repair to his workshop for the morning, breaking it with his regular and leisurely partaking of coffee and cake at Tom Usherwood's Coffee House on Church Side. There, in the company of Constable Wray who was always quite willing to tolerate Twygge's holding forth about this or that, they would probably talk about the murders. Wray had arranged a quiet table where they'd be out of earshot.

Within minutes of Crosswell arriving a young lad charged through the door.

'Mr Twygge, Mr Twygge, I've......'

'Whoa, hold your horses young man. Calm down. Don't I know you? Of course, the Cross Keys Inn weeks ago, you're... er... Heron, Joseph Heron. Am I right?'

'Yes, sir, yes, but I've got something to tell you, sir. I came straight here on Saturday night after I'd seen them but you were not here. A lady told me to come back today as you wouldn't be in yesterday so I came as quick as I could this morning but I've only got two minutes or Mr Baker will sack me if I don't...'

'Slow down, steady Joseph. No need to be in haste, take your time. I shall take you back to the hotel myself and explain to Mr Baker. He won't fire you.'

'Yes, thank you, sir.'

'Now, you say you saw *them*, who were *them*, Joseph?'

'The two men, sir, you know, the two who were following that swell in the blue coat. It *was* weeks ago. Perhaps you've forgotten, sir?'

'No, no,' Twygge gave a little laugh, 'I have not forgotten at all. If you only knew! Anyway, Joseph, tell me the whole story, slowly and carefully. Oh, and in future don't use slang words like *swell*. Respect your mother tongue.'

'I beg your pardon, sir?' He clearly didn't understand what Twygge was talking about.

'Never mind, Joseph, just carry on.'

'Well, sir, it was Saturday night, sir. I was leaving the inn to go home when I passed two men, sir. They were coming from High Street up Grimsby Lane. I'd been on an errand for Mr Baker, sir. There were quite a few people around so I thought they must've just got off the ferry, sir.'

'The Barton ferry?'

'Yes, sir.'

'What exactly did you see, Joseph, every detail you can remember.'

'They stood out, sir, just like when I saw them last in their seamen's slops, but one of them was different. He was much smaller. The other one was the same. I remembered their faces, sir.'

'Anything else?'

'Yes, sir, they were carrying sailor's bags and one of them, sir, had a parcel tied up with string under one arm.'

' How big a parcel?'

'Oh, about that big, sir.' Joseph held his hands about twelve inches apart.

'What shape was it?'

'It was like a box, sir.'

'What did it look like on the outside? I mean what was covering the parcel, was it paper, cloth or what, Joseph?'

'I couldn't be certain, sir, but it was dark-coloured I think.'

'Did you happen to see them again?'

'No, sir.'

'Could they have stayed at the Hotel?'

'I don't think so, sir. It's not their sort of place.'

'Well, Joseph, that's very interesting indeed. I wish I could tell you how very useful you've been to me but I cannot, so I shall give you sixpence instead. Tell your mother and father exactly who gave it to you and why, but don't mention the seamen. Do you promise?' He took a sixpence out of his purse and handed it to Joseph.

'Ooh, thank you, sir, I promise. Thank you very much, sir.' His eyes shone and his mouth gaped as he looked at it.

'Now, let's get you back to the Hotel and I'll explain everything to Mr Baker.'

He led Joseph out and they walked together the short distance across the Market Place and into the Cross Keys.

At eleven o'clock Twygge entered Sam's Coffee Shop, walked briskly over to a table far enough away so they wouldn't be heard by other customers. Wray was already ensconced. Most of the regular customers were used to Twygge and Wray's daily get-together, and they'd exchanged the odd nod and *good morning* here and there, as they entered. Most of them had probably already forgotten the events of several weeks ago, although there were one or two who paid a more than passing interest in the two men.

'Do you know, Robert, I could kick myself.'

'Settle down first, Nick, you're too excited. Have your coffee and cake.'

'This is incredible. You won't believe it. On Saturday when we arrived in Barton do you know who was there?'

'Yes, the Chief Constable. I didn't know anybody else, except you!'

'Don't be foolish, Robert.' Twygge, in almost a whisper, '*On or near the Waterside, at the same time we were there, so were the two murderers!*'

'Now who's being foolish. How on earth do you know that?'

'Think back to December. We went to make enquiries at the Cross Keys.'

'Yes.'

'Do you remember that lad who works there, Joseph Heron, who told us about those suspicious seamen?'

'Yes.'

'Well, Robert, he came to the shop this morning and told me something most remarkable.'

Twygge told Wray everything Joseph had said.

'How do you know he was telling the truth?' said the ever-cautious Wray.

'Why would he lie? He risked his job at the Inn coming to see me. I know he wasn't lying – it's not difficult to tell, especially in a young lad. So let us assume, Robert, that he *was* telling us the truth. We can work out a strategy based on that assumption.'

'It could all be a waste of time. Look, Nick, you haven't touched your coffee, it's getting cold.'

Twygge took a large sip.

'Not necessarily *our* time, Robert, we could use others. That lad for example.'

He took a bite of the Shrewsbury cake.

'Assuming that these two men are still in Hull, Joseph could try to hunt them out. We could inform the Excise men and they could keep their eyes out among the boats due to sail. I could use Samuel. We could ask the Captain to lend us some men, and so on. Oh, and there are all the other constables.'

'You can't use Joseph Heron, he's working at the Hotel all hours.'

'I know, Robert, but we could pay-off Mr Baker temporarily and he could easily find a stand-in for a few days. I've already explained to Mr Baker what an intelligent and honest lad he is, he'll understand.'

'You're astonishing, Nick, how do you do it? You've convinced me. I'm only sorry I can't devote as much time as I would like to this business but your ideas certainly take the burden off our shoulders. You know, many times I've wished the Captain had never palmed off this responsibility on to us.'

'Now, Robert, we both know if he and his men had been left with it very little would've be done. He really didn't think it should have been him and his men's job in the first place. Or even anything to do with this town.'

'Maybe he's right.'

'Well, it's too late now. We can't just give up. Two, nay three men...' Wray interrupted.

'Three? How come three? You remember in London and Mr Harris?'

'Of course, it'd slipped my mind. Three men have been brutally murdered and we must discover why. Anyway, I *need* to know why, Robert, I couldn't let it go now we've come this far.'

'Well, Nick, I shall leave it to you to organise those people to do the hunting. Although, on second thoughts, perhaps I should speak to Captain Sanderson. Maybe I should also see the Chief Constable first and then the Excise Collector. You can organise the rest.'

'Thank you, Robert. I think I knew somehow that you wouldn't let it go either.'

'We will meet tomorrow morning in my office at the usual time. I really don't feel at ease discussing these things in a public place.'

'Yes, I agree. I shall eat another cake and then to business!'

'Do you mind if I leave you now? I need to see to the books.'

'Yes, Robert, you take care of your books and I'll take care of mine – yours for the riches of the body, mine for the riches of the mind.'

'Yes, but which does man need most?'

'Well, we could talk about that for hours. Another day maybe?'

'Perhaps, when we're old with nothing else to do.'

'Be off with you, Philistine!'

'Good day, bookworm!' Wray left smiling. He enjoyed having the last word for once!

Whilst this meeting was taking place, Benjamin Sachs of Dagger Lane had called at Twygge's shop to order a book. Henry Crosswell took the order: *Shilush Leshonoth* by Sebastian Münster, Basel 1530. Sachs had explain to him that the book was extremely rare and he transcribed the title in order to make it easier for the London dealer to locate it. Sam Parker was in his study with his head in the Classics. He wasn't aware of Sachs' visit until the day the book arrived in Hull.

14

The next day, Tuesday 19th January

'Gentlemen, you must somehow try to speed up your investigations. The leaders of the Corporation are becoming impatient. People are getting agitated about this latest murder. Since the weekend they've been starting to bother the Burgesses and the Magistrates. Even the Chief Constable has been to see me. There is a ripple of discontent running through the town that could grow into a torrent if things are not brought to a conclusion.'

'*The man is almost a poet*,' thought Twygge'. Socratic irony was not normally part of Twygge's store of figures of speech, but he resented being accused, albeit indirectly, of slackness and incompetence when he and Wray had voluntarily devoted hour after hour of work for Sanderson.

'I want to know everything,' continued the Captain, 'Constable Wray, please tell me how near you are to discovering and apprehending the murderers.'

'Well, sir, we may be very close.'

Wray was trying to mollify the Captain and, at the same time, he was aware of how vague is the word *may* is. Twygge detected this and was impressed by Wray's self-control and diplomacy.

'We have scores of men scouring the town looking out for the two men, Captain. Mr Twygge and I believe that the ones described to you are the actual culprits. All the sources of evidence, from December at Bishop Burton to this past weekend in Barton, show this almost conclusively to be the case. I know you're not interested in detail, Captain, but Mr Twygge has something to add concerning the cause of death of the two victims.'

'Well, Mr Twygge, let's hear it. Is this another one of your theories or is it fact? And, more importantly, does it have any bearing on the outcome?'

'It could have, sir, because every single detail is vital in order to put together a complete picture of the events, and so bring us nearer to a conclusion.'

'Yes, Mr Twygge, do get on with it. My time is valuable.'

'*Isn't everybody's?*' thought Twygge. 'Well, Captain, the victims were strangled before they were beheaded, in fact garrotted.'

'Why on earth garrotte a man then cut his head off? This sounds like nonsense to me.'

'It was confirmed by Mr Melling, Captain. A more competent, experienced and knowledgeable surgeon there never was in our Town.'

'Yes, continue.'

'I consulted another surgeon, Mr Bacchus Huntington of Dock Street, and was informed that after the heart stops beating at the moment of death there would be some pressure left in the blood vessels, but that would slowly drop. He said it would take a few minutes for the blood to stop pouring out of an open vessel, and shorter through a major artery. That would explain the cut wrist of the dead man.'

'But if he's dead why go to all *that* trouble and then chop his head off?' interrupted the Captain.

'Because the murderers knew this and had to take precautions to prevent themselves and the head of the victim from being covered in blood. To do this, strangle the man first, wait awhile, the when the heart stops beating, cut the wrist to release the pressure, then chop the head off without releasing too much blood! And the murderers have been seen carrying a box.'

'A box? What sort of box? How is this relevant? '

'A box big enough to put a head in, Captain.'

'You mean they were carrying the head of the victim around in this box? This is more balderdash.'

'Is it, Captain? Why were the heads not found? If they were

buried where are they buried? There are no answers. I believe they had a very good reason for keeping the heads.'

'And what, pray, could that possibly be? For keepsakes? For bleeding trophies?'

'I haven't fully resolved that yet but we *will* find out.'

'That may be what happened but does it bring us any nearer to stopping it? How will you do that?'

'As I said, Captain, it's more detail and it gives us more bricks to build the foundations of a solution.'

'We need a quicker result. You must find those two men. Now, gentlemen, I must get on with other things. Would you excuse me?'

Twygge and Wray got up from their seats.

'We are giving our men three days, Captain. They are searching the docks and the wharfs on the River Hull, others are making enquiries at hotels and inns. They have a clear description of the culprits. If they are still in the town they shall be found.'

'You sound very confident, Constable, I hope you don't disappoint me.'

'I did say *if* they are still in the town, Captain. If they've flown the coop then we won't catch them.' Wray was becoming agitated by the Captain's continual flow of pompous demands.

'Hmph! Well, good day, gentlemen. I expect to hear from you by the end of this week, one way or the other.'

'Yes, Captain. Good day to you.'

Both men left Sanderson's office and made their way to the ferry.

'One would think we were a pair of raw recruits, the way he talks to us,' said Wray.

'That's the way he is, Robert. He is not a contented man. As I said before he would probably prefer to be in front-line action. He also needs a wife and family.'

'What woman would have him, Nick?'

'You never know, Robert, he may have another side to him

that we haven't yet seen.'

'You always make allowances for people don't you? But, I have noticed that even you get irritated by him often as well.'

'I admit it, but it's only briefly, Robert, and I don't let it fester. It's not like Othello's *green eyed monster that mocks the meat it feeds on.*'

'And thereby hangs a tail, Nick!'

Once again Twygge was speechless.

'I see I've surprised you. No, I haven't read *Othello*, Nick, I remembered you used that *tail* tale once before, more than once, I might add!'

'Guilty as charged! Repeating the same old lines, dear, dear! Well, Robert, I'm ready for my dinner. Here's the ferry man.'

15

The next day, Wednesday 20th January
Joseph Heron rapped on the door of Nicholas Twygge's bookshop at seven o'clock in the evening. Mrs Field heard it first. She and Twygge were having supper together in the upstairs dining room.

'Nicholas, can you hear that?'

'What, my dear? Oh... yes, I just heard it. Someone knocking at the door? I shall go and see. Who can it be at this hour?' He arose from the table and went downstairs. The knocking continued until he opened the door.

'Who are......' It took him a few seconds in the subdued evening light to recognise the lad. 'Joseph Heron. Do come in...'

'I found..., I found...'

'Calm down, Joseph. One thing at a time. Come with me and then you can tell me all about it. Take your coat off and leave it on that hook.'

He closed the door and then led Joseph up the stairs.

'It's them, sir...'

'Joseph, shush, wait awhile longer.'

'Sorry, sir, I can't wait to tell you. '

'All in good time, Joseph.'

He opened the door to the dining room and invited the lad to sit at the table.

'Now, I'm sure you're hungry. Hannah, this is a young man called Joseph Heron, he is an assistant of mine. Joseph, this is Mrs Field.'

'Very pleased to meet you, Missus.'

'I'm very pleased to meet you, Joseph. I didn't know Mr Twygge had a young assistant. I don't believe I've met you before.'

'Joseph works on the streets for me, Hannah. You know, that other business?'

Twygge had confided in Mrs Field but only given her a vague outline of the events he was investigating.

'Now, Joseph, have some cold veal and pickles. Mrs Field's bread cakes are delicious so have some of these.'

'Thank you, sir, thank you, Missus.'

He took some food and put it on the plate. This clearly was a treat for him.

'When we've finished eating, Joseph, you can tell me what you've found. And please take some cheese. Then there's pumpkin pie and whipped cream to finish.'

'Wow, sir!'

Whenever pumpkins were mentioned Twygge was reminded of Sir John Falstaff, *this unwholesome humidity, this gross watery pumpion......*

When they'd all finished their supper Mrs Field cleared the table and left Twygge and Joseph alone.

'Come, sit by the fire.'

Twygge pointed to Mrs Field's chair.

'Now you can me tell your story, Joseph. And speak slowly and steadily, I want to hear clearly the account of your discoveries.'

'Well, sir...'

It was apparent to Twygge that Joseph had calmed down considerably, was full of food, and, no doubt, was feeling a little lethargic.

'...it's like this, Sir – I was going home down High Street, Sir. It was very busy as usual.'

'Carry on.'

'Then I saw them, sir, the two sailors. I saw them coming out of the Black Boy and then walk up High Street so I followed them up High Street, then up Salthouse Lane and onto the Dock Side, Sir.'

'I hope they didn't see you?'

'Oh no, Sir, it was busy and I kept well back.'

'Excellent. Describe them for me.'

'They were just the same as before, sir.'

'Where they carrying anything?'

'No, sir.'

'Not the parcel you saw them with before?'

'No, sir, they weren't carrying anything.'

'What happened next?'

'Eventually they came to a ship, sir, and went up the gang-plank.'

'What sort of vessel was it?'

'It was a brig, I think.'

'Two- or three-masted?'

'It was big, Sir, so probably three.'

'Good, so what did you do next? Come straight here?'

'Oh no, Sir, I thought it would be a good idea to find out about the ship – where'd it come from or where it was going.'

'I never cease to be amazed at your ingenuity, Joseph. Do continue.'

'Well, Sir…'

'Joseph, please don't keep calling *Sir* - it's not necessary and I haven't been knighted - well, not yet anyway!'

'Sorry, Sir… whoops, I mean sorry Mr Twygge. I spoke to a man who was standing by the gang-plank.'

'Were they loading or unloading?'

'Neither, it looked to me as if they'd finished loading. There was not much stuff on the wharf and the crew were busy on deck.'

'What did the man tell you?'

'He said the ship was about to sail with the tide very soon.'

'Oh dear, we must be too late. Where was it sailing too?'

'He said Hamburg.'

'I wonder why Hamburg?' Twygge asked himself.

'I don't know.'

'Of course you don't, Joseph, I was thinking aloud. Did you see the name of the ship?'

'Yes, but I couldn't read it so I asked the man. He said it was the *Frederika Louisa* or something like that.'

'Well done Joseph. I wonder if she's set sail yet.'

'It probably has now.'

'Well, even if she hasn't sailed what could I do? I couldn't have demanded to go on board and takes the two suspects off, could I? Even if I did what proof have I that they are guilty of anything? No, Joseph, we haven't caught them yet, but we have some new and valuable information, thanks to you.'

'Yes. What do we do next?'

'We shall have to call off the search first thing tomorrow morning. I shall see Constable Wray and explain to him what you've found out. Then we shall have to rethink our strategies.'

'But if they've fled what else *can* we do?'

'I don't know, Joseph, but we mustn't think it is all over, although we don't want any more people killed, do we? Somehow or another we may be able to stop any further murders.'

'How?'

'I don't know yet, but don't give up hope. Now, Joseph, it's time you returned home. What will your mother and father say if you return this late?'

'Nothing, I sometimes work this late at the Hotel.'

Twygge dipped into his pocket. 'Look, Joseph, here is a shilling for all your hard and excellent work, spend it wisely.'

'Ooh, thank you!'

'We shall have to find some way to get you to learn how to read and write, won't we? Then you can do better than slaving away all hours of the day in a hotel. What do you say to that?'

'I... I don't know. I don't think my father would like it.'

'Never mind now, Joseph, we shall see. Now off you go home.'

Twygge got up from his chair and Joseph followed him downstairs.

'And remember, not a word to anyone.'

Joseph put on his coat.

'Not a word I promise. And thank you and Mrs Field for the delicious supper, and for the shilling.'

'You're most welcome. I shall see Mr Baker in the morning and tell him you'll be returning to the Hotel. Good night, Joseph.'

'Good night.'

And off he went into the night.

16

The next day, Thursday 21st January
Early the following morning Twygge went to the offices of the various Excise men to call off the surveillance. He then immediately called on Robert Wray at the Coach and Horses to tell him about Joseph Heron's discovery and to call off the constables.

'I'll go to see the Chief Constable straight away, Nick. But if the ship has sailed already what can we do?'

'We can talk about that later this morning at the usual place. Will that suit you?'

'Yes, Nick. Eleven o'clock then. I better be off to see the Chief.'

They both left the Coach and Horses, Wray turning up Fish Street and then onto King Street and past the Trinity House, to reach the office of John Clarkson, his Chief, on Silver Street. He explained to him the latest developments.

'Mr Wray, both Captain Sanderson and I believe that there has been far too much time wasted on this business to the detriment of law and order in this town. Neither murders have anything to do with us. I know that the members of the Hull Corporation made the original request of the Captain but that was many weeks ago now and nothing has been achieved. Those two men you mentioned may have nothing whatever to do with it. And to take the word of a boy seems to me to be rash.'

'Well, sir, I know it's been slow but this lad is very astute and both Twygge and I have full confidence in him.'

'Even so, I can't imagine for one minute what you can possibly achieve next. The ship has sailed, and in three or four days will be in Hamburg. What can you do about that, Robert?'

'I don't know, sir, but Mr Twygge will come up with something, he always does.'

'It's always Mr Twygge this and Mr Twygge that, Robert. I don't mind what you do in your own time and if you're not available to attend a major incident when required it will be seen as a dereliction of your duty and will have to suffer the consequences. You are aware of the restlessness of the people because of the flour and the bread prices? We all have to be ready to deal with any disturbances that might arise. I know the militia are there to deal with mobs and rioting, as they did last year, but it's the constables who can nip it in the bud. We cannot underestimate the value of local men dealing with local people – without that there would be much more disorder and law-breaking and the like. The militia are confrontational, they can control people by sheer numbers but they are seen by the people as alien, they are resented, they cannot command respect in the same way you and I can.'

There was a pause.

'Well, I apologise for the lecture, Robert, but I feel strongly about this. I know you're a good Constable and I know that people respect you, that's why I don't want you to lose that by acting in a way that might put it at risk.'

'I completely agree with what you've just said, sir, no one could agree more, and I shall make sure that my duties will be carried out fully. However, from what I've seen and learned from the murder of that man at Bishop Burton and the other one at Barton, sir, I would not like to see another one happen. I also know that this town *has* been involved in it. We are in the middle of something here that links both murders. I'm aware that Captain Sanderson believes it's not our business but that of the Beverley and Barton authorities, but I believe otherwise, and so does Mr Twygge. There is something going on and Hull is at the heart of it. The next killing, if there is one, could well happen here.'

'I see, Robert. Well, in that case if it's a possibility then it would be my job to try to prevent it happening again, especially our doorsteps. But why do you think it might happen again?'

'Well, you remember I told you something very similar happened at the London docks some weeks ago? That makes three almost identical killings with more than just the manner of their deaths in common as I explained to you about the clothing. Do you not think, sir, that it is more than a coincidence when three similar events occur within a relatively short period of time?'

'Well, coincidences do occur in life. However, as we do appear to be involved, as you believe, then I cannot ignore it. The best thing I can do is to see the Magistrates and give them a clear account of all we know. If they then believe that we should continue then we can work something out. But you and Twygge cannot do it all by yourselves.'

'We haven't though, have we, sir? The other constables and the Excise have been helping us only yesterday.'

'It seems to me that you've got this investigation fully under control. Depending on what the Magistrates say I will allow you to continue. But, there must always be a Constable on duty in your area so I shall speak to all the others nearby and come to some arrangement. One word of advice, Robert, don't endanger yourself. If things do turned bad and you're in the middle of it you must get out and hand it over to Captain Sanderson to deal with. Is that clear?'

'Yes, sir, and I must thank you. I shall try my best to bring this matter to a conclusion as soon as possible, although it won't be quickly from the way we see it at the moment. The more we can find out the quicker we can find these murderers. Delay would mean we could lose our way and never find it again.'

'Quite. Now that we've come to an understanding I shall go immediately to the higher authorities and let you know their instructions straight away. Anything else, Robert?'

'No, sir. I shall await their answers and act accordingly.'

He got up to leave. 'Thank you again, sir.'

'Good day, Robert.'

He opened the door and stepped out into Silver Street to be met with the usual hustle and bustle of daily life.

Twygge was late arriving at Sam's Coffee House.

'I do apologise, Robert, it took me a long time to find all the Excise men. Young Joseph is back at the Cross Keys this morning. What did the Chief have to say?'

'We can continue doing what we're doing as long as the Magistrates agree.'

'Splendid! Well done. Did he take much convincing?'

'Not really. You see, he has to consider his duty to the town and the Magistrates first but when I pointed out to him that Hull could be in the centre of all this he then softened his attitude. This morning we have some French biscuits, have one.'

'I do hope they're not revolting!'

'Don't you ever cease your punning?'

'Sorry, Robert.'

He takes a bite.

'Nice and lemony. Good old Mrs Usherwood, and good old Chief Constable! Now, Robert, I have an idea. It's wild and extravagant but I think it would be worth doing.'

'I'm not sure I like the sound of that. Your ideas are often wildly extravagant, without you're saying so, Nick. Saying so probably means they're completely impossible.'

'Aha, a sceptic! Yes, I agree upon the latter but let me tell you anyway. We should go to Hamburg.'

Wray nearly choked on his biscuit.

'No, wait, Robert, don't have a fit, just listen.'

'Totally absurd... out of the question, especially after what the Chief said.'

'What did he say?'

'The constables' duties are to the town of Hull. I may have

won my argument on that basis but asking him if we could go to Hamburg is unthinkable. He *would* have a fit, *and* he'd take my job away.'

'Well, I shall have to go alone.'

'You can't do that, you will find *yourself* without a head one morning, if you haven't lost it all ready.'

'This is one of the most intriguing puzzles I have ever had, Robert, I cannot give up now. It's *the first attack of Satan.*'

'What are you talking about, Nick, are you still sane?'

'Sane as I'll ever be now that Mrs Field has agreed to marry me. No, I was quoting Samuel Johnson, Robert, *obsession*: *the antecedent to possession*. I'm becoming obsessed with solving these murders.'

'Whatever Samuel Johnson says...'

Twygge interrupted, '*Said*, Robert, he's dead.'

'*Said*, then, obsession is not healthy, you will lose your judgement, you will do rash things, you will...'

'Robert, I am using hyperbole. I'm not obsessed in that sense, an evil spirit hasn't made my mind his abode, I'm just very excited about it.'

'What on earth do you expect to find if you do go to Hamburg? Are you going to wander the streets hoping to catch a glimpse of the two men, neither of whom you've ever seen? Impossible, Nick.'

'Of course, that would be a ridiculous notion. Look, we know the name of the ship, we know where it's going, we know who was on it. It only sailed yesterday evening so if I could find another vessel going to Hamburg, or even Bremen, today or tomorrow, I could get to it and find out what happened to the two men.'

'No, no, Nick, it's too far-fetched. You will be wasting a lot of money on a fruitless journey. What if nobody remembers the two men? And even if someone did how would you know where to find them? It will be like looking for a needle in a bottle of hay.'

'But what *if*, Robert, I *do* find where they are and what they're doing? That would make it all worthwhile.'

'You think that you can stop it all on your own? This time, Nick, you cannot convince me. I cannot be involved because my position as Constable is at stake and because I think what you propose to do would be a complete waste of time. I'm sorry to oppose you on this matter but this is one time when I really do think you'll be doing the wrong thing.'

There were a few moments of silence.

'Well, Robert, I honestly don't blame you for taking that stance. I shall respect your view at all times, but I'm going anyway!'

It wasn't until Twygge had looked in the newspapers and visited Isaac Pleasance, the Excise Collector, that he discovered that there were no ships going to or coming from either Hamburg or Bremen within the following six days. He thus had to abandon his plan and he returned to inform Wray of the change and to revise his strategy.

'We shall just have to wait until the next boat arrives, Robert, and hope it's the same vessel and the same skipper, unlikely though it is. Six days is probably insufficient time to unload, load *and* make the crossing.'

'You shall have to wait until such a boat arrives, Nick, and then we shall see.'

17

Four days later, Monday 25th January
Among Saturday morning's delivery of post, amidst a number of parcels and various missives, Nicholas Twygge found a letter from Isaac Townend of York. He would be coming to Hull again on business. He would arrive at Mr Winter's Neptune Inn on White Friar Gate in the early afternoon on Monday and could he call in to see Nicholas? Of course it would be too late now for Twygge to get a reply to Isaac in time so he decided he would meet the coach personally.

The coach had arrived by the time Twygge got to the Inn. The building was new and almost as large as a mansion - four storeys of superb Georgian architecture, a symbol of the wealth and power of that Age. Over the front door was a carved bearded head of Neptune himself, and crowning the façade was a rectangular pediment of elaborate Adamesque carvings on the parapet. It could barely be seen from the street but it was planned to stand and command a regal view for people coming down the proposed new Parliament Street. This was a street that was being created out of an area of extreme poverty and squalor, the residents being forcibly removed from Mughouse Entry, a step that could only be achieved by an Act of Parliament. Only Twygge was aware of the disparity, and yet, at the same time, he was moved by the sheer splendour of this edifice.

He entered the building and found Townend with his bag waiting in the lobby.

'Ah, Isaac, how pleased I am to see you. Are you staying in this palace? You know, you could have stayed with me.'

'Good day, Nicholas, pleased to meet you too. I didn't have time otherwise I would've let you know I was coming sooner.

No, I'm not staying here, I can't afford it. I have to find a much cheaper place.'

'Nonsense, Isaac, you can stay with me. How long will you be in Hull?'

'Only two days.'

'The usual business visit?'

'Partly, but I do need to talk to you.'

'Oh, what about, may I ask? I detect a note of urgency in your voice.'

'We can't talk here, Nicholas, we need privacy.'

'In that case, come to my house.'

They left the Inn and turned right down White Friar Gate.

'We can get Mrs Field to make up a bed for you and we can talk in my office. Have you had any dinner?'

'I brought some pie with me to eat on the coach.'

'Was that enough? You need more than that to see yourself through until supper tonight.'

'That's very kind of you, Nicholas. I got quite chilled on top of that coach. But I haven't come here to beg anything of you, I merely need some information.'

'On top, Isaac? Was there not a seat inside?'

'I left it too late, besides it's much cheaper outside.'

'It does sound to me as though you're in some kind of difficulty.'

'I am, that's why I wanted to speak to you.'

They reached Silver Street. It was always a bottleneck and they had to dodge, single file, through the throng before they reached the Market Place.

'Well, Isaac, we've known each other now for many years. If you need any help in any way you can depend on me. But now, let's get you to my house and you can warm up and fill up. Mrs Field and Sam and I are going to the Assembly Rooms this evening. There is a Chamber Concert, they'll be playing some string quartets and you can join us. It'll be a pleasant distraction for you, just what you need I think. You know your Shakespeare... *if music be the food of love, play on; give me excess of it......*'

'Yes, I know it, Nicholas, and I know what follows... *that, surfeiting, the appetite may......*'

'Yes, yes, Isaac,' interrupted Twygge, 'I know. Perhaps not the most appropriate of quotations, but I do like the initial metaphor.'

The Holy Trinity clock struck half past the hour of one as Twygge and Townend were passing by.

They soon reached Twygge's shop. Inside there were one or two customers but it was generally quiet, being a Monday.

'Good day, Mr Crosswell, I'm very pleased to meet you again.'

'Good day, Mr Townend. Have you had a good journey from York?'

'The usual, Mr Crosswell, long and tedious, but there we are!'

'Yes, indeed, sir. Fortunately, I need to travel little, but I do know how it is.'

'Can you manage without me, Henry? Samuel should be back quite soon.'

'Certainly, Mr Twygge. As you can see we are not very busy.'

'Mr Townend and I shall be in my office if you need me.'

The two men went through a door on the right at the rear of the shop and entered the office.

'Take a seat, Isaac. I shall go and arrange with Mrs Field for you to stay. Two nights you say?'

'If I may, Nicholas?'

'Certainly you may. I shall return shortly.'

He left the office by another door into the side passage and climb the stairs. He found Hannah in the kitchen still clearing away after their dinner.

'Hannah, my dear, I brought Mr Townend of York. He'll be staying for two nights. Is the guest bed made up?'

'It is, Nicholas, all prepared. With you I never know who or when somebody will appear so it's always ready. He'll be here for supper as well?'

'He will, Hannah, and don't forget where we are going tonight, so we shall have our supper a little earlier if we may?'

'Your word is my command, Master.'

'I do hope not, *thus spake the Fiend, and with necessity, the tyrant's plea, excused his devilish deeds.*'

He gave her a gentle one-armed hug.

'One more thing, my Mistress, would you please bring some tea for Mr Townend and myself? *Please*, I beg you on my knees.'

'Oh, go on, out of my kitchen, slave.'

'I'm going, My Lady. We'll be in my office.'

He gave a bow and left, and returned to his office and Mr Townend.

'Now, Isaac, you must tell me what has been causing you such concern.'

'Part of the problem is, Nicholas, as in my previous visit, I cannot tell you everything, and that will make it impossible for you to help.'

'Now here is a conundrum if ever I heard one. You obviously need my assistance but you cannot tell me why?'

'I'm afraid so. If I told you everything my life would be at risk.'

'Come, come, Isaac, that cannot possibly be, surely?'

'There is no doubt about it, Nicholas. I told you before that I brought it on myself because my business was slowly failing. Being in business yourself you know how that can happen - once it begins to slide it's extremely difficult to stop it. I have no resources to stop it. So, I resorted to an easy way out – make some money another way.'

'What on earth was your idea for doing that? Why didn't you approach your friends? I would've very happily helped you out.'

'I'm not the type of person to beg for financial assistance, Nicholas. I just couldn't do it. Anyway, it's happened now so it's too late.'

'So what was your scheme?'

'That is what I cannot tell you, absolutely not.'

'That just doesn't make any sense to me, Isaac. How can I help if I don't know what the problem is?'

'I'm sorry, Nicholas, but that's how it has to be. You may be able to help if you can give me some information.'

'That should not be too difficult, I can tell you anything I know about anything, quite willingly.'

'You may not, you don't know yet what information I need.'

'Well, you had better tell me now and we can get everything sorted out, and maybe then you will be rid of your problem.'

At this point Mrs Field arrived at the door with the tea. Twygge went to open it. 'Come in, my dear Hannah.'

'Good afternoon, Mr Townend.'

'Good afternoon, Mrs Field, how pleasant it is to see you again.'

She nodded and put down the tray on Twygge's desk.

'Those stairs will be the death of me. I shall tumble down one day, you'll see.'

'Oh dear, Hannah, I didn't realise. Now look, you mustn't do it again. If I order food or drink in the future you must insist that we be served in the parlour. If I forget you must sternly remind me.'

'I shall, Mr Twygge, you may depend on it. Now, gentlemen, enjoy your tea and cake.'

She left the room.

'I must tell you, Isaac, because I don't believe you know. Hannah and I are engaged to be married. It's set for April and you shall be receiving an invitation.'

'I'm not surprised, Nicholas, because you may not remember but you said as much when I was here previously in December.'

'Did I really? I do believe I'd forgotten that. Now, have some tea and cake.'

He poured the tea and offered Townend some plum cake.

'Now, what do you wish to know?'

'Well, Nicholas, I would like you to tell me all you know about those two men who were murdered and beheaded.'

18

The same day, Monday 25th January

As Twygge and Townend were leaving their meeting in the office Sam was keeping shop with Mr Crosswell. The latest delivery of post had arrived and Sam was opening the parcels of books. One of them was an old tome very carefully wrapped and on the spine was what he recognised now as a title in Hebrew. When he opened it he found it was also in Greek and Latin. Inside the parcel was an invoice for three pounds.

'Goodness me,' he thought, 'who could this be for? Would Mr Sachs want such an expensive book? No, it must be for one of the wealthy gentry.'

He took it over to Mr Crosswell.

'Sir, would you look at this and could you tell me who has ordered it, then I could deliver it?'

'Yes, Sam, let me check my order book.'

He took out a ledger from under the counter.

'Here we are, *Three Languages*, ordered by Mr Sachs only a week ago. My, that was a rapid delivery! How disturbing to see the world moving at such a frightening speed these days. What with Mail Coaches hurtling through the towns and countryside and the like we're all going to be spun off the face of the earth soon.'

'Yes, Mr Crosswell. Could I deliver this now?'

'There is an invoice, I presume?'

'Yes, sir, here, for three pounds.'

'Well, I suppose you could, but don't forget to give an invoice to Mr Sachs this time. Give me a moment then I shall write one out for him.'

'I'll not forget it. I shall keep it in my hand all the time.'

'Wrap it up again, then you may take it.'

He wrapped the book and tied the string around it while Henry Crosswell wrote out a new invoice, then Sam left the shop. There were a few light flakes of snow falling gently as he made his way down Myton Gate. When he arrived at the house of Mr Sachs he knocked once, waited awhile then knocked again. Shortly he heard someone approach and unbolt the door. His heart began to race. The door opened and there was Rachel Sachs.

'Well, good afternoon, Mr Parker, I see you bring a parcel, it must be some books.'

'It is Rachel. How... how very nice to see you again.'

'Do come in out of the snow.'

He stepped in and she closed the door.

'My father is not in at the moment but my mother will give you the money. You do have an invoice this time?'

She smiled. Sam blushed slightly but he did admire the gentle way she delivered the irony.

'Yes, Rachel, I do, it's here in my hand.'

He handed it to her. Their fingers touched briefly and Sam reddened again.

'Thank you.'

She looked him in the eye and smiled again but he didn't know whether she'd noticed him blush or not. He couldn't think of anything to say. She took Sam into a room at the back of the house where an old lady was sunk deep into a chair, appearing to be asleep. There was the sound of children's voices in an adjoining room.

'Bubbe, dos iz her Parker.'

The old lady opened her eyes and nodded an acknowledgement then closed them again.

'This is my grandmother, Mr Parker.'

'Please call me Sam,' he said quietly to Rachel.

'I shall go and get my mother from the kitchen.'

She went into the next room and returned with her mother

followed by two children.

'Dos iz her Parker mit a buch un mit a faktoier. My mother doesn't speak English, Mr Parker, so just please say good afternoon.'

'Good afternoon, Mrs Sachs, I'm very pleased to meet you.'

'And these are my sisters, Rebecca and Tena.'

Sam smiled at them but didn't know what to say. The two girls remained silent.

'Gehen ir in di kich, maine meidlech,' said their mother and the girls returned to the other room.

'Give the invoice to my mother, Mr Parker, and she will get the money for you.'

He handed it over and Mrs Sachs went out of the room.

'You don't have to pay now, Rachel, you know. Mr Twygge doesn't mind waiting for it. You could bring it to the shop later.'

'No, no, my father always likes to pay straight away, Mr Parker, it is best that way. It means every bill is settled so no debts are allowed to build up. Do you understand how important that is?'

'Of course I do, Rachel, it is a very wise way to conduct business. Would you care to come for a little walk outside when this is settled, the snow is quite gentle?'

'Well, I don't know, Mr Parker, I shall have to ask my mother.'

Sam felt that that was likely to lead to an answer he didn't necessarily want.

'Do you need to go to the shops for anything? I could accompany you.'

At this point Mrs Sachs returned. She handed the money and the bill to Rachel.

'Here you are, Mr Parker.'

Sam signed the invoice as paid.

'Now I'll show you to the door.'

'Good day, Mrs Sachs it was nice to have met you and your children, and the other lady.'

'Good day, Mr Parker,' she said in her broken English with just a slight hint of a smile.

Sam felt somewhat encouraged by that. They left the room, Rachel closed the door and they went down the corridor. She opened the front door.

'Mr Parker, if you wait around for several moments I may be able to come out.'

At that she closed the door and bolted it. Sam was elated, his mind was suddenly in a fuzz. He walked slowly down towards Postern Gate, quite unaware that the snow was falling more heavily now. He looked back several times but there was no Rachel. Before he reached the end he turned around and walked slowly back on the other side of the road. Before he'd reached the point opposite the Sachs' residence he saw her coming out. She was bundled up in a long black coat and a fur hat. She looked both ways, didn't see him, and set off walking in the opposite direction towards Myton Gate. Sam dashed across the road, avoiding two near-collisions as carts and waggons were passing. The snow was falling more heavily now.

'Rachel,' he called.

She turned and saw him and stopped.

'Rachel, I'm very pleased you came out. I didn't think you would.'

'I shall have to tell you why I did, Sam, but you may not be so pleased when I have. I told my mother I was going to the shops.'

He noticed she'd addressed him as Sam and not Mr Parker and yet his heart still sank.

'I thought you told me the snow was gentle, I think that was the word you used.'

'Yes, it was when I arrived at your house, but what do you have to tell me?'

His impatience was obvious.

'I must tell you, Sam, for your own sake. I know you will be hurt but it cannot possibly be avoided.'

'First, Rachel,' he interrupted, 'let me tell you, you are the most beautiful woman I've ever seen. I think of you all the time. I take walks along here whenever I can to see if you ever come out, but I only saw you that one time.'

He had to tell her this before he heard the bad news.

'You mustn't talk like this, Sam. I cannot be friends with you, my mother and father wouldn't allow it.'

'Why not? Is it because I'm a Gentile, is that the word?'

'No, no, Sam, not to me, but *yes* to my parents. But that is not the real reason. You see, Sam, I'm engaged to be married.'

Sam was so stunned he felt a giddiness come over him.

'Engaged, but to whom?'

'He's in Prussia, he lives there. His mother and father are friends of my parents. They've been to England once or twice over the years, and we've been there. His name is Moritz Lewin.'

'Do you love him, Rachel?'

'That doesn't matter, Sam. In these marriages people learn to love each other over time. My father and mother's marriage was arranged and now they love each other very much.'

'It doesn't seem natural to me, Rachel surely they don't always lead to love?'

'They do seem to, usually.'

'What does this Moritz do for a living?'

'He's a jeweller.'

'Is this marriage going to take place soon?'

'Next year, Sam'

'Next year, that's a long time from now. Could we not be just friends and go for walks now and then? We could just talk, and I promise I shall not say things to you again as I did just now.'

'I don't know, Sam, I don't think it would be right. It would be deceiving my mother and father.'

'Are you are not doing that now, talking to me?'

'Only a little, because I came out to tell you I shall be getting married. You had to know, you see, because I could see in your eyes when you look at me, you know?'

'You mean... you could see how I felt, just in my eyes?'

'Yes, but also in your voice.'

'You are very perceptive, Rachel, and so very clever.'

'I'm just average, Sam, just a normal Jewish daughter who cares about her family.

'Don't we all do that?'

'Well, yes, of course.'

There was a pause.

'I must leave you now, Sam, we've reached the Market Place. I am very sorry for you, Sam, sorry for how this must hurt you. You're a nice boy, I do like you, but you do understand my position don't you?'

'Of course I do, Rachel, and I shall respect it.'

She looked at him with such a gentle softness in her eyes that he felt a tear welling within.

'Goodbye, Sam,' she touched his hand, 'Don't be sad. Peace be with you.'

She turned and walked into the Market Place.

The following morning Nicholas Twygge entered the Coach and Horses and found Robert Wray in his office.

'Good morning, Robert. Don't be surprised, nothing untoward has occurred.'

'Good morning, Nick. What brings you here this early? Couldn't it wait until eleven o'clock?'

'It could but I want you to be prepared, but we also need the privacy. Can you spare some time now?'

'Well, if it doesn't take very long.'

'I shall be as quick as I can. Firstly, I don't believe I shall be going to Hamburg just now. I saw Mr Pleasance and he informed me that the sailing time each way is almost four days, depending on the weather of course. So, allowing for unloading and loading and one thing and another it will be too late, the birds will probably have flown the coop. Unless we have another incident I fear this may be the end.'

'That doesn't sound at all like you, Nick.'

'Maybe but I've begun to think it is so. Secondly though, much more interesting, a friend of mine from York, Isaac Townend, is in Hull again. He came yesterday on business but also to tell me something, something I found utterly amazing. It appears he was involved with the two murdered men. He is not guilty of anything, he's not committed any crime as far as I can tell but he is involved. Not only that, he goes in fear of his life. He was paid a considerable amount of money, I might add, to book a ticket for a coach from York to Liverpool. He was to meet a man at the York Tavern, the Hull Mail Coach terminal, on the evening of November 23rd, then take him to the Black Swan Inn where he'd booked a room for the man, and then to see that he got on the Liverpool coach the following morning. The man never appeared. This happened again in January, the man failed to appear.'

'Had he been doing this previously, I mean before the December incident?'

'Apparently, yes. He had met several men in this way and got them safely on their ways.'

'What makes him think that those murdered men were the ones he was due to meet?'

'It has happened twice, Robert, on the same days. That's too much to believe it could be a coincidence, surely?'

'I suppose it is, but why is he afraid?'

'He must feel responsible. He was paid to fulfil an

agreement and he didn't, or rather couldn't, because the men didn't appear when they should have.'

'But that was not his fault, if that is the case.'

'That *is* the case, Robert. I know Mr Townend well enough now to know he wouldn't be dishonest. We'll have to help him as best we can.'

'How can we do that?'

'By finding the murderers.'

'Isn't that too late now?'

'It may seem so but who knows what may turn up if we keep working on it? Anyway, he's staying with me until tomorrow. He's gone out on business at the moment but I would like you to come by my house, Robert, early this evening if you can where the three of us can talk together. I have asked Mr Townend and he's agreed. By the way, Robert, you should have accepted my invitation to join us at the Assembly Rooms yesterday, the music was absolutely splendid, so uplifting, it was nectar and ambrosia for the soul. Mr Haydn and Mr Mozart transport one to the Elysian Fields, *far from the madding crowd's ignoble strife, to the......*'

'Come, come, Nick, you are mocking. You know very well I couldn't go with you. But this other thing, *is* intriguing. Wherever you go, whatever you do, Nick, there is always a surprise. Yes, I am free this evening and I shall be at your house, at what time?'

'Come to supper about seven o'clock'

'I shall be there. This is a meeting that cannot be missed at any price.'

Part II

Bleeding Trophies

It will have blood, they say; blood will have blood.

19

The same day, Tuesday 26th January
At seven o'clock there was a tinkle of Twygge's doorbell. Sam went out of the parlour door, down the stairs and opened the door to Constable Wray.

'A good evening to you, Sam. Winter's with us at last – a good two inches of snow!'

'Good evening, Constable, do come in. You can hang your coat here. There's a brush for your boots just there. The snow certainly brightens up the towns, sir – makes it appear quite cosy, if not rather cold.'

'It is very pleasant, Sam, as long as we have plenty of warm clothes upon us.'

Sam led Wray up the stairs and into the parlour. There was a fire roaring in the hearth, and around it were placed four easy chairs in an arc. Already seated where Mr Twygge and Mr Townend.

'Good evening, Robert, do come over and sit by the fire. Warm yourself up. Sam, fill a glass with punch for Mr Wray, would you?'

'Good evening, gentlemen, I'm pleased to meet you again. Here's a good fire and good company for a pleasant evening, I'm sure. I am honoured.'

'Thank you, Robert, we are also honoured by your presence. Now take a chair,' Twygge indicated one of the chairs nearest the fire, 'and warm yourself up.'

'Thank you, Nicholas.'

'*Nick*, please, Robert, no formalities here.'

'Mr Townend, I hear you're in some difficulties?'

'Yes, sir, but nothing I cannot sort out, I shall…'

'Now, gentlemen, please, this is a topic of discussion for later. Let us first enjoy our punch and then we can have our supper, if Hannah deigns to serve us, that is, and we'll talk about Mr Townend's predicament when we've finished our repast.'

'Sam, I'm glad to see that you are with us. Perhaps we should now address you as the *gentleman*, Mr Parker?'

'Well, Constable Wray, honoured as I am to be invited to be present in this illustrious company and very pleased to be so, I still feel somewhat of an intruder. I'm still young and inexperienced– I haven't the confidence to engage with you on an equal footing.'

'That may be so, Sam,' said Twygge, 'and we can understand your feelings. We've all been through that part of youth, that *no-man's land* where one doesn't know where one fits in, except with one's peers, of course. But, *please*, Sam, relax. We shall treat you as an equal now. we're aware that you've grown up and matured, not to mention well-learned and sensible. You may not be of age but I know you have more qualities of full adulthood than many an older man that I have been acquainted with.'

Sam felt somewhat embarrassed and suddenly he was being the centre of attention in this way and couldn't think of anything to say. Twygge was aware of this so he continued, 'Gentlemen, let us drink a toast. Raise your glasses to...... Success in whatever we do!'

In unison, 'Success in whatever we do!'

'Please sit, gentlemen. You here, Isaac. Robert....here. Sam, would you care to sit there? Splendid.'

'This must be like dining at the Worshipful Mayor's annual banquet.'

'Indeed, Robert, only the food will most likely be better!'

'Well said!' These were the first words from Isaac Townend since Constable Wray had entered the room. He appeared to be more at ease.

'Now, gentlemen, I have a very special announcement to

make. You all know that Hannah and I are the affianced. It is my great pleasure to inform you that on Saturday the first of May we are to be married. And, of course, you all shall be invited.'

The three men applauded and offered their congratulations.

'I have a special bottle of Rhenish Hock for us all this evening. I hope you shall enjoy it. It was given to me by Mr Benjamin Outram in return for a favour.'

'I can't say I've ever tasted it, Nick,' said the Constable, 'is it white or red?'

'Oh, white, Robert. The best of the wines from the Rhine are all white. They use a grape that gives their wines the most exquisite flavour of summer and...... and the full bounty of the grape itself. They are superb, but I cannot afford to buy them.'

'We are privileged, Nicholas,' said Townend, 'I too have never tasted Rhenish. I shall look forward to it.'

'Excellent. Would you gentlemen please excuse me while I go to the kitchen to assist Hannah? I try not to make her feel she's being taken advantage of – after all, she's not a mere cook and housekeeper any more!'

He smiled as he got up and left the room.

'Mr Townend,' said Wray, 'do you get to visit our town very often? I know it's a very different place to your city of York.'

'Not that often, Constable, but I do enjoy the change. You have a very interesting town here. It's far more cosmopolitan, and there's a much greater variety of people and things going on than in York.'

'Yes, but not as genteel by a long way. Call me *Robert*, by the way.'

'Certainly, Robert, and please call me Isaac. More genteel, you say, well, yes, perhaps, but I do find your citizens much more friendly, and, how shall I put it... down-to-earth. I suppose it comes from being a port. You have a multitude of ships of all shapes and sizes coming and going now on three sides of the town. In fact, you're not very far off being a virtual island.'

'I suppose if you look at it that way, Isaac, that is all true. What do you say, Sam?'

'Well, sir, I believe Hull to be very exciting town. I enjoy all the different things going on around us. I love to see, *and* hear all the different kinds of folk there are busying themselves with this and that. I love all the…er… hurry-scurry.'

'Very well put, Sam. You are fortunate too that you enjoy it so much,' said Townend. 'Do feel the same about your town, Robert?'

'Well, I… suppose I do. I've never given it much thought. I do believe Sam is right, although I've never been in any other town for any length of time. This is all we know, is it not, Sam?'

'Yes, sir, but one day I *should* like to see other places. Perhaps I shall go to sea.'

'Oh, that *is* a tough life, Sam. I'm not sure that would suit you. You've seen all the rough sailors about town, do you want to be one of them?'

'No, indeed, sir, but I have seen the officers, that might suit me.'

'My, you do have ambitions, Sam. Mr Wray is right, it would not suit you.'

'Well, maybe just for a few years. I really do want to see some of the rest of the world. I love to learn about other lands, and their people, of course.'

At this point the door to the kitchen opened and in came Twygge with a tray bearing four bowls and a tureen of soup.

'Hot soup, gentlemen, to warm your cockles.'

'So it is *sea-food* soup then, sir?'

'You caught that one in your net quickly, Sam. No, it's green pea.'

Twygge place the tray on the sideboard and served the soup, gave out the bowls then sat down himself.

'Now, gentlemen, let me begin. Shall we give Sam here the honour of choosing for us a topic for discussion? This is your first time with us three together so you would feel most comfortable in a subject of your own choosing. Do you agree, gentlemen? But let us eat our soup first to allow Sam some time to think.'

'I think that's a splendid idea,' said Townend with a smile, 'it relieves us of the risk of choosing the wrong thing, does it not, Nicholas?'

'Indeed not, Isaac, there is no such thing as a wrong topic for debate, surely – everything is there for the taking, everything from the structure of the universe to the mating habits of the common toad, if you would pardon me!'

'I'm not sure,' added Wray, 'I believe some topics can lead to serious disagreement, even the falling-out of friends.'

'Yes, Robert, but only amongst the most narrow and intolerant of people. I'm sure *we* can disagree on things and yet amicably agreed to differ. Is that not what civilised people do? What do you think, Isaac?'

'I tend to agree with you, Nicholas, but I do believe certain things, by their very nature, can lead to very serious disagreements.'

'What, for example, Isaac?'

'Well, politics for one. We read in the newspapers about the dreadful behaviour in the Parliament when two parties disagree strongly on some political issue or another. Have not duels been fought occasionally?'

'Oh, yes, Isaac, but I didn't qualify my statement by using the word *civilised*. It is evident to me that many people in Parliament fall short of that epithet, do they not, merely by their behaviour?'

'Well, Nicholas, here we are again - trapped in the net of your logic, to repeat your earlier metaphor.'

'No, no, Robert, not trapped, merely enlightened. That may

sound very arrogant but that is how I've been able to get to the very heart of some things by thinking them through carefully, weighing this against that and so on until a clear conclusion is reached. But, very large *but*, gentlemen, I am wrong as often as I am right, as are we all. *And*, often my conclusions may be different from someone else's who has equally thought things through. So where lies the difference?'

'If I may, sir,' said Sam, 'is not the difference due to the way we see things? Each of us has a unique point of view. Is that not the nature of our minds, our individualness, for want of a better word, the way we are born?'

'Well put, Sam, that is exactly why we either agree or disagree on matters, I believe.'

'I agree with that, Isaac, but you have forgotten one small thing, gentlemen - logic, that word you yourself used, Robert. Logic is supposed to eliminate this business of individual points of view.'

'But does it always work, Nick?'

'Precisely, Robert! It doesn't always work, in fact, it rarely does work. That is the beauty of the human mind – if we all thought logically about everything we would all think the same way, we would have no individual identity, life would be hardly worth living.'

'The sad thing,' put in Townend, 'is that not seeing everything in the same way is often very destructive: wars, murders, fights, quarrels, squabbles and so on, these things cause unhappiness, misery and suffering to people, that is the consequence of our so-called individualness, as Sam so nicely put it, not individuality which I believe isn't quite the same thing.'

'You see, gentlemen, how we have all begun to use our minds in a way that we normally wouldn't - we have *cleared* our minds in this process of discussion. I can't think of a better way of doing so. My only regret so far is that Sam hasn't had a chance to proffer his own choice of subject for debate - we have purloined it!'

'Not at all, sir, I am happy to discuss anything at all.'

'Well, I see our soup bowls are empty. I shall take them away and Hannah and I shall return with the next course. Excuse me, gentlemen.'

'Tell Hannah her soup was delicious.'

'I shall tell her, Robert, it certainly was. Sam, do you mind putting some more logs on the fire?'

'Yes, Sir.'

Twygge gathered the accoutrements, place them on the tray and left the room. A few moments later he and Hannah returned with an array of cold meats and cheeses, a Cheshire porkpie and a bottle of claret.

At the end of the meal, Twygge arose from his chair.

'I shall say a little grace now, gentlemen. I discovered this one in the book by a young Scottish bard by the name of Robert Burns. I've changed it slightly to be a little more comprehensible to us Anglo-Saxons, or, a recent addition to our vocabulary, us *Sassenachs*. I have to leave in the final word in its original form to keep the rhyme but the sense will be clear, I'm sure:

Some have meat and cannot eat
And some would eat that want it.
But we have meat and we can eat
So to the Lord be thankit.

Now let us repair to the parlour and more comfortable chairs around a warm fire. Isaac shall tell us all about his predicament.'

'That was a splendid supper – congratulations to Hannah the perfect, and yourself, Nick, for being the perfect waiter at table.'

'Thank you, Robert, you may return the favour some day.'

'Of course, Nick, but my rooms are not as quiet and homely

as this.'

'No matter, it is the company that makes for a successful evening, is it not? Please be seated, gentlemen. And we shall have another little treat – a glass of old red port, a generous gift from one of my more financially endowed customers.'

When the others were seated in the parlour Twygge went to the sideboard poured four glasses of port and gave them out.

'Please smoke if you wish.'

'It is good fortune that I live so nearby, Nick, I don't think I could walk very far after all this. I'm not accustomed to such volumes of food and drink.'

'Well, Robert, if you can't walk home you may take your repose for the night on the sofa there.'

'Thank you for the offer, Nick, but I must be on duty at the Inn.'

'Isaac, I believe now is the time to tell us all about the peck of troubles you've got yourself into in York. Please take your time and let us have all the details.'

'Well, Nicholas, I shall try not to omit anything, although I have been told, in no uncertain terms, not to talk about this to anyone.'

'Do not concern yourself on that score, Isaac, none of it will leave the four walls of this parlour, will it not, gentlemen?'

In unison, 'Of course.'

'You have our word, Isaac.'

'Well,' Townend took a sip of port, 'it all began in October. I was approached one day in my shop by a foreign gentleman. I didn't then know why I was chosen but I do now - it gradually dawned on me - he could sense my business was not doing so well and, more importantly, my shop is in close proximity to the White Swan Inn, a main coach terminal, as I'm sure you know.'

'Could you tell by his speech what country he came from?' asked Wray.

'I'm sorry, gentlemen, I'm not so good at these matters, and his English was very good. He put a proposition to me – he offered me 30 guineas to meet a certain gentlemen who would be arriving by coach from Hull at the White Swan on certain days. I was to escort them to the York Tavern in St Helen's Square. I was to buy them tickets for the coach to Liverpool the following day and I was to make sure that they got onto the coach safely.'

'That's a lot of money for a simple task, sir,' said Sam.

'It is indeed, but I dared not question the arrangement – I needed the money. He told me that I should do exactly the same each time one of them was due to appear. I'd be given prior notice in good time when they were to arrive, and I would be paid accordingly, 30 guineas for each one. It was too good to be true!'

'Did you think that something highly suspect was going on?'

'Of course I did, Robert, but as I said I needed the money, and that sort of money would relieve me of my difficulties.'

'So what happened to upset such a lucrative arrangement?'

'Well, Nicholas, after the first three were dealt with as instructed in October and November, I can't remember the dates exactly, but the next one was due to arrive on 23rd November.'

'But how come you remember that particular date?'

'Well, Sam, that was because from that day on things started to go wrong.'

'In what way?' asked Twygge.

'The man did not appear. I was confused. I didn't know what to do. I had no way of contacting anyone connected with this business. Every day for a whole week I went to meet every coach that arrived at the York Tavern but he didn't appear. You see, for each arrival I was paid in advance. I had the money but I hadn't earned it and it started to prey on my mind. And then it happened again on 16th January.'

'There is one factor, if I may be so bold,' said Sam, 'that you haven't told us – how would you identify these men when they arrived?'

'That's an excellent question, Sam. I was hoping someone would think of that. However, if *I* may be so bold, I think I know the answer to that,' said Twygge.

'You do?' said Townend with surprise.

'Let me guess – he would be wearing a blue coat bearing buttons embossed with the initials **MS**. Am I correct?'

Townend was clearly stunned by Twygge's response.

'I don't know about the buttons, Nicholas, but you're correct about the coats they wore. How on earth did you know?'

'More of that later, Isaac. Please continue your tale.'

By his expression Townend was still disturbed by what Twygge had said. He wanted to know how he knew but he had to let Twygge keep matters under control in spite of himself.

'Well, gentlemen, nothing happened for several weeks, then I had a visit from the same foreign gentleman, the one who told me of the arrival dates and the one who paid me. He asked me if the travelling gentlemen had all arrived at York and had they got onto the coaches safely. I had to say, of course, that was the case except for the one due on 23rd November. He became suspicious, he questioned me. I had to tell him I knew nothing - the man did not appear, that was it, that was the truth. I think he believed me in the end, but he was clearly angry.'

'Did he threaten you?'

'No, but it frightened me.'

'That may have been your conscience, Isaac. And then?'

'He asked me if the most recent one, the one due on 16th January, had arrived. I had to say *yes*.'

'Why did you lie, Isaac?'

'Because I was afraid. I just dared not tell him the truth – for fear of my life, Nicholas!'

'I think I can understand that. What happened next'

'He looked me in the eye for a long time, then turned around and left my office.'

'What day was this visit, Isaac?' asked Wray.

'It was Wednesday last. But what seems strange to me, Robert, is why he did not seem to know that the second man had not arrived when he was due *before* he came to see me.'

'Well,' interposed Twygge, 'I think that was because there was not sufficient time for him to have been informed. We don't know where he came from to visit you in York. We don't know where these travellers go to after they arrive in Liverpool. There are too many questions we don't know the answers to, gentlemen, but what I believe we *can* be sure of is that the two murdered and beheaded victims were the very same two who failed to turn up at York.'

'And the fact that Isaac lied to him put him in a very dangerous situation,' added Wray, 'What can we do about that? Obviously he can't remain at his bookshop.'

'You're probably right, Robert. We must conceive of a plan that would remove him from any danger. Have you had any ideas yourself, Isaac?'

'I have thought of going away into hiding. My wife came from the village of Everingham, do you know it?'

'No, but I believe it's off the York Road somewhere near Market Weighton, is it not?'

'Yes. My Wife's family are still there. We could stay with them.'

'But what about your business, Mr Townend?' asked Sam.

'I shall have to leave it in the hands of my assistant.'

'But what does he know about you? Does he know, for example, that your wife came from Everingham? You see, Isaac, you mustn't leave behind any trace of where you will be hiding. These are desperate men, they would stop at nothing to find you, especially since your disappearance would make them think that you were guilty of something.'

'No, my assistant has not been with me long enough to know anything about my family. I had to let my previous assistant go when the business started floundering, but since those little windfalls recently I employed a cheaper and younger assistant. No, I do believe I shall be safe in Everingham.'

'If you're certain, Isaac, then you should arrange to move as soon as you can. I'm just pleased that you came to me. Between the four of us we shall ensure your safety and try to put an end to this dreadful... this, how shall I put it...*Ah*, if I may lighten the atmosphere with some words of that *wicked imp they call a poet*, Thomas Gray: *Papers and books, a huge imbroglio* – this dreadful *imbroglio!*'

There were a few seconds when the room went silent, when the significance of these recent revelations were being digested, alongside their suppers.

'Now, gentlemen, this is the point in the evening that I feel moved to explain, as much as I know, of this whole business as I see it. That does mean, of course,' began Twygge with some solemnity, 'that not a word of any of this must leave the four walls of this room.'

All three heads nodded in acquiescence.

'Good. One more glass of port to see us through the rest of the evening. Do the honours please, Sam.'

'Certainly.'

He went for the bottle, filled their glasses and sat down.

'This is a very gruesome tale, gentlemen. I believe Isaac might already have some suspicions so we shall see. But be prepared to be shocked and confounded as you may never have been before.'

The air of melodrama in Twygge's address was not intended but he had to convey the events of previous months with the gravity they bore. It took him nearly half an hour to give his account during which time not a word was uttered nor a glass raised by the other three until he had finished.

Then Isaac Townend spoke, 'But why would anyone want to murder someone then take away their heads? Could they be gruesome trophies of some sort do you think?'

'We have not the slightest idea,' answered Twygge, 'but it is my intention to find out – with the assistance of Constable Wray of course. And I have no doubt that we have not seen the last one – there will be more blood, I am certain..'

20

Wednesday 27th January
The next morning Twygge, Townend and Sam were seated at the breakfast table.

'How did you sleep, Isaac?'

'Very badly, Nicholas.'

'Yes, I can quite understand how this business would be preying on your mind. I must say, I too lost some sleep. I was desperately trying to devise a plan of action, but each time it turned out to be not feasible so I tried another and, likewise, it went nowhere. I spent what seemed like hours going around circle after circle until, eventually, I must have drifted into sleep through mental exhaustion. How did you sleep, Sam?'

'Not well at first, sir. I had these gruesome images in my mind of men being beheaded. It was as though they wouldn't go away. Like yourself I must have drifted off eventually.'

'I'm just sorry that I've put you through this disturbing business, gentlemen. It's all my fault,' said Townend, 'I should not have come to you with my burden and upset you all in this way.'

'Nonsense, Isaac. Robert and I were involved long before you came on the scene. And to some extent so was Sam when he did do some investigations for us. No, you shall not take any blame, in fact, you've helped us *because* you've been involved. We now have more information and, how shall I put it...a much larger piece of the narrative – not a complete view but enough to give us firmer foundations to build upon.'

'Well, that's very kind of you to say so, Nicholas, but I don't feel any better because I put *myself* in a very dangerous situation and if these people discover that you're involved also, your lives may be in great danger too. That possibility makes me responsible. But don't forget, my wife and my assistant are also now exposed.'

'Look, Isaac, what's done is done, we can't turn back the clock. So, please, Isaac, drop this burden of guilt you're carrying around and concentrate your mind on what we *can* do, not what *has* been done, for all our sakes. You know, I have a belief, Isaac, that I only wish everyone would convert to, it is this - in life there is no problem that cannot be solved. I have had this belief for many years and I've yet to find it flawed. It works because I *know* it will. If one frets and worries over a problem it'll never be solved. So let us get our heads together, look forward, and with all the facts we have we can build up step by step a strategy that will bring this to an end once and for all. It may take a long time but we must persevere.'

'Well, that's telling me, Nicholas. Deep down I know you're right. I shall try now on to be less of a hindrance.'

'That's the spirit, Isaac. You're one of a team now, one of us, and we shall work together.'

There was a moment's silence. Then a knock was heard at the door from the landing. Sam got up and went through the parlour to answer it.

'Good morning, Constable. Do come in. We're just finishing breakfast.'

'Good morning, Sam, good morning gentlemen. I hope I'm not disturbing you.'

'Not all, Robert. Bring that chair up and have something to eat.'

'I've had my breakfast, Nick, but that coffee smells good. May I?'

'Of course. I'll get you a cup and saucer.' He went over to the sideboard. 'How are you this morning, Robert? Did you sleep well?'

'As it happens I did. Yesterday evening's conversation tired me out.'

'Excellent. But what gives us the honour of your presence this early?'

'Well, I have been somewhat perturbed by Isaac's predicament. I thought we should work together for the sake of his safety. I have some time to spare this morning so I came to offer my services.'

'That is extremely kind and considerate of you, Robert,' said Townend, 'but I shall return to York today and explain everything to my wife and my assistant. Then we can prepare to leave for Everingham. We shall try to find a coach or waggon tomorrow that can take us as far as Hayton and then we can take a dog-cart to Everingham.'

'But, Isaac, is that feasible? Can you just appear at your parents' door without warning? And can you manage all your personal items? Do all this in one day?'

'It *can* be done, Robert. I know my wife's mother and father. They have a room that is always ready for visitors. They are Catholics, as I am as you know, their sense of family is somewhat stronger, I believe.'

'Well, there's a topic for debate if ever there was one! So I see you have thought this through, Isaac. But returning to York may expose you to possible dangers.'

'I doubt that, Nicholas, after having had such a recent visit from the foreign gentleman. But what else can I do? I cannot just abandon everything immediately and not return to York.'

'Of course not, but I believe one of us should accompany you tomorrow. What do you say? Here's your coffee, Robert.'

'Thank you, Nick. I agree, you do need to be accompanied. After all, as was agreed yesterday, we shall do everything we can to help you.'

'The question is - who can accompany Isaac to York? Sam, do you think this adventure would suit you?'

'Er...I...I never thought for a moment that I should be the one. I don't know what to say.'

'Just say yes, Sam.'

'But Nick, do you think...'

'Of course, Robert,' interrupted Twygge, 'Sam would be the perfect one. He's young enough not to arouse suspicion, yet old enough to take care of himself. What do you say, Sam, is this to your liking?'

'Yes, sir, I would be honoured to accept.'

'But what if both of us should come face to face with danger in some form? Is it better to expose only one person rather than risk two?'

'I suppose logically, yes, that could be true. But, as they say, there can be safety in numbers - it may be two against one.'

'Well, I'm resigned to accepting your kind assistance, gentlemen. I could never argue my way out of it anyway.'

'Now that's agreed we can start making the necessary arrangements as soon as breakfast is over. *And*, we do have a certain advantage.'

'How so, Nick?'

'It is a flaw in the scheme for moving these foreign gentlemen. They have organised transport to be carried out in a routine fashion - that is their weakness. There is a consistent pattern in this scheme and when a scheme like that is put into practice the plans become vulnerable because they can become *predictable*, and, hence, can be interfered with. That is to our benefit. Anyway, now, gentlemen, I shall just go and inform Hannah of what we shall be doing, but not the reasons of course. Heaven forbid we should involve Hannah in all this!'

21

Almost two months later, Monday 15th March
The Marquis Ducantal was on the latest ferry of the day from Barton. The sky was clear and the stars were at their brightest, with just a hint of a sliver of the moon. The River Humber was calm and the air was still, crisp and cold. The Marquis was on the next stage of a long and arduous journey. It started in Koblenz where the Mosel flows into the Rhine, where a boat took him down river to Cologne. Then several coach rides took him the four hundred miles or so to Hamburg. He had been travelling for more than four weeks but it would be a long time before his journey would be over. It would be many more weeks before he reached Montréal, if the ship wasn't sunk by the Americans first.

He managed to find somewhere to sit for the two hours it took to cross the seven miles of the river from Barton to Hull. The ferry was not full by a long way and when it reached the pier at the South End there was not the usual bustling crowd. When he stepped onto the pier with his one piece of luggage he stopped, looked around and appeared to be looking for someone, someone who should have recognised him and be there to meet him. He could hear the boisterous noise of drinkers at the inn nearby, full of sailors most likely.

A man approached the Marquis from the direction of the Ropery to his left.

'I beg your pardon, sir, I believe I'm your escort to take you to York. My name is...'

'Just one moment, gentlemen,' interrupted another man.

He was one of two who had suddenly appeared from the High Street on the right.

'We are here to take this gentleman and make sure he gets to York safely. Who are you?'

'I am the gentleman's escort. I must ask who you are. You must...'

'No you're not, you are an impostor. We know that you have tried this deception before.'

Then he addressed his colleague.

'Take this rogue away. Take him straight to a constable, or a militiaman if you find one and have him locked up.'

'One moment, all of you,' commanded the lone traveller, whose foreign accent was revealed immediately, 'How do I know which of you is my escort and who is the rogue? You two look like seamen, this one here appears to be a gentleman. You two are the rogues.'

At this point the Marquis brought out a pistol.

'No, sir, we are not rogues. We are disguised. This is a dangerous area of the town at this time of night, robberies are common. We didn't want to be noticed, for the sake of your own safety, sir.'

'I protest. I have authority to see that this gentleman gets to...'

'No you haven't. Take him away.'

The second seaman took him by the arm and held a pistol to his back.

'This way you, we'll soon sort this out with a constable.'

He pushed him along towards the Back Ropery and out of sight.

The Marquis appeared to be perturbed.

'Sir, please accept my humble apologies. We knew this was likely to happen, it's been tried before. That's why they sent two of us this time to give you better protection. You do know where you shall be staying for the night?'

Several drunken men stepped out of the New Whale Inn nearby, singing loudly as they started to make their way towards the end of High Street.

'It's called the Cross Keys Hotel. There will be a coach

tomorrow to take me to York, yes?'

Not being fully convinced as to who was who he felt as though he had better tread carefully.

'Yes indeed, sir. We shall take you to the inn and make sure that you're well guarded. You won't need your pistol, sir, you can put it away. We are both well armed.'

He took out a double-barrelled pistol from underneath his sailor's coat.

'What about your other man? When will he be back?'

'He'll be joining us soon, once he's found an officer. It shouldn't be many minutes. I'm glad we stopped that rogue before he took you away. Your life was in great danger. Now, sir, shall we start to make our way to the Cross Keys?'

He led the Marquis towards Queen Street.

'This is the safest way. Have you had a comfortable journey so far, sir?'

'I have not. It has been an...what do you English call it...*un cauchemar*, a night horse?'

'A nightmare, sir. A female horse.'

'Endless days of the most uncomfortable coaches along the worst of roads. Terrible sailings on the worst of waters. Noisy, dirty inns. Abominable food...'

'Take no mind, sir, the Cross Keys is a fine inn with the best of food in the town.'

'You English, you don't know what proper food is, you eat slops.'

The Marquis had regained his composure and confidence.

'You must be hungry, sir. There will be plenty of sustenance at the inn.'

They reached the end of Queen Street when they were joined by the other sailor.

'I found a small group of soldiers on the Humber Bank. They're going to take that impostor to the gaol.'

'I do believe we've saved your life, sir, and just in time.'

They continued along the Butchery. Just before they reached the Market Place they stopped.

'There's a lane here, sir, that will take us to the inn more quickly and keep you away from prying eyes.'

He took a lantern out of the box he was carrying and lit it.

They turned right into an alley through the Fish Shambles, pungent as usual with its pervading stench like the f'c'sle of a Dutch onion boat. There was always the smell of fish in the Old Town, and elsewhere on market days, but the people of Hull were used to it.

They soon reached the corner where they met another dark and narrow thoroughfare, Grimsby Lane. They turned left and facing them were the ruins of the Augustinian Friary, lately being demolished.

'Just behind that tower, sir, is the yard of the Cross Keys. Follow me.'

He led the way through rubble of bricks, broken tiles and lengths of splintered timbers.

'Sirs, this cannot be the way. Where are you taking me?'

'We do apologise, sir, but it is for your own good - it's safe and no-one will see you. We're nearly there. You can hear people in the yard – a coach has probably just arrived. We'll soon be completely safe.'

'I cannot imagine what it is I am in danger of.'

'There are murdering kidnappers on the prowl, sir. There was an incident not long ago. No doubt they can tell you about it when you reach the inn. And we'll be there to escort you to York tomorrow. We've been paid to protect you, sir.'

The Marquis hesitated. He thought, 'Escorts for this kind of work are usually paid *after* they have delivered, not before.'

At this point, as they scrambled behind the tower, the Marquis suddenly went in the opposite direction but the rubble hindered his progress and he was stopped in his tracks by something that caught him around his neck. He tried to shout for help but no words came out, only coughing and choking noises. He made a grab at the thing around his neck but his fingers couldn't get inside it. A slight gurgling sound came out of his gaping mouth, and in an instant the garrotte tightened and tightened until he could no longer make a sound, and very soon he could no longer struggle nor feel the pain and he slowly sank to the ground.

'Now, quiet!' one of the men whispered, 'Can you hear anything?'

'No, only the sounds from the inn-yard.'

'Right, now, you do the wrist, quickly.'

He stood back. The other man took out a dagger from under his coat.

'Bring that lantern closer but hold it just at arm's length. Now..'

He lifted the dead man's right hand, felt for the pulse but there was none. He then turned the hand so the underside of the wrist was away from him and facing into the rubble. With a swift and accurate slice of his dagger he cut the wrist and straight away slapped it down onto the ground. Blood squirted out into the rubble but slowly as the pressure dropped it became a mere gentle ooze until eventually there was hardly a trickle.

The other man took his sword out of its scabbard. He reached down and positioned the dead man's head so it was clear of any obstructions. He placed some bricks underneath it to raise it and give it a solid base. When he was satisfied with the positioning he raised his sword as though it were an executioner's axe and slashed it down with enormous force, taking the head completely off in one swing. The dead Marquis's wig fell off as the head rolled away. It was clear from the accuracy and skill of the performance that the executioner was well practised in his art.

'Get the box ready. Give me those covers.'

He wiped his sword on the dead man's wig. The other man handed him a large cloth and a sheet of tarpaulin.

'Have the box ready.'

He laid out the cloth and placed the head on it. He wrapped it carefully and wrapped it again in the tarpaulin. He placed the bundle in the box and stuffed in the wig with it. He closed the lid and wrapped the box in more tarpaulin and tied it up with tarred string.

They covered the headless body with rubble until it was barely visible. They looked around for any prying eyes, listened, but no-one seemed to be anywhere near. One of the men took his knife and cut off one of the buttons from the Marquis's coat and slipped it into his own coat pocket.

'Time to be away. Come!'

They made off in the direction of Grimsby Lane Alley, turned right into Grimsby Lane and marched off towards the High Street.

They were not staying at the Black Boy Inn this time – they never repeated any part of their missions if they could help it.

22

The same evening, Monday 15th March
Isaac Townend had gone with Sam back to York and arranged his move to Everingham with his wife. His assistant was left to run his bookshop. He'd not heard a word from Townend - that was the arrangement - he would carry on until he heard otherwise. Townend had not wanted anybody to know where he was hiding, except, of course, Twygge, Wray and Sam Parker. Further information regarding the earlier murders had not surfaced so Twygge and Wray were waiting patiently, sending out repeated requests now and again for various parties to keep an eye on the ferries and the ships using the staithes and the New Dock, but, as yet, nothing had come of it. Captain Sanderson appeared to have abandoned the whole affair, believing and hoping that that was the end of it. Twygge, however did not believe that that was the end of it. He assumed that the activities of the past weeks had either been postponed because of the disappearances of the travelling gentlemen or, perhaps, been diverted to other routes. He kept a close eye on all the sources of news to see if there were any signs of any other incidents that may have had possible connections but nothing came to light. He'd had one letter from James Harris of the GPO in London telling of another beheading. The *modus operandi* - the beheading, the blue coats, the buttons embossed with **MS** and one of them removed, handkerchiefs embroidered with **VL**, and so on. This murder had been just the same as the others, and this led him to the contemplation of the *modus vivandi* of the perpetrators - how could people live like this? Nothing had been gleaned that had been of any use to Twygge. He resigned himself to accepting that whatever happened so far away was beyond his scope. There was nothing he could do, he would have to wait for events that

would happen nearer to home. It wasn't until later that evening that the body of the third victim would be found.

Twygge was working late in his office. He was thinking of his wedding. It was approaching midnight. This was the only time of day when he could catch up with his orders and bookkeeping. He was just about to wipe his quill and finish for the night when he heard a vigorous knocking on his door. The urgency of the knocking made him rise from his chair quickly and go to the side door. He lifted the latch and opened the door. There was Joseph Heron looking distressed and extremely agitated in the light of Twygge's candle.

'Come in, Joseph, come in. What on earth has happened to you?'

'Sir, I...I've seen the...I...' He suddenly collapsed in a heap in the doorway. Twygge placed his candle on the stairs, gathered up Joseph in his arms and carried him into his office. For the want of anywhere to put him he carefully laid him on the floor, dashed out of his office, grabbed his candle and ran up the stairs and into the parlour. As he was laying Joseph down on the sofa Sam came into the parlour in his nightdress.

'Sorry you were awakened by the noise, Sam. It's Joseph Heron. He knocked on the door and when I opened it he fainted. I hope it's not from lack of food, and what can he be doing out this late at night? Go and fetch a blanket so we can keep him warm.'

'Yes, sir.' Sam went up to his room just as Hannah was coming the other way down the stairs.

'What is it, Sam? Such a commotion at this time of night!'

'In the parlour, Mrs Field, you will see.'

She entered the parlour to find Twygge standing over Joseph.

'Nicholas, who is it? Is he dead?'

'No, Hannah, I believe he just fainted. It's Joseph Heron, he works at the Cross Keys. He's been helping us.'

'Why would he come here at this time of night?'

'I don't know. Should we try to give him some brandy?'

'I think smelling-salts should do the job if he's just fainted. My, though, he does look ill. I shall go to fetch them.' She left the room.

Sam came in with a blanket and placed it over Joseph.

There came a moan from Joseph and he moved his head slightly to one side and his arms stirred.

'I believe he's coming back to consciousness, Sam. Let's just wait for a few moments.'

Shortly Hannah came back in with a small bottle.

'This should revive him. Oh, I see he's moving. Perhaps he'll wake up without this. Should I give him a sniff, Nicholas?'

'Yes, Hannah it won't do any harm.'

She took the top off the bottle and placed the open neck by Joseph's nose. After a few seconds he stirred again, moved his head from side to side and opened his eyes.

'Joseph, it's Mr Twygge. It's all right, you're safe here. Hannah, I believe some hot broth would do him good. Could you, Please?'

'Certainly, as quickly as I can.' And off she went into the kitchen.

'This is Sam, Joseph, you know him don't you?'

'Yes, sir, a little.'

'Now, you're going to warm yourself up with some nice hot broth, and then you can tell us why you're here. How does that sound?'

'Yes, sir, thank you, sir.'

'Sam, do you know where Joseph's house is?'

'No, I don't think so.'

'In that case I'd better go. It's on Grimsby Lane, I won't be long. We must let his father and mother know what's happened. You watch Joseph until Hannah brings the broth, do you mind?'

'Not at all. I shall keep a close eye on him.'

Twygge left the parlour, went downstairs, grabbed his coat and scarf and left the building.

Ten minutes later Hannah came into the parlour with a bowl of steaming broth.

'Where's Mr Twygge, Sam?'

'He's gone to tell Joseph's mother and father where he is. He shouldn't be long, it's just down Grimsby Lane.'

'I don't know, Sam, the weirdest comings and goings in this house. It's a mystery to me what it's all about.' She started to give Joseph some broth.

'I'm sure you lap it all up, Mrs Field – not the broth, I mean all the excitement. It makes our lives, er, interesting does it not?'

'I don't know about that, Sam, life could never be dull as long as Mr Twygge is around. But I do like things to be in order. I do like a routine.'

'I think I can take this broth by myself now, Mrs Field,' said Joseph as he began to sit up.

'So, you're feeling better are you? That's good. Now, here you are.' She handed him the bowl and spoon. 'Are you warm enough now?'

'Yes, thank you, very comfortable.'

He began consuming the broth with vigour and colour was returning to his cheeks.

'Where's Mr Twygge? I've something very important to tell him, it's very urgent.'

'He's gone to your house. Don't fret, he'll be back very soon. Eat up your broth then you can tell us all about it when Mr Twygge gets back.'

Hannah was thinking - she'd noticed how Sam treated Joseph, almost like a father.

'I shall go back to my room now, Sam. I'm sure you can cope with Joseph on your own. You know where to find me if you need me.'

'Of course, Mrs Field.' She left the parlour.

Minutes later Twygge came into the parlour. Joseph had finished his broth and was telling Sam about his work at the Hotel.

'I'm glad to see you've recovered, Joseph. I've explained everything to your mother and father, and told them you can stay here tonight. Would you like to do that?'

'Yes, sir, very much. It's nice and warm in here. My room at home is very cold.'

'I'm sorry to hear that.'

Having just come from the house in Grimsby Lane he new what semi-squalor they lived in.

'Now, Sam, I want Joseph here to tell me everything he's seen tonight, and I believe, if my assumptions are correct, that it will not be a pleasant account to hear. Do you think you are prepared to hear a very bloody and disturbing story?'

'Well, sir, I have a very good idea of what to expect. Having been involved from the sidelines I've been able to piece together various bits of information from here and there and made what I may call a theory.'

'That does not surprise me in the least, Sam. Good for you! So I assume you wish to remain? Don't answer, there's no need to. Joseph, are you in a fit state to be able go through all the details you saw this evening? I don't want you to do it if it will be too painful. It could wait until tomorrow when you've had a good rest.'

'I can to you all, sir, now. I must tell someone.'

'That's very brave of you, Joseph. It will be best. If we wait until tomorrow you may have forgotten some important details. Try not to miss anything out however unimportant it may seem to you. When did it all start?'

Joseph Heron recounted everything he'd seen from the ferry

from Barton arriving to the murder in the Friary grounds, and the men leaving the scene and crossing the Market Place from where they entered Silver Street. There they went down a narrow alley to the White Hart Tavern. He'd followed them in the shadows throughout without being seen. He then came straight to Mr Twygge's house. His account was very detailed and not a word was said by either by Twygge or Sam during the whole twenty minutes it took. When he'd finished there was a pause. The atmosphere had an intensity that pervaded the whole room.

'What a dreadful thing for you to see, Joseph, no wonder you fainted away. But now, immediately, I must go to the Coach and Horses and get Constable Wray. If we act with celerity we may be in time to apprehend these men whilst they're at the tavern. Sam, would you mind keeping an eye on Joseph? Stay with him as long as you can. He's in a state of shock and needs someone with him.'

'I will, sir.'

'One more thing, Joseph, and I apologise for having to ask you to recall these awful events again, but what about the third man, the one who first met the murdered man off the ferry?'

'I don't know, sir, he was just led him away with a pistol in his back down the Back Ropery. I never saw him again, I had to stay with the other two. The other man came and joined his partner with the victim at the end of Queen Street.'

'Thank you, Joseph, now you must lie down and rest. I'll be going out now and I don't know when I shall be back, but Sam here is going to stay with you.'

'Thank You, sir.' His voice was fading, his eyes were wanting to close, so Twygge left the parlour quietly, donned his coat and left his house.

His excitement was apparent from his demeanour and the haste in his steps along Myton Gate. Two minutes later he was entering the Coach and Horses. Wray was not in his bed, he was on constable duty in his office.

'Nicholas! What on earth are you doing here at this time of night?'

'Robert, I think we've got them, the murderers. They're staying at the White Hart.'

Twygge sat down then gave Wray a full account just as he'd heard it from Joseph.

'We must get some of the militia to help us, and also we need to send some down the Back Ropery - I, suspect we shall find another body there. Captain Sanderson also needs to be informed, unfortunately.'

'Nick, if all this is true it's what we've been waiting for all these months. Let me get my coat and boots and we shall get the Chief Constable and Constable Smart.'

'Smart by name and smart by nature, eh, Robert?'

'This is no time for humour, Nick.'

'If you say so, Robert.'

'We must also get Sheriff Walton, he's on Lime House Street, we need him to make the arrest. Would you go and fetch him now, Nick? Bring him to the Chief Constable's where we shall all meet.'

'But do you think we should drag him out of his bed at this time of night? We haven't much to go on.'

'These are unusual circumstances, Nick, he must be informed as should everybody in this town *and* some beyond. I'm certain he should be there to make the arrest.'

'What about the militia and Captain Sanderson?'

'I think we can manage without them, don't you, Nick? There are enough constables.'

'Well, I suppose it would to our credit. If you're sure there'll be enough people to handle all this.'

'Yes, I'm sure there is. If we take them by surprise we'll get these two murderers into the House of Correction in no time.'

'But what about the Back Ropery, we can't leave a body lying there, if that's where it is? There must be a search.'

'Or even if there is one. We have no proof.'

'And don't forget the victim, he will need removing before anyone else finds him.'

'Of course, you're right. I'll call up Constable Johnson at his inn on the Market Place, he can search the Ropery. I must get to the Chief Constable right away and pick up Smart and Johnson on the way and you can get the Sheriff.'

They left the Coach and Horses in considerable haste. Wray gave Twygge a dog-cart and he drove it down Myton Gate and headed for the Sheriff's residence in Lime House Street. Wray had to drag Constable Smart out of bed but Johnson was still up and about at his inn and he sent him off in the direction of the Ropery. Wray and Smart continued down the Market Place towards Silver Street. The Chief Constable was abed and he had to be aroused by his housekeeper.

'Gentlemen,' he said as he came down the stairs three-quarters dressed, 'what brings you here so late and obviously so urgently?'

Wray explained the situation in full if somewhat speedily. By the end the Chief was fully dressed.

'We must not delay any longer but we do need more assistance. We must find some more constables. These murderers must not be allowed to escape for want of manpower.'

'Mr Twygge has gone to fetch the Sheriff, and I've also told everyone to meet in the yard of the George Hotel. It's the best place, being just around the corner. We should not be seen by anyone coming and going from the White Hart. We mustn't risk alerting the suspects to our presence.'

'An excellent suggestion, Constable. Also someone must go immediately to the Citadel and inform Captain Sanderson. Also, gentlemen, we must be armed. I shall get a brace of pistols if you would wait here for a few moments.' He went to the back of his house and emerged soon after with the weapons, some powder and lead shot. Also two pairs of wrist manacles, lately known as *cuffs*. The three left the building, turned right and in a minute were entering the yard of the George. Constable Smart was sent to gather more constables.

It took the best part of half an hour before there was a small handful of men gathered in the yard. The Chief gave a brief outline of what they were intending to do, speaking almost in a whisper. He had also informed the landlady of the George, Mrs Bamford, of their presence but not the reasons for it.

'Gentlemen, if you must speak to each other you must keep your voices very low as I am doing at this moment. We must be patient and bide our time until the Sheriff arrives. We must also have one of you watching the entrance to White Hart Entry on Silver Street and another watching the entrance on Bowlalley Lane. Under no circumstances should we allow these two men to escape our clutches. We do have pistols, but I'd rather we capture these men alive. Also be aware that they will be armed themselves. Not since the Civil War and the refusal to let King Charles enter our town has the White Hart been so important to us. We have one the most law-abiding towns in the country so let us live up to that reputation and get those two men.

By the time Twygge arrived at the George with Sheriff Walton there had gathered in the yard four constables, two militiamen and the Chief. Twygge had explained everything to the Sheriff on their ride to the yard. The Chief then explained to the Sheriff his plan of action.

'Chief Constable, I shall leave you completely in charge. Your plan is excellent. I shall make the arrest when the time comes but there must be at least two witnesses. But also their must be some evidence of their crime, without any we shall be wasting our time. Are we all ready?' There was a nodding of heads.

'Chief Constable, I'm not cognizant with your plans,' said Twygge, 'do you have a task for me, sir?'

'I'm afraid not, Mr Twygge. You have been extremely helpful over the past months and everyone here, nay the whole town, is grateful for what you have done. But I cannot allow your life to be put at risk. But I would like you to stand by and keep that dog-cart at hand on Silver Street once we've entered the White Hart.'

'Yes, sir, I'm very pleased to be of service.' Twygge was clearly disappointed but he knew that he had to stay in the sidelines. Nonetheless his excitement was mounting, as it had been doing since Joseph Heron appeared at his door.

He waited in the yard until all the men had left to take up their positions. He then walked the dog-cart out and into Silver Street, turned it at the Market Place end so he could see White Hart Entry and climbed on. He sat there in the cold night air and waited.

23

The same day, Monday 15th March
In April 1642 an event occurred in Hull which many believe was the trigger that eventually led to the Civil War. It started in a room on the first floor of the White Hart Tavern. The differences between Charles I and his Parliament had grown greater over recent years, and the King's wars with Spain and France and, latterly, troubles with Scotland over the rise of the Covenanters had led to depletions of the contents of his coffers and stores of arms and ammunition. The magazine of the Citadel of Hull was the largest in the country by the nature of its strategic position, even including the Tower of London. The King wanted the magazine moved to London but, obviously, there was strong resistance from Hull and the Parliament, and the tensions became so great that both sides realised that whoever held the Hull garrison would have the upper hand if ever it came to a revolution. Parliament appointed Sir John Hotham to be the Governor of Hull. At first the town resisted his appointment - they were already well-governed - but gave in after a threat of treason was issued. As the King and Parliament became more and more at odds with each other the threat of revolution was in the air. In April the King came up north with his court to Beverley and then proceeded to ride to Hull with the intention of taking over the town and its garrison.

On 22nd April at 11 o'clock in the morning the King arrived at Hull's Beverley Gate and demanded entry to the town. Sir John Hotham, Sir Peregrine Pelham MP and Mr Hull an Alderman, together with some friends met at Sir John's house, now the White Hart Tavern, where they agreed to Parliament's previous instruction to deny the King entry into the town. When this was declared the King tried negotiating with Sir John but after several hours with no agreement the King finally ordered two Heralds-at-Arms to proclaim Sir John Hotham a traitor and all those who assisted him guilty of high treason. He then returned to Beverley.

The siege of the town which followed later that year was carried out with vicious malice and lasted for over a year. The suffering of the townspeople was not as severe as expected but the inhabitants of the surrounding villages suffered more, being in the middle of Royalist actions outside the walls of Hull. Eventually the Royalists were defeated in the area and the siege ended on 12th October 1643, a date that was to be celebrated annually in the town for many years to come.

Almost 160 years later Chief Constable Stanley, Sheriff Walton and two constables were following John Clarkson, the landlord, up the stairs of the White Hart Tavern. They passed the very room on the left where Sir John Hotham and his men had had their meeting. Three of them were armed and all four of them felt their hearts pounding, but not John Clarkson, he wasn't aware of what the fuss was all about, nor the depths of evil that the occupants on the next floor had perpetrated. No-one spoke a word.

The Tavern had been panelled in oak in Jacobean times and had darkened with age giving the whole building a deep gloom at this time of night. There were no people about at this hour and the occasional creek of a step on the stairs sounded as though it would wake up the whole place. They reached the top floor. Clarkson warned them to be aware of the *stranger's step* at the very top - if anyone stumbled on it it would wake everyone up. Clarkson held his lantern up as they approached the door of a room on the right at the top of the stairs. The Chief Constable indicated with his hands where the others were to stand at each side of Clarkson. He then nodded to Clarkson who then knocked gently on the door. There was silence. He knocked again a little more loudly. Still there was no sound of stirring. He knocked a third time and spoke just loud enough to be heard inside the room, 'Gentlemen, may I have a word with you?'

There was a pause but no reply nor sounds of movement were forthcoming.

The Chief Constable signalled Clarkson to move aside. He then approached the door and waved Wray to his side. Pistols were poised and he took hold of the doorknob. He turned it and with a sudden movement pushed it open and dashed into the room. The others followed close behind. It was dark, no sound came from within, not a hint of anybody being disturbed. They felt a slight relief but also disappointment that their quarry had escaped capture.

Clarkson was standing in the doorway. The Chief grabbed his lantern and held it up inside the room. There were two beds to the left and between them a small cabinet. On the right there was a small chest of drawers and a wash stand against the back wall to the right of the beds. It appeared that two persons were in the beds.

'Let's have some candles lit,' said the Chief. Two were on a chest of drawers and were lit. The Chief then signalled Wray to approach one of the beds whilst he approached the other, slowly, pistol cocked. He bent down, took hold of the covers and suddenly yanked them off. Wray did the same with the other bed. Then there was a stunned silence. Nobody spoke, nobody moved.

24

The same evening, Monday 15th March
Outside, on Silver Street, sat a very cold and anxious Nicholas Twygge on a dog-cart. He was beginning to get agitated. He had the feeling that he was being cheated. All that thought and time he had devoted over several months to this business and here he was, sitting outside in the bitter night air like some lackey or some naughty schoolboy being punished. It was a very rare thing for him to feel resentment about anything. His live-and-let-live philosophy and his generally relaxed *persona* got him through life with few tensions, but tonight those were being stretched towards breaking-point, his equilibrium was being challenged. He was also concerned at the irrational nature of his feelings. Try as he may he couldn't overcome it and the fact that he was being weak-minded at that moment annoyed him.

When he was at the peak of his anxiety two constables emerged from the White Hart Entry and approached Twygge.

'Sir, the Chief Constable would like you to go into the tavern. They're on the top floor. We shall look after the dog-cart.'

'What has happened up there? Anyone in custody?'

'We don't know, sir, we were not in the room but I don't think there were any disturbances. You'd better go up now, sir.'

'Thank you, constable, I shall.'

His mood instantly changed. He dashed down the Entry and into the tavern, climbed the stairs two at a time and reached the top.

'Ah, Nick,' said Wray, 'here's a surprise for us. Come in and have a look for yourself.' He led Twygge into the room.

Inside was the Chief constable and the Sheriff.

'We didn't expect this, said Wray, 'these two men are dead. They were dead when we burst into the room and it appears they were strangled. Have a look for yourself.'

Twygge approached one of the beds. He had become himself again. He had a close look at the body.

'It looks to me that this man was garrotted.'

'That is our conclusion, Mr Twygge,' said the Chief, 'both of them.'

'Well, there is a puzzle!'

'We were all hoping,' said the Sheriff, ' that tonight would see an end to this very unpleasant affair that has beleaguered our town, but we are in a worst situation that ever. I shall leave it to you now, gentlemen. In the present circumstances there are no duties for me to perform. If someone would drive me back to my home?'

'Yes, sir,' said Twygge, 'there are two constables standing by the dog-cart on Silver Street. I'm sure one of them will take you.'

'Thank you. I will bid you good night, gentlemen.' He left the room.

'A good night it *isn't*,' said the Chief after the Sheriff had left.

'Have you searched the room yet?'

'No, there's been no time, Nick. Perhaps we can start now, chief?'

'Is there something in particular that you expect to find?'

'Well, there are several things. If we search the men's pockets there could be something or other that could tell us who they are or where they're from, or even where they were going to next. Also, there should be a box or a package of some description of just the right size to hold a human head.'

'So, you believe they haven't disposed of it already somewhere else?'

'They may have got rid of it but then my question would be

- why behead the man in the first place? The latest victim and the other two appear to have been strangers, and probably French or German maybe. It appeared they were merely passing through on to a further destination. It seems unlikely that he would have been recognised anyway.'

'They may have hidden the head in a safe place elsewhere to collect later,' said Wray.

'Of course, Robert, that certainly is a possibility but I do very much doubt it.'

'Well, gentlemen, if it's in the room we shall find it. First we must search their clothing. Constable, you search that one,' said the Chief, pointing to the bed nearest the window, 'and I shall search this one. Mr Twygge, would you search elsewhere and see what you can find?'

Neither of the victims had changed into bed clothes, their kitbags were lying on the floor by their beds. They were still wearing their sailors' slops which told Twygge that they were the murderers from what Joseph had told him earlier. Unless these two are another pair of sailors.

'How did you know this was the room of the murderers, gentlemen?'

'The landlord led us to it,' said the Chief.

'What exactly did you tell him?'

'That we were looking for two sailors and would he show us their room.'

'So we can assume that there were no other sailors staying in the tavern tonight.'

'Yes, that must be the case.'

It didn't take Twygge long to realise that there was no box containing a head. The Chief and Wray were still rummaging through the men's pockets.

'This not what I expected,' said Twygge, 'there is no box and therefore I'm baffled. I would have sworn the head would have been in this room tonight. Also, what I didn't expect to find is them dead.'

'Aha,' ejaculated Wray, 'I've found a piece of paper.'

'Let us finish our searches,' said the Chief, 'and then we can see what we've got.'

The contents of the men's bags were now scattered over the floor. The Chief and Wray checked each item carefully before putting them back in the bags.

'When we've finished we must get these bodies to an undertaker as soon as possible. Mr Twygge, would you mind calling off the other constables from their stations and have them gather downstairs? Oh, and would you send one of them up here as soon as possible?'

'Yes, sir.' He left the room.

When their searches were complete the Chief and Wray had found five separate items - two purses, one on each of the victims, containing a significant amount of money, a piece of paper with two names and addresses on it, a ticket for two berths on the *Prinz Ferdinand* sailing later this morning with the tide from the New Dock to Hamburg under Captain Bergedorf, and, finally, a coat button bearing the initials **MS**.

By the time the Chief and Wray had tidied up the room, covered up the bodies, and ensured that every nook and cranny had been searched thoroughly a constable knocked and entered.

'Ah, Constable Waite, no doubt the word has spread and you know what we have here. I would like you to take up a position outside this room. Keep the door closed and make sure nobody starts to poke their noses in or starts to ask questions. Is that clear?'

'Perfectly, sir.'

'The rest of us will be downstairs in the tap-room but you must wait here until an undertaker arrives or you receive further instructions from me.'

'Yes, sir.'

'Good, now we'll leave you on guard.'

The three of them went out of the door, closed it and went down the dark winding staircase and entered the tap-room.

The Chief Constable addressed the assembled men.

'There is nothing more for you to do tonight so you may now return to your beds or whatever you were doing. *But*, you must not say a word to anyone, not even your wives, about what you've seen and done tonight. Do not repeat or even contradict any gossip that you may hear, in fact, do not even talk to each other about it. There are very good reasons for doing as I say. What has happened in this town in recent months is not the fault of the town or its people, it is just unfortunate that Hull was chosen to be where these things were to take place rather than somewhere else. As you are aware, gentlemen, this is a very orderly town. You rarely get called out for any serious disturbances so let us hope that after tonight we can all return to our normal lives. Thank you all for what you've done, and I bid you good night. Constable Wray and Mr Twygge, would you please remain behind?'

All except those three left the tap-room one by one in silence and walked out of the tavern, going their separate ways. Although the night sky was not blanketed with clouds there was a new moon making for a heavier darkness. The streets were mostly empty. Those who were awake would have heard the bells of Trinity Church strike 2 o'clock.

25

The same evening, Monday 15th March
While the events at the White Hart were taking place Joseph Heron was having nightmares as he lay on the sofa in Twygge's parlour. Several times he woke up screaming, startling Sam and causing him to leap up out of his reveries. Sam was able to raise his latent paternal instincts and he gently coaxed Joseph out of his troubled state.

When Twygge eventually returned home he climbed the first flight of stairs as carefully as he could but wasn't able to prevent the many creaks no matter how much he tried. He slowly opened the parlour door. There was stillness broken only by the usual aspirant sounds of the sleeping. He gently closed the door and climbed the stairs to his own room.

The following morning Twygge, feeling the worse for wear, left his building, crossed the Market Place and went straight down Grimsby Lane to the home of Mr and Mrs Heron.

He told them of the events of the previous evening, without the gory details, and it would be best if Joseph remained where he was for the rest of the day. He gave them a shilling to compensate for Joseph's loss of earnings. He then returned to the Market Place, turned right and marched off towards Silver Street to the Chief Constable's office where a meeting had been arranged.

He wasn't the first or the last to arrive. There was the Chief of course, the two constables Johnson and Waite, and, of all people, Captain Sanderson.

'Good morning, Mr Twygge,' greeted the Chief.

'Good morning, gentlemen.'

At this point there was a knock on the door and in came Robert Wray and Constable Smart.

'Now we have a full complement we can began. Good morning constables, please take a seat.'

When they were all settled the Chief continued.

'Firstly, I shall run through the details of what has been happening in recent weeks, nay, months. I shall also give you a full account of what happened yesterday evening. Not all of you know everything by a long way, in fact I don't believe any one of us does. This is the purpose of this meeting, to ensure that we all know every detail of what's been happening when and where. I shall be calling on each of you individually to add what you do know that others don't. This is all on the understanding that none of what is said here goes beyond these four walls. If any of you are later found to have said *anything whatsoever* to anyone else who is not in this room you will lose your positions as constables. I shall begin first. Are there any questions, gentlemen?'

One or two of the gathering looked around at each other but nobody spoke. Twygge was tempted, as was his wont, to give a speech but he resisted, thinking that tact was a better option in the circumstances - he didn't want to upset anybody before they'd even started.

Once they'd begun it took a considerable length of time for each of those who knew anything to add their particular piece of the puzzle. By the time it was concluded an hour and a half had elapsed.

'Well, gentlemen, there you have it – probably the worst thing that has ever happened in this town for many, many years. In spite of having the details and the evidence we still don't know a thing of what it is all about. When we've finished this morning I would like you to go away and give it some thought and if anything comes to mind I want to hear it. But not now, if you don't mind, I still have a lot of work to do for the aldermen and the Sheriff. So let us disperse and return to our usual duties. If there are no questions I would like to thank you all for your assistance and bid you good day.'

Twygge joined Wray as they left the office but not much was said as they walked down Silver Street towards the Market Place. When they turned right Twygge spoke.

'Robert, there was one thing that suddenly shone out like a bright lantern in a dark cavern just now in that office.'

'What might that be?'

'The button. The button embossed **MS**. Without the discovery of that last night we would have no evidence whatsoever that these two men had garrotted and beheaded that unfortunate soul in the Friary ruins. And *also* that other poor soul down in the Back Ropery.'

'I suppose that must be the case, Nick.'

'Robert, I detect a decided degree of detachment in your voice. Is all not well?'

'I suppose so. I hardly slept the short time I was in bed last night. I think I've had more than my fill of unpleasantness lately.'

'Me too, Robert. I'm trying to pull myself out of it by applying my mind to the puzzle of it all.' That was not intended as a rebuke but Robert thought it was.

'Don't preach to me, Nick, it only makes things worse.'

'I'm not preaching to you, Robert. I was just trying to keep my own mind from drifting into gloom. I apologise if I gave offence.'

'No, no, no, Nick, you're quite right. I shall pull myself together. It's not having anyone at home to talk to, I'm...I'm...oh, I don't know. Perhaps I should give up this constable business and just run the inn.'

'Everybody thinks that about their work now and then, it's quite natural. I bet there's been more than once that you felt like giving up your inn. There have been times when I thought about giving up the shop and just doing the bookbinding. But these moments are fleeting and soon dissolve away, as I'm sure you know.'

'Well, yes, but just let us get to my parlour and we can get some coffee down us, that might help.'

'And some cake?'

'But of course!'

Their pace was quite rapid down the Market Place and soon they turned down Myton Gate and reached the Coach and Horses. On their way in Wray went to speak to someone in the kitchen.

Ten minutes later when they were both seated in the parlour by a warm fire a maid knocked and brought in a tray bearing a pot of hot steaming coffee and a hedgehog on a dish.

'I was tempted by something a bit stronger but common sense prevailed.'

'Not really, at this time of day. But where's the cake?'

'I felt like something rich this morning, something to give us a lift - this hedgehog will certainly do that.'

'I'm sure it will but is it not a bit unusual to have a dessert in mid-morning? But why not? So let's tuck in.'

Twygge wondered while he was partaking of the rich *mélange* of almonds, sherry, eggs, cream, sugar, butter, currants and orange flower water whether he would be 'lifted' or, more likely, laid out for the rest of the day.

'Good, Nick?'

'Er...certainly,' he mumbled through a mouthful of the stuff.

Little more was said until their dishes were empty.

'Now I shall pour the coffee.' Wray went over to the table.

'You know, Robert, there is one other item you discovered last night besides the button that I find quite exciting.'

'Well, if you must talk about it, what was that?'

'That piece of paper with the names and addresses on it.'

'Yes, but what use is that to anybody?'

'Another thing occurred to me - what if these two men last

night were murdered by blood-hunters?'

'Wouldn't that mean an end to it all now?'

'It could have but I don't think so. It wouldn't fit my theory. I believe they were murdered because they've been very careless, and as a result they've exposed this business to public scrutiny.'

'And that bit of paper you mentioned?'

'I was thinking about it in bed last night when I was trying to sleep - not the best way, I might add, to try to sleep!'

'Oh, I know what you're going to say. I can read you like a book. You want to go to those addresses in Hamburg that are on that piece of paper. Am I right?'

'Yes, absolutely right! This may be the only means by which this business can be brought to an end. Don't you see that, Robert?'

'It may also be the means by which someone will bring an end to *you* in the process. Here, drink your coffee and forget about such a silly idea. Anyway the Chief's got that piece of paper and I bet you can't remember exactly what's on it after such a fleeting glance at it last night.'

'Ah, that's where you're wrong, Robert, I wrote them down as soon as I had the opportunity. When he passed it around the room I caught a glimpse and memorised them.'

'I might have guessed!' He said resignedly.

Twygge read from his piece of paper.

'You do realise that this means we shall *have* go to Hamburg.'

'You must be ready for the madhouse if you're serious. The minute you step aboard a ship for Hamburg you'll be done for. Don't you realise there will be spies about now we seen everything? Who'll take care of Sam and your business? There'll be no more morning get-togethers for coffee and cake. The whole town will miss you. And what about your wedding?

How will Mrs Field feel when you've left her stranded, a newly-wed and a widow at the same time?'

'Come, come, Robert! You're exaggerating. Look, we're two intelligent people - well, at least one of us is – we can take care of ourselves.'

Wray was stunned into silence. He was flabbergasted, his jaw dropped, his eyes opened so wide that, for a second, Twygge thought he was going into some sort of paralytic seizure.

'Let me get you some more coffee.' He took Wray's cup and saucer over to the table.

'No, no, no...a hundred times *no!*' spluttered Wray as he recovered from his 'seizure'. 'Are you listening, Nick...NO, NO, I will not go with you. And that's that!'

26

The next day, Wednesday 17th March

'Sam, would you mind foregoing your literature studies this morning? I've had a delivery of the most magnificent book, one that needs to be delivered to Mr Boyes of Anlaby as soon as possible.'

'I don't mind at all, sir. Well...I do a little, but I think I would enjoy the journey more, as a change, of course.'

'I would have liked to have gone myself but there are too many things I need to do. Have some more tea.'

'Thank you. What is this magnificent book?'

'It is the Reverend Tickell's *History of the Town and County of Kingston upon Hull*. Mr Boyes is one of the subscribers. Constable Wray's brother is too, and many others but they'll get their copies from other booksellers.'

'Shall we have a copy for ourselves?'

'In spite of my probably ending up in the debtors' prison I did buy one for us, Sam. But there we are - according to Mr Johnson, *booksellers are generous liberal-minded men* - so what if it does lead to bankruptcy? You'll take care of me won't you, Sam?'

'Of course, Mr Twygge, in return for giving me your library?'

'''Tis yours!'

'Thank you, sir. Can I have it now?'

Sam smiled at Twygge - they both relished this kind of gentle humorous banter.

'But now, how to get to Mr Boyes' house. I don't believe you've been to Anlaby before have you?'

'No, sir.'

'Get a shay-cart from Mr Wray. The hood will give you some protection from the weather. Go to the Beverley Gate then take the road to Cave, Carr Lane. Then just keep going until you come to the end and you'll be in the centre of Anlaby. It's about four or five miles. Turn left and very soon you'll see a lane to the right with a large house on the right of it – that's Beech Lawn. Keep going for another 200 yards and on your left you should see another big house – that's Anlaby House, the home of Mr Boyes. If you leave soon you should be back by dinner time, unless you get lost of course.'

Twygge knew that Sam wouldn't get lost, it was just a little more banter.

It was about 9 o'clock when Sam left his house and collected the shay-cart from the Coach and Horses. He decided the best way to get to the Beverley Gate would be to go down Myton Gate, turn right down Dagger Lane then at the end turn left into Postern Gate and towards the Town Wall.

It just so happened that as he was leaving the yard of the Coach and Horses he saw Rachel Sachs on the opposite side of the road walking in the direction of the Market Place with her shopping basket over her arm. He stopped the cart, got down and shouted Rachel's name. He couldn't believe his luck - he thought this was meant to be.

Rachel turned, looked around and saw Sam. She didn't wait for him to come to her, she crossed the road and came to him. He was holding the horse's harness.

'Good morning, Miss Sachs. How very pleasant it is to see you again.'

'Good morning, Sam, but please, you may now call me Rachel, as I told you before.'

'Of course, Rachel. I see you're going shopping?'

'Yes, my usual task. My mother rarely leaves the house, except to go to the shul.'

'Shul, what's a shul?'

'Oh, I beg your pardon, Sam. It's what we call the synagogue.'

Once again he was transfixed by those magnificent dark eyes and that beautiful face. He was staring at her.

'Is there anything the matter, Sam?'

'No, no! How would you like to come for a ride with me on the cart? I... we... er..'

He couldn't believe what he was just saying so he became confused and stumbled over his words as he struggled to finish the sentence. 'I... er...have to go to Anlaby. Please come with me.'

He felt like a childish fool saying that and he blushed.

'I don't know that place Anlaby. Where is it? I never go out of town.'

He realised once again that Rachel was ignoring his embarrassment, so he regained some composure.

'It's not very far. We could be there and back in less than two hours.'

'Why are you going there?'

'I have to deliver a book to Mr Boyes. It's in here in this box,' pointing underneath the seat, 'It's big and heavy.'

'I couldn't go with you, Sam. It's too long a journey and my family would worry about me.'

'Could you not tell them that the shopping took longer than usual?'

'That would be untrue. I couldn't lie to my parents.'

'Well then, tell them the truth Rachel, what harm could come to you? You are a grown woman, you know. And it's always refreshing to get out of town now and again. It'll be good for both of us.'

'Oh, I don't know, Sam. I don't like to upset my family.'

'Please!' His plea was genuine, his whole heart went into it. Rachel hesitated, then succumbed.

'Yes, Sam, I will.' Her eyes twinkled and she added a smile. Sam could tell that she was happy to concur with his wishes in spite of her reservations.

'Here let me give you a hand up.'

She got into the cart, placed her basket on her lap and they set off towards the Beverley Gate, bypassing Dagger Lane.

Once Sam had paid the toll and driven through the Gate and its surrounding heaps of rubble they travelled along Waterworks Street and into Carr Lane that would take them straight to Anlaby. As they left the town and its buildings on its outskirts they both felt a change - the freedom of open spaces, of freshness in the air, of peace as the noises receded, of escape from everything that was part of mundane everyday life. Here they were alone and together, side by side, with time to themselves. They didn't speak as they left the town behind until they had become adjusted to the new surroundings and they'd become more relaxed. Rachel had cast off her concerns about the possible consequences and Sam was exalted just to be alone with her.

They were passing through the flat landscape of fields, small woods, marshes, dykes and ditches. There was the occasional farm here and there.

'This is like travelling through another world, Sam. Do you not feel as though you don't belong here? I feel like an intruder in someone else's land.'

'That's because you never get out of the town as you said, Rachel. There is a new-found pleasure in a ride. I feel it every time I go out, whether to Hessle, Beverley or elsewhere. I went to York on the coach in January. What a wonderful journey that was.'

'What did you see? Was it different to this?'

'Very different. When you get past Beverley the land begins to rise and you enter a beautiful country of rolling hills and dales. You should have been with me. We dropped down from the hills when we approached Shipton but they were still visible on the right of us for miles.'

'I can tell you were happy.'

'I was. But one is continually brought down to earth in a coach - it can be very uncomfortable at times, especially if the road is in need of repair. But what about you, Rachel? Tell me things, anything about yourself, your family. I want to know more about you.'

'Well, Sam, I think you know everything.'

'Not really very much. Tell me about the man you're going to marry.'

'There's not much to tell. I've told you everything already.'

'Do you know him well?'

'Not really.'

'How can you marry a man you don't know very well?'

'That's how it works in our families, Sam.'

'Always?'

'Not always but mostly.'

'It sounds strange to me. My master, Mr Twygge, is getting married in a few weeks but he knows her very well. She's been his cook and housekeeper for along time. They both seem to be very happy about it. I don't detect any happiness in your voice when you when you talked about your betrothed.'

'What does *betrothed* mean?'

'I beg your pardon, Rachel. It's the person you are engaged to be married to. You haven't answered my question.'

'I don't have an answer. May we talk about something else?'

Sam was aware that this diversion of Rachel's was a sign, a sign had pleased him. But he kept his thoughts to himself.

'Yes, of course we may.'

It was apparent that Rachel was happy to change the subject.

'Your religion, tell me about that.'

'That's not very interesting either, Sam. It's only the men that do it really.'

'How do you mean? Don't the women go to church?'

'Synagogue, Sam. Oh yes, the women go but but all they do is sit together separate from the men. The men say everything that needs to be said - prayers, reading from the Torah, and so on.'

'What is the Torah?'

'It's the sacred text, the five books of Moses.'

'It does sound very different, but interesting. But, of course, we only have men running the churches - vicars, rectors, vergers and so on.'

'You're not telling me about yourself, Sam.'

'Oh dear, I'm not doing very well, am I?'

'Of course you are. I want to hear *you* talk - about anything, anything you like.'

'Well, I live with Mr Twygge and Mrs Field, they're soon to be married. Oh, I just told you that didn't I? I've lived there for many years. My father died at sea many years ago, he was a mariner. My mother lives on her own. She couldn't manage to feed us both so Mr Twygge offered her an allowance if he could take me to live in his home and be brought up there. That's about all there is.'

A noise could be heard in the distance coming from the estuary. As it got closer it became a gaggling mixture of screams and yells. There was flock of seabirds approaching. They circled and then some landed on the water on the left. It made Rachel start. She moved closer to Sam and grabbed hold of his arm.

'What are those birds doing?'

Sam could sense that she was anxious. He put both reins in one hand and put his other hand on hers on his arm.

'Are you frightened? There's no need to be, they won't hurt you they're only sea-gulls.'

He could feel how cold Rachel's hand was. When she realised what she'd done she quickly removed her hand. She relaxed somewhat.

'Of course they are, Sam. I've seen them over the town often, but not so many all at once, they were quite frightening. And what a loud noise they made.'

'See, they're ignoring us, they're not bothered at all about us driving along. I doubt if they even know we're here.'

Rachel turned her body and looked behind her. She could see nothing of the town but the faint projection in the sky of the Holy Trinity tower. She looked ahead and only saw the road, marshes to the left, and meadows to the right, and a few trees scattered here and there.

Sam thought he could detect that something was wrong. Rachel was agitated.

'What's the matter? Is something bothering you?'

'No,' she replied hesitantly, 'I'm... just wondering when we'll be there. Is it far?'

Sam had heard of people who were afraid of wide open spaces, and wondered whether Rachel was one of them.

'Not far at all. We should begin to see the houses of Anlaby shortly.'

As he spoke another cart appeared ahead of them coming their way.

'There you see, we're not alone.'

It was this cart that made Sam realise that there had been very little traffic on the journey so far this morning, not quite what he would have expected. He could now understand Rachel's concern. *'She's a town girl,'* he thought, 'through and through. She must think this is an absolute wilderness out here. Perhaps I shouldn't have brought her.'

The cart turned out to be a waggon heavily laden.

'A good mornin' to you, young uns, said the driver as they passed each other.

'Good morning to you,' replied Sam. He glanced at Rachel, she appeared to be more relaxed now.

Soon they approached the first of the houses of Anlaby.

They passed a very large house on the right.

'That's Grove Lodge I believe. I've never seen it, only heard about it. I don't know who lives there.'

'Who would want to live out here so far from the town?'

'Oh, lots of people do, Rachel. Apart from the villagers who are scattered all around there are quite a few Hull families out here, all wealthy ones, of course. They all have large houses - they live out here like lords and ladies.'

'There can't be much to do here can there?'

'Well, they must do something. Of course the men-folk go into town every day to work.'

They came to the end of the road. Sam turned the cart left and in a few minutes they were approaching the lane that went off to the right. Sam immediately saw the first big house. There were some magnificent beech trees in the grounds, not a common sight in the town! In another minute they came to a double bend, then beyond that the house of Mr Boyes made itself visible. He turned the cart into a small drive at the side of the main entrance - he knew better than to go straight to the front door. He stopped the cart.

'You wait here, Rachel.' He got down from the cart and retrieved the box containing Mr Boyes' book. He went to a side door and rang the bell.

On their return journey Rachel was much more at ease. She talked a lot, Sam talked a lot – the ice had finally been broken, they were united in companionship for the next hour.

When they arrived back and were passing through the Beverley Gate Sam had a twinge of apprehension – what will Rachel's family say? Will she be in serious trouble?

'I shall take you to your house and explain where we've been. I shall say it was my fault. I'll say that I talked you into it. I don't want you to be in any trouble.'

'It doesn't matter, Sam. I can explain to them. I won't be in trouble. Anyway, I can't go home now, I have to finish what I set out to do and buy food.'

She smiled at Sam.

'Just take me back down Myton Gate and leave me where we started. I shall go on from there.'

'Are you sure, Rachel?'

He was not sure of himself, he couldn't decide what was the right thing to do. And he felt guilty now.

'Of course I'm sure, Sam. Now drive me down Myton Gate.'

She was so calm and positive about it but Sam's guilt wouldn't go away.

'What a strong woman she is,' he thought, 'a *princess* of a woman.'

When he'd dropped Rachel off and said their goodbyes he returned the shay-cart to the Coach and Horses and went back to his house. On the way he began to think, 'What if Mr Sachs comes to the shop and starts baying for my blood? What'll happen then? I shouldn't have talked Rachel into going with me. I've made trouble for both of us. I'll upset Mr Twygge and Mrs Field, *and* Rachel's family. I won't be allowed to see her again.'

These worries lingered on in his mind for the rest of the day and into the night.

27

Nine days later, Friday 25th March

It took Nicholas Twygge over a week to convince Robert Wray, the Chief Constable, Sheriff Walton, the aldermen, *and* Captain Sanderson that going to Hamburg was necessary to find the answers to the mystery of the murders. He formulated his argument with great care on the day following the events at the White Hart Tavern and the following morning meeting with Wray. He used one particular issue as the focal point of his argument, one that would appeal to everyone if presented in a detailed and persuasive manner, like a salesman trying to sell his wares to reluctant customers – namely a means by which the killings could be stopped and the reputation of Hull be returned to its previous status of general lawfulness, as well as taking away the anxiety, worry and concern about the safety of the people. He had convinced them all that he had worked out, using all the evidence that had been gleaned since the first murder at Bishop Burton the previous November, why these men had been killed. He had tried to avoid going into the details of his theory but managed to convey to them in essence.

At the end of his presentation he was asked to leave the Sheriff's office where they had been ensconced to discuss the matter amongst themselves. There were reservations all round of course, but it was Captain Sanderson who presented the strongest objections, almost swaying the others to his way of thinking. But in the end it was the Sheriff himself with his aldermen who were more concerned about the town than Sanderson who won the day for Twygge.

Robert Wray was not quite so sure but he had his duty to think of. But once he had resigned himself to the decision he softened, accepted it and worked with his full co-operation while they were making their plans shortly after the meeting ended.

Twygge had told them that he would pay his own expenses but the Sheriff denied him that, saying that if he succeeded the town would be very grateful and should pay him accordingly. The Sheriff also offered the Chief Constable extra funds for Wray's part in the affair. The Chief then offered to go to Hamburg with them to supervise the venture but the Sheriff said that three would be too many, too conspicuous and, besides, the town needed his continued presence. Not only that, Constable Wray and Mr Twygge had been working on this more than anybody and, therefore, would be the most suited to carry on with it.

After hearing all this Twygge felt somewhat elated – at last he felt his work had been appreciated. He knew now that he'd got the Sheriff and the aldermen on his side. It gave him a boost of confidence and determination to do the best he could, rather like a schoolboy after being praised for good work. He was going to prove his theory and stop the killings.

28

The same day, Friday 26th March
Twygge had obtained two tickets for berths on the barque *Frederick Louis*, sailing for Hamburg with the tide on Sunday next. He was pleased that he'd found an English ship, it would make it easier to communicate with the Captain and his crew. He might also be able to pick up come colloquial German on the way. He'd obtained a German dictionary and a grammar but he found them something of a struggle. He'd managed to commit to memory a list of words which he felt would be the most useful. Having overheard smatterings of German over the years in various parts of the town he felt confident that he could get by. What words did they need, he thought, - items related to rooms, food, directions, and a few others that would likely crop up. Armed with these he felt certain that their journey would not be a waste of time. He couldn't find a map of Hamburg but there was a travellers' guide to the Continent he'd discovered in Richard Millson's bookshop on the Butchery. The section on Hamburg was brief but it did offer some snippets of useful information.

Twygge had to be back in Hull by 11th April, the day of the first reading of the wedding banns. If they arrived in Hamburg on 1st April they would have to leave no later than the 5th – that would give them only four days to find all the information they would need. Having the two addresses should give them all they needed to know, *but*, Twygge was not going to be too sure of himself in thinking it would all be easy – there would be the risks to their lives if they had to confront dangerous men. He and Wray would have to be armed.

He was pondering these matters in his office after dinner when a knock came on the side door that led to the street.

'Come in,' he called, and in came Isaac Townend.

'Isaac, how good to see you again. Come in, sit down. This is a surprise. It's fortunate that you found me at home.'

'Good day to you, Nicholas. I do apologise for not giving you advance notice of my arrival but it all happened so quickly. I thought you should be the first to know.'

'Know what, Isaac?'

'That I'm safe now.'

'Well, that is very good news indeed. Look, let us go into the next room, it's more comfortable. I'll get Mrs Field to bring some refreshments.'

They both got up and entered Twygge's parlour. Twygge rang for Mrs Field.

'Now, Isaac, you sit there and let me get this fire going, then we'll have something to drink. We'll make ourselves comfortable and you can tell me your tale, of mystery and suspense no doubt? After that I can tell you mine. I imagine both our tales could be the makings of one of these new Gothic novels.'

'If it *were* a story in a Gothic novel I would be inclined to read it as pure invention, not real life.'

'Indeed, if this were to be played on the stage I would condemn it as nothing but totally improbable nonsense, *thus spoke Fabian*. You know, Isaac, I do believe there is not a single facet of the human condition that Mr Shakespeare has not made a brilliant and concise pithy comment upon. Every time I encounter one it gives me a tingle up the spine. Such a unique ability to capture the very essence in just a few perfectly honed words or phrases. There will never be such another.' Twygge finished making the fire and lit it.

Townend looked baffled but before he could comment Mrs Field entered from the dining room.

'Hannah, my dear, Mr Townend has arrived. Would you be so kind as to rustle up some tea and cake for us?

'Good day, Mr Townend.'

'Good day to you, Mrs Field. I hope I find you well?'

'Very well thank you, Mr Townend. I shall now do your bidding, my Lord,' she said in the direction of Nicholas, 'tea and cake will be forthcoming,' and out she swept.

'Isn't she a treasure? Soon to be Mrs Twygge, Isaac.'

'Yes I know.'

'Now then, tell me *your* latest chapter of this Gothic novel.'

'Well, as you know, Nicholas, my assistant has been keeping the shop for me. He sends me messages via a family my wife knows who live in Seaton Ross. She collects them and brings them to Everingham. That way the trail to me should be difficult to follow. He tells me that nothing has been happening out of the ordinary, no visits from suspicious strangers or foreigners or such - until Tuesday.'

'Ah, I thought something must have happened to bring you here, especially without prior notice.'

'Yes, I apologise for that, but it's good news I bring. I had no time to let you know I was coming. What happened is this - my assistant had a visit from a gentleman. He gave no name, he was well-dressed, and spoke with a slight accent. He asked for me but he was told I'd gone away and it wasn't known when I'd be back. This man then told my assistant that I need not hide any more as it now known that I was not involved in the disappearances of the men I was supposed to be sending to Liverpool. He made it clear that he had guessed that I'd gone away to avoid the consequences. I couldn't be certain that he was genuine and not just trying some sort of scheme to get me to appear again in York. But I could tell he'd detected my fears and tried to convince me that he was telling the truth, and I could tell by his manner, his demeanour, and his voice that he must have been. Then he left the shop.'

'That's very interesting, Isaac. You may not know it but we had another dreadful murder and beheading just over a week ago. But, *believe this or not*, the two men who committed the murder were murdered themselves the same night. It seems to me that this Gothic novel is going to become the best-seller in its class. Anyway, I can't help but think that the visit to your shop was linked to this, in fact, I would venture to say that I am certain of it.'

'No, I hadn't heard about these latest murders. Not much news of the outside world gets to Everingham. Maybe you are right.'

'I'm quite convinced that I'm right. I shall explain shortly when we have our tea.'

When Hannah had been in with the refreshments and left Twygge proceeded to tell Townend the story of the events that had occurred after he'd moved to Everingham, including his plan to go to Hamburg. However he did not tell him the details of his theory as to what it was all about. As Isaac had been involved, albeit unwittingly, he didn't want him to carry the burden of knowing more than he needed to at this point.

'Well, Nicholas, I do hope your visit to Hamburg is a success. I mean I do hope that it will bring an end to this dreadful murdering. As you well know, I like a quiet life, and now I'm free of worries concerning my safety and sorting out my financial problems as well, peace of mind may be just around the corner.'

'For your sake, Isaac, I hope so too. Now, let us put all that behind us and have a game of backgammon. By the way, are you going to stay the night?'

'I have already got a room thank you, Nicholas, at the Blue Bell in the Market Place. I didn't want to burden you and Mrs Field when your wedding is so fast approaching.'

'As you wish, Isaac. However, I hope you *will* join us this evening for supper. The four of us and Robert Wray can go to the Assembly Rooms in Dagger Lane. There is some unusual entertainment coming to Hull, and it's not to be missed.'

'Thank you for the invitation. What is it that you've got in store for us? I remember you took me to a Chamber Concert on my previous visit in January. Are you always out in the evenings?'

'Only when something is worth going out see. We must take every opportunity we can to enjoy and enlighten ourselves in our spare time, should we not? A satisfying diversion is good for the soul.'

'So, what is on tonight?'

'A gentleman called Mr Philip Breslau will be performing mysterious acts.'

'I'm not sure I can stomach any more mysterious acts, Nicholas.'

'No, no...this is purely light-hearted entertainment. Wait here, I shall get the bill-sheet from the shop window.'

He leapt up and dashed out of the room, and returned within minutes.

'See whether this doesn't intrigue you.' He handed the bill to Townend. He started to read.

'*New amazing deceptions with pocket-pieces, rings, sleeve buttons...*He is a conjuror...*watches, particularly a leg of mutton...*This man must be a fake, Nicholas, or a joker.'

'Of course he is, it's purely for entertainment. Does it not appeal to your imagination. Look,' he took the bill out of Townend's hands, 'it says he has his own premises in London - *BRESLAU'S EXHIBITION ROOMS* - he must be popular therefore worthy of attention. Will you join us then?'

'I shall. It may be as good as you say.'

'Excellent. Now I shall get the backgammon board.'

'Yes, Nicholas, but I won't play for money – I've learned a lesson!'

29

The next day, Saturday 27th March
It was several weeks since Sam had begun to dismantle the book during the Saturday mornings in the workshop. It had taken three of the mornings to separate all the sections of pages and arrange the parts neatly ready for the next step – 'to put it all back!' It took another two sessions to sew all the pages back together. This was probably the hardest part - keeping them perfectly aligned and sewn firmly together, keeping the cords in place on the spine and the coloured headband at the top. Then came the rounding and backing of the spine, another delicate operation. When Twygge had approved and congratulated him on his work he instructed Sam in the next stage of attaching the boards. By the end of March he was ready to put on the leather cover.

'I think we should try to match the original colour with the finest morocco, don't you, Sam?'

'Certainly. I haven't been allowed to work with that yet at Mr Bell's.'

'There has to be a first time, and it is now. So you select the leather and cut it to size. How are your paring skills?'

'Good – I *think*. Well-practised.'

'I'm sure I can trust you, we can't afford to ruin a piece of expensive morocco. Not only that - to *pare* does not require the *pair* of us.'

Sam groaned.

'I'm peckish, Mr Twygge, may I eat a pear before I pare and then the pair of us can get on with what we're going to do?'

'Any more puns on that word are now *per impossibile!*'

'*Per contra...*' but Twygge was leaving the room hastily before Sam could finish.

Disappointed that he couldn't get in what he thought would be the *coup de grace* he would save it for another time. He went over to the drawers where the leather was kept and extracted a piece of rich brown morocco. He took it over to the table and proceeded to take measurements. Once the leather was marked out and cut to size he drew faint lines to show where the paring should begin. This process was designed to thin the edges of the leather gradually down to paper-thinness where they were to be glued down on the inside of the boards to prevent hard edges sticking up through the endpapers. All this took him the rest of the morning.

The trouble he'd had over Rachel was now forgotten by everyone except himself. He could not forget, and every day he relived those two hours that he was alone with her on their journey to Anlaby ten days ago. Mr Sachs did come to the house to see Mr Twygge in the afternoon of the same day. He'd explained to Nicholas what Sam had done but he was not angry, in fact, he almost apologised for what had happened, shifting the blame onto Rachel. He then explained that Rachel was going to be married in the autumn and shouldn't have gone with Sam the way she did. Sam was not there when this meeting took place and when Nicholas told Mr Sachs that he'd call Sam in to see what he had to say about it, Mr Sachs told him not to bother, it was not really that important. Mr Sachs then left, again apologising as he went through the door. Twygge admired his gentle humility.

When he told Sam about the visit and questioned him he too didn't show any anger. Sam told Nicholas exactly what had happened, taking all the blame, and when he'd finished Nicholas told him not to do such a thing again. He said it would only lead to more upset. He didn't want to lose Mr Sachs' business - he was good customer and a nice person. He didn't want to upset the family and, anyway, it wouldn't be good for Sam to become involved any more, it would only cause hurt later when Rachel's future husband appeared on the scene, no matter how innocent it might have been at the time. The life of the Hebrews was so different to theirs he could never fit in and become one of them. Sam could understand all this and he took the blame for what he'd done. He apologised to Nicholas expressing his appreciation of the kind way he had been treated – he'd expected worse. He'd felt so much guilt after realising what he'd done that fateful day that it grew as the day went on, and his anguish grew as he'd imagined what dire punishments were likely to be forthcoming. But now the relief at being treated so kindly by both Mr Twygge and Mr Sachs made him elated and he spent the rest of the day jauntily going about his business with an air of lightness and humour. But, lying in bed that night, he recalled again his journey with Rachel and it made him both happy and sad. Simmering at the back of his mind, so far back that he wasn't aware of it yet, was the notion that Rachel was not going to be out of his life forever. This notion would finally manifest itself because his desire to see her and speak to her again was going to be more powerful than his loyalty to Mr Twygge and Mr Sachs. And when it happened he would find himself in a painful struggle as these two desires were fighting for supremacy. It took a long time before sleep came to the rescue and crept over him.

Later at supper Nicholas was telling Sam what he should be doing whilst he and Constable Wray were in Hamburg.

'You shall have to suspend your morning studies, Sam, and work with Mr Crosswell in the shop, and keep Mrs Field entertained in the evenings. I know what you can do, you can read to her, she likes that. How about trying *The Castle of Otranto*, we haven't read that have we? Or perhaps the new *Mysteries of Udolpho*? Or something a little more gentle and amusing, Mr Fielding perhaps?'

'I shall see what we have and try to pick the most appropriate.'

'Good. You may even try some poetry occasionally. You know she quite enjoys something light, some narrative poetry... she should enjoy *John Gilpin*. I shall leave it up to you.'

It seemed to Sam that Nicholas was being pernickety about Mrs Field's evening comforts. At the same time he recognised how much Nicholas was fond of her and concerned for her contentment, but he would make up his own mind as to the reading matter.

'I do envy your adventure, I only wish I could come with you.'

'I do too, Sam, but it's not practicable, in more ways that one, as I'm sure you appreciate. I know you have this urge to travel, and there's nothing wrong with that, and one day you shall. We can arrange a special journey for the three of us - as long as my business keeps thriving, that is.'

'Yes, sir, I shall relish that thought greatly. Now that you've sown the seed of that suggestion I shall be waiting patiently, or even perhaps impatiently, for it to germinate.'

'Nicely put, Sam, but it may be slow to germinate. This journey to Hamburg is going to cost a considerable sum.'

'I realise that, sir - the my patience shall sit on a monument like Viola's.'

'Oh, one more thing, Sam. I've left a new book for you on the desk in your room. It's title is *Caleb Williams*. It's quite newly published. I've been reading it at night before sleep. It's by William Godwin. I think you'll enjoy it. It has some very interesting and thought-provoking ideas about modern life - the way people conduct themselves and behave towards each other.'

'Thank you, sir.'

'You can use your Wednesday morning Literature sessions for the reading of it.'

He took a sip of his coffee.

'It's Palm Sunday tomorrow so what a pleasant way to begin an adventure into foreign lands. I hope it bodes well, although I doubt that anyone will be laying down their cloaks and palm branches before *us* as we enter the town.'

30

The next day, Sunday 28th March
The barque *Frederick Louis* looked majestic sitting proudly by the quay, like a queen among the other ships. She was berthed at the northwest corner of the New Dock. Twygge and Wray were walking along the quay with Sam. Twygge pointed out to Sam which ship it was.

'That's the largest ship in the dock, look at those masts, and such a massive tangle of rigging.'

'Not a tangle, Sam,' said Wray, 'each and every rope has a precise function. But I do believe that there are ships here that maybe larger than this one. Look across the dock – you see the one third from the left, it's full ship-rigged somewhat also splendid.'

'Of course, sir. You know, when we live in the midst of all this shipping day in and day out do we really take any notice of it?'

'I suppose we don't,' said Twygge, 'we take everyday things for granted. That is until they suddenly take on a special meaning. I must add though that the sheer size is enough to give one a certain degree of consolation, does it not? Bobbing about on the North Sea for nearly four days in a small tub would not.'

'This is a ship that one *could* sail around the world in. I wish I could.'

'Dreams, Sam,' said Wray, ever the pragmatist, '*dreams!*'.

'I know, but without dreams would people ever advance themselves, achieve anything great? Isn't it a dream that drives every explorer?'

They'd arrived at the gang-plank so Sam's question remained unanswered, but he really did know the answer himself anyway.

'Well, Sam, we shall have to bid you farewell. Take good care of Mrs Field for me and make sure the house doesn't burn down!'

'Goodbye, Sam,' added Wray, 'I hope we can return with some good news for everyone.'

'Goodbye, sirs, and *bon voyage* as they say.'

Twygge and Wray started to climb the gang-plank. At the top they turned and waved to Sam. He returned their waves. He saw them being met by a member of the crew who took them across the deck and they disappeared down below.

Instead of feeling sad Sam felt cheerful. He looked around at all the activity in and around the dock – the jungle of masts and rigging, and he could feel the excitement that journeying to distant parts could bring. He imagined himself boarding a vessel, sailing slowly and steadily out of the dock, down the river and into the estuary, and out towards the open sea.

Twygge and Wray's embarkation had sparked his imagination and he knew that one day he would be the one who was embarking, just as his own father had done many times when Sam was a small boy. His father had never sailed beyond the inland waterways of the Humber estuary but still he felt that sailing was in his blood. Maybe he could begin his adult working life as a mariner on the keels or sloops of the river trade? He could then, after enough experience, move on to sailing the oceans of the world.

He wound his way back along the quay, dodging the people, barrels, boxes, ropes, chests and other assorted clutter on the dockside. He reached the small bascule bridge that spanned the short channel between the dock and the River Hull. The bridge was up and a trading ketch was passing through into the lock pit on its way out, taking advantage of the rising tide. When the bridge was lowered Sam crossed over to the South Quay and made his way towards Low Gate, thence homewards and his studies. For a moment he considered going via Postern Gate and Dagger Lane but immediately he thought better of it.

31

The same day, Sunday 28th March

> *They that go down to the sea in ships,*
> *That do business in mighty waters,*
> *These see the works of the Lord,*
> *And his wonders in the deep.*

The landlubbers Twygge and Wray were not taking the voyage across the sea well. This first day was easy, a little choppy but that was to be expected. The sky was clear and the sun kept the air warmer than it otherwise would be for March. The five passengers were able to entertain themselves on the poop-deck.

Twygge, ever curious as usual, was enquiring of the Chief Mate what cargoes they were carrying to Hamburg.

'Oh, all manner of goods, sir. Well, I suppose more of anything are the manufactured goods – you know, things made of iron, cloth goods of all kinds, er..., pottery, even barrels of ale, the list is endless. I sometimes think we haven't enough ships to move everything. Back and forth, back and forth across this sea. Of course, a ship of this size goes much further afield than the Elbe. Now that the trade with the Americas is picking up we may be doing some Atlantic trips. I don't really know what will come next. I sometimes think a beautiful ship of this size is wasted doing these short hops.'

'Do you often sail further afield then?'

'Yes, we've been on the Baltic runs for several years but the owner, Mr Sykes, has put us in a pool of eight doing the Hamburg runs now.'

'What does a pool of eight mean, Chief?'

'Well, it allows an equal distribution of the values of the cargoes, so one ship doesn't come off worse than any other in terms of profits.'

'I see. What a splendid idea. Well, this is a magnificent ship, and how well she sails.'

'*Twygge was hardly a seasoned sea-going traveller*', thought Wray, who hadn't said a word throughout this conversation, so how would he know?

'Tell me,' continued Twygge, 'when you return to Hull, if indeed you do, what will you be carrying on the way back?'

'Well, sir, usually, recently anyway, we've been bringing a considerable amount of wine from the Rhine. Linen has been coming in great quantities, although this is slowing down now. Hemp is increasing, I suppose for the growing number of boats and ships being built these days. Then we often have chemical substances of all kinds, oh, and cotton wool as well.'

'I thought cotton was produced in America,' said Wray.

'It is but they do something with it somewhere – I don't know what and where I'm afraid.'

'It's all very interesting,' said Twygge, 'thank you very much for the information.'

'You are most welcome, gentlemen, it's not often people ask about these things. Please excuse me, there's work to be done. It appears that the wind is changing.'

He walked off towards the steps to the main deck.

'So, she sails well, Nick?'

'Of course, don't *you* think so?'

'I don't know, not having been on anything as big as this before.'

'I was only comparing it with the Barton ferry, Robert. You know what that was like the last time we were on it.'

'Yes, but this is completely different.'

'Do you really think so – choppy water is choppy water wherever you are, is it not?'

'Not necessarily. Look how this sea swells, albeit slightly today so far, but you don't see that kind of swelling on the Humber.'

'Well, Robert, I do believe you're correct on that point. But this ship is so magnificent, so solid, it inspires confidence. And if it weren't a good sailor it would hardly be used to sail the great oceans of the world, would it?'

'No, but I don't believe your very limited experience warrants any comments about the qualities of a sea-going vessel. That's all, Nick.'

'Maybe you're right. Shall we leave it at that? It's not exactly a great issue to disagree upon, is it? It sounds to me, Robert, that you might have got out of bed on the wrong side today.'

'Well, yes, I do feel a little tetchy today. To be honest with you, Nick, I didn't want to come with you on this jaunt. I don't want to be responsible for our safety. We may be having to deal with some very dangerous and violent men. I just don't believe it's our job to get involved. It's become too big, too big for the likes of you and me. Don't you see that? I think we should disembark at Hamburg, find another ship straight away that's sailing for Hull and get on it.'

Twygge could detect in Wray a hint of fear in his voice. He knew he was not a man who was usually fearful of anything, so why now?

'Robert, it would be such a waste of the money we've already paid for the return journey next Monday. Not to mention the duty we owe to the people of Hull.'

'Yes, but the people of Hull are not the victims, are they?'

'No, but do they *really* believe they think that they're not going to be victims? No matter what they've been told there would be many who would not believe that they'd been told the truth. It's human nature – to fear the worst!'

'Well, we may be wasting our money by going straight back but we may be saving something much more valuable – our own lives! Is that worth paying for?'

'Of course not, Robert. But I believe you are exaggerating the danger. When we get there and find those two addresses we have, and when we knock on the doors we'll have some carefully thought-out simple questions to ask. Do we not look like two harmless people, people of middle-age with a certain air of benign friendship? You don't even have to be with me – you could linger further down the street. I must admit I shall no doubt have a measure of trepidation myself, but my urge to search out the truth behind these murders is far greater.'

'But what makes you think we might find the truth, Nick? Just two addresses – they might come to nothing!'

Twygge was aware of Wray's streak of pessimism, it was apparent during the early stages of their friendship. But he also knew that he had the ability to talk Wray out of it. So instead of continuing the debate he changed the subject. He would begin the conversation again later, at a time when Wray's mind was more receptive.

They were standing against the rail at the back of the poop-deck, looking over the stern. The pitching and rolling were sufficiently active to cause them to hold on firmly. Nothing was said for several minutes. Then Twygge spoke.

'What an unusual sensation this is, Robert. You know, for the first time in my life I am in the middle of a wilderness of water and no land in view whatsoever. Don't you feel a powerful sense of isolation? Does the thought not disturb you?'

'Not really, Nick. We're in the lap of the gods at sea, aren't we? If anything happens to this ship we're done for – that's the disturbing part.'

'That's true, Robert, but the sea can be kind as well – and a life-saver. You remember Xenophon's horde of Greek soldiers who fought their way across Mesopotamia to get to the Euxine

Sea? That sea was their saviour, it allowed them to escape their enemies. Ah, Thalassa! Thalassa! Isn't it magnificent? Come, let's go down to the Main Deck, there may be some shelter from the wind down there.'

It was the following morning when it hit them. Twygge was worse than Wray. The first to run out of his cabin and discharge the contents of his stomach was Twygge. He put his head over the scuppers – he was too much doubled over in agony to stretch his head over the gunnels – and offered all the half-digested food to the creatures of the sea.

Wray soon followed. It must have been Twygge's rapid exit that triggered Wray's *mal de mer*. For the rest of the day Twygge was in and out of the cabin more times than anyone could count. By late afternoon his agony and despair were such that he briefly considered throwing himself, as well as the foul liquid that was continually ejecting itself from his stomach, into the sea to rid himself of his suffering.

Wray had recovered some measure of equilibrium by the afternoon and was engaging in a conversation with two of the passengers on the Main Deck. By early evening Twygge was feeling a little better. The vomiting had abated but his guts felt as though they'd been through Hannah Field's mangle. He remained in his cabin. He certainly could not face supper. It appeared that one of the other passengers had been too ill the come to breakfast – that made him feel a little better.

'That was the worst day I've ever had to suffer in my whole life. I never wish to have that experience again. How do you two gentlemen feel?'

'I feel back to normal, Nick, thank you – one might even say a little cheerful. Does that surprise you?'

Twygge struggled to smile.

'I am surprised and much pleased that you are.'

Mr Moxon, the other passenger with them smiled too.

'I know what it's like, gentlemen, and never to be forgotten. But that was a long time ago now. I've lost count of how many voyages like this I've made. If it's any consolation, the next time you sail you should not suffer as much as the first time again.'

'So, you're a frequent traveller, Mr Moxon?' enquired Wray.

'Oh, yes. As a merchant and a banker, you see, I like to see who I'm doing business with and visit my banking colleagues.'

'Does all this travelling not take away a significant portion of your profits?'

'Yes, but not in the long term. Doing business face to face brings strength to our dealings and brings in more business. I shall be looking at some of the best French wines when we reach Hamburg.'

'Do you get the best French wines through Hamburg? It must be very difficult because of the problems in France - indeed, *with* France.'

'It has been but there is a network of transport now. You see, gentlemen, in spite of a revolution a country cannot afford to cut off its trade, it would be suicide.'

'Of course,' said Twygge, 'The American Revolution did see a reduction in trade with us but merchants had the goods diverted to European ports and then they were re-shipped.'

'That's correct, Mr Twygge. Business has no boundaries, the wheels will always keep turning no matter what happens.'

32

The next day, Tuesday 30th March
Whilst Nicholas Twygge was recovering from seasickness and beginning to feel that a full recovery might be not many hours away there was an incident at the Cross Keys Hotel in the Market Place in Hull. Joseph Heron was slaving away at his usual menial tasks, one of which brought him into the foyer of the Hotel, he was alerted to take his attention away from his task and look up towards the reception counter. He'd overheard the word *murder*. He tried to work his way towards the conversation without attracting anyone's attention. Joseph was bright enough to have realised long ago that the likes of him in a place like this make him quite invisible to the guests. Sometimes it had its distinct advantages.

'Yes, sir, terrible it was. The worst thing that's ever happened in this town,' said the gentleman at the reception desk.

'Can you say exactly when it was?'

'Yes, sir, how can we forget? It shall be remembered for years to come. It was very late in the evening. It was a Monday, er..., March the fifteenth I believe, sir.'

'So, two weeks ago then?'

Joseph heard all this and he recognised something in the man's voice that told him he was not English. The accent was barely noticeable but it was there nonetheless to those with a discerning ear.

'Would you be able to tell me who is in charge of such matters? Who would be required to make inquiries and such like?'

'Well, I know the constables deal with the usual problems but not usually murders. The Sheriff is obliged to take charge of such things.'

'Could that be because there are no murders, usually, as you put it?'

'Of course, sir, but the law is enforced by the Sheriff and the Justices.'

'Yes, but I believe that there hasn't been anyone who's been brought to justice, has there? So there would be no need for the Sheriff and Justices to be involved.'

'That's true, sir, but the murderers were found.'

'Oh, I did not know that.' He was clearly surprised. 'So were they brought to justice in this town?'

'No, sir. It wouldn't have been possible because when they were found they had been murdered themselves. Strangled they were, sir.'

Joseph continued to appear to be working around in the vicinity of this conversation. He missed the occasional word or phrase but managed to keep up with the gist of it.

'That indeed I did not know either,' said the stranger. He appeared to have received a blow of some sort. He turned his head this way and that, looked down, then up, and didn't quite know what to say next.

'Yes, sir, that's what happened. The whole town was relieved. You couldn't believe how much we were all afraid after that third murder. Although one of them did occur over the river yonder. But it was near enough to home to cause consternation. Now it's all over.'

'Is it? Are you sure? How did the Sheriff know that those two men who were strangled were the murderers?'

'I don't know that, sir. You would have to ask the Sheriff himself, or the Chief Constable.' He began to feel a little wary about all this questioning. He started to have suspicions about who this man was and what he wanted to know and why. He knew he was not the person who should be answering so many questions.

'Where would I find the Sheriff?'

'He should be in his office in the Town Hall, sir.'

'What's his name?'

'Thomas Walton, sir.'

'How can I find the Town Hall?'

'Well, it's not very far from here. I think it would be easier to have someone take you there.'

He looked around the room and spotted Joseph with his brush.

'Heron, come here.'

Joseph stopped his work and approached the counter.

'This gentleman would like to speak to the Sheriff. You know where his office is don't you?'

'Yes, sir, in the Town Hall, sir.'

'Now, put your brush down behind the desk and take this gentleman there. And be quick about it. I want you back here in five minutes.'

'Yes, sir, straight away, sir.'

Joseph placed his brush behind the counter and the two left the Hotel. The man did not say a single word on the way to the end of the Market Place, not even when they entered the Town Hall, a somewhat decrepit building destined eventually to be converted into rubble.

Joseph addressed the man sitting at a desk inside the foyer.

'There's a gentleman here to see the Sheriff, sir. I've just brought him from the Cross Keys.'

'Good day, sir. You wish to see Mr Walton?'

'Yes, I do. I have been led to believe that he is the Sheriff of this town.'

'Indeed he is, sir. Just one moment please, I shall go and tell him.' He went up some stairs.

Joseph could not be seen to be lingering so he left and returned hastily to the hotel. He vowed that when he had the opportunity he would dash over to Mr Twygge's and tell him what had just happened. Unfortunately that opportunity did not arise until the early evening and even then he discovered that Mr Twygge and Mr Wray had gone over the sea to Hamburg so he had no-one to tell his story to. He did contemplate going over to the Chief Constable's but he could think of no reason why the Chief would be interested or even able to do anything about it. So he went home sad and disappointed.

'Sheriff, my name is Monsieur Chevalley. It is not my real name. If I revealed my real name my life would be in danger, as would the life of anyone who I was connected with. I *can* tell you that I was once employed several years ago in London as an *envoi* for the French Government. Needless to say, that post ceased to exist not long after the start of the Revolution.'

'Monsieur Chevalley, may I interrupt? Why are you telling me this? I have no wish to endanger myself by being here in your company, if what you say is true. I am merely a sheriff of this town, and then only for one year. We are an important port here but quite remote otherwise. We have no dealings with what goes on between governments far away. I am a very busy man, Monsieur, my rôle is merely to ensure that local justice is done when the need arises, with the stress on *local*.'

'I quite understand, Sheriff, but I am here for that very reason – *justice*. I too am here to try to ensure that justice will be done – for the benefit of this town.'

Thomas Walton was uneasy. He sensed that something bigger than whatever he could deal with was looming. What business has he to do with revolutions and what went on between nations?

'Sir, I do not think that I am are your man. From the little you have said so far this sounds to me to be a matter for more important bodies. Why Hull? You should go to London if your concerns are of an international nature.'

'Precisely, Sheriff. My concerns rest here, in the town of Hull. Someone else from my country is in London doing what I am doing here.'

At this point Walton was unable to summon up a response. Instead he directed his mind to being a good host.

'May I get you some refreshment? Clearly, you have travelled a long way and must need something. May I offer you some tea?'

'That is very kind of you, Sheriff. I would enjoy some tea.'

Walton was somewhat relieved that he could get out of his office for a moment. Was he getting himself embroiled in some international intrigue and villainy? He composed himself, realising he'd been over-reacting and then ordered tea. He returned to his office.

'Tea will be along shortly, Monsieur Chevalley. Now perhaps you can tell me in more detail what brings you here and how I may be of assistance.'

'Thank you, Sheriff, your co-operation will be appreciated by many people, as you will eventually discover. Some of them have turned up in parts of your country. They have been found murdered, at least we believe so. Reports of this have taken many weeks, even months in one or two cases, to reach France and then to me. The duty I have been given is to find out as much as I can about what happened to them. I am here because we have been informed that at least three of these murders have occurred in the vicinity of this town. Now, sir, I hope you will understand the situation I am in and be able to tell me everything you can, every little detail of what has occurred here that may be connected with my inquiries. I can understand your reserve. Your country is at war with France. You're bound to be cautious in dealing with a Frenchman but I can assure you that I am on your side. You will not in any way be jeopardising yourself, your town, or your country. In fact, probably the opposite, at least I hope so.'

Although the Sheriff was slowly becoming convinced by this man's demeanour that he was being completely honest, yet there was still a corner of his mind that would not fully submit – a corner where the drive of self-preservation was situated.

'Very well, sir, I shall help you. There is a lot of information involved so I need to retrieve my files. We also need a third party so I shall call for one of the Justices to be present shortly.'

He left the room and the tea to Monsieur Chevalley.

When the three of them were seated and ready to proceed it took a considerable amount of time for the Sheriff to cover all the ground of the previous events in detail, from the first murder in November up to the present time. Monsieur Chevalley was taking copious notes throughout.

When it was finished Chevalley expressed a serious and protracted interest in the piece of paper which was found in the White Hart Tavern bearing two sets of names and addresses.

'May I see that piece of paper, Sheriff?'

'I do not have it,' he lied. This was one piece of evidence that he thought was too dangerous to reveal to someone he didn't know anything about. He could not risk the lives of Constable Wray and Mr Twygge.

'And why would that be?'

'Because similar murders have been committed in London, so it was felt that it should be dealt with by higher authorities. This was a decision made by the Justices and myself.'

'I understand, Sheriff. So there is nothing more you can tell me?'

'No, sir, that is all we know.'

The Sheriff refrained from telling M. Chevalley about the mission currently being undertaken by Twygge and Wray.

'Thank you for your assistance. What you have told me is very valuable, although that piece of paper may have contained enough information to solve our problem. However,

I have a colleague in London at the moment, as I mentioned, so he will be able to discover what it contains and can then act upon it.'

He stood up.

'Thank you for the refreshments, gentlemen. I have to go to York next so I shall be bidding you both *adieu*.'

'Goodbye, Monsieur Chevalley, and good luck with your inquiries. Please keep us informed if you hear of anything that would concern this town, good or bad.'

'I shall indeed, Sheriff. Good day to you.'

He left the room and returned to the Cross Keys Hotel.

33

Two days later, Thursday 1ˢᵗ April
The *Frederick Louis* sailed gently into the gaping mouth of the River Elbe at about 4 o'clock in the morning. For most of the voyage the winds were against them but this changed as they approached the coast, allowing the passengers a more restful night at last.

For Robert Wray the journey had been tedious in the extreme. He'd not had much to occupy himself with and spent most of the time wandering around the ship and staring out to sea for long periods. He was accustomed to keeping himself busy and on this voyage he could find nothing to do – he was not in control of anything that was going on around him. There were times when it was more tolerable, such as meal times in the cuddy and in the evenings when the room served as a sort of lounge for the passengers and when an officer or two would join them. On one occasion Captain Storm honoured them with his company.

For Nicholas Twygge, however, after he'd recovered from his hellish bout of sea-sickness, the voyage brought a lot of interesting things to busy his mind with. He would pester officers and crew, bombarding them with questions about the ship and life at sea. He'd learned about tops'ls, mains'ls, mizzens, halliards, cro'jacks, futtock shrouds, tyes and Turk's heads and much more until his own head became a knot of jumbled information. He was in his element. At quiet moments he'd spend some time in his cabin reading Dryden, a poet of depth, he thought, a Puritan *and* a Parliamentarian, but not a fanatic. Pope had agreed:

Hear how Timotheus' vary'd Lays surprise,
And bid alternate passions fall and rise –
The power of music all our hearts allow,

And what Timotheus was, is Dryden now.

This was the one and only book he'd brought with him – it was one of John Bell's *Little Trifling Editions* of the poets of Great Britain, miniature volumes handy to keep in one's pocket.

His fellow passengers and officers were good company, except Mr Moxon, the merchant, who he found excruciatingly boring with his endless dull tales about himself. The other passenger, Herr Longen, was good company and helped Twygge with some useful colloquial German. Longen was an architect who'd heard about the splendid new buildings which were being erected in their hundreds in the new part of Hull beyond the New Dock. He'd been to inspect them himself as Hamburg was also undergoing considerable modernisation. It was equal to if not greater than Hull in its wealth and expansion, but, as Twygge was to discover, the styles of buildings both old and new were very different to those of Hull.

The estuary of the River Elbe was magnificent – an enormous ram's horn. Its banks so far apart at its mouth that it was not possible to see them both at the same time when sailing in. It was a giant compared with the Humber.

The *Frederick Louis* entered at the south side of the estuary and by the time the passengers had got out of their beds the dawn light was bright enough to see the land, but it wouldn't be for another hour or two before the mouth narrowed sufficiently to see both banks, to convince the travellers that it was a river and not the open sea. The ship had to anchor off Brunsbüttel until the tide turned. It was in full sail again by the time the sun was in the sky and the day lightened.

This was the day of disembarkation. When that thought struck him Twygge could sense a fluttering in his stomach and rise in the heart beat. At breakfast the four passengers chatted away with a touch more vigour than the previous two mornings – only the hardened sailors took it in their stride, although the first sight of land usually evoked a slight thrill depending on how long they'd been at sea.

'...And Mr Wray and Mr Twygge, where will you be staying whilst you're in this town?' enquired Moxon.

'We don't yet know. When we arrive we shall find the nearest inn we can.'

'May I be so bold as to recommend a fine hotel?'

'Well,' replied Wray, 'we don't want anywhere expensive. We'll only be here for a short time, and this voyage has cost us a large sum already.'

'Of course,' said Moxon, 'I understand. I am intrigued though by the mystery you've made of the reason for your visit to Hamburg. Are you not going to give us just the tiniest inkling of what you're about?'

'I'm afraid not,' said Twygge firmly, 'You may hear of it one way or another eventually. Now, Herr Longen, what are your plans on arrival?'

'Oh, gentlemen, just the usual routine. I shall go to my office and write an account of what I've seen in Hull. Of course, like Hull, our town is growing very quickly – increased trade, more wealth, people coming into the town to find work. We have a lot of building to do to keep up with the changes. Too many people living within a small area is not good, as I'm sure you know from what's been happening in Hull over recent years. There is no mystery about that,' he added with a wry smile.

'No indeed,' said Twygge, no mystery at all, sir.'

Twygge was anxious to finish breakfast and go on deck to observe the scene. For the first time in his life he would be seeing a new country, new ways of living, fresh landscapes, all of these things were capturing his interest even before he'd stepped ashore.

'Would you please excuse me now, gentlemen, I need to take the air. We shall meet again on the deck no doubt.'

'Certainly, Mr Twygge,' said Herr Longen, 'I shall be coming outside myself shortly. Soon I shall be spending most of my time indoors so I must make the most of this opportunity to taste some freedom from the shackles of toil whilst I can.'

Twygge was very impressed by Herr Longen. He'd shown himself in these few days to be a man of learning, and his mastery of the English language put Twygge to shame. All he'd been able to arm himself with for the time when he would came face to face with the impending alien culture were a meagre few words and phrases of German. He didn't think he could even summon up enough to make a complete sentence.

The cruise down the Elbe seemed interminable. The day was beginning to darken by the time they approached the mouth of the Alster River which flowed into the Elbe on the north side. Many ships and boats were coming and going. Unlike Hull Hamburg was built on and around the mouth of the Alster with a series of linked canals and enclosed areas of water, such as the harbour to the southwest end to the large Binnenalster or inland side of the river at the northeast, the whole of it being defensively walled, almost blocking access to the Alster from the Elbe.

Twygge and Wray and the other passengers were standing on the port side of the poop-deck, keeping clear of the bustle of activity as the ship was being prepared to enter the harbour. As they approached the harbour entrance they saw what appeared to be a long row of pillars sunk into the riverbed forming a wall closing off most of the harbour.

'What a strange thing that is,' observed Twygge, 'look at those, are they tree-trunks?'

'They are indeed,' replied the much-travelled Mr Moxon, 'it's a wall of trees. In German it's called the *Baumwall*, cleverly designed as part of the town's defences. It's really an alternative to having to build the rest of the stone walls in the water – a very difficult thing to do as you can imagine.'

'How interesting. I believe the city of Venice was built on tree-trunks, was it not?'

'I believe it is, Mr Twygge, but I've not travelled their myself.'

'It is quite amazing – the ingenuity of Man! But it's a shame such defences are needed – man can create marvels but can kill his fellow man in pointless wars.'

'Oh, are you a pacifist then, Mr Twygge?' asked the ship's bore, 'Do you not think we should fight our enemies who do us harm?'

'I am not a pacifist, sir. I am a realist. I was merely observing that it is a great pity that we have to kill each other whilst, at the same time, be so creative and imaginative. Is it not incongruous?'

'That is life, Mr Twygge, you have to accept it.'

Twygge was annoyed at the man's condescending and dismissive tone and refrained from honouring that remark with a retort.

'There are many splendid churches, Nick. Look at all those towers and spires. Certainly many more than we have in Hull by all appearances.'

'Indeed, Robert. I do believe we are entering a town considerably larger than our own.'

'Yes,' added Mr Moxon, 'at least twice the size I would say. This a free Hanseatic city, Mr Twygge, it rules itself so it is able to use its wealth in ways that it thinks fit without outside interference. Although, perhaps, the Holy Roman Emperor may have a say in it if he wishes.'

'It appears we are approaching our berth, gentlemen,' observed Mr Moxon.

The ship slowly moved towards the north side of the harbour.

'This is the Niederhafen, Mr Twygge. When you disembark you should go along the harbour side towards the city. You should find somewhere to stay for the night before you go very far.'

'Thank you, Mr Moxon, you have been most helpful.'

'Not at all, Mr Twygge. The next time I'm in Hull with time to spare I may visit your shop. I have a brother, Richard, who lives there, on High Street. Perhaps you know him?'

'Indeed I do. You would be most welcome, sir. And if you do and find that I am not in the shop then ask my assistant Mr Crosswell or my ward Samuel of my whereabouts – I may well be in my workshop in the back.'

Although it was not yet completely dark there were plenty of harbour lights. Twygge and Wray would have no difficulty finding their way towards the centre of the city.

'I'm ready for a good meal, a good bed that doesn't move of its own volition, in a room that stands still and a good solid night's sleep.'

'Me too, Robert. Even a drop of some spirit or other as well perhaps?'

'Without a doubt.'

It took quite a long time before the barque was securely moored and the gang-plank placed in position. As the four men headed for the exit there was Captain Storm and another officer standing by.

They bade their farewells and descended onto *terra firma*. As they left the ship behind, Twygge and Wray both had feelings of apprehension, both began to wonder, and in Wray's case not for the first time, why they were there, in a foreign land, on a mission fraught with dangers. But they *were* there and were now committed, so they had to get on with it.

34

The same day, Thursday 1ˢᵗ April
It was about two weeks since Sam had last seen Rachel when he'd dropped her off in Myton Gate after their ride to Anlaby. He'd thought about her every day and even ventured out occasionally at dinner time into the Market Place to see if she was anywhere to be seen doing her shopping. But he never found her. This morning he was pouring over maps of Europe at his desk in his room. It was Thursday, Geography day.

'There are two possible ways to get to Hull,' he thought as he moved his finger along the page of the atlas, 'this way would be a very long journey, and this one not so long.' His finger first followed a line from the southern Baltic coast, up between Sweden and Denmark and around into the North Sea, thence across to the River Humber. Then it followed a line, almost straight, west from Prussia, through Hamburg and then into the North Sea.

'How curious,' he pondered, 'Mr Twygge and Mr Wray may very well be in that town at this very moment, or at least very soon will be.'

This exercise had two purposes, apart from the geography lesson – first to see how the Sachs family might have travelled to Hull all those years ago, and the other was to see the route that Moritz Lewin might be taking. The latter thought brought with it a twinge of sadness which he felt in his stomach and in his chest. To try to take his mind away from these thoughts he focussed on the other cartographic features in front of him – the major towns, the rivers, the mountains, the countries and how they were shaped. It was very difficult for anyone to grasp the full extent of the boundaries, particularly of Germany. There were countless States scattered over a vast area, some with names he didn't know how to pronounce: *Schleswig,*

Württemberg, and the Prussian ones were harder still – *Szczecin* – he didn't even know where to start with that one!

At the end of his morning session he hadn't mastered all the details but he had got a good overall image of the general form of Northern Europe and its major cities and rivers fixed in his mind. He felt satisfied with what he'd achieved, but what it also did was to make him think more about Rachel and her impending marriage, diluting the pleasure he'd got from his studies with a dose of dolour.

What Sam didn't know and what he wasn't to learn about for several weeks was an event that occurred at the same time that he was studying his atlas and at the very premises he had just been thinking about.

At the house of the Silversmith in Dagger Lane a letter had arrived. It was addressed to Herr Sachs and bore the postmark on the back of *Chodziesen* printed in a circle with the date, **17 MÄ**, at the centre. Near to the postmark the letter was sealed with red wax bearing the letter ***L***.

Mr Sachs recognised the seal immediately and proceeded to cut around it and unfold the letter.

'Fun vanent izer?' enquired Mrs Sachs, looking over his shoulder.

'Er iz fun her Lewin, main libling.'

The conversation continued along these lines:

'What does he say?'

'I don't know yet, my dear, I haven't read it yet.' He'd just finished opening out the double-page missive.

'Now it's open. What does he say?'

'Give me time, give me time, my dear.'

'It is bad news. I know it is bad news.'

'Why would it bad news?'

'I know it, a letter is always bad news.'

'Don't be silly, my love, of course they aren't.'

There was a brief period of silence whilst the letter was read. Then Mr Sachs started to read it aloud

'*We are arranging to reach you by the end of September...*'

'The end of September! Why the end of September. I though they were coming next year?'

'It seems to me, my dear, that they have changed their plans.'

He continued to recount what he was reading.

'Moritz wants to have the marriage sooner and is anxious to establish himself in his business here before they get married. He will be travelling alone..., The Lewins will come later when the date of the marriage has been arranged.'

He finished reading, turned and smiled at his wife.

'There, you see, this is not bad news. It's good news for Rokhele, for us all. She going to be married sooner than she thought.'

'Yes, but have we time to get everything ready so soon?'

'Of course we have. They're not going to be married as soon as Moritz arrives, are they? He needs to settle in. He and Rokhele need to get to know each other. He'll be staying with us, of course.'

'Yes, yes, of course...'

Mrs Sachs was beginning to mellow. The initial surprise and panic were ebbing away.

'We must tell her immediately, when she returns. She'll be very happy. I've noticed she's been less cheerful lately, haven't you? She must have been longing for Moritz to get here so they could marry.'

'Yes indeed, my dear. I've noticed her moments of quietness as well. Anyway, now I must get back to my work.'

He put the letter down on the table and left the parlour. Rivke picked it up and peered at it. She couldn't read but she felt she had to have it in her hands and see it with her eyes. At that point her mood changed, she realised the full significance of the message and a wave of elation swept over her.

'Ah, thank you, God, my first daughter is getting married at last! Oh, thank you.'

After his dinner and before he was due to work in the shop Sam left the house and took a rather brisk walk down Myton Gate, down Dagger Lane, up to the end and back again, a route he had taken many times recently. Not once had he found Rachel and nor did he this day. He wished he'd had time to walk the Market Place but he couldn't let down Mr Crosswell, so he returned to the house yet once again with bitter disappointment.

35

The next morning, Friday 2nd April

Twygge was extremely surprised when he went down to breakfast to find Robert Wray in an exuberant mood.

They had managed to find an inn with rooms soon after they'd disembarked and wandered along the Niederhafen up towards the end of the harbour. It was a raucous place when they arrived but it didn't take long for them to find sleep – the need for a good night's sleep in a bed that didn't pitch and roll overcame the noise.

'A very good morning to you, Nick. I presume you slept well?'

'Good morning, Robert. Indeed I did. But pray, what has happened to make you so jovial this morning?'

'Well, Nick, a good night's sleep works wonders, to the body and the soul!'

'Yes, yes, but I believe there's more to it than that. Come on, own up. What has changed? You were quite morose for the whole of the sea voyage.'

'Oh, that's over and done with now. I feel a certain excitement this morning. We are on a mission are we not? That in itself is cause enough, don't you think?'

'Naturally, I continued to feel that way all the time, except of course when *mal de mer* had struck me down. But you've been thinking all along that the whole thing was a waste of time and money.'

'This morning when I awoke I realised I was feeling differently – at least pleased to be on dry land at last! But also because we are here now, we have a job to do, we are responsible for the lives of other people back home, and it's my duty. Do you understand now?'

'Of course I do, Robert, and very pleased indeed that you feel this way. It will make it much easier for the both of us now. Remember, though, we only have four days. Now, what do we have for breakfast? I'm famished.'

Twygge was aware of how easily bachelors of middle-age can change moods more readily than those who are happily married. This morning Wray was a different man.

During their meal they decided to find a more salubrious inn to stay at. After settling their bill they set off toward what appeared to be the centre of the town. There were many church spires visible from the open area of the Niederhafen so it was decided to go in the direction of the middle one. It bore the highest tower from where they were looking. It was rather early in the day to look for rooms but they thought it would be worth trying to find somewhere on the way so they could leave their bags without being burdened with them all day. They tried to keep the tall spire in view but it was not always easy once they'd arrived at the dense and narrow streets.

It took a long time for them to negotiate their way through the streets, turning down this one then that one, not sure whether they were going in the right direction or not until they could see the tower once again, continually fighting crowds of people and traffic. The sun was popping out from behind clouds now and then so Twygge was trying to use it as a guide to navigation, and also trying to remember which way they'd come in case they had to retrace their steps. Because they didn't actually know where they were going they couldn't very well stop people to ask for directions.

'You know, Robert, I don't quite understand why Herr Longen would want to see the buildings of Hull.'

'What do you mean?'

'Do you not see how different they are? Look at this old building.' He stopped in front of a timber-framed shop. 'Similar to some of ours is it not, particularly those on High

Street. But look more carefully – you see the wooden crosspieces between the verticals and horizontals, they're different to ours? And the shape of the whole building is different.'

'I don't see it, it looks the same to me.'

'Well, have a good look, and when we get back to Hull have a good look at one of ours and you'll see.'

They continued on their way.

It was almost mid-morning when Twygge suddenly stopped.

'This looks like a coffee-house to me, Robert. Shall we go in?'

'Why not? I'm ready for one, *and* some cake, just as though we were back at Usherwood's.'

'And we can begin to use all those Schillings from Messrs Smith and Thompson's.'

They entered the coffee-house. It was almost full but there was an empty table just on the right by the open side of the door. Twygge closed the door.

'Do you want to sit here or try somewhere else? You know why this table's empty?'

'That's obvious, but I don't mind.'

'Beggars can't be choosers, so let's be seated. We shall keep our coats on.'

They arranged themselves and a waitress promptly appeared.

'Gut'n Morgen, meinen Herren.'

A verbal struggle ensued between Twygge and the waitress but after many *ers* and some vigorous movements of hands and the slight raising of voices the orders were taken. Twygge was not absolutely certain what he'd ordered apart from the coffee but it didn't sound like cake.

'Well, Nick, how did you manage that? What are we having?'

'Er, well, coffee, and, er, to be truthful, Robert, I'm not sure. Are you hungry?'

'Not very, we had a hearty breakfast, especially all that meat and cheese.'

'Good, neither am I. But whatever arrives on a plate I shall be willing to take a bite. Now, I think we should work on our strategy. If we keep our voices down and don't name names we should be safe. We have limited time so we should begin what we set out to do as soon as we find somewhere to stay.'

'I agree.'

'I think we should first determine where we are. I shall endeavour to ask the waitress the name of this street we're on now and go from there.'

'Go where, Nick?'

'Very humorous, Robert. Tell me what you think.'

'I don't think it's difficult. We have two names and addresses, nothing more, so the obvious thing is to find where the first one on the slip of paper is, knock on the door and ask questions.'

'I don't believe it is as simple as that, Robert. We must be very careful what we ask and how we ask it. That is what I meant by strategy. If we're not very careful the wrong question could lead us into serious trouble. We need to feign ignorance, in fact, I believe we should invent a lie as to why we are in Hamburg in the first place and that the names and addresses – sorry, I mean each name and address –- must not be revealed to the other party on the list. We could say that we were given it by a merchant or some such person we know because he'd found it somewhere and thought we should enquire about it while we are here. How does that sound?'

At this point the waitress arrived with a smile and a tray.

'Meinen Herren...' she put down the cups and plates before them, 'Danke schön,' gave them another smile and took the tray away. They smiled back.

'Well, well, well, this looks interesting, whatever it is. It's warm and it's certainly not cake of any kind. It looks rather like a cake of minced meat on a slice of bread.'

'The bread's very dark. I can smell onion, Nick. It's a very highly pressed piece of minced meat, if that's what it is.' He cut himself a chunk. 'Mmm, this is delicious. Try it.'

Nicholas took a piece.

'Well, what do you think of it?'

'I agree, Robert, absolutely delicious.'

After the first taste of ecstasy began to dissolve Twygge continued.

'Questions and lies! What do you think, Robert?'

'I'm not sure. Couldn't we say the name and address was given to us by Sam Usherwood. Say he found it on the floor of his coffee-house and as we were there and knew that we were going to go to Hamburg he gave it to us.'

'Yes..., a good suggestion, but don't you think it sounds like too much of a coincidence – Hamburg *and* Hamburg, as it were? If somebody told you that would you believe it? That's the test.'

'Hmm, perhaps not. Do you have any thoughts then?'

Wray polished off his last piece of savoury and took a sip of his coffee.

'Talking of Sam Usherwood, Nick, we could tell him his coffee's not good enough. This coffee is heavenly. Shall we have another one, *and* another slice of this..., er, whatever it is?'

'Not me, Robert, but please do have some yourself. Now, what do you think of this idea? Tell the truth initially – the piece of paper with one name and address on it was found by the landlord of the White Hart. He handed it over to the Chief Constable whose house is nearby and the Chief put out a request for anyone sailing for Hamburg to look into it, without saying why, of course, and not mentioning anything about murder. We are here because we are wine-buyers, just like Mr

Moxon on the ship. One more thing, I think we should obtain some evidence. To be fully convincing we should be able to say who we are dealing with.'

'What do you mean?'

'We need to find the name and street of a wine merchant, one who exports, a genuine one in case anyone asks.'

'We could ask the waitress.'

'Better still – the owner, Robert. We shall ask the waitress to speak to the owner when we pay the bill.'

'So, that's it, we have it. I think you should do more of the talking than me – you'd make a better liar than I would!'

'Ouch, that hurt! But these lies are not meant to deceive or harm anybody, in fact the opposite, so my conscience is clear. It's all about acting the part, and the ends justify the means, do they not?'

'Of course, Nick, I was only jesting.'

'I know you were, and please, Robert, jest as much as you like – it lightens the mood and lifts one's heart, at appropriate times of course. You recall John Gay's epitaph? –
Life is a jest, and all things show it.
I thought so once, but now I know it.'

'That is somewhat extreme, Nick. There must be times when we need to be serious otherwise everyday life would fall to pieces.'

'Of course it would. It's just a philosophy, another way of looking at life, a way of making life more bearable at times, that's all, Robert.'

'I see. I also see the waitress. Are you sure you don't want any more, Nick?'

'You've talked me into it. Just coffee though. You can do the ordering this time.'

Wray caught her eye and she came over. He managed to make her understand, more by gestures than words.

When they had finished and just about to pay the bill Twygge attempted to find out from the waitress which street they were on.

'Diese ist die Deichstrasse.'

'Deichstrasse! I don't believe it, Robert, the gods are with us. Do you realise where we are?'

'Yes, it's one of the two!' Wray wasn't a particularly religious man but this shook him – coincidences like this are not believable, he was stunned.

'Well, I believe we did take the widest and what appears to be the wealthiest thoroughfare and we were lucky.'

Twygge tried to make the waitress understand that he wanted to see the owner of the coffee-house. He didn't succeed until, in frustration, he said *proprietor*.

'Ah, ja, ja, der Inhaber. Ein Moment.' She went away and shortly returned with a gentleman.

'English, ja? I speak some English.'

With great relief Twygge made his request and obtained the name and the address of a wine-merchant Herr von Fürstenstein of Wölberstieg, near the Trostbrücke. Twygge committed it to memory. It was very close to the Church of St Nikolai.

Once outside the coffee-house they got their bearings and continued to walk in the direction of the church.

'We should have look at all the premises along here as we pass, businesses and houses. We can do the other side of the street later when we've found rooms. Look for the name *Chevalley*.'

'Yes, I know, Nick, I too committed them to memory.'

At the end of Deichstrasse the streets weren't quite so busy but being narrower it still meant slow progress. The church loomed into view and they soon reached it. It was massive, far larger than Hull's Holy Trinity. The spire was the tallest thing they'd ever seen. Outside the main entrance was a stone set into the wall, *Hauptkirche Sankt Nikolai.*

'Who was St Nicholas, do you know?'

'Apart from an ancestor of mine I believe he was the Saint of Christmas.'

'Was he really?'

'I don't know, Robert, I wasn't being serious. There may well be more than one St Nicholas. But it is an enormous edifice, much larger than York Minster even, I should think. Anyway did you spot any inns or suchlike, I didn't?'

'No. I think we should try some of the streets around here and use this church as a point of navigation.'

'I agree. Wherever we find ourselves it shouldn't be too difficult to get back to this place. We shall take each street that leads from here in turn.'

They set off in a north-easterly direction then took the first street on then right. It wasn't long before they came to what appeared to be an inn. Outside was the sign *Gasthaus St Nikolai.*

'Well, I have very little German but that tells me this must be a guest-house. Shall we try it?'

'Have you brought your book of German words?'

'I couldn't, Robert, it was too big and heavy to carry around. But I did commit to memory some of the commoner words we would need. I shall now endeavour to put some more of them to good use. Come. Wish me luck.'

They entered the foyer. It wasn't very busy. There was a desk on the left and a woman standing behind it, writing. Twygge approached the desk.

'Guten Tag. Zimmer... for us?' He pointed to Robert and himself.

'Gut'nTag, meinen Herren. You want a room? It is very early, they will be doing the, er...room cleaning.'

'Ja, two Zimmer bitte, for four nights.' He held up four fingers.

'Vier Nächte, ja? Gut, I check for you now.' She had an open ledger on the desk. 'Ja, we have rooms. You have nummers acht und elf, ja? Aber Sie müssen, er, you put the...' she pointed to their bags. 'hier bitte.' She went to a door near the back of the desk. It was a large cupboard. 'Ja, verstehen?'

Twygge quite understood what she meant.

'She said we can leave our bags in this cupboard until, I presume, the rooms have been made ready.'

They put their bags inside.

'At what time,' he took out his pocket-watch and pointed to it, 'can we...?'

'Ah, ja, um drei Uhr, ja?' She showed three fingers.

'Ja, danke schön.'

'Bitte schön.' And they left.

Once outside they retraced their steps back to Deichstrasse. It was a long street, slightly curved. There were some magnificent modern houses, clearly belonging to persons of wealth. However the name *Chevalley* did not reveal itself on any of the plates on any of the frontages. Twygge and Wray were disappointed.

It took four attempts before they found someone who knew where Chevalley lived. It was at a bookshop where they found a man who could speak good English. He and Twygge talked at great length about German wine, he was not going to risk talking about bookselling. Wray was left to drift around the shop peering at book spines whose titles were meaningless. Twygge enquired of the owner whether he had anything on his shelves that might help with his German. He bought a small primer in German for learning English. In spite of it Twygge saw that he would be able to learn by simply reversing the process of translation. Eventually he got around to the main task of asking about M. Chevalley.

'Yes, yes, I know Monsieur Chevalley. I buy books for him, mostly in French.'

'Does he live nearby?'

'Yes, yes, his house is six doors down on the left side. There is a small coat-of-arms on the door, it has a *fleur-de-Lys* on it.'

'Has he lived there long?'

'I think so, yes. Perhaps three or four years. Why do you ask?'

'Well, his name came up when I was talking to a friend of mine in England about our coming to Hamburg to buy wine. I thought it would be pleasant to call on him as we have a mutual acquaintance. Well, we shall have to be on our way. I shall study this book and maybe then I can return and I shall be able to have a conversation with you in German?'

'That would be good, but you must get a book in English for learning the German, yes?'

'Of course, but when we return to Hamburg in the future, maybe then?'

'But I am selfish, I want to speak to you in order to practise my English, yes?' He smiled and Twygge smiled.

'Of course you do. I would want to do the same in your position. Thank you again for your kind assistance.'

They shook hands and Twygge and Wray left the shop.

By the time they had settled into the hotel, tidied themselves up and gone out to have a meal it was beginning to get dark. They would call on M. Chevalley after breakfast in the morning.

Twygge spent the evening studying his German primer in his room. He assumed M. Chevalley would wish to converse in French and Twygge had learned enough over the years to be able to manage at a simple level. However, what he really hoped for was that Chevalley could speak English – it would be more likely that misunderstandings would be less likely to occur. Twygge knew how important it was that they should convey precisely the information that he and Wray had agreed upon. Any confusions in that regard could make their mission abort instantly, even put their lives at risk.

36

The same day, Friday 2nd April
Sam reddened as soon as he saw Mr Sachs enter the shop. His instinct told him to make a bolt to the workroom but Mr Sachs had spotted him straight away, so he was prevented from making his escape. He stood where he was, looked down and continued what he was doing pretending he hadn't seen him.

Mr Sachs walked over to the counter and addressed Mr Crosswell.

'Good day, sir.'

'A very good day to you, Mr Sachs. Do we find you well?'

'Very well, Mr Crosswell, thank you.'

'What can we do for you today, sir?'

Sam could see that Mr Sachs' attention was not on him so he thought he could make his way slowly to the door of the workroom. However, as soon as he turned away he heard Mr Sachs address him.

'Good day, Mr Samuel.'

Sam turned around.

'Good day, Mr Sachs, how pleasant to see you again.' The inner guilt he felt for trying to pretend he hadn't seen Mr Sachs was hurting. 'It must be many weeks since we last met.'

'I think so, Mr Samuel. May I speak with you after I've finished my business with Mr Crosswell?'

'Certainly, sir, I shall remain here.' He continued to sort out the pile of books he'd been handling. But he was nervous and he fumbled with them, not really knowing what he was doing. He listened to what was being said.

'I have money now, Mr Crosswell, so we can buy the next volume of our *Talmud*. It is number three we want next please.'

'I shall write out the order immediately, sir.' He took the order book from below the counter. 'This time it should not take more than ten days to two weeks, Mr Sachs. Do you mind waiting?'

'No, no, sir. We will wait as long as necessary.'

'There, it is on order. When it arrives we shall have it delivered to your house immediately. Thank you for your business, Mr Sachs, it has been a pleasure to serve you.'

'The pleasure is for me, Mr Crosswell. Thank you. Now may I have a talk with Mr Samuel?'

'Of course you may. Sam, would you mind having a word with Mr Sachs?

'No, sir, of course not.'

Sam was aware of the other customers and of Mr Crosswell and he didn't relish the idea of his conversation with Mr Sachs being overheard. So he made his way towards the workroom door.

'Would you come this way please, sir? We can talk in here.'

Sam was also aware that people around would be wondering why he and Mr Sachs had to go into another room to talk. This was perfect fodder for gossip, he thought. Wherever Mr Sachs went he stood out from the crowds as did all of his co-religionists, mainly just by their dress. This made Sam self-conscious. It was with some trepidation that he opened the door and let Mr Sachs go before him into the workroom. He followed and closed the door behind him.

'This is very interesting, Mr Samuel. What do you do in here?'

'Please sir, there is no need to call me Mister, everybody calls me just Sam. Er, we do some book-binding, we repair worn or damaged books, that sort of thing. We also have a small printing press over here.' He walked over to the far corner where the press was as though he were trying to get as far away as possible from Mr Sachs.   'It's not used very much, only for posters for our shop and the like.'

'You do work in here?'

'Yes, sir, I am learning how to bind books at Mr Bell's once a week and I work in here on Saturday mornings. Please take that chair, Mr Sachs.'

'Thank you, I shall. You are very clever, Mr Samuel, to make books.'

'Not as clever as making things out of silver, sir.' Sam was pleased with that retort. It made him feel a little more relaxed and confident. Perhaps it would appease Mr Sachs a little, although he showed no signs of being angry.

'I have wanted to talk to you about my Rokhele, Mr Sam.'

Sam immediately reddened and tensed again.

'Oh, sir, why? I haven't seen her for... er...oh, quite a long time. How is she? Is she well?'

'Not much. She has been changed, Mr Sam, she is not full of joy any more. My wife is sad, I am sad. She has become so...so...*unterschiedlich*. Do you speak German?'

'No, sir. Please, sir, would you call me just Sam? Mr Sam makes me seem too important.'

'Yes, Sam. You know, I think I know why she is sad. Do you know why?'

'Me, sir? I have no notion of it whatsoever. Why should I know, sir?'

'My Rokhele is going to be wife, Sam. She will marry in a few months.'

'I didn't know, sir, I thought it was next year.'

'It is changed. Mr Lewin is coming soon.'

Sam's heart sank so low it felt as though it had descended into the floor beneath his feet. It was several seconds before he could say anything.

'I see you very surprised, Sam, yes?'

'Er... a little, sir...' He stopped speaking, afraid he would say too much or the wrong thing.

'I think she is sad because she thinks of you, all the time, Sam. She should be happy – she is to be wife – but she is not happy.'

Sam remained silent.

'I am not giving you blame, Sam, it is not really your fault. You have done nothing wrong.'

'No, sir, but perhaps I did when I took her to Anlaby that morning. I should not have taken her.'

'I don't think that is important, Sam. I and my wife want to beg of you to do something to help our Rokhele. We want you to come to my house when you can and talk to Rokhele. Would you come? We want you to tell her that you will never be able to see her again. Tell her that you cannot be friends, she is betrothed to someone else. Tell her that her life and your life are a long way apart. You know, Sam, that has much truth – we are very much apart, aren't we? We talk a different tongue at home, we dress different, we have a different God, we go to our church on Saturday, you go on Sunday, we eat different food, we have many, er...*yomtoivim*, er... how do you say..., special days. We can say *good morning* and *good evening* to you but we cannot be more near, Sam, our lives are not the same. Do you understand? Please come and talk to Rokhele. It is to make her better again. She must be happy again. And you are the only one who can do it. I know no other way.'

Sam was very moved by Mr Sachs' plea. He felt sad for him and for his family, and for himself. He felt guilty about imposing himself upon Rachel.

'I shall help you, sir, and all your family. I shall come when you say and talk to her as you requested. I too want to see her happy.'

'Thank you, Sam, you are a good boy, I knew that when I first saw you. When can you come to my house?'

'I could come tomorrow evening when my work is finished.'

'No, no, Sam, tomorrow is *Shabbes*,.. your word is *Sabbath*, I think?'

'Of course, Mr Sachs, how stupid of me to forget. I could perhaps come on Sunday afternoon?'

'Yes, that time would be good.' He arose from his chair. 'Thank you for listening to me and for your, er..., *mitgefühl*, er... *simpatye*, how do you say?'

'I think the word is sympathy, Herr Sachs.'

'Yes, yes, sympathy. You have made me very happy. I shall go now.'

Sam crossed the room and opened the door for Mr Sachs. He walked out.

'Good day, Sam.'

'Good day, Mr Sachs. I shall be at your house on Sunday afternoon.'

Sam closed the door and went back into the workroom. He flopped down into a chair and wept.

Part III

The Web is Wove

*Let the wicked fall into their nets
While I alone come through.*

37

The next morning, Saturday 3rd April

'Now, this is it, this is the impending moment of truth, Robert. We are approaching our *Nemesis*, she will dole out her retribution for all our meddling in these matters. Well..., I *hope* she won't.'

'What on earth are you muttering about? I don't understand a word of it.'

'I beg your pardon, it's this heavy burden of apprehension that I'm carrying with me at the moment. Do you not feel it?'

'Of course I feel it, I've felt it ever since we left Hull, but it doesn't make me utter nonsense.'

They were walking towards the Deichstrasse, staying on the right-hand side. They would be at the house of M. Chevalley within ten minutes.

'One doesn't know how very alien it is to be in a foreign country until one has actually been in it for a day or two. Everything is alien – these buildings, the language, the food, the dress.... I can understand how people love to be back home after a long sojourn abroad.'

'I don't know, Nick. We haven't been here long enough to know. We also have the knowledge that in two days we shall be returning to Hull.'

'But can you not imagine how difficult life would be if we were to be here for months or even years?'

'I think people adapt when they must. Many people move to live in other countries for various reasons, do they not?'

'Yes, of course they do. I was thinking of myself, Robert. I would find it very difficult to adapt. The main problem is the language, that's the greatest barrier against adapting that I can feel at this moment. It's certainly a barrier to our communicating with any confidence and clarity with whoever we shall be dealing with. I mean in-depth communication, not just mundane chit-chat. We are isolated, as on a desert island. You see, Robert, I *live* by communication – friendships, business, and, of course, reading. These I could not live without. Now, if we talk about moving to some of the Colonies where English is spoken, that would be different.'

'Well, Nick, I must admit you are not quite the average person, are you? You have a mind that never rests, the wheels are forever turning like some engine running day and night.'

'How poetic, Robert, very impressive, a splendid simile. I don't know about my mind though, it is what it is. One can never be in the mind of another to know what it's like. In that sense we really are, each one of us, on a desert island. We are all Robinson Crusoes.'

'But now, Nick, you *must* apply your mind to another way of thinking – in a foreign language. We have arrived. Everything is in your hands now.'

They stopped outside the house that was set back a little way from the street. They went up to the door and Twygge pulled the bell-knob. There was no response so he tried it again. Shortly the door opened.

'Bon jour. Monsieur Chevalley?'

'Was wollen Sie? Wer sind Sie?'

'Escusez moi, Monsieur, la Francais. Je suis Mr Twygge, il est Mr Wray. Nous sommes Angleterre et nous...' Twygge couldn't think of the next word. He was so nervous his mind felt as though it were in a maelstrom, all his thoughts jumbled up and swirling around. He reverted to English to escape the confusion that was in his head.

'Monsieur, I am very sorry, my French is not very good, as you can tell, and my German is even worse. Do you speak English?'

'Of course, what do you want?' He was very brusque.

News of what has been happening in England must have reached them here by now so it must be expected, thought Twygge, that whichever side they are on, good or evil, they must be suspicious of every stranger who calls on them.

'We are here in Hamburg on business, sir. We come from the town of Hull. We are wine merchants, well, at least we are here to buy wine.' *That was an awkward stumble*, thought Twygge, it showed a hint of doubt in the veracity of his account of himself.

'What has that to do with me? Please tell me what you want of *me* or I shall have to close this door.'

'Are you Monsieur Chevalley, sir?'

'No, he is not here.'

'Oh, we must see him. When will he be back?'

'Not for many days. Now what exactly do you want of him? I work with him so you can tell me.'

Twygge decided to throw caution to the winds.

'We have been asked by the Chief Constable and the Sheriff of Hull to talk to Monsieur Chevalley about a very serious matter.'

Now, thought Twygge, it's now or never - we shall soon find out whether this man is on our side, or, if he's the enemy? There was a considerable pause while the man eyed them up and down and seemed to consider the situation with great caution. Twygge and Wray could both detect a slight change in the man's demeanour.

'Come inside.'

He stepped aside and let them through the door. They both entered with considerable trepidation.

'Come this way.'

Once inside Twygge realised that they had burned their bridges. There was no going back now that the door was closed behind them.

They entered as large entrance hall, splendidly furnished, with doors leading off to the left and right of a central staircase. The man led them towards the door on the right and they entered what appeared to be a study, with books lining the walls on three sides.

'Please be seated, Messieurs. Would you care for some coffee?'

'Yes, sir, very much.'

The man rang a bell.

'Now, I am taking a great risk bringing you into this house, a risk to me and to yourselves. I am not giving you my name until I hear what you have to say. Do you understand why I am cautious?'

'Indeed we do, sir.'

'If I discover, for whatever reason, that you are lying or that you are not what you seem to be you may find yourselves unable to leave this house, or this world. Is that clear to you?'

This made Twygge and Wray very nervous. Caution was needed on both sides, thought Twygge.

'What has been happening in Hull is so serious, sir, that we must all be cautious,' began Twygge. 'It is difficult for us to know who is responsible for what. It must be the same for you.'

'Quite, but this is not getting us anywhere. I think you should now make it quite clear why you are here, why you came to this house. I do not believe you are wine merchants, but neither do I believe that you are both villains. That's the risk I am taking. But it really matters not because whoever you are, as I said, you will not leave this house without my permission. Now, gentlemen, we know where we stand so will you tell me why you are here?'

Twygge was very impressed by this man's command of English. He then proceeded to introduce themselves properly, pointing out Wray's role as a Constable. He then gave an outline of what had been happening in Hull over the previous months. He did not reveal what he himself believed had been the reasons for those events. Nor did he include details of the blue coats and the buttons, but he did mention that the victims had been beheaded and their heads had never been found.

Twygge's account was interrupted in mid-stream by the arrival of the coffee. After it had been served they settled down again and Twygge continued.

The man listened intently, keeping a careful watch on their faces. Eventually Twygge got to the point where they had decided that the matter had needed further investigation, including the need for them to come to Hamburg.

'That is very interesting indeed but you have missed out two very important details, Monsieur Twygge – how did you know about this house and the name of Monsieur Chevalley?'

'It was on a piece of paper, sir, found in the pocket of one of the murdered men, who, we believe, were the actual murderers of the other victims.' He did not mention that there were two names and addresses.

'I understand. If it means what I think then this is very useful to us indeed. I must now tell you that M. Chevalley should at this moment be on his way to Koblenz. He has been to Hull doing what you are doing. It is an unfortunate twist of fate that your paths haven't crossed.'

This announcement came as a shock to Twygge and Wray. Did this mean that their journey had been a waste of time? Where is Koblenz and what has it got to do with it? Twygge felt helpless suddenly in the face of so many unanswered questions.

'I see that you are surprised to hear it, gentlemen. It is quite possible that M. Chevalley will return with the same knowledge that you have just brought to me.'

Twygge wondered if he would. He then thought that they should begin the next stage of their mission as soon as possible

– go to the second address before events become more complicated.

'Yes, sir, it does sound as though we may have wasted our time coming to Hamburg. But at least we are having the pleasure of seeing this beautiful city and enjoying its food and hospitality. We shall not waste any more of your time, sir. It now remains for us to bide our time until we return to Hull on Monday. I think we shall visit some of the wonderful churches that you have here.'

'If you two gentlemen happen upon any more information you must inform me, yes?'

'Of course we shall, sir, but I don't see how we are likely to – our work here seems to be concluded.'

Twygge had the feeling that this man knew that they knew more than they were saying but he didn't know how he possibly could. Maybe it was Twygge's conscience affecting him.

'There is one other matter, sir. You haven't told us who the murdered men were and why they were murdered. With that knowledge we may well be able to prevent any more crimes being committed.'

'I was wondering when you would ask me that. I was beginning to think you knew already.'

'Indeed not, sir. The main reason for us being in Hamburg is to find out. I had to ensure that you believed who we were and why we were here before I could ask that question.'

'I quite understand. Had you come here and started asking blunt questions from the start I would have been more suspicious than I was. Now I believe you to be genuine, although Constable Wray is conspicuous by his silence I shall assume he is too, I shall tell as much as feel able to.'

'The Constable, sir, is one who says little but learns a lot.'

'That's probably very wise of him.'

The man, who still hadn't revealed his name which, thought Twygge, gave him an advantage, proceeded to explain what had been happening over recent years and why some men had been murdered. It didn't take long, it was quite simple.

'So you have never been able to ascertain who is responsible for the murders?'

'Ah, Monsieur Wray, you do speak! Yes, we have tried but the trail is a tangle that we have not yet been able to unravel. We do believe the source of it is here in Hamburg, hence this is where were reside at the moment.'

'Two more things, sir, if you don't mind?'

'Not at all, Mr Twygge.'

'Where is Koblenz and what is its importance that it takes M. Chevalley there?'

'Ah, I cannot explain it all to you now other than to say it is a city on the River Rhine at the mouth of the Mosel River. I shall tell M. Chevalley to clarify all the details for you when we have cleared things up. And the second question?'

'Do you have any idea what might have happened to the missing heads of the murder victims?'

'Well, we have our suspicions but I'm afraid I can't say until things are over, it might jeopardise our strategies if word got out.'

'Thank you for your frankness, sir. You have been most generous with your time, your knowledge, and your hospitality, so we should not keep you any longer from your business.'

'Gentlemen, between us all I am sure we can reach a satisfactory conclusion eventually. I am hoping that Monsieur Chevalley will return with some of the answers.'

He rose and led them to the door. They crossed the foyer and reached the front door. There was no sign of any other person in the house.

'Good day, gentlemen, and *bon voyage*.'

'Good day to you, sir, and *au revoir*.'

Once back on Deichstrasse they turned left and began to walk back in the direction they had come earlier.

'I get the distinct impression, Robert, that Monsieur Chevalley is in the process of weaving a web to catch the killers. We will find out eventually, no doubt.'

38

The same day, Saturday 3rd April

'Well, well, well, Nick, fate certainly dealt us a trump card today. At one point I did believe that we may not have left that house alive, *and* without our heads still on our shoulders.'

'We could not have left the house alive without our heads, could we, Robert?'

'Ha, ha, very droll! How can you be so..., so full of levity when we might have been so near to death?'

'We were not, Robert. I must admit I entered that house with a touch of fear and trepidation at first but soon dissolved away.'

'Explain yourself.'

'The house for a start – the grandeur of it. And then, when we'd been in the company of that gentleman for a while I realised we were not in the room with a villain. Did you not detect his imposing and regal demeanour? I knew within minutes that one half of my theory was correct, so I relaxed. As you say, Robert, we have been dealt a trump card.'

'I see, but the difference between us is that you have a theory, and from previous experience I'm expecting it to be proved, but I have *no* theory.'

'In that case I shall cast all caution aside and explain it to you this evening in the privacy of our rooms. I apologise for not telling you sooner, Robert, but had I been wrong you may not have recognised danger when it was there. You may easily have misinterpreted situations and made an error that might have brought us serious trouble. I felt we should face all situations with open minds and considerable caution. Do you understand now?'

'Of course, Nick, you're right again. I'm afraid I was not born with the subtlety of mind that you possess.'

'Nonsense, you are an equal part of our doings, don't forget that. Do you think I could ever have had the courage to do all these things without you at my side? You give me moral support and physical protection if needed. Now let us change the subject and decide what we should do next, and hope it too deals us a trump card.'

'It's obvious – we must go to that other address that we have, whether or not we get a trump card.'

'I was hoping you would suggest that. Now where is it?'

He rummaged about in his waistcoat pocket and withdrew a small document.

'Here we are, Reimerstwiete. I have no idea how to pronounce it – I get the *ei*s and the *ie*s confused. But using a little logic, we know now that this street we're on is Deichstrasse – you've heard the waitress say it and seen the sign – pronounced *die*, which we don't want to do, of course! So, *Reimer* must be *rye* and *twiete* must be *tweet*. So there we have it - *rhymerstweet*! How does that sound to you? I have occasionally come across verses by rhymers who tweet.' Wray groaned audibly. 'But I don't know what a *twiete* is so I hope we shall soon find out.'

'You're rambling, Nick. Let's have some dinner and we can ask inside where it is, however it's pronounced.'

'But I must know how it's pronounced. I dare not risk showing this piece of paper to anybody.'

'Whatever you say. Now, we need somewhere to eat. Look across the street Nick, there!' He pointed, 'Just next to that shop with all the hardware outside.'

'I see it. Now, can we get across?'

Being a wide street, Deichstrasse, although busy with traffic, did not seem to be as crowded as the narrower lanes where their hotel was. They soon found a gap in the traffic and dashed across.

At the end of the meal Twygge asked the waitress as best he could the whereabouts of Reimerstwiete. After a considerable struggle to convey the meaning of his question she finally understood.

'Ah, ja, ja. Gehen Sie auf diese Strasse,' pause, Twygge nodded, 'auf diese Weise,' she pointed to the right, 'dann rechts abbiegen. Dann nehmen Sie die erste Strasse links, Katherinenstrasse. Reimerstwiete ist die nächste Strasse über.'

'Danke schön, very much, Miss.'

'Bitte schön.'

'There, Robert, communication is not so difficult, is it?'

'Well, if you can understand what she was saying, I'm a Dutchman, or you *can* speak German after all. You should have seen yourselves, it was like a one-act drama – you call that easy?'

'Yes, I do. The only words I *had* learned were *links* and *rechts*, left and right, but other words were obvious – *erste* probably *first*, *nächste* is obvious, and so on. I thought she and I did very well. Now let's be on our way.'

They left the café and Twygge turned to the right down Deichstrasse.

'We go to the end of this street, turn right, and then we take the first street on the left, called Katherinenstrasse. Then the next street we see should be the one we want.'

'Up here, then right, then left?'

'Precisely. It will be precisely *if* we find it, not so if we get lost. There is a maze of narrow streets at the end of here, as you know.'

Reimerstwiete was not difficult. They found themselves in the midst of very old buildings, not unlike High Street in Hull – timber-framed with cowering jetties over narrow lanes.

'Which way do we turn, Robert, left or right?'

Reimerstwiete ran 90° across Katherinenstrasse.

'Either way, does it matter? We don't know the house so we shall have to ask people where this Monsieur... whoever-he-is... lives.' He looked at his piece of paper: *Monsieur Boillot*.

'May I suggest we start here on the left-hand side, then when we reach the end we can return on the opposite side of the road, then cross this Katherine Street or whatever it's called and do the same down that side?'

'Yes, we shall do that. There are lots of people about, plenty of activity, it shouldn't be too hard to find someone who knows. But do remember, this could be the most dangerous part of our work. Shall we begin?'

'I'm ready, Nick. I shall try to make myself look as fierce as possible in the face of anything threatening.'

'No need to try, Robert.'

'Thank you – such kind words from a friend.'

It seemed as though they both knew instinctively that to begin in a good humour and optimistic would fare them better than showing any signs of apprehension or anxiety. If they did confront any of the *enemy* the greatest danger would be in showing signs of fear. Just like wild animals villains can sense fear in their adversaries when it's there.

It took the best part of an hour and many difficult attempts to get their questions understood before they found someone who had heard of M. Boillot.

'Ja, ja, der Franzose. Dort, er wohnt in das großes Haus, über die Strasse.' He pointed to a double-fronted building, further down on the other side of Reimerstwiete.

'Danke schön, sir.'

'Bitte schön.'

Twygge and Wray went off, leaving the man standing in the street, smoking his pipe and watching them.

'A rough type, wouldn't you say? Someone not to meddle with.'

'Well, I don't know, Nick. I couldn't judge the man just on a few words spoken in a few seconds, and in a foreign language.'

'But didn't you see his eyes – full of suspicion?'

'No. Perhaps he eyes all strangers, especially foreign ones, with suspicion. It's only natural in some people.'

They crossed the street between the traffic in three quick long strides.

'Here's the door. This looks to me like some sort of rooming-house. Are you prepared?'

'As well as I'll ever be.'

As they entered they saw a large middle-aged lady sitting at a desk reading a newspaper. She looked up as they went in.

'Gut'n Tag, meinen Herren. Kann ich helfen Sie?'

'Guten Tag, Madame.' Twygge suddenly flustered slightly after mixing his German with French. 'Ist der ein Monsieur Boillot hier?'

'Warum?'

He couldn't work out what she was asking, although from the way she said it it was clearly a question.

'We... er, wir sprechen mit Monsieur Boillot.'

'Er ist nicht hier. Er hat ein Büro bei der Niederhafen.'

Twygge recognised the name immediately.

'Ah, danke schön.'

'Bitte schön. Auf wiedersehen.'

They left the rooming-house.

'It appears we have to go back to the harbour. She said Boillot had an office, I think. What else could the word *Büro* mean?'

'So, another long walk, Nick. Can we find the harbour again?'

'Well, if we go back onto Deichstrasse we can retrace our steps from when we first arrived. You remember we came upon it by accident? It shouldn't be very difficult to find the way we came in reverse. Try to keep going southwest and watch out for ships' masts above the roof-tops.'

'So, back we go to Katherine Street?'

'I think it's the only way.'

After another lengthy trek they eventually emerged into the large open expanse of the harbour basin. For a port of the size and importance of Hamburg it was, as to be expected, extremely busy. The Niederhafen was lined with warehouses and offices, and many ships were being loaded and unloaded. There were horse-drawn waggons of all shapes and sizes, men pushing hand-carts hither and thither and the harbour-side was littered with crates, bales, and barrels of all descriptions, and the noise was deafening. It was, of course, a very familiar scene for Twygge and Wray.

'It seems as though most of these buildings have the names of the owners outside. Let's hope we can find a sign reading *Boillot*.'

After battling their through all the hustle and bustle for most of the length of the Niederhafen the name of *C. Boillot* suddenly loomed before them. Underneath in equally large letters were the words *Ausfuhr und Einfuhrwaren*.

The office door was open as were the large doors to the warehouse next to it. Crates and sack-barrows were being taken in from the harbour-side.

'Now, Robert, shall we enter?'

'Now or never, Nick. I shall lead the way.'

39

The same day, Saturday 3rd April
Twygge and Wray walked into the office of *C. Boillot*. A man was sitting behind a high desk with stacks of papers and ledgers. He was talking to a well-dressed man standing in front of the desk. When Twygge and Wray entered they stopped talking and turn to look at them.

'G't'n Tag,' said the well-dressed man.

'Guten Tag, meinen Herren.' He'd heard that latter phrase enough times now to be confident enough to use it. He thought it would be better to come straight to the point.

'Monsieur Boillot?'

'And who are you?'

'Oh, you speak English, sir?'

'Yes, and French and German, and a little Flemish. Do you wish to do business with me?'

'Not exactly business, sir. Are you free to talk in private?'

This made the man look at them both with obvious suspicion.

'Is it necessary?'

'We think it is, sir.'

'Then come with me.'

He took them through a door at the back, across another room furnished as a parlour and then opened a door into an office.

'Be seated, gentlemen.'

He took up a position behind a desk and sat down.

'Would you introduce yourselves, please, and explain why you're here?'

'Certainly, sir. You haven't said so yet but I presume you *are* Monsieur Boillot?'

'Yes. Please would you speak quickly. I have to leave Hamburg on business later today. I have little time to spare.'

Twygge had seen what he thought was a travelling bag at the side of the man's desk when they came into the room.

'I am Mr Twygge and this is Mr Wray and our visit to you concerns the town of Hull in the north of England.. You know of it?'

'Of course, my business is in imports and exports. I know of it well, as I know many other parts of the world.'

'Well, sir, this is not really very important. We are here in Hamburg on our own business – to buy wine. We happened upon the Niederhafen as we got off the ship.'

'What has this to do with me?'

'Well, sir, it's simply that a piece of paper has been found with your name and address on it.'

This startled M. Boillot considerably. Twygge and Wray saw him squirm a little in his chair. He appeared to fiddle with something under his desk.

'It was found,' continued Twygge, 'just outside the door of my office in Hull and someone found it and handed it to me. And as we had planned this trip to Hamburg I thought I could help you in case it may be of some importance.'

'I cannot think of one possible reason why a bit of paper with my name and address on it could be of any importance to me. It was probably dropped by someone I was doing business with. And anyway, there is nothing now that anyone can do about it without any more facts, is there? Are you certain that that is the only reason why you have come to my office?'

Twygge and Wray could detect that M. Boillot was not convinced by this lie.

'We are sorry Monsieur Boillot then for wasting your time. We were merely trying to help. Of course it is of no importance and we do beg your pardon. We shall be on our way now.'

Twygge was very conscious of his own nervousness and that M. Boillot could tell by his manner of speech that he suddenly wanted to leave.

'No, you shall not!'

The man raised his right hand from his lap and pointed a pistol straight at Twygge's chest. He stood up and moved towards a door on his right and opened it.

'In here.'

Twygge went into what appeared to be a small dark closet. Boillot closed the door and turned the key in the lock.

'You,' he growled at Wray, 'this way!'

Boillot pushed Wray in the back with his pistol towards a narrow corridor. They reached a flight of stairs also narrow with a hatch a few feet at the top.

'Push that open and get in.'

Wray hesitated, turned his head to face Boillot and was about to speak…

'Silence! In there!' The pistol dug into his back harder.

Wray pushed open the hatch and scrambled through on his knees into a dark space.

'Close the hatch!'

Wray dropped it shut. He then heard what he thought was a bolt being slid into place. He heard Boillot step back down the stairs and walk away. He fumbled about, feeling his way around. The room was quite small, maybe 7 or 8 feet long and about 5 feet wide. It appeared to be entirely empty. The roof was higher than he could reach and it was pitch-black without the slightest hint of light anywhere. He could hear the noises of the haven outside.

40

The same day, Saturday 3rd April
Mr Sachs had decided to talk to Rachel in the evening. He had no wish to taint the hours of *Shabbes* with unpleasantness. He fully understood the condition in which Rachel found her mind and her heart. He knew that what he had to say to her would cause her considerable pain.

Rachel herself was unaware that her father had been to talk to Sam Parker, so when he asked to have a word with her alone in his office she was a little taken aback. Their conversation was in Yiddish.

'Please sit next to me here, my dear Rokhele.'

She looked at him quizzically – this had never happened before. Whenever anything had to be said it was said together with the family, or at least, with her mother there as well. This situation made her somewhat anxious and her father noticed this.

'You are a beautiful girl, and a wonderful and dutiful daughter. Everyone loves you, everyone in this house and in our community, Rokhele.'

'You're very kind, tatte, and this is the best family anyone could wish for, I know that. But why are we here?'

'Because what I want to talk to you about is going to hurt you, my child.'

She turned a little pale. She looked straight at him and he saw the pain in her eyes begin to appear. He looked down.

'You know what I'm going to say, don't you?'

'Yes, tatte, I think I do.' She turned her eyes away from him.

'Rokhele, I know that over recent weeks you have changed. You've become quieter, you've not been full of the joy and fun that you've always had before. Your mother and I are sad that you are like this. We worry about you day and night. The atmosphere in our house is not what it was. We feel that something inside of you has died and we want you to return to being the Rokhele you were.'

There was a pause. Rachel was now looking down. She said nothing.

'Please, please, try to forget Mr Parker. You are going to be married to another man, and we're sure *he* wants to marry *you*. We all want this to be a happy marriage, it's what we know everybody wants. Please don't ruin everyone's lives, and your own. You cannot marry a Gentile, you cannot be with one, Rokhele, it is not done, it's never been known. Don't you understand?'

'I do understand, tatte, but...'

'Your life would be miserable – our people would disown you. Mr Parker's family would disown you because you'd not be Christian. Where would you go? Where would you live? You're both very young, Rokhele, to live life in such a way.'

'Mr Levy married a Gentile, didn't he? And what about Ahab?'

'Its different for men, you know that. Besides, look at what Ahab's wife, Jezebel, wrought on Israel with her corrupt pagan beliefs and trying to eliminate God from the Holy Land. But that isn't the question, Rokhele, it's your life and happiness, your own family's happiness and the happiness of our people and friends. Aren't those the most important things in the world? And what about your children? Don't forget that they too would be outcasts, subject to taunts and mockery. Our family would be a subject of gossip as long as you lived in Hull, and probably wherever you lived. Would you want your children to bear that?'

Tears welled up in Rachel's eyes and she began to sob.

'Please don't cry, Rokhele. It pains me greatly to see you cry. I won't say any more. I shall...' He reached over and put his arms around her and hugged her tightly. It was plain to see that he was just as pained as she was. Rachel put her arms around her father.

Nothing was said for some time.

'I'm sorry, tatteshi, I know I've done wrong, please forgive me. You and mamme have always been so kind to me I don't want to hurt you.'

'There, there, my darling, there, there.'

'I will do as you say, tatte, I will not see Mr Parker again, I promise. I will marry Mr Lewin. I shall do everything you and mamme say. I will try to become happy again.'

Her father knew what she was saying – she was admitting to herself that she had not been happy in recent times. He thought that her own recognition of her present state and the effects this has had on the family would give her the strength to overcome and recover from the discomposure and perturbations that had afflicted her since meeting Mr Parker. He felt content now that things would slowly return to normal. The whole family would have to be very patient with her. Perhaps, he thought, she could go away for a while. He would try to talk her into going to London where Mrs Sachs has a cousin – just for a few weeks until Mr Lewin arrived.

Rachel stopped crying. Her father released her from his arms. She wiped her eyes, looked at him and smiled.

'See, tatte, I am better. Shall we go back to mamme now? I will show her I am better.'

They got up and Mr Sachs put his arm around her as he led her through the door, down the hall and into the parlour.

Sam Parker had been comforting himself by immersing his mind in the story of *Caleb Williams*. He had started reading it the previous Saturday evening in his room, the night before Mr Twygge left for Hamburg. He was gripped by the story – it was the most exciting thing he had ever read. He *was* Caleb as he read and reached the point in the book where there appeared to be no hope of the lad escaping from the executioner a second time. Sam had to keep on reading, he couldn't put the book down. He was, even now, on this Friday morning, relinquishing his morning session of Arithmetic to sit and read when Mrs Field knocked and entered.

'Do excuse me, Sam, but dinner is nearly ready and we have a visitor.'

'Oh, yes, Mrs Field, and who might that be?'

His reaction was to think it was Mr Sachs again.

'Mr Townend from York. He arrived unexpectedly to see Mr Twygge so I begged him to stay for dinner.'

Sam was considerably relieved.

'I shall be right there, Mrs Field, thank you.'

She left the room and Sam put his book down on his desk and followed her out.

As they sat at the table, indulging in deep-fried oyster loaves in wine sauce, Mr Townend, after hearing about the Hamburg venture and its purpose, was giving an account of a recent murder in York in which a foreign gentleman had been found headless beneath Clifford's Tower.

'Mr Townend, please,' interrupted Mrs Field, 'you're putting me off my food!'

'I do apologise, Mrs Field, but this is the purpose of my visit. I was hoping to inform Mr Twygge but he is not here. I believe he must be told about it the minute he returns. I shall ask you, Sam, if you would be so kind as to inform him for me?'

'Certainly, Mr Townend. Could you tell me more?'

'Well, if I endeavour not to upset Mrs Field, may I continue?'

'Yes, but no gory details, please.'

'No gory details then. The dead man was wearing a green coat. I managed to find out from the constables that one of the buttons was missing from the coat. I'd told them about Mr Twygge and Constable Wray's discoveries and that they were friends of mine. But all I know was in the following day's newspapers.'

'Apart from the coat colour it certainly seems to be the same as all the other murders.'

'It does indeed, that is why I came here.'

'I thought,' said Sam, 'that the discovery of the *murdered* murderers was going to be the end of it.'

'It appears not to be so. When are Mr Twygge and the Constable due back in Hull?'

'It should be Wednesday or Thursday, Mr Townend, *if* they are not murdered themselves!'

'Now, now, Mrs Field, don't be so much of a pessimist. I have every faith in their succeeding in their mission. Now let us leave this unpleasantness behind us and talk about other matters. Mrs Field, tell me about your wedding plans. And after that, Sam, you can tell me how you are getting on.'

41

The same day, Saturday 3rd April
It was several hours before Twygge and heard sounds in the room outside his 'prison'. He was tired, thirsty, aching and uncomfortable. There had been nowhere to sit, and hardly room to squat or sit on the floor, let alone stretch out.

There was the sound of several voices and what sounded like the moving of furniture. Twygge has his ear to the door. The people outside were talking French, that much he could make out, but there was no hope of getting the meaning of it.

Eventually the key turned in the lock and the door opened. Twygge attempted to stand up but he struggled, and was dazzled by the bright light.

'Come in, gentlemen, and stand by the door.'

He moved forward and took up a position side by side in front of the closet doorway. No-one spoke. As his eyes became adjusted to the light he could make out a semicircle of men, seated in chairs arranged around him.

M. Boillot was the first to speak.

'We are here to ask you questions. You will answer them fully and truthfully. If, at the end of our questioning, we are satisfied with your explanations you may be released and allowed to go your ways. If we are not satisfied, well, what will happen to you remains to be seen. Is that all absolutely clear?'

Twygge didn't move, there was merely a slight nod of his head.

'Now Monsieur,' began Boillot, addressing the man on the far left side of the semicircle, 'would you begin?'

Twygge counted six men, four of them very well-dressed and two not so.

'Why have you come to Hamburg?' He was one of the well-dressed quartet.

Twygge gave exactly the same reasons he and Wray had given Boillot earlier in the day.

'How did you get the address of this place and the name of Monsieur Boillot?'

He gave the same explanation as before.

This questioning went on for some time – the same questions followed by the same answers. The only thing he omitted was the fact that Wray was a Constable. He had by now begun to believe their own little white lies, *and* their innocence. Twygge was thoroughly immersed in acting a part. He even attempted to create an innocence in his face and body language.

'I you are a bookseller, as you say you are, why did you come here to buy wines?'

'I had never been to Hamburg before, sir. Mr Wray invited me to accompany him – he needed to stock up the wine-cellar of his hotel. I am also a devotee of fine French wines. We happen to be very good friends. The way things are in the present circumstances buying wines in France is impossible, as I'm sure you understand. All the wines we need have to be bought through this town.' Twygge was pleased with himself by his quick-thinking – to add a small gesture of support for France.

The questions ceased while two of the men engaged in a brief whispered conversation. Then one of them addressed Twygge.

'Is not being a bookseller quite a modest occupation? How can you afford to buy expensive wines and to pay for a voyage to this country?'

'Well, sir, I do have a very well-stocked shop and valuable and faithful customers, many of them wealthy merchants who enjoy good books. And we deliver to several large houses in East Yorkshire. Also I have another side to my business, I repair and rebind expensive volumes. This has proved to be very lucrative.'

There was another pause. All six men were looking intently at Twygge. This made him uneasy and so he looked around, at the floor, at the walls, and glanced at the men in between, trying as hard as he could to appear innocent.

After a few moments M. Boillot spoke.

'Do you have any idea why we have been keeping you here, why we have interrogated you so thoroughly?'

Twygge looked at them with a puzzled expression.

'No, sir,' he replied, 'maybe you mistook us for some other people. We are utterly ignorant of who you are or what we may be guilty of.'

'It is curious that a piece of paper with a name and address on it appears out of nowhere in Hull, then brings you all the way to Hamburg.'

'It was found, sir,' said Twygge, '*after* we had planned this trip and bought our tickets. It was entirely a coincidence. If we had thought that it would have caused so much concern to you gentlemen we would not have bothered ourselves. I'd have just thrown the piece of paper away.'

The six men looked at each other.

M. Boillot continued, 'What are your opinions concerning the Revolution in France?'

This took Twygge by surprise. He thought that this was a very dangerous question for them to answer. He had to think quickly. There were two possible answers, and one of them would be the wrong one – the one that could lead to their rapid demise – and the other to their freedom. Twygge thought he knew the answer that these men wanted but he was not totally convinced and hence a hint of fear rippled through him as he answered.

'Well, sir, you may be aware that we had our own Revolution in England, over a hundred years ago. It was called a Civil War but it amounted to the same thing. Actually, we had a previous Civil War briefly in the early 12th century but...'

'Mr Twygge, would you keep it short – I'm not interested in the history of England.'

'I do apologise, Monsieur Boillot. Well, we had a tyrannical King and an arrogant lot of lords, earls and dukes and the like, just at the time when we were creating our own Parliament of the People. The people rose up under a strong leader with lots of support. Eventually the King and his followers were defeated and England became free of tyranny and the Parliament was reinstated. This, gentlemen, is what I believe is happening in France. As ordinary simple folk we must support such events against tyranny and abuse.'

Once again glances were exchanged between the six gentlemen.

'But I believe your Civil War, as you call it, failed – you reverted to a monarchy shortly afterwards.'

'We did, sir,' added Twygge, 'but by then we had developed a strong Parliament with many powers of control. The King was no longer able to rule with total power as they had been previously. Once our Parliament became established its power has grown and grown, and new laws created, until we have the full and total freedoms that we enjoy today. Our monarchies since the Civil War have generally been benign, almost merely figureheads.'

'If people are greatly oppressed do you believe that severe violence is justified against the oppressors?'

'If it is necessary and is the only way that they can overcome their oppression then, yes, I agree.'

'I must request that you now return to the closet.'

M. Boillot got up from his chair and approached him. He held the door open and Twygge went back in. The door was closed and locked. He heard the muffled sounds of chairs being moved, men talking and the gradual fading of the sounds as they all seemed to be leaving the room.

It must have been after about another 10 minutes or so in his *cell* that Twygge nearly jumped out of his skin. He'd heard a pistol shot not far away. This was followed by the sounds of shuffling feet passing by the door. After these sounds faded away everything went quiet. Twygge knew immediately what had happened --- Wray had been shot! He was devastated. He knew it was his fault, he should never have talked Wray into joining this stupid venture.

Before he could think himself further into depths of sorrow and guilt he heard the sound of a key going into the lock in his door.

'Come out!'

This time the six men were not sitting but standing in various parts of the room looking at Twygge as he emerged from his prison..

M. Boillot spoke, 'We have discussed your situation and what you have said to us in reply to our questions. We are not all convinced of your total innocence – some of us believe that you have not been fully honest with us and you're holding something back. You both may well be spies. As for you, Mr Twygge, I was not fooled by your attempts at flattery concerning French wine. It seems to me, sir, that you were attempting too vigorously to appear innocent which means you know something which makes you believe your lives may be in danger in this house. If you were innocent flattery would have been unnecessary.'

'But, sir…'

'Be quiet, I have not finished. Don't dig a deeper hole for yourself, Mr Twygge, or should I say *grave*. This is what's going to happen. You have tickets to sail to England on Sunday – you will be on that ship. For the remaining time that you are here in Hamburg you will be followed wherever you go. Some of us would not have been so lenient, so think yourselves fortunate that we are letting you go. We have people in England so you will be watched when you return. Now leave.'

'What about Mr Wray, sir?' asked Twygge.

'We've dealt with him. So you're on your own now.'

'But, sir,...'

'*The door!*'

Boillot pointed to the door on the opposite side of the room. Twygge began to walk towards it. As he crossed the room another man opened the door and followed him out as he left.

Once outside he stood on the dockside. He looked right, then left, then he started walking towards the town.

42

The same day Saturday 3rd April
Once out on to Niederhafen again Twygge didn't know which way to turn --- turn right and look for the next ship home, or to turn left and go back to the hotel? Should he inform the police about the shooting of Wray? His mind was in a mental maelstrom --- fear, guilt, shame, all fighting together inside his head. He felt that his life was now ruined, that nothing could repair the damage he'd wreaked, life could never be the same again. Would life be worth living now? Would it be worth returning to Hull? Why not disappear and take the whole mess with him into oblivion?

Without realising it he'd started walking towards the town. Not aware of where he was going he eventually finished up outside his hotel. Then seeing the door his mind came out of its darkness into the light of reality, the maelstrom had abated.

'How did I get here?' he thought.

He went through the door then hesitated, not knowing quite what to say to the lady at the reception.

'Mr Twygge, I thought you were dead!'

Twygge spun around, knocking over a chair, stared and said nothing.

'Nick, what *have* you been doing? That chap Boillot told me he'd kicked you out of the building, and…'

'Robert, Robert, you're alive.'

'Well, I do believe so, and so are you apparently. Am I glad to see you, Nick.'

'Robert,' he reached out his hand, 'Robert, I thought you'd been shot?'

'I thought *you'd* been shot!'

They took hold of both of their hands.

'However, Robert, you left me in a right pickle. There I was not knowing what on earth I could do and then I walk in here and there you are back from the dead. Anyway, here you are, and here I am and what a relief! I don't know what to say.'

'I know what you can say - let's get our things and get out of here, get out of this town, get out of this country, *now*!'

'Certainly we must. But let's try to regain some composure first. I believe some food and drink would be in order.'

Half an hour later they were sitting in Twygge's room with a plate of splendid German cakes and a jug of coffee. They'd told each other their stories in full.

'Well, Robert, they certainly played a nasty trick on us. Obviously they tried to frighten us off altogether.'

'Not *tried*, Nick they *did*!'

'Well, I'm not sure.'

Wray groaned, 'Oh, no, no, no, no, Nick, not again! We should get a ticket back to Hull immediately, today, or whenever one's leaving next. Have you completely forgotten what happened today? Have you lost your mind?'

'We can't just run now, Robert, that'll make them think we have something to hide, that we're not here to buy wine. No, we must bide our time. Do nothing untoward, and wait until Sunday.'

'Perhaps we should stay in our rooms.'

'No, we have things to do.'

'Oh, don't tell me, you're going to carry on? You're going to get us shot for real this time. Didn't you grasp what Boillot and his men were saying back there?'

'Of course I did. But if we don't continue with the original plan those murders in Hull, and elsewhere, will just continue. Don't we owe a debt to the people of Hull, and to those unfortunate Frenchmen?'

'How can you be so sure that we *can* stop it?'

'I know, Robert, I've worked it out. My little chat with our friends at the Niederhafen was very enlightening, although I must admit at one point I didn't expect to get out alive after I heard the pistol shot and thought you were dead. I'm more than ever convinced that my theory is correct.'

'Your theory? *Our friends*? Are you mad? We were both as near to extinction today as we ever have been and you're treating it like some, like some..., I don't know, some garden party game.'

'Calm yourself, we are free now aren't we? You exaggerate.'

'You don't see it, do you? Those men are *very* clever, and *very* dangerous. They saw through your little bit of smarminess.'

'Yes, but it is true, it wasn't meant to prove anything.'

'Well, it sounded false to me at the time. There is probably, nay, most likely *definitely*, somebody at this very moment only a few yards behind us, carrying a weapon, and you say I exaggerate?'

'No, no, you're right of course. But if we stay calm and act normally but with care we'll be in no danger. And besides, isn't it our duty to try to carry this through to the end?'

Wray said nothing, he was too exasperated with Twygge. He knew he would win his argument, nor could he be stubborn and refuse to go on.

'Now, Robert, we don't really have much time left. There are two things at least that we must do.'

He paused, waiting for some sort of response from Wray but none was forthcoming so he continued.

'Firstly, we *must* get information to Monsieur Chevalley, that is absolutely crucial. Secondly, we must get to see Herr von Fürstenstein. If we don't show an interest in buying wine we will be scuppered. In fact, Robert, to be totally safe we must order some.'

'The latter, Nick, will be easy, but as far as going to see Monsieur Chevalley whilst we're being followed will be madness. It's out of the question!'

'There are ways and means. We must do it at all costs. Anyway it's too late in the day now. So back to our rooms now and then supper. What say you?'

Wray said nothing.

43

The same day, Saturday 3rd April
It was after sunset. The Shabbes candles had been lit and blessed by Mrs Sachs. Mr Sachs blessed the children, *A Woman of Valour* was recited, a hymn sung, the prayer over the wine said, hands washed, the bread blessed, and the meal started.

Two tables had to be placed together for tonight's meal – there were seven members of the Sachs family and six guests. Sitting with them at the table were Aaron Jacobs, a jeweller of Manor Alley, and his family. Jacobs was the uncrowned king of the Jewish Community and a special guest at the house of Benjamin Sachs. It was Aaron Jacobs who organised the production of the splendid gold crown that adorned the statue of *King Billy* in the Market Place.

Although the Jewish Community at this time consisted only of about forty people it was growing rapidly and many of the families were becoming very successful in their business ventures, allowing them to invest more and more money into the synagogue and its appurtenances, as well into the formation of a *cheder*, a school for the young Jewish children.

At the end of the meal Aaron Jacobs recited the Grace, *Birkat ha-Mazon*, then Benjamin began to make an announcement.

'I wish to let you all know something that has happened today and something that has made me very happy and, I'm sure, will you all happy too.'

The Sachs family knew already what it was, of course, and were looking directly at Rachel.

'My beautiful and clever daughter, Rhokele, has come back to us. She has been away for too long and we have missed her very much. The light that always shone about her head had faded into gloom. But now it is shining bright again and we can rejoice.'

Mr Jacobs then made a little speech.

'We are so glad that you are with us again, Rhokele. You can see how it has made us all happy. We are a community of wonderful people, people who work hard for their families, people who all love each other and have a special strength that comes from that love. By keeping together we can hold onto that strength and that makes us what we are. So this is a special night in more senses than one. Now, let us all enjoy this Shabbes.'

Throughout the meal Rachel had been conscious of being the centre of attention, albeit subtly, and she'd noticed more eyes catching her attention than she would normally. By the end of the announcements she realised that her father had been right. She felt the warmth, the joy, the love that all these people exuded. It was her family, her friends, her life – she couldn't give it all up and make everyone unhappy and finish up unhappy herself. She had resolved to marry Mr Lewin, she would raise her own wonderful family. She would not think of Sam Parker again. She would not visit his bookshop, she would not answer the door just in case it might be him with a book, nor try to meet him in the street. She would forget him completely.

At the home of Mr Twygge that same evening there was Mrs Field sitting in the parlour in front of a warm fire doing something with needle and thread. Sam was sitting opposite her with his head buried in a book.

'What are you reading today, Master Sam, something interesting?'

'Very interesting, Mrs Field, and very, what shall I say, ...exciting.'

'How can a book be exciting? I can understand it can be humorous or entertaining, but not exciting or even interesting as you call it.'

'Well, let me explain. This is a new kind of story. Mr Twygge said I should read it and I'm very grateful that he did. You see, it's about a young man called Caleb who is very bright but from a humble family and...'

'Just like yourself Sam.'

'Er, I don't know about that. Anyway, he has to work as a sort of manservant in the house of a rich gentleman. He is falsely accused of stealing from his master and sent to prison.'

'How can that be exciting? It sounds like a rather miserable tale to me.'

'You would have to read it yourself. You see, he escapes from prison and has an adventure but he gets captured and is sent back to prison and faces a possible hanging. That's as far as I've got and I can't stop reading and put it down until I find out what happens to him.'

'In that case, Sam, I am sorry that I interrupted you. I shall continue with my sewing and let you get on with it.'

'Not at all, Mrs Field. I suppose it is rather ill-mannered of me to sit here with you all this time and not talk.'

'No, no, Sam, please do continue.'

'I shall not. I have read enough for tonight and besides, I may not find out what happens to Caleb for hours yet.'

He placed a slip of paper between the pages he was up to, closed the book and paced it on the table.

'I wonder how Mr Twygge and Constable Wray are getting on. They should be sailing back home on Sunday.'

'If they've not been murdered and beheaded in their beds, Sam. They should never have gone in the first place. What are we to do if they don't come back? Tell me that.'

'They will come back, Mrs Field, you may rest assured. Mr Twygge is very astute and Mr Wray is strong and between them they will be able to take care of themselves whatever happens.'

'I do hope you are right. And our marriage is looming up and there he is gadding about in some far-off land full of villains and murderers. I don't know what to make of it.'

'Make nothing of it. They'll be completely safe. Now let me read you a poem.'

He got up and went across to a small pile of books sitting on a side table by the door to the dining-room. He picked up a copy of Cowper, returned to his seat and opened it at the contents page.

'This will amuse you, Mrs Field, *and* excite you – *The Diverting History of John Gilpin*, by Mr Cowper, *Showing how He went further than He intended and came Home safe again.*'

By the time Sam had got to the end of the poem Mrs Field had stopped her sewing. Her head was resting on the back of her chair, her eyes were closed and she was smiling:

> *Now let us sing – long live the king,*
> *And Gilpin, long live he;*
> *And, when he next doth ride abroad,*
> *May I be there to see!*

44

The next day, Sunday 4th April
By the next morning Twygge had a devised a means to send a message to the house of M. Chevalley on Deichstrasse explaining what had happened to him and Wray on the Niederhafen together with the address of Boillot on Reimerstwiete. He was also going to give Chevalley's assistant the full details of his theories of what had been happening. The missive would also request a reply from him as soon as possible as they were soon to sail back to Hull by the next day's tide.

Twygge had prepared his letter early the previous evening. He had obtained some paper and sealing wax from the innkeeper. He had also been eyeing up the various members of staff to see if he could find anyone who he thought could be trusted to take the message to Deichstrasse and wait for a reply for a small remuneration. He'd decided that a mature woman would be the best choice and maybe the least likely to arouse suspicion. From his own experience Twygge knew that men, particularly young men, in general are less honest than most women, with exceptions of course – Joseph Heron sprung to mind. Women were also more susceptible to a little charm. He'd thus set his sights on the lady behind the desk in the foyer. When they'd first arrived at the Gasthaus St Nikolai he'd recognised in this woman a certain warmth and a hint of mutual attraction, and there was also the fact that she spoke some English, albeit limited. He'd ascertained that this woman was not the innkeeper's wife but did reside at the inn. Twygge then made a request of the innkeeper whether she could be relieved of her duties for a while. Twygge also offered to pay him compensation for the loss of her services. The innkeeper had agreed and arranged with the woman that Twygge's letter would be delivered the following morning. None of this was going to be easy – there would be Boillot's spies about – so Twygge had to make all the necessary arrangements with diligence and a considerable amount of caution.

It was early in the morning when Twygge knocked gently on Robert Wray's door. There was no sound so he knocked again. Twygge heard some shuffling and the floor creaking then the door opened. He quickly entered and closed the door behind him quietly.

'Good morning, Robert. Did I wake you?'

'Good morning, Nick. Yes, you did, but no matter. I was wanting to be up early anyway after such an early night. What did you do with yourself yesterday evening?'

'Oh, not much really. I wrote a long letter to Monsieur Chevalley's assistant. I arranged with the innkeeper to have it delivered this morning by that attractive lady behind the front desk. That's all. We just need to wait for a reply. But we also need to be going together to see the wine merchant, Herr von Fürstenstein. That way we can divert attention from that compromising letter.'

'My, you have been busy. I hope you managed to arrange all this without any of Boillot's men watching and listening. They could be lurking everywhere.'

'I did. It was all conducted in private rooms. The innkeeper promised to be careful. It was quite difficult to get him to understand but in the end I'm convinced he did. He seemed to be an honest fellow.'

'Let's hope he is, otherwise we'll be done for.'

During this conversation Wray was dressing and dousing his face with water from the ewer.

'Indeed, Robert, I do believe that this is going to be the climax of our little venture. We shall not know the outcome for quite some time if my understanding of the situation is correct. We shall now wait and see, as they say. If the reply from Monsieur Chevalley's house is what I am expecting and we are not discovered we can sail home with light hearts and a self-satisfied sense of achievement.'

'You're very confident, as usual, Nick.'

'One must be, there is no alternative. If one thinks something is not likely to work it usually doesn't. Positive thoughts produce positive results. And I am famished – shall we have breakfast?'

'Now the sermon is over and I've finished putting on my boots, yes.'

'Of course. I'm not hurrying you. Do keep an eye open though for Boillot's men or anyone who seems to be paying us any attention. There may be only one but could be more. And I'm sure he would have placed someone as a resident of this inn. At a suitable moment we need to check who booked in yesterday evening after we returned here, or this morning. We must act normally at all costs. No whispering or surreptitious glancing around. We must give the impression that we have forgotten our meeting with Boillot and have no secrets or anything to hide. It is possible to spot a potential spy without making an obvious scrutiny of everyone.'

'Yes, yes, yes, yes, yes, yes....'

'Sorry, Robert, I'm lecturing again. But we *must* be very careful. Are you ready now? You know, Robert, I think the best way to behave normally is to forget everything else and just focus on whatever we are doing today, moment by moment.'

'Yes, M'lud, lead on.'

They lingered over breakfast. The dining-room was not full but enough people, mostly men, were there to give the room an air of busyness. Twygge and Wray made small-talk – about their impressions of Hamburg, what they could see in the time they had left, and about wine. It was after 9 o'clock before they left the inn.

On their way to the wine-merchants they both knew that they mustn't turn around without a good reason, in spite of the overpowering urge to do so. The morning air was cold and sharp but the sky was as clear as German crystal, and the sun was bright, promising a rise in temperature as the day moved on.

Having ascertained the way to the Trostbrücke from the innkeeper they made their way towards Wölberstieg, then turned right in the direction of the bridge, keeping a watch for the premises of Herr von Fürstenstein. The Trostbrücke went over the Nikolai Fleet, one of the many waterways of the city. However they didn't have to cross it as they spotted the building they were looking for before they got to it. The building was large and impressive with an elaborate gold-painted sign over the central doorway. The much smaller sign on the door read *Geöffnet*. Twygge opened the door and allowed Wray to enter first.

'G't'n Morgen, meinen Herren.' A middle-aged man was sitting at a desk on the left-hand side. In front of them was a long curved bar behind which was a large array of pigeon-holes containing dozens of wine bottles. Each of the holes was numbered. Some tables and chairs were placed on the right side of the room. On each table some small stacks of paper and pens were set out.

'Guten Morgen, mein Herr,' Twygge was left to do the talking, 'ist Herr von Fürstenstein hier?'

'Ah, gentlemen, I assume you are English, yes?'

'Yes, sir. I'm afraid my German is very poor.'

'We have many English come here, especially in recent years. My name is Herr Pfeiffer – at your service. Herr von Fürstenstein is not here, he is down the Rhine. But I can help you if it is wine you wish to buy.'

'It is indeed, Herr Pfeiffer. I am Mr Twygge and this is Mr Wray.'

'I am very pleased to meet you, gentlemen, and we can do some business, yes? You are wine-merchants I presume?'

'Not merchants exactly – Mr Wray here is the owner of an inn and coaching house. I am merely a lover of fine wines. We are both from the town of Hull on the northeast coast.'

'Ah, Hull, yes. We have business with Hull. Are you familiar with Mr Outram, sirs?'

Twygge had the feeling that Herr Pfeiffer was testing them. Could he possibly think they were hucksters or such-like, or was it Twygge's imagination?

'Indeed we do, sir, and his massive vaults in Quay Street. But we do not buy on the scale of Mr Outram. However, we do have Bills of Exchange from Smith & Thompson's if these are acceptable?'

'Of course they are, Mr Twygge. Mr Wray, I believe there is a person with your name in the Hull bank of Pease, Harrison & Pease, is there not? Does that happen to be you, sir?'

Wray was taken aback by Herr Pfeiffer's depth of knowledge of Hull business.

'No, it is my brother John. He is much more involved in various affairs in Hull than I.'

'But you are not using the Bills of Exchange from his bank?'

'That is correct. It is because I have been using Smith & Thompson's for many years. I believe it is wise to stay faithful to one bank when it has been very helpful. Besides, my brother only joined Pease's bank long after I had been with Smith & Thompson.'

'Of course, Mr Wray, I fully understand. Now, you both have gone to a lot of trouble coming all this way to Hamburg to buy some wines just for yourselves.'

'Well, as I said, Herr Pfeiffer, Mr Wray owns a busy inn and felt he would like to make the trip here himself for a change. Of course, France is out of the question.'

'My stocks are getting low, Herr Pfeiffer. I usually buy through one of the Hull merchants, but, as Mr Twygge said, I just had this urge to visit Hamburg. It has a reputation of being a fine and important city and I know several people who have already been here.'

'Yes, it is a fine city and, as you may know, once a member of the powerful Hanseatic League. But you are the first men from Hull who are not wine-merchants to come to do business with me. But no matter, business is business, and we do have a lot of local customers who are not wine-merchants either. Are you here for long?'

'Until tomorrow', said Wray, 'We arrived on Thursday. We've already seen a lot of your fair city and we shall see some more before we sail tomorrow.'

'Excellent, gentlemen. Have you visited the church of St Nikolai? It is, I believe, one of the tallest buildings in the world.'

'We have, sir, our inn is nearby. But we didn't know it is the tallest in the world. We shall tell everyone when we get back – they will be impressed.'

'You must also visit the church of St Michel before you leave, it is quite new and magnificent. It is directly to the west from here.'

'We shall do so. Thank you. Now to business?'

By the time Herr Pfeiffer had explained what he thought would be the best wines for Wray's inn, and after he'd given Twygge an account of recent developments in wine production in Germany, they were ready to place an order. The best of the French wines were becoming questionable. Since the Revolution the ownership of vineyards had been passed on to the peasants who had worked them. This had led to considerable turmoil in the wine market. On the other hand, there had been some excellent new wines being produced in Germany, particularly in the Rheingau at the Schloss

Johannisberg. These were all produced from the Riesling grape and were semi-sweet to sweet but had a magnificent richness of flavour that counteracted any excessive sweetness which made them suitable for wider use than mere dessert wines. Hock had always been popular in England, and because many people in Hull, including Twygge, had a preference for wines that were not very dry. These new wines were becoming very popular indeed, not only in England but throughout Europe.

They placed orders for cases of these even though they were more highly priced than the standard hocks they usually bought from the Hull merchants. They both felt the pain of the final cost. But, Twygge thought, what is the cost of wines compared to the cost of lives? They had said that they'd come to Hamburg to buy wine so that is what they had to do in a convincing manner.

'Please remember, gentlemen, that these wines are best drunk within the next five or six years. They will spoil if kept much longer than that.'

'I have no doubt,' said Twygge, 'that there will be no danger of that. Will you be able to get our cases down to the Niederhafen ready for loading by later today? Our ship is the *Frederick Louis*?'

'I shall organise their shipment down to the docks immediately. They should be there by this afternoon.'

'Thank you Mr Pfeiffer, you have been most helpful and it's been a pleasure doing business with you.'

When they left Herr Pfeiffer Twygge thought it would be quite natural to look right and left as they came out onto Wölberstieg without appearing to be suspicious. The street was very busy so he couldn't tell whether they'd been followed or not.

'Now, Robert, a coffee-house could be next don't you think?'

'I say, most certainly, *and* some cake.'

'You've forgotten, haven't you? Savouries in the morning.'

'Oh yes, well... an extra large something or other would do nicely.'

'I think we should go in the direction of St Michel's church.'

'I believe we've already seen it, Nick, when we were sailing into the harbour. You remember all those church spires, they were quite conspicuous?'

'I saw lots of church spires, some of then very tall.'

'Yes, but there was one further from the others to the left. It had a great copper-covered dome on top. And it seemed like the nearest one to us.'

'Well, well, Robert, how observant of you. Can you see it now?'

'No, these buildings are too tall and close together.'

'You see there on the right, there are steps up the to the bridge? Perhaps we can see it from there.'

They set off towards the Trostbrücke. They walked down the street a short distance and Twygge decided to cross the street to give them an opportunity to look both ways again. As he turned his head to the left he saw a man entering the wine-merchant's. He didn't allow his eyes to linger long so he immediately looked to the right. The street was narrow but there was not a lot of traffic apart from people so he went straight across.

Once they were on the bridge the copper dome of the church spire was quite visible due west of them.

'Now, we can navigate this maze of canals and streets and get to the church.'

'I don't see why not, and find a coffee-house on the way.'

'Of course, the stomach comes first. Can you stomach a long walk?'

'No more, Nick, I've had a bellyful of your puns.'

'Well, I'll eat my hat, you're doing it too. You've changed your mood.'

'We're sailing tomorrow so I *can* stomach it.'

'I see. Now, do we go back down Wölberstieg or do we cross the bridge and hope we can find our way?'

'I would cross the bridge. If we go back we would be returning to the risky area.'

'Maybe, but isn't there danger everywhere for us now? We must be being followed.'

'Thank you for that happy thought. No, let us take the new route. I would feel more at ease, safer or not.'

They crossed the bridge, turned left and made their way as best they could until they found a coffee-house.

After finishing their refreshments they continued the search for the church, and after many turns down several streets and crossing more canals they eventually arrived at the splendid new church of St Michel. By this time it was well past noon.

'A very modern building. We don't see new churches of this stature being built back home. Quite magnificent! You know, Robert, this building is a clear indication of the commercial power and wealth in this city. It's quite amazing.'

'Yes, but look, Nick, it reads *St Michaelis* here. Mr Pfeiffer called it St Michel.'

'So he did. I've no idea why. St Michael – the conqueror of the devil. Are we two not trying to do just that – trying to conquer devils?'

'In a way, yes, I suppose we are.'

'Shall we walk around the outside and then go inside and see the rest?'

'You lead and I shall follow.'

'Then some dinner perhaps?'

After exploring the church and some more of the city they made their way to the harbour to check on the sailing time of the *Frederick Louis*. Neither of them had been able to detect whether or not they had been followed.

By the time they got back to their inn it was late in the afternoon. The woman at the reception handed Twygge a letter which he swiftly slid into his coat pocket and he and Wray went to their rooms.

'Come into my room,' ordered Twygge.

'Certainly.'

When the door was closed Twygge took the letter out of his pocket, broke the seal and unfolded the sheet of pale blue paper. He read it to himself.

'Well, this is somewhat disappointing, very terse.'

'What does it say?'

'Read it for yourself.'

There was a pause.

'Have we wasted our time, Nick? Gone to all this trouble and danger for nothing?'

'No, no, I don't think that. It means we just have to be patient and wait. It may take several weeks – that's the disappointing part. I am convinced, though, that we have begun a process that *will* eventually see an end to these murders. We must bide our time.'

'He didn't even tell us when this Monsieur Chevalley will be back in Hamburg. That could have been the least he could do after all the trouble we been through.'

'I know. He was just being extra cautious. It seems there has to be caution at every turn. I can understand that. Now we must destroy this document. The maid will be lighting a fire while we're having our supper. I shall burn it then.'

'In the meantime I shall conceal it in my waistcoat. Now for a wash and a scrub up, and then to supper.'

45

Two days later, Tuesday 6th April
The Sheriff of Hull was listening intently, with two aldermen sitting beside him on his right and the Chief Constable and Captain Sanderson on his left. They were in the Sheriff's office in the Town Hall.

M. Chevalley was giving an account of what he had been doing since Thursday last. He had been in York to make further enquiries after his brief stay in Hull. He thought he would make a return visit to the Sheriff before he took his ship back to Hamburg. He didn't add any extra detail about who the murdered men were, he described them merely as *colleagues*.

The Sheriff then proceeded to explain to M. Chevalley who Twygge and Wray were and what they were doing at the present time in Hamburg.

'They may be in the middle of the North Sea at this moment on their way back,' said the Sheriff.

The story of Twygge and Wray came as a great shock to M. Chevalley and he was visibly taken aback. The Sheriff thought it wise not to mention the mysterious piece of paper that started it all.

'I am at a loss for words, gentlemen. May I enquire again whether any of you, including Mr Twygge and Mr Wray, know the *precise* reasons for these murders?'

'I'm afraid not, sir. Mr Twygge told us he had a theory but was not willing to tell us until they had accomplished their mission in Hamburg and discovered whether his theory was correct.'

'So, you have no ideas yourselves at all?'

'No, Monsieur Chevalley, none whatsoever. It is all a mystery to us.'

'This, then, has made my journey all this way rather a waste of time. The only thing that's happened that does not seem to be a part of my enquiries is the death of the two men at that inn. That I cannot account for. They appear to me to be part of a separate crime unrelated to the others.'

'Pardon me, sir,' interrupted Captain Sanderson, 'that is extremely unlikely. Our town is a very law-abiding one, sir. There is little crime and never any murders. It cannot possibly be a coincidence when men have been beheaded in the way they were.'

'Is anything impossible in this life, sir? I believe not.'

'I believe you have been influenced too much by your country being in revolt in recent times – mass murders, assassinations – you have become too sceptical, sir. I can assure you that beheadings like these do not occur in our quiet peaceful country by coincidence.'

'Without evidence we cannot come to any conclusions, Captain. Surely that is logical is it not?'

'Not everything can be accounted for by pure logic, Monsieur Chevalley.'

'Well, perhaps Mr Twygge will be able to enlighten us when they return. Do you know, Sheriff, when that will be?'

'Not exactly, sir, but it will probably be Wednesday or Thursday.'

'That is unfortunate. I must take my ship to Hamburg tomorrow. I would be very grateful if you could write to me as soon as you have all the information from Mr Twygge and Mr Wray. I shall give you an address. Do you have pen and paper, please?'

He proceeded to write down an address – it was not on Deichstrasse.

'I must thank you all for your time and assistance, gentlemen. I regret that I have not discovered much more about the murders of my colleagues. I also regret not being able to talk to Constable Wray and Mr Twygge. But I shall pursue the matter and not stop until I can bring about a definite end to it all. I must leave now, gentlemen. I pray that Mr Twygge and Mr Wray are safe.'

He got up and the others arose to bid him farewell, then he left the Town Hall.

'Well,' said the Sheriff, 'what do you make of that? You do realise don't you that the address that Monsieur Chevalley just gave me is not the same as the one on the piece of paper?'

'That is easy to explain,' said Captain Sanderson, 'the man's a fraud, he's not who he said he is.'

'That's a considerable assumption, Captain, if you don't mind my saying so. He may just be protecting himself. He struck me as being very honest, a gentlemen, and a man of honour.'

'I doubt it, Chief Constable. One cannot trust a Frenchman. It is most likely that he is a spy for the enemy.'

The Sheriff interrupted, 'Does it really matter? There is nothing we can do. As I explained to Monsieur Chevalley this business is beyond us, it is too big for us to be involved in, save for the local issues. All I am concerned about is the safety of Mr Twygge and Constable Wray, and of this town, of course. Now, I have other work to do if you please, gentlemen? Thank you all for attending.'

They others left the room and carried on with their usual daily business.

46

Two days later, Thursday 8th April
The barque *Frederick Louis* didn't reach the New Dock in Hull until late the following Thursday morning. The voyage across the North Sea was slow and it rained continuously. This ship had to sail close-hauled to the wind for most of the way, with the tacks and bowlines bowsed tight for'ards. The passengers were confined to below decks for long periods and boredom crept up on them. By the time they berthed the rain had stopped and the sun was shining. The respite from the endless rainfall and the endless days came as a blessing and brought with it a light-hearted mood among the passengers and crew.

'There's no place on this earth I'd rather be in, Nick,' said Wray as they watched the gang-plank being put into place, 'Isn't it a splendid town?'

'It is, Robert, it is a fine town. So, you're pleased to be back then?'

'You know, there was a time when I thought we'd never see it again.'

'Would it happen to be when we were locked in that cupboard?'

'Well, yes, but before that – as soon as we stepped off the ship at the Niederhafen, that was when I felt fear sweep over me.'

'That was probably because you hadn't put a foot down on alien soil before. I must admit, Robert, that I felt quite the opposite – excited. Anyway, whatever it was it's over and we can disembark with considerable relief.'

Sam had been trying to find out the arrival time so he could meet them at the dock but the agent was unable to. He decided it would be a waste of his own time lingering about the dockside waiting for them so he stayed at home and pursued his geography studies.

There was no-one to greet Twygge and Wray as they got off the ship, just the usual busyness – the noise, the smells, the bustling activity. It always gave Twygge a thrill to be in the dock – all human life was there, it was full of fascination, people of all types, cargoes of all shapes and sizes. He felt that people living in land-locked towns were missing so much of life and he felt sorry for them.

When they reached the Market Place they said their goodbyes and agreed to return to their regular routine and meet at Tom`s Coffee House the next morning. In the afternoon they would go to see the Sheriff to explain everything.

Twygge entered his property by the shop door. The bell tinkled and Henry Crosswell looked up from serving a customer.

'Welcome back, Mr Twygge, how pleased I am to see you safe and sound.'

'Good day, Henry, how pleased I am to *be* back. How has the business been since I've been away?'

There was no-one else in the shop at that moment apart from the one customer, it being dinner-time.

'Very well, Mr Twygge.'

'Nothing untoward has happened then?'

'No indeed, everything has been just as it always is. However, there has been a rumour that there's been a Frenchman in the town but that is all.'

'Really, Henry, that is unusual these days. I presume you mean a Frenchman of some importance?'

'It seems so, yes.'

'Well, I mustn't delay you any longer, this gentleman will be getting impatient.'

'Not all, Mr Twygge,' the man replied, 'I too am pleased to see you back. There were many people who thought you probably wouldn't be back, except in a coffin. You've become the talk-of-the-town.'

'*Oh dear*, thought Twygge.

'Well, here I am all in one piece, alive and safe, and so is Constable Wray. Please excuse me, gentlemen, I must go up to see Mrs Field and Sam.'

I expect they'll be having their dinners at the moment, I'm sure you're ready for yours.'

'I am indeed, Henry. Good day, gentlemen.'

He went through the door to his office then into the passageway, climbed the stairs to the apartments and entered the parlour. He heard voices coming from the dining-room. He crept as quietly as he could towards the door then entered abruptly.

'Good day to you both.'

Mrs Field and Sam, startled, jumped in their seats.

'Oh, Mr Twygge, you made me nearly knock over my dish. I'm all of a shiver.'

'I'm sorry, Hannah.'

He put his bag down, went to the table and gave her a kiss on the cheek.

'Now is that better? You both look well, *and* well-fed. And how are you, Sam?'

'Very well indeed, sir, and all the better for seeing you back safe. Has Mr Wray arrived safely as well.'

'Yes, he has. Now, is there any of that delicious food left, I'm famished?'

'There is, the stew's in that tureen on the side. I'll get another dish for you.'

'No, no, Hannah, I shall get one, you stay where you are and finish your dinner. Then I shall tell you all about our adventure.'

After they'd all finished their dinner Twygge told them everything, barring names. Mrs Field repeated her belief that they had been extremely foolish to go in the first place, but Sam was thrilled and envious of them.

'Now we must just wait patiently. I have been promised a letter that will explain what has been happening in Hamburg but it'll be some weeks before it arrives. In the meantime we must hope that there are going to be no more murders. This afternoon Constable Wray and I must visit the Sheriff and tell him the whole story. But please, Hannah and Sam, you must not say a word of what I've been telling you to anyone. I know I can trust you to do that.'

'Of course,' said Sam.

'Now we can leave all that behind for now and get on with our normal lives. We also have a wedding to think about! The first banns are going to be read this coming Sunday.'

'Yes they are, Nicholas, and I nearly thought of cancelling everything – I didn't think you would return.'

Twygge noticed the sparkle of a tear in her eyes.

'Oh, Hannah, I had no idea that you were going to be so upset. I *am* sorry. Please forgive me and accept my apologies. I didn't really think...'

'I know, I know, Nicholas, but you're back now and that's all that matters. I don't know – you men, what shall we do with you?'

Twygge went over to her, move a chair up and put an arm around her.

Later in the day when the house had regained its former equilibrium and Hannah and Sam had learned everything about Twygge and Wray's exploits, and Twygge had heard what had been happening in Hull while they were away, which was of very little interest, the three of them were sitting by the fire in the parlour. Supper was over and the evening had reached that time when all was peaceful, cosy and warm.

'How have your studies been since I left, Sam?'

'Very well, sir, although I must admit I did steal some of my morning time reading *Caleb Williams* – I wanted to get to the end. I hope you don't mind?'

'Not at all, Sam, it is time well spent. And Hannah, has Sam been keeping you entertained in the evenings?'

'He has, Nicholas, he has been very attentive and read to me while I sewed.'

'I am pleased to hear it. Now tell me, Sam, what are your opinions about *Caleb Williams*?'

'It was very exciting – the imprisonments, the escapes and then the pursuits. But on top of that I was angry inside at all the injustices he had to suffer. Let me get the book and show you.'

He went over to the side-table where several books lay. He sat down and flicked through some pages.

'Take this, for example,' he started to read aloud, '*Strange, that men from age to age should consent to hold their lives at the breath of another, merely that each in his turn may have the power of acting the tyrant according to law!*' And there are many more such sentiments. Mr Godwin has shown me a world the way it is. He's brought to the light so much of what is wrong in this life.'

'That is precisely what I had hoped this book would teach you, Sam. I'm very pleased that you've benefitted from it, and also enjoyed reading it of course.'

'Yes. It does seem to be a contradiction though that one can read a book so full of injustices that it makes you angry yet enjoy it at the same time. I suppose it's the excitement and the need to know how it ends that makes keeps one enthralled. But it has made me think that I would like to change everything. I want to be in charge, I want to put everything right so there'll be no misery and suffering, whatever the cause.'

'Those are worthy sentiments, Sam, and it pleases me that the book affected you in that way. But, *putting everything right*, as you say is the hardest thing on this earth to attempt. Politicians and preachers have been trying it for centuries, as history shows us, but it is good that you recognise these things. Don't become too obsessed though – just behave in everyday life with these thoughts at the back of your mind – that's the best we can hope to do.'

Hannah had been sitting very quietly in the background as it were, sewing away and listening to the two men. *'Yes,'* she thought, *'Sam is a man now. But what is it about men,'* she pondered, *'that they're always talking about wanting to change the world? I don't know, perhaps that is the problem – men always want to do instead of just getting on with it. Still, these are two good men and I'm fortunate to have them. If only they would leave things alone...if only!'*

47

Five weeks later, Wednesday 12th May

It wasn't until the second week in May that Twygge received a reply to the letter he'd written in Hamburg to M. Chevalley. The letter came as a package firmly wrapped and sealed but the opportunity to open it didn't arrive until the late afternoon of 12th May when he returned home from a meeting.

During the previous two weeks the Twygge household had undergone a sea-change – Hannah had become Mrs Twygge and moved into Nicholas's bedroom. Nicholas had persuaded Sam to stop calling him *Sir* and use *Nicholas* instead. Sam found this very difficult at first but was slowly becoming inured to the idea. Twygge didn't feel it was now necessary for Sam to call Hannah *Mrs Field* so it was agreed that he call her Hannah. Hannah herself seemed to become a new woman. She sang to herself more in the kitchen, she joined in more conversations, and she seemed to exude more of a sparkle. Nicholas too was more jolly, if that were possible. The only thing to mar this domestic bliss was another murder and beheading. It occurred a week after the wedding when the 3 o'clock Mail Coach to York had been held up between the villages of Woodmansey and Beverley. It was broad daylight and the driver had to bring his coach to a halt when he'd seen an obstruction in the road ahead of him. It was an upturned waggon *across* the road leaving no room to get around. The guard was shot from behind as the coach slowed down. A man was abducted by two masked men on horses, and then they rode off at speed down a lane eastwards with the victim sitting behind one the kidnappers. The remaining men on the coach were then employed to shift the waggon to the side. The coach reached Beverley seven minutes late and was delayed even more by having to report the hold-up. The naked headless body was discovered the following day trapped in a reed-bed in the River Hull near the village of Wawne. It was brought to the garrison in Hull, much to the chagrin of Captain Sanderson. It was agreed that this was the only suitable place, being sufficiently removed from the town and secure from prying eyes. This came as no great surprise to Twygge, he knew that Chevalley could not have stopped everything in such a short time.

The usual group had been called to inspect the body: the Captain of course, Twygge and Wray, Mr Melling the surgeon, the Chief Constable and the Sheriff. The Captain began to describe the body:

'As you see, gentlemen, the murderers have become wise and left this body with no personal items, not even a ring on a finger. However, the beheading itself has quite clearly been executed by the same means as all the others.'

'*Beheading and execute! Does the Captain recognise his pun?*' wondered Twygge.

'If you look carefully you can see the lines where the garrotte has been and the flesh of the neck has been cut with a sharp instrument, a sword of course.' The Captain had assumed the air of an expert on these matters, 'And also, you must observe, the usual cut on the wrist there. This tells me one thing, gentlemen, that beyond all doubt the original murderers are still at large and those other two men who were found strangled at the White Hart Tavern were not responsible. There you have it.'

'*Indeed,*' thought Twygge, '*there we have it, have we?*'

'How can you be so sure, Captain,' put in the Sheriff, 'when the *modus operandi* may have been prescribed by the leaders of this, er,... whatever it is? The murderers may well have been instructed in detail how to perform this, er,...this bloody butchering. Is that not a possibility?'

'I agree with the Sheriff,' said the Chief, 'all of the events connected to all the four beheadings, and the two stranglings, must be related. They must all be parts of a much bigger saga.'

'I do believe,' added Twygge, 'that the Sheriff and the Chief constable are correct in their assumptions. My theory supports that.'

'Your theory, Mr Twygge, your theory? We've heard a lot about your theory but we never have had the good fortune to hear what it is. When will you deign to offer it to us – *after* more murders have been committed?'

There was no letting down of the Captain's gall. Twygge was baffled: what had he done? What had he said to warrant such bitterness? Will he ever know the reason?

'I apologise, gentlemen, for the delay,' said Twygge, 'It is only a matter of time now before I receive a communication from Hamburg. When I do you will all be informed immediately. And I feel certain all will become clear and the murders *will* stop once and for all.'

There was not much more to be said. There was nothing anyone could do except bury this naked headless body and wait... perhaps for another murder? The frustration felt by all the men was apparent in their demeanours, caused mainly by their impuissance, the utter inability to do anything. If there were going to be another murder no-one could prepare for it, no-one could know where it would happen. How could they explain to the justices, what could they tell the people, the newspapers? The only source of relief they could offer to alleviate their concern and the fears of the people was to emphasise that not one of the men murdered was of this town, nor was it in any way to do with this town other than by unfortunate coincidence. They could attempt to be Job's Comforters and just hope that it would prevent any unnecessary anxieties.

Twygge left the garrison on his own, leaving Wray and the Chief talking with the Sheriff. He came away with a feeling of emptiness and a sense of failure. He realised that it was not logical to feel that way because he bore no blame for anything, but it was the Captain's outburst that offended his sensibilities – by implication in figuratively pointing an accusative finger at him and virtually accusing him of incompetence. He'd lost his appetite for his supper.

The package from Chevalley was waiting for him when he arrived back at his house. Mr Crosswell handed it to him as he came into the shop just before it was due to close for the day. He saw several postmarks on it, one of them, Hamburg, was quite distinct.

'You look morose, Mr Twygge, is anything the matter?'

'No, no, Henry, I've just had an unpleasant encounter, 'tis nothing. Thank you for the mail. I shall go straight upstairs with it and leave you to close up.'

'Very well, Mr Twygge. I shall say good evening to you then.'

'Have a good evening yourself, Henry.'

He went through the door to his office and up the stairs to the parlour. There was no-one there so he went through to the dining-room, then into the kitchen.

'Hannah, my dear, I've returned. Where's Sam?'

'He must still be in the workshop. Is anything wrong? You're very glum.'

'No, Hannah, just a very serious visit to the garrison this afternoon. I shall soon be back to my normal self.'

'Please do, Nicholas, I don't want any dark clouds hanging over us during dinner. It's nearly ready.'

Twygge began to feel better already. Hannah was a balm that soothed all ills.

'I shall go and get Sam and we'll take our seats at the table for supper immediately, my Mistress.'

He wanted to open the package there and then but he knew it would have to wait so he left it in his coat pocket for later. He was uncomfortable concealing it, he didn't like any type of deception. But these were exceptional circumstances and he had to read it in the privacy of his office.

He went back down the stairs to fetch Sam from the workshop. Within ten minutes they were sitting down in the dining-room to a supper of potted venison and pickles, with fresh bread.

48

The same evening, Wednesday 12th May
It was with considerable apprehension that Twygge took the package out of his pocket and broke the seals. He opened up the bundle of papers. There were six sheets altogether with a strong outer sheet that was blank apart from Twygge's name and address. He opened them all out, flattened them with his hands and started to read.

It wasn't long before he realised that M. Chevalley's written English was inferior to his spoken. Nevertheless he was able to distil the essence. Firstly, he explained at some length his position regarding the French Revolution. Then he went on to try to explain the role that M. Boillot was playing as the prime controller of the network, equally at considerable length. By the time Twygge had got to the fourth page he realised that his theory had been almost correct all the way along, apart from knowing exactly who was who and which parts they were playing until they'd been to Hamburg. This made him pleased with himself. Twygge was not a conceited or vindictive man by any means, but... he would take great pleasure in relating the contents of this letter to the others, particularly in the presence of Captain James Sanderson! The remaining two pages of the letter described the way in which Chevalley had set about to bring an end to it all. He expressed his confidence that they were achieving that and that it would be concluded in a short time. The process of finishing off had begun several weeks before Twygge and Wray had gone to Hamburg, and involved Chevalley's trip to Koblenz. But there was, in the closing paragraph, something that Chevalley had written that had given Twygge a jolt just as he was believing that the murders were over – they were not going to stop immediately after all! One man, a Vicomte de Brassen, had left Hamburg for Hull via London before Chevalley had been able to organise the rounding-up of Boillot's ring and, therefore, before he had had time to stop the Vicomte and warn him and offer protection. The Vicomte would be travelling by coach from London to Hull and would be in great danger, either in London or Hull. This meant that Twygge would not be able to reveal to the Sheriff and the others immediately what was in the letter except for the imminent arrival of the Vicomte. He would inform the Sheriff tomorrow. They would have to wait for further developments and these could well take several days.

He refolded the letter and put it in his desk drawer and locked it. It was not that he didn't trust the people around him but more to prevent it being stolen in case of a break-in. There were dangerous men out there, and desperate now they were being hunted down. He went up to the parlour where Sam was sitting reading. Hannah was still in the kitchen clearing up. Sam looked up as Twygge walked in.

'You look unhappy, what's the matter?'

'Oh, nothing much, Sam.' Once again he felt a twinge of guilt at having to tell a white lie. 'Just the usual business. I shall have to tell you – it'll be all around the town in no time. The newspapers and the tattlers will be out in force once the word gets out.'

'Not another murder?'

'I'm afraid so, Sam, yes. Monday afternoon's Mail Coach was held up and a man was abducted, killed and beheaded, just like the others.'

'Where did this happen?'

'Between here and Beverley, somewhere near Woodmansey. Let's not talk about in case Hannah comes in. I don't want to spoil the evening.'

'Of course not, sir.'

'Samuel, I have not been knighted – *yet*! Remember?'

'I am sorry, sir,... whoops... Nicholas! I really do find it difficult to say that, it makes me feel impertinent.'

'You'll get over that, Sam. Remember to us and the world you are a man. Now, what are you reading?'

'Well, it was my literature session this morning and I'm studying Andrew Marvell's life and works at the moment.'

'Ah, yes, our very own Andrew Marvell. I believe he *was* a marvel, even praised by the great Milton, *and vice versa*.'

'I know, sir, I have...'

'Samuel!'

Sam blushed as he felt like a fool.

'*Nicholas*, yes. I have Marvell's lines here at the beginning of this book.'

'Read them to me.'

Sam turned the pages back to the front and read:

'When I behold the Poet blind, yet bold,
In slender Book his vast Design unfold,...'

When Sam had finished reading the poem Twygge was very moved by Marvell's words and by Sam's faultless reading as well. What also moved him was the fact that Andrew Marvell had been a close friend of the greatest poet in the land, and who was also a man who lived in this town and attended the Grammar School, not five minutes walk from where they were sitting.

'Very well read indeed, Sam. You have a talent that not many people have – the ability to read and bring out the meaning and the beauty of the verse with feeling, almost as if Marvell himself were addressing Milton in person. I couldn't have done it so well myself.'

'Thank you, Nicholas, that is praise indeed.'

'Now, Sam, it has been a difficult day for me, although your reading has made me feel much better. I shall now repair to my bed and leave you and Hannah to entertain yourselves. I bid you good night.'

'Good night, Nicholas.'
Twygge departed and went upstairs.

49

The following week, Tuesday 18th May
The Sachs family were surprised by a letter from Moritz Lewin that arrived in the afternoon. Moritz would be travelling to Hull and would arrive sometime towards the end of May. He was leaving Chodziesen on the 9th May and didn't know how long his journey was going to take. So when the letter arrived he had already been travelling for nine days. He didn't say how he was travelling so the family had no idea when he would be arriving.

'We shall have to wait and see. It could be a few days, *az Got vil*, or much longer.'

The family had gathered in the parlour. The letter was brief and little more was in it apart from some affectionate regards directed at the family and to Rachel in particular. Her father watched her face take on a shocked expression.

'What's the matter, my Rhokele, are you not pleased? I thought this news would make you happy. It is the Eve of Shavuos – a good omen don't you think?'

'I am pleased, tatte, just surprised it is so soon.' She made an effort to smile but it did not convince her father.

'I know it is a surprise, my darling,' said her mother as she put an arm around her, 'you weren't expecting him this month, none of us were. But when the surprise wears off she will be happy, won't you?'

'Of course she will, Rivke, you'll see.'

'We have the room nearly ready for him and we can have you both married in no time.'

'Yes, mamme, that is good,' said Rachel, but there was no joy in her voice. Her father and mother knew that the surprise would be slow to melt away. Her mother knew what it was like for a young girl facing marriage – the anxiety and apprehension when the two didn't know each other. Once Moritz had arrived the ice would be broken they would soon get to know each other. Rachel was resigned to the inevitable.

The Vicomte de Brassen was a passenger on the same Mail Coach that brought the letter from Moritz to the Barton Ferry for transport across the river to Hull.

For five days excisemen, militia and constables had been deployed to watch all coach and ferry arrivals. All the main hotels had been asked to keep a watch out for any man who had the likely appearance of being the Vicomte de Brassen, to take down details and immediately inform one of the officials. All this was a very time- and manpower-consuming strategy but it was believed to be the only way to save the Vicomte, *and*, hopefully, apprehend the potential killers.

As the day was coming to a close and no further ferries or coaches were due the Chief Constable had received no messages regarding the arrival of anyone who could be the Vicomte.

50

The following day, Wednesday 19th May
The ferry from Barton had plied through dismal rain, louring clouds and wind. The sharp coldness of the rain drops were pecking at the passengers' faces. It was not typical weather for this time of year and people were bundled up as though winter had returned and come back to taunt them.

The ferry moored at the South End at about 3 o'clock. Several people were waiting at the pier. Some were excise or militia and appeared to be in a sad state, standing there in little pools of rain, saturated and cold. The passengers began to disembark. One or two were stopped and questioned as they left the gang-plank and their details were noted down. A tall man dressed in a black coat and wearing a black hat, looking bedraggled, and carrying a large bag in his right hand and a Bible in his left came down the gang-plank and started to walk towards the centre of the town. He had the air of a member of the clergy. He was not stopped and questioned by anyone. He was aiming for the Trinity Church whose tower he had spotted from the ferry as they approached the pier. When he reached the end of Queen Street the church came straight into his view. He turned left, partly to avoid the rain that was throwing itself at him with full force from the north. He hadn't gone far when he saw the Coach and Horses. He looked it over and decided it would suit his purposes for one night. When he entered the inn Wray's desk-clerk stood up.

'Good day, sir, may I help you?'
'Good day, Monsieur. I wish to have a room for the night.'
The clerk sat down and picked up his quill.
'Certainly, sir. Your name please?'
'Yes, my name if Pfarrer Schmidt.'

The clerk entered the name *Farrier Shmit* – although he looked less like a person who would look after horses than the clerk himself.

'And you are from, sir?'

'Er,' there was a distinct hesitation, 'London.'

'I see.' The clerk wrote it down. 'You live there do you, sir?'

'Yes, it is my home now. May I have the key now?'

'Yes, sir. I have given you Room 7, on the first floor. How long will you be staying for, sir?'

'One night only.'

The clerk handed him the key.

'Thank you, sir. The room will be four shillings and sixpence. You may pay when you leave in the morning. Would you like dinner later, sir?'

'Yes, I think I will have dinner, in my room if that is possible?'

'We can arrange that for you, sir. I will show you to your room. Let me carry your bag. I will send someone to make up the fire for you to dry your clothes. We don't normally need a fire at this time of year of course.'

'Oh, one more thing. Where can I buy a ticket for the coach?'

'When you are dried out and settled in I shall send you a boy who will take you to the ticket agent, Mr Pybus on Silver Street.'

'Thank you.'

As soon as the clerk returned downstairs he picked up the hotel register and knocked on the door of Robert Wray's office.

'Come in.'

'Mr Wray, I believe we may have someone you might be interested in. He's just arrived. I put him in Room 7. Have a look as the register.'

'*Farrier Shmit*! Well, James, that is interesting. We shall have to learn a little bit more about him. So, he's from London?'

'So he said. Another thing, Mr Wray, he called me *Monsieur* when he first came in. I know that is French but his name looks German to me.'

'It is, James. But *Farrier* doesn't sound like man's name, and I doubt he is a farrier – he wouldn't be staying here, would he? Are you sure you spelt it correctly?'

'Well, sir, that's what it sounded like.'

'Well done, James, I think you may well have spotted someone important here. I shall leave my desk for a while. I'll be back as soon as I can. If Mr Shmit happens to leave before I get back get Francis to follow him.'

'Oh, that reminds me, Mr Shmit wanted to know where he could buy a ticket for a coach.'

'Did he say to where?'

'No, but I was going to send Francis with him anyway to show him the way to Mr Pybus' s office.'

'Splendid, James. Just one thing, do be *very* careful about how you go about things – just act naturally and don't do anything that would arouse Herr Shmit's suspicions.'

'Certainly not, Mr Wray.'

When Wray entered Twygge's shop the first person he saw was Sam Parker.

'Good afternoon, Sam, can I see Mr Twygge, it's important?'

'Yes, Mr Wray, he's in his office. You know the way.'

He found Wray bowed over his desk scratching away with his pen.

'Good afternoon, Robert, this is an unexpected visit. What brings you here?'

'I believe we have someone at the Coach and Horses who's just arrived who we may be interested in. He calls himself *Farrier Shmit*, according to James, my desk clerk.'

'Yes, I know James.'

'He's staying in Room 7, just for one night apparently. He told James he wanted to find where he could by a coach ticket.'

'Where to?'

'We don't know yet. One of my boys will take him to Mr Pybus when he's ready. Then we'll find out.'

'Did you happen to see this man?'

'No, I was working in my office when he arrived.'

'Well, I think we should go to your place immediately, Robert. I shall get my coat. Has it stopped raining?'

'Just about. I think we should inform the Chief. So I'll go to see him now and you can go straight to the inn and we'll join you there.'

'Don't you think we should find out more about this man before we go to see the Chief? He may be quite innocent.'

'I should let him know what we're doing, Nick. Many people are involved now. We can't just take on everything on our own any more.'

'We did in Hamburg, Robert, and they all knew what we were doing then. I just prefer to deal with things myself first, you know that. I can think more clearly, I can ask any questions I think appropriate without asking a committee first. Other people just keep butting in and generally get in the way. *The more cooks the worse the potage*, is that not so?'

'Well, on your head be it. We'd better be off.'

When they arrived at the Coach and Horses Mr Shmit had not yet left his room. Wray went into his office and Twygge took a seat against the wall opposite the clerk's desk and waited.

It was a good half hour before Twygge saw a man dressed all in black come down the stairs. The desk clerk gave Twygge a surreptitious nod. As the man approached the desk Twygge spotted the Bible he was carrying.

'Ah, Mr Shmit, you have dried off I see. How is your room?'

'It will do. Now, I wish to buy a ticket for the coach.'

'Oh, yes, of course. My boy is not available to take you but this gentleman will, he's a friend of the innkeeper, Mr Wray. He's going himself to buy tickets as well.'

'Good evening, sir. I am Nicholas Twygge. Pleased to be of service. It is only five minutes walk to the agent's and he'll be closing soon. The rain has stopped now.'

Schmidt hesitated. It was obvious to Twygge that he was not comfortable.

'I see you carry a Bible, Herr Schmidt. That is one reason I need to buy coach tickets. I'm a bookseller and I need to go to York to restock my Bible supply, also to visit a good friend who is also a bookseller who sells only religious volumes. Are you a clergyman, Herr Schmidt?' Twygge was trying his best to make the man feel at ease and win his confidence.

'Yes, I am a priest. Shall we go now?'

They left the inn, turned right into Myton Gate towards the Market Place.

'You will see our modest church soon, Father, the Holy Trinity. It is just around the corner. That is the Church of England, of course, but we also have various dissenting chapels. We even have a small Catholic congregation. Perhaps you would like to visit it? You *are* a Catholic, I presume?'

'Why do you say that?'

'I beg your pardon, Father, it was very presumptuous of me. I thought being from the Continent...'

'No, sir, I am a Lutheran, and please don't address me as *Father*.'

'Ah, a follower of Mr Luther, yes. I have heard a little, but tell me about it.'

'I believe it is not unlike your Protestant beliefs.'

'I don't know whether you know but our country would be now entirely Catholic had it not been for our King Henry VIII. I think I would find that very difficult to live with. Many of us, like yourself, find Papism not to our taste.'

'I do not know, sir. It has a lot to be said for it. It has brought whole nations together into one faith. It has happened in France.'

'France may be unifying its religion, but at what cost? The country is in turmoil.'

'I agree it is in turmoil. It will never be the same again.'

Twygge thought he could detect a note of sadness.

'Should there not be room for people to believe in and practice whatever they wish, if it does no harm to others?'

'You are a liberal, sir, that is not good. Liberals bring disorder and discontent. We must have order. There is no order in France, she is, as you say, in turmoil.'

The man was distinctly becoming annoyed. He had revealed enough to allow Twygge to take the plunge into deep seething waters.

'Monsieur le Vicomte, do not be alarmed, we are your friends. We were warned of your arrival and we 're here to protect you.. You will be safe.'

The Vicomte said nothing for several seconds. His face darkened, he looked around, he clearly was afraid for his life.

'I, er,... what it this? I don't understand. I am a priest from Germany. I...'

'Monsieur, we have constables, militia, and many people who are ready in Hull to protect you. I have been to Hamburg. We have met with Monsieur Chevalley and we are helping each other. That is the truth, sir.'

The Vicomte seemed to relax a little as they approached Silver Street. The rain clouds were beginning to disperse and hints of blue sky were promising a brighter end to the day.

'We have had three of your compatriots murdered hereabouts in the last six months. We had to do something about it. We have had to go to great pains to discover what has been happening and now we are prepared to prevent another death, which could have been you, Vicomte.'

'I am, how do you say, astonished. I did know of the danger, that is why I am dressed like this, but I didn't know what that danger was.'

'Yes, sir, but now we are at the ticket agent's. We shall enter and see Mr Pybus.'

They obtained four tickets for the York coach leaving tomorrow. There was not enough room left on the Mail Coach so they had to settle for a slower light coach that left from Mr Moor's on the Land of Green Ginger at 6 o'clock in the morning. Twygge had referred Mr Pybus to the Sheriff who had agreed that three of the fares would be paid out of public funds. Twygge signed a docket to that effect. He also asked Mr Pybus not to mention anything about him and the Vicomte to anyone else. If anyone happened to come in asking questions about either of them he should tell them the truth about the stranger in black but not mention that three other tickets had been sold.

After Twygge and the Vicomte left the office and had just reached the Market Place Twygge spotted two men in sailors' dress walking out of Scale Lane opposite and starting to cross the road. They may have been harmless, there was no way of knowing. He dared not look around, just in case.

Robert Wray was standing behind the front desk as Twygge and the Vicomte entered the inn.

'May we use your office, Robert?'

'Of course. Mr Newton will be back shortly'

'Ah, here is your clerk.'

'James, we shall be in my office for a while. I know you will be finishing soon but would you be so kind as to wait until we've had our meeting? It shouldn't take long.'

'Certainly, Mr Wray.'

The three men sat down in Wray's office.

'Would you gentlemen care for some sherry sack? I keep it for special guests.'

Wray assumed that by now that Twygge had determined that the new guest in black was indeed the Vicomte de Brassen.

'That would be splendid. I'm sure the Vicomte would welcome some sack after his long and rather soggy journey. Vicomte?'

'Yes, I would.'

'Mr Wray, may I introduce you formally to the Vicomte de Brassen. Vicomte, this is the landlord of this inn and also Constable of this town, Robert Wray.'

'If you are who you say you are, Messieurs, and I am beginning to believe you are, then I shall be happy to drink with you.'

Wray poured the drinks.

'Did you get the tickets?' he asked.

'Yes, the light coach that leaves at six in the morning.'

'Excellent.'

'Now, may I offer a toast?' said Twygge, 'To the Vicomte and to wishing him a safe journey to his final destination, wherever that may be.'

'To the Vicomte!'

'Now, Robert, I believe there are two matters to deal with that are urgent. Firstly, we must inform the Chief Constable and the Sheriff as soon as possible. Secondly, we must move the Vicomte from Room 7 to another room and do it without others seeing us – is that possible?'

'I believe so. There is a room at the top next to mine.'

'It seems quiet at the moment, we should do it straight away. But don't, please, tell anyone, Robert, not even your staff. Just tell them not to put anyone in that room.

'If you think that's necessary then certainly, Nick.'

'I am reluctant to let you leave the inn, Robert, so would you stay whilst I go to see the Chief?'

'I'm usually at the front desk after James goes home anyway. Would you want me to ask him to stay longer until we've finished the moving?'

'Yes, I think so. We had better start as soon as our glasses are empty. I shall try to arrange for the Chief and the Sheriff to come here – the Vicomte needs careful guarding.'

There was a knock on the door.

'Who is it?'

The door opened and in walked the Chief Constable. They were taken by surprise.

'Good evening, gentlemen, excuse me for charging in but I have something to tell you. Who is this gentleman?'

'Chief, good evening. Er,... this gentleman is the Vicomte de Brassen.'

'Ah, I understand now. Is he likely to be the next target?'

'There is no doubt about it, sir', said Twygge, 'We were intending to inform you and the Sheriff shortly. What brings you here?'

'I had a visit from a very frightened Mr Pybus not long ago. He told me that two men came into his office asking about coach tickets and who had bought any. When he refused to disclose that information they became violent and threatened him to the point where he had to tell them about you, Mr Twygge, and a stranger, who I now realise must be this gentleman.'

'Oh, dear, well,' said Wray, 'we now know where we stand and what needs to be done. Chief, we were going to go up to my room shortly to plan a means by which we can stop the Vicomte coming to any harm and to arrest and arraign the potential killers.'

'In that case, Constable, I shall leave you in charge and I'll go to see the Sheriff, and you can wait for our return.'

He left the room with haste.

It was not until 7 o'clock that they were all gathered in Wray's room on the top floor of the Coach and Horses and the Vicomte had been moved to the room next door. It wasn't until 9 o'clock that a plan of action had been agreed upon, after some considerable effort on the part of Nicholas in trying to persuade them to accept his scheme.

There would be just four of them on the coach. The Chief, being the nearest in physical size to the Vicomte, would be dressed in a black coat and hat and a muffler to cover most of his face. The Chief and Wray would be armed with pistols. They would meet at Mr Moor's coach terminus on the Land of Green Ginger at a quarter to six the following morning.

After the meeting, at about 10 o'clock, Nicholas returned to his house and told Hannah and Sam that he would be leaving early the next morning for York. He apologised profusely about not being able to tell them why. He also told them that if anyone came to the shop to ask where he was to tell them he was on a business trip to buy some books. Hannah was much disturbed by this news.

'Nicholas, you don't need to tell me why you're going because I know that whatever it is you'll be in jeopardy. Why do you get yourself involved in these things? Why don't you just be what you're supposed to be – the man I married, not just a bookseller but a kind and nice man who everybody loves? Why?'

Nicholas put his arms around his wife.

'This *will* be the last time, Hannah, my dear. I give you my word it will be over by tomorrow. There is little danger so please don't worry about me. I'm not quite sure when we shall be back but we *will* be back, safe and sound. There is no doubt about it.'

He knew that he was really not able to convince Hannah so he changed the subject.

'Sam, what's that you've been reading this evening?'

'Oh, it's Mr Gibbon's *Decline and Fall*, the new abridged version. I couldn't face the whole six volumes.'

'I agree, Sam, neither could I – life's too short. I don't usually go along with the idea of the abridgement of great works but I think this one is justified, unless, that is, you're going to be a classical scholar and historian. I doubt very much if that is what you want to be.'

Hannah left the room not saying another word and not at all happy. She doubted whether she would be able to sleep that night.

At the same time that the Twygge household was temporarily losing its equanimity, two sailors rode their horses into the yard of the King's Head, Market Weighton, at nigh on a quarter past ten. They realised that trying to find the man dressed in black in Hull was proving too difficult, even after threatening Mr Pybus to the point of his revealing the information about Twygge's tickets. So they hired horses to conclude their work in a secluded spot on the road to York the next day.

51

Early the next morning, Thursday 20th May
No attempt had been made during the night by anyone to get into Room 7 or any other room at the Coach and Horses. It was cold for a late May morning, with a brisk wind blowing from the northeast, scudding the scattered clouds overhead towards Lincolnshire:
> *But winter ling'ring chills the lap of May.*

Nicholas Twygge was nervous, more nervous than when he'd confronted M. Boillot in Hamburg and been locked in a closet. He bore an aura of seriousness that was unusual for him as he walked along, looking at the ground, saying little, on their way to the Land of Green Ginger. It was busy for such an early hour, even though it wasn't a market day. As they approached the Holy Trinity Church he looked up and thought to himself:

'*What is a church? - Our honest sexton tells, 'Tis a tall building, with a tower and bells.*'

Twygge was attempting to ease his tenseness by conjuring up lines of verse of a humorous nature, however inappropriate they may have seemed to Wray had he spoken them aloud. The Vicomte, appearing somewhat uncomfortable in the Chief's clothes, did not say a word all the way to the coach. Wray, on the other hand, was humming some unrecognisable strings of notes, looking totally at ease. Twygge thought this was not like him at all, he must be concealing his anxiety. The most incongruous figure of all was the Chief Constable dressed in a black cloak. He was standing in John Moor's yard as they arrived.

'Good morning, gentlemen,' said the Chief, 'I hope you're well prepared.'

'As prepared as we ever shall be, Chief Constable.'

'Pistols loaded?'

'Yes, sir.'

'Mr Twygge, you do not look as though you wish to be here? You may change your mind if you wish. You do not need to come.'

'No, no, Chief, I am well. It's the early hour and the cold wind that have cooled my ardour. One doesn't expect it to be this cold in May. I shall be all right,' he said with feigned cheerfulness, *'I am afeard there are few die well that die in a battle...'* he thought.

The Chief Constable had taken the Vicomte aside and was talking to him in a low voice which Twygge couldn't hear, then they returned to the group. The Chief gathered them close together and spoke.

'The coach-driver is armed and I've also given the Vicomte a pistol. Constable Wray and I have two each, so now the odds will be six bullets against our six, assuming there will be two of them, which is likely. If they carry single-barrelled pistols then it'll be six against four. Even so, when you shoot make sure you're going to hit your targets. Now, let us be away.'

The men then got onto the coach. The Chief and Wray sat inside facing the front, Wray on the left, and Twygge and the Vicomte sat facing them. Twygge was perking up after hearing about the weapons.

The black and yellow coach left the Land of Green Ginger promptly at 6 o'clock. There was no time for any of the four passengers to rest. Full diligence was necessary for every mile of the thirty nine miles to York – the hold-up could occur anywhere along that route. The horses were changed at Market Weighton at about nine-fifty and brief refreshments were taken. The coach resumed its journey at five minutes past ten. It was not long before they reached the toll-booth at Shipton, close by the Black Swan Inn. The terrain by now had levelled out and there would be flat moorland for several more miles. The coach soon passed the hamlet of Thorpe le Street and continued towards Hayton. One or two carts and slow waggons and men on horseback were coming and going in both directions but the road was generally quiet. The men inside the coach had become uncomfortable – continuous concentration and the craning of necks out of the windows every minute of the way had taken their toll. Twygge was becoming lost in an array of thoughts and his discomfort was exacerbated by having to face the rear.

They were about half a mile beyond Hayton as the coach was coming towards a narrow lane cutting across the main road when the Chief and Wray each saw a man on horseback approaching them, one from the left and one from the right. The coach-driver knocked twice behind him on the rear of the coach with his pistol butt.

'There's the signal. Prepare yourselves, gentlemen, cock your pistols, this may well be the time. Keep calm but don't hesitate when the time is ripe, and don't assume that this is them and shoot too soon. To begin with act innocent then we can take them by surprise.'

Twygge didn't have a pistol so there was nothing he could do but keep out of the way, and besides, he and the Vicomte couldn't see anything from their positions because the Chief and Wray were blocking the windows. He turned his legs to the side to keep them well away from the door and tucked his arms in close to his body. To his surprise he was not afraid, in fact, he began to feel a dash of excitement rise within him.

The driver rapped on the coach again. The coach slowed down a little – the driver had been instructed to do so if he thought there was a threat.

'Just stay still and don't say anything,' said the Chief.

Before they reached the crossroads there came a loud and menacing order:

'Stop the coach, driver!'

The Chief and Wray put their heads out of the windows.

'The one on the right is carrying a pistol, he's about thirty yards away and aiming at us,' said the Chief in a loud whisper.

'The same on the left,' said Wray.

'Now, ready everybody. Leave the talking to Constable Wray.'

The coach braked and came to a halt.

'Driver, get up on top and lay flat face down,' yelled the man on the right, 'and don't move.'

Wray put out his head. 'What's going on?'

'Be quiet and stay in the coach!'

The driver stood up and appeared to make a move to climb up onto the top but as he raised his foot, just as the man was yelling at Wray, he swung around and fired at the second man on the left, then leapt down off the coach and rolled underneath, all in a few seconds. The horse of the man who was shot at reared and threw him off, his pistol went off as he hit the ground. Then confusion arose. The coach's horses were disturbed by the ructions. Wray leapt out and aimed his pistol at the man on the ground but he didn't fire – the man was not moving.

The chief leapt out at the same time, just as the other man was moving around to the left. The Chief fired from at him from his side and Wray fired his second pistol from the left and the man dropped down off his horse. The Vicomte got out of the coach, his pistol at the ready and stood there. The sounds of the pistol shots faded away leaving a still and eerie silence.

Ahead of them was a waggon in the road about fifty yards away, stopped, with the driver lying down on the seat.

The Chief walked carefully towards the two men lying on the ground. There was a groan from one of them.

'I think one of them is dead,' he told the others, 'Cover me while I get their pistols. This other one might survive.'

At this point the driver crawled out from under the coach.

'Are you hit, sir?' asked the Chief.

'I don't think so, but I've twisted my ankle.'

'That was very brave of you, what you did, but also very stupid. Nevertheless, it was you and Wray's quick thinking and speedy actions that deserve our gratitude. Well done, both of you.'

Twygge came out of the coach.

'Gentlemen, we need to get these two onto the coach. We'll put the dead one on the top and cover him up. Vicomte, would you mind helping Wray to do that? We'll get the wounded one tied up and inside the coach. Driver, do you think you can take the reins as far as Market Weighton?'

'I'm sure I can manage that, sir.'

'Good. Mr Twygge, would you mind sitting with the driver, there's hardly room for five inside?'

'Yes, Chief, I don't mind at all – pleased to be of some use.'

'Oh, just a minute, leave that dead man for a while.'

He then walked down the road towards the stationary waggon. As he got there the driver was just getting onto it.

'Excuse me, sir, I would like you to do us a favour.'

When they'd introduced themselves and the Chief had explained very briefly what had been going on he walked back to the coach.

'The man with the waggon, Mr Gospel, has agreed to carry the dead man on his waggon for us as far as Market Weighton. Will you help him load when he gets here? As quickly as possible, please, we need to get this other man to a doctor – we don't want him dying before we've thoroughly interrogated him, do we?' He then collected the kidnappers' pistols, put them in a bag and placed it in the coach. With Wray's help they tied him up – his moaning continued.

The Vicomte was almost recovered from the shock of the events when he addressed the Chief:

'Chief Constable, shall I be able to get to York today?'

'I'm afraid not, sir, you must return to Hull with us to act as a witness. You will not have to stay there long, just until you can give the justices and the Sheriff a full account of what happened.'

'I understand.'

'Now, sir, I believe I have no further use for your clothes. Shall we change?'

'Yes, although I hope I shall not need to wear black anymore.'

'I am confident that this is the end, sir. According to our information you are the last one to have left Hamburg without protection. There should be no more deaths, or even attempts.'

Mr Gospel's waggon approached the scene.

'Gentlemen, this is Mr Gospel. Can you tell us what you saw, we may need you as a witness as well?'

'I didn't see anything, sir. As soon as I heard a shot I laid meself down and closed my eyes. I didn't open them again until you came, sir.'

'That's all right then, Mr Gospel. We won't bother with you as a witness. We'll give you a little something for your troubles when we get to Market Weighton.'

'Oh, that's very kind of you, sir.'

'Vicomte, can you find a way to stop this man's bleeding? Would you mind? He doesn't appear to be seriously injured. Coach-driver, you do realise that we cannot take this coach to York now, don't you? We're all going to be needed in Hull.'

'Yes, sir, but will I be compensated for the loss of return passengers?'

'Well, there would have been only room for one. Without this hold-up the Vicomte would get off at York and we three would be returning with you, wouldn't we?'

'Oh, of course, that is correct, sir.'

'We shall see you get the money for one passenger.'

Various chests and sacks were shuffled about on the waggon and the body placed on it safely out of sight.

The coach set off with the waggon on its tail. Progress was slower, hindered by the inability of the single horse pulling the loaded waggon to go any faster.

After two hours at Market Weighton all the necessary reporting had been done and a makeshift coffin containing the dead man had been tied to the top of the coach. The injured man had had his wound dressed. It was such a short range between Wray's gun and the bullet that hit the man – it went straight through his chest near his right shoulder – there was no chance that he would die and avoid a trial. Twygge realised, though, that it was unlikely that this man would hang – there was nobody kidnapped or murdered, and he doubted whether there was any evidence that could connect him to any of the other murders. He wasn't sure what the sentence for an attempted hold-up would be but he doubted it be long enough. At least Twygge would now be looking forward to a return to a normal, if generally uneventful, life. When that occurred to him he was wondering whether that was what he really wanted.

It wasn't until 7 o'clock in the evening that the coach arrived back in Hull.

52

Two days later, Saturday 22nd May

In the mid-afternoon there were gathered together in the Meeting Room in the Town Hall: the Sheriff, all the Justices of the Peace and Aldermen, the Chief Constable, Constable Wray, Captain Sanderson, and Nicholas Twygge.

'Now, gentlemen, you know why we are here but I would like to thank you all for coming to this very important meeting, a meeting of great significance to everybody in this town and its surrounding areas. Constable Wray and Mr Twygge are the two men who have worked the hardest and the longest, and travelled the farthest in the pursuit of a solution to the murders that have been committed since November of last year. They alone know all the answers so I shall ask them shortly to explain it all to you. Constable Wray has requested that Mr Twygge should tell most of it because it was his so-called *theory* that provided a means by which they could proceed and, therefore, he can explain it more thoroughly. Shall we begin? Mr Twygge.'

Twygge stood up.

'Thank you, Sheriff. If I may be so bold – could I possibly remain seated? There is so much to explain and my legs and feet have been exceedingly busy recently that I fear I may become exhausted before I get to the end.'

'I think we could allow that, Mr Twygge. Would you please come over here next to me where you can be more clearly seen and heard? Gentlemen, would you please move down the table one place to make room?'

'Thank you, Sheriff.'

He took up his papers and went over to the big table, sat down, and began to address the gathering.

'I shall try to weave the circumstances of the murders into the larger tapestry of the major events of the French Revolution in order for us to understand clearly what has been happening that has affected us all here today. However, I will have to talk at some length and if, at any time, you have a question or you want something explained in more detail, please do stop me and ask as we go, rather than leave it until the end. Everything that has happened has to do with the French Revolution. All the men who have been murdered were members of the French Aristocracy, saving the two who were murdered at the White Hart Tavern and that was in-fighting and doesn't really concern us at the moment.'

'But please explain that briefly, Mr Twygge,' said one of the Aldermen.

'Yes, sir. There was a very large amount of money to be had, which I shall explain later, and, clearly, you would expect that the greed of others would enter into it at sometime or another. It was simply that two men had discovered what was going on in the transport of the victims through England and had decided that they were going to take over the work, which of course they did.'

'I see. Thank you. And what do you think that piece of paper with the two names and addresses on it was doing on the murdered men?'

'That is not easy to explain, other than as a reminder for them when they got back with the head to Hamburg. But we can't really explain why Monsieur Chevalley's name and address was on it. It is something we could ask Monsieur Chevalley at a later date. Perhaps he was an intended victim himself?'

'I understand. I suppose in such a complex affair as this not everything can be explained fully.'

'Quite so, sir.' Twygge continued with his account. 'The problems in France were the result of the exploitation and ill-treatment of the peasants over centuries. There were many *very* wealthy landowners, mainly members of the aristocracy – dukes, marquises, counts, viscounts, and so on, down to princes. In addition vast areas of land, as much as a fifth of whole of France, were owned by the Church which itself was also extremely wealthy. The rest of the population were peasants, slaves really, who were burdened with enormous taxes, taxes which were not controlled centrally but determined by the whims of the local powers. The worst of the taxes was the *taille*, which could exact from the peasants as much as 53% of their meagre earnings. So you see, gentlemen, it was inevitable that eventually one day there would be stirrings of an uprising against this evil abuse.'

'I do believe, Mr Twygge, that we are all familiar with these events in France. May we get down to the relevant facts?'

'These are relevant facts, Captain Sanderson, and maybe not all of us are so well-informed as yourself. I have no wish to leave anyone in this room in the dark in the matter of detail. The politics involved are not simple and it is too easy to form opinions without adequate information. Even in this country we have eminent people who don't agree – Mr Fox, for example, who speaks out *for* the Revolution, and Mr Burke who is against it. Do they know *all* the facts? One would hope so, but we can't be sure.'

'I agree with Mr Twygge,' said the Sheriff, 'This town has been seriously disturbed by the murders and many of them quite frightened by it all, so we *do* need to understand everything. We need to know because we have to present it to the rest of the town, including the newspapers, and also to York, all the facts. We need as well to convince everyone that it all has now been brought to a final conclusion. So please, Mr Twygge, do continue as you think fit.'

'Thank you, Sheriff.'

Twygge now felt more at ease, having got the full support of the Sheriff. He continued:

'As a consequence of the abuse of the peasants for so long there arose groups who were wanting to do something about it. The first of these was the Jacobin Club. These people were extremely radical and wanted to change the country completely, by violence and death, or by whatever means. A couple of years later a more moderate group was formed, the Girondists, by some members of the French Assembly. Needless to say, you *are* aware of the Reign of Terror in 1793 – that was initiated by the Jacobins. Over the following years thousands upon thousands of people have been carried on the tumbrels to their deaths on the guillotine, during and since the Revolution, many of them being the greedy and tyrannical aristocrats whom the Revolutionaries wanted rid of forever. The worst of them were taken away from their great houses, and their land and property confiscated. There were some who were considered benevolent enough to remain alive, although vast swathes of their lands were given to the peasants. There were some of the aristocrats who were deemed by the extreme Jacobins to be disposable. There were others who were frightened for their lives and made attempts to seek refuge outside France. There were other Frenchmen who had escaped earlier who endeavoured to help as many as they could get across the borders and into safe keeping. You may recall, gentlemen, the nobleman called the Marquis de Sierre who had escaped from France and was passed through Hull in '94. I believe that that was the first attempt to use Hull as an entry point to England. Where he or others went after that we don't know. Anyway, after the Revolution was over a cabal of some remnants of the extreme Jacobins remained, their aim being to get rid of all the remaining aristocratic families. At the same time a network had been formed by a gentlemen you have met, Monsieur Chevalley. That is not his real name though, and what his real name is remains a secret. He has spent two or three years putting together this network. It spreads throughout France and Germany and beyond. Its aim was to give the remaining noblemen a means of escape. Nowhere on the continent is completely safe – the Revolutionaries have spies everywhere, all parts of the Continent have been infiltrated by them. The Jacobin cabal had discovered Monsieur Chevalley's network, infiltrated it and substituted their own men to take over the transport in Hamburg. Monsieur Boillot was the leader of that group and of the whole network. He organised the transport to Hull and employed the Yorkshire men to do the killing.'

'Excuse me, Mr Twygge,' interrupted Alderman Osborne, 'but why were the Frenchmen beheaded, do you know that?'

'Yes indeed, sir, – for 30 pieces of silver! That was one of the puzzles at the beginning in November that got me thinking, *and* the missing buttons and the blue coats, and so on. Monsieur Chevalley informed me that he'd discovered from Boillot's men that 500 Louis d'Ors was being offered for the head of each man that was taken back to Hamburg. The blue coats were worn as a means of identification, and the buttons were used just in case there was more than one man wearing such a coat.'

'How much is 500 Louis d'Ors in Guineas, Mr Twygge?'

'Well, I believe that one Louis d'Or is more or less equivalent to one guinea, Sheriff. So you see, gentlemen, that amount of money would tempt an angel. Of course, this money came from the sale of the purloined property of the rich and the privileged.'

'I'm interested in the routes of travelling from France to England, can you tell us?'

'Only vaguely, sir. The one I know, from Monsieur Chevalley's letter is from the River Mosel, which starts in France where it's called the Moselle. It joins the River Rhine and there they'd change boats and sail downstream to

Cologne. From there they would travel overland to Hamburg. However, these men must travel alone and under assumed names, for their own safety. I was given the name of the Vicomte, who we saved this week, by Monsieur Chevalley because it was assumed he would be safe. They used to travel, before the Revolution, with large retinues for service and protection, but those days are now over.'

He took a breath before he continued.

'Well, gentlemen, that brings me to the end of the story. Do we have any more questions?'

'Before any more discussion I believe we should have some refreshments. Mr Porter, would you mind arranging for us to have some tea brought in?'

'Certainly, Sheriff, and something more solid as well, if we may?' said John Porter, one of the Aldermen.

The Sheriff made a request of Twygge to talk about what they did in Hamburg. Twygge said he would. He then took advantage of the intermission by taking himself off to the toilet. He felt regret that the Captain had been put down by the Sheriff but the inimical nature of his attitude towards him was now irreparable. The others talked among themselves until the refreshments arrived.

After tea and cake, Twygge continued.

'Gentlemen, I have been asked to relate to you what Constable Wray and I did in Hamburg. I shall keep it as brief as possible, and, again, please ask questions. When we'd arrived and found ourselves somewhere to stay we decided to visit Monsieur Boillot, the first name on that famous piece of paper. That proved quite threatening...'

Twygge continued until he'd reached the point where they boarded the *Frederick Louis* for the return journey.

'I have a question,' said the Chief, 'Can you explain to me, Mr Twygge, why it is that these men were murdered in

England and not nearer to their homeland? It seems to me it would have saved them, and us, a lot of time and effort.'

'A very good question, Chief Constable. It did occur to me too so I put the question to Monsieur Chevalley. He explained that by having these men murdered *en route*, as it were, well away from home, their identities would not be known once they'd left France and their network more difficult to discover. This caused Monsieur Chevalley serious difficulties – he lost contact with the links in his network and the men who were in Boillot's way were disposed of. It took Monsieur Chevalley several months to make any progress in stopping Boillot. In fact, without boasting, it was Constable Wray and I who led him directly to Boillot. The whole problem was solved by that famous, (or infamous?), piece of paper found near the dead men at the White Hart Tavern on that terrible night. It has saved many lives.'

'Well, I'm sure,' said the Sheriff, 'that there are many, many people, on both sides of the North Sea, who are grateful to you both, Mr Twygge, for having achieved so much. It is highly commendable. Well, gentlemen, I believe it is now time to close the meeting. As I said earlier we are all extremely grateful for the splendid work done by Mr Twygge and Constable Wray and I believe that now all they want to do is go home and have a long rest – there will be no more murders for them to think about, no more mysteries for them to solve. There is a lot to be said for a simple life and now the whole town can go back to just that. I believe the two men who were caught will get the condign punishment they deserve after the trial at York and be hanged.'

'I do beg your pardon, Sheriff, but I doubt that,' interrupted Twygge, 'because they didn't murder anyone. Nobody can prove they were involved in any of the other murders. I am sorry to say they will only be charged with attempted abduction. I don't know the precise punishment for that but I doubt they will hang, and none of the other murderers have ever been caught.'

'Well, we shall let the courts decide and wait and see. Thank you all for sitting here patiently, but I'm sure you have all found it very interesting, and enlightening as well. Thank you in particular, Constable Wray and you Mr Twygge. I bid you good day, gentlemen.'

53

The following week, Saturday 29th May

At the Twygge's house equanimity had returned. They were all settled into their usual routines once again. Hannah had forgiven Nicholas his schoolboy antics and, in fact, she had forgotten them by the end of the week. After the meeting held in the Town Hall the previous week the town officials had decided to send the injured criminal to York for trial. Sam was disappointed that he had been left out of the recent Vicomte affair, but he *was* happy because during the week he had come across Rachel in the Market – it had been such a long time since they last met. They had a long talk. As they talked it became clear to Sam that Rachel was glad to see him. Her eyes were bright and smiling, and she was standing quite close to him, closer than he would have expected. He was also a little uneasy – after what he'd promised Herr Sachs should he be talking to her? She didn't mention her future husband and he didn't ask. The memory of their encounter would remain vivid and linger in his mind for months to come.

Robert Wray had been invited to supper at Twygge's home and the four of them were seated at the dining-table. In the middle of the table, instead of the usual cold meats, sat a steaming dish. Hannah had just brought it in, sat down and taken off the lid.

'There you are, gentlemen, this will warm your cockles.'

'It may be the end of May, my dear, and such a fine warm day it has been, but I do believe our cockles *are* in need of warming, are they not, Robert, with what we've been through recently?'

'Indeed, that is true, Mrs Twygge.'

'Please call me Hannah, Constable, we've known each other long enough now.'

'Yes we have, Hannah. Please call me Robert. The hours we've had to sit and wait and repeat things over and over again in that courtroom – such a waste of time, And now they're sending him to York.'

'Well, 'tis over now, Robert. We can celebrate and offer a toast to ourselves for our accomplishments. Are you not proud of what we have achieved?'

'Of course, Nick. Now, Hannah, do I detect the odour of a stew with sausages and red cabbage there?'

After the meal, fully fed and watered, all four of them repaired to the parlour and settled down to enjoy a glass of port wine brought for them by Robert Wray.

'Now, just to bring our special evening to a jovial conclusion let me tell you one of *Joe Miller's Jests*.'

'Oh, no!' came a collective groan.

'Good, I'm glad you can't wait,' retorted Twygge, 'you haven't heard this one.'

He starts to recite, 'A woman who had two gallants, one of them with a wooden leg, the question was put: which of the two should father the child? He who had the wooden leg offered to do it in the following manner - if the child, says he, comes into the world with a wooden leg, I will father it, if not then it must be yours.'

Another, louder, collective groan resounded.

'Excellent, I'm glad you enjoyed it. Clearly you wish for another….'

Before he could finish he saw that all four had their fingers in their ears and a communal 'Noooooo!' issued forth. Then silence.

'Have I told you the one about the Irishman……..'

54

The same day, Saturday 29th May
A small man in a long black coat tied with a belt around its middle and wearing a heavy black hat came down the gangplank. He was carrying a box of considerable size by a handle in one hand and a stick in other. He came with a few other passengers from a brig recently moored at the quay of Mr Porter, merchant, on the side of the River Hull. He looked most incongruous to be dressed as he was on such a warm day. He had a long straggly beard, partly grey, and in his worn-out shoes, he walked slowly with his head bowed. When he reached the solid ground he stopped and looked around. He saw a man standing in the doorway of one of the countless warehouses stretching along the riverside from the New Dock to the River Humber. He approached him, put down his box, removed a piece of paper from his coat pocket and showed it to the man. The man looked at it and then started to point towards one of the staithes, waving a hand and indicating as though giving directions. The man in black nodded and bowed in gratitude, placed the piece of paper back in his pocket, picked up his box and ambled unsteadily towards the staithe.

When he reached the High Street he walked straight across between the traffic and went down Chapel Lane. On entering Low Gate he put down his box again, took out the piece of paper and offered it to a passer-by. After more pointing and arm waving he proceeded down Low Gate into the turmoil of the madding crowd of the Market. He saw the golden figure of *King Billy* glittering in the sun above the crowd and weaved his way through the masses towards it. Once more the piece of paper came out. In a few moments he was ambling down Myton Gate. When he was approaching the end he saw the name of Dagger Lane on the side of a building on the end of a street on the right. He turned into it and was soon standing in front of a house, looking at the door. Moritz Lewin put down his box and knocked on it.

NOTES

Many of the characters in this story were real people who do the same jobs as they did in the period that this was written.

Thanks must go to Osher Osdoba for his valuable help with the Yiddish.

Most thanks must go to my wife and family for their invaluable support.